Genevieve Lyo  where she began her came one of Ireland's nders of the Dublin C cting career to bring ught drama and writ ....ginal plays for schoolchildren.

She lives in London, but spends much of the year travelling abroad.

THE PERFECT FAMILY

Genevieve Lyons

WARNER BOOKS

A *Warner* Book

First published in Great Britain in 1996
by Little, Brown and Company
This edition published by Warner Books in 1998

A CIP catalogue record for this book
is available from the British Library.

ISBN 0 7515 2148 5

Typeset in Baskerville by
Palimpsest Book Production Limited,
Polmont, Stirlingshire
Printed and bound in Great Britain by
Mackays of Chatham PLC, Chatham, Kent

Warner Books
A Division of
Little, Brown and Company (UK)
Brettenham House
Lancaster Place
London WC2E 7EN

This book is for my friend
Barbara Doris,
my wonderful agents,
Mike and Alice Sharland,
my equally wonderful editor,
Helen Goodwin,
and Michele.

THE PERFECT FAMILY

Chapter One

❧ ❧

Everyone agreed the Floods of Rossbeg were the perfect family. Not that they aspired to such a title, oh no! Roddy Flood would be the first to scoff at any such suggestion. His good-humoured face would split in an infectious smile and he would shake his head, saying, 'You've got to be kidding!' It was simply the way their friends and acquaintances saw them, how they presented themselves to the world, how they *seemed* to be rather than how they actually were. Assessed on the impression they gave to outsiders the title was thrust upon them – but, it had to be said, they did not actually reject it. Roddy's beguiling smile was simply self-deprecating, not contradictory.

They certainly appeared perfect. Roddy Flood was an affable, even-tempered man, radiating health with his brilliant white teeth and pampered skin. A man you could trust. A loving man who provided more than adequately for his family. Rich, able to live in comfort – not to say luxury – in his beautiful house on the Dalkey coast outside Dublin, nevertheless, to his credit, not many were jealous of Roddy. He was too generous, too nice, too good-humoured.

Cora, his wife, *was* perfect. People always fell back on that word when they talked of Cora Flood. No one had ever heard her utter an unkind word about anyone, and if her expression sometimes revealed her inner contempt for her less-than-perfect sisters, she restrained herself from uttering a single criticism and that in itself showed enormous self-control.

Everything Cora Flood did she did with taste and style. Beautiful, always elegantly groomed, always calm and a little remote, she was the 'very glass of fashion and the mould of form'; she was the one who triggered the word *perfect* in people's minds.

1

Their children too were considered exceptional, and, one had to admit, the four that were *seen* were enviably admirable.

Ossian, the eldest, was twenty-one and beautiful. You could not describe him otherwise. He had gone to be a priest, and all the girls in Dalkey and Dublin – in fact any of the girls in Ireland who had met him – lamented that fact. It was a terrible loss, they said. A total waste. But their mothers envied Cora Flood. What mother in Ireland would not give anything for her eldest, to be a priest? And Ossian would go far, so tall and fair and charming was he.

Fidelma, nineteen, the oldest girl, was as exquisite as her mother; the perfect daughter. Some people thought her hair was too thick, her eyes too large and blue, the colour too violent. Some decided her lips were too pouty, her nose too small for *real* beauty, and some even said she lacked vitality. She was *too* tranquil, *too* sweet.

She was doing a line with Harry Devereau, the most eligible boy in Dublin or Wicklow. He was *the* most desirable catch, and so handsome. If Ossian Flood was a beautiful man, Harry Devereau was handsome and dashing, and there wasn't much to choose between them except that Ossian Flood had pledged his life to God and Harry Devereau was available. Most thought Fidelma Flood would marry Harry, and, though they agreed it was perfect, like a fairy-tale, nevertheless it didn't seem *fair*! She had never caused her parents a moment's anxiety. It was an education, people said, to look at those two beautiful creatures, Ossian and Fidelma Flood, watch them defer to their parents, hold the chair out for their mother, listen respectfully to their father, and thus to be quite certain your own judgement was sound when you pronounced them perfect.

What had Cora Flood done to deserve such children? She must be the holiest woman in Ireland, for didn't Father Mulligan constantly remind them from the pulpit that 'as ye sow so shall ye reap'? Therefore it followed that the Floods' piety must be unassailable. True, Roddy Flood had what *he* thought of as a little secret, but then, people agreed, the male sex was weak – well, in *that* department. Wives were not passionate creatures, after all, and couldn't be expected to satisfy a man's more basic needs, nor should they be expected to, and sure wasn't Roddy Flood only human? And didn't it give him a bit of class, having the luck like that? And it was, after all, Cora who set the tone for the Flood family, and weren't they as near ideal as you could expect in this vale of tears?

The youngest Flood, Eamonn, was only nine, bright as a button and such a good little boy. Always behaved himself. An after-thought, he was, born so far behind the others.

Decla Flood, who came after Fidelma and was seventeen, was not as *perfectly* beautiful as her mother or sister, but then that would be asking too much! Nevertheless, she had a lot in common with the current favourites of the silver screen and although Cora Flood pronounced Lana Turner and Yvonne De Carlo common, in any other family Decla Flood would be considered ravishing.

She was, with her father, the most popular of the Floods. Those who admired Ossian, Cora and Fidelma but found them a touch daunting were drawn to Decla and Roddy. Those who stood back in awe at the eldest children's and their mother's perfect beauty warmed to Decla and Roddy, to their friendliness, their sweetness, their warmth – for perfection is not *so* endearing, and beauty can be offputting.

Yes, everyone seeing the Flood family together – smiling faces, well-groomed bodies, perfect manners – at the tennis club, at the dances, at dinners, the theatre and the races, looked upon them as the ideal. If only their children were as biddable as the Flood children! If only they had a gorgeous house like Rossbeg! If only their wives were as beautiful as Cora Flood! If only they, or their husbands, were as rich as Roddy!

But no one talked about Cecie. She tended to be forgotten. Cecie, who must now, by people's reckoning, be sweet sixteen. Poor Cecie who was sick. Poor Cecie who was never seen.

For people did not really include Cecie in the Flood family group. She was not on their minds when they dubbed the Flood family perfect. They smiled in admiration, turning their heads to stare at Cora Flood making an entrance, slim as a racehorse, elegant in Dior or Hartnell, leaving a waft of Schiaparelli 'Shocking' as she walked past a little ahead of Roddy, who was sleek in his cashmere and tweed, or his linen and silk. They gazed as behind them the stunning son and daughter followed, a pair so glamorous they took the breath away, and, after them, the delightful Decla and Eamonn, eyes bright with a dash of mischief, and they shook their heads at the unbelievable luck of some people as they once more murmured to themselves that the Floods were indeed the perfect family.

And being the perfect family naturally must mean that they were happy. That must, *ipso facto*, follow. So no one asked the Floods about that. They simply assumed it to be true. And they assumed that the Floods, one and all, (except of course Cecie), must be in a state of constant bliss.

Appearances, as the wise man said, can be misleading. In Rossbeg, as Cora Flood awakened in the huge four-poster in the master bedroom, her first instinctive action was to shrink away from her husband. She recoiled from Roddy Flood, grimacing as if he were the Monster from Forty Thousand Fathoms. 'Ugh!' she breathed as she wrinkled her face in distaste and shoved his warm and slightly sweating body away from her. It got worse with the years, not better, this revulsion she felt for her husband on awakening. It should have become easier, but it had not.

Roddy rolled over in his sleep as he often did. Cora told him many times with a slight frown that he was an untidy sleeper. It was a cross Cora Flood had to bear. If Roddy was anywhere near her she moved hastily and with disgust away from him and was glad when it was morning and she could get up and leave the bed.

Cora would have had separate rooms only Father Mulligan spoke often of the sanctity of the marriage-bed. He had so often propounded this fact to her, drummed into her head her duty to Roddy, that even when Monsignor Robert Maguire told her that God was not, in his opinion, remotely interested in whether she, having provided her husband with two sons and three daughters, slept in the same room as Roddy or not, she could not summon up the courage to defy her parish priest. Though she wanted badly to believe the Monsignor, and actually, if she was honest, *did* believe him – for he was a very clever man and her PP was *not* – still she did not feel up to challenging Father Mulligan. She was too afraid of Hell or Purgatory to take the chance.

And so she lay on her side of the bed all night, worried in case her husband got an 'urge', awakening instantly if Roddy encroached into her space, slipping out of bed very early each morning. It had become a habit.

She often wondered whether other women felt as she did. Or was she weird? It upset her, this feeling of physical distaste she felt for Roddy. She knew she shouldn't feel like that, it was not natural. She tried so hard to suppress it and mostly she succeeded, but during the day, not the night. And, as she made her way to the bathroom that Saturday morning in nineteen fifty, she implored God's forgiveness, if it was a sin. She was not sure it actually *was* a sin, but hedging her bets said her 'I Confess' anyhow. *A woman shall leave her Mother and her Father and cleave to her husband and they two shall become one flesh.* The words terrified her, always had. 'Cleave' especially. Cleave seemed to her excessive, sort of getting *stuck* to Roddy in that awful sweaty way, but she knew exactly what Father Mulligan would say if she asked him about the exact degree of commitment required of her, for he preached it often enough from the pulpit, and could have accused her, with justification, of not listening if she pretended to be ignorant of his, and therefore the Church's, views on that particular subject.

'A woman is her husband's chattel. His possession. And she must obey him in all things. Bend to his will. Bear him children and love him, as the Church loves you. Then she will truly be a pearl of great price. Oh, man has his duties too.' Father Mulligan would fix his male parishioners with a steely eye. 'Obligations he must fulfil. He must look after this pearl of great price, for she is above the price of rubies. He must provide for her. Love her . . .'

Tell that to Shona Monaghan below in the pub whose husband beat her up every Friday night and went to confession next morning and got instant absolution, going scrub-faced to communion on Sunday, holier than thou. No escape for poor Shona.

'If the husband is a brute,' Father Mulligan informed them, 'then that is a cross the good but unfortunate wife has to

5

bear. But she will be rewarded in Heaven for her patience and fortitude.'

Well that, in Cora's opinion, was not good enough, and she thanked her Creator that she had no such worries about Roddy. Her husband was gentle as a lamb, and she liked and respected him. Why then did she find contact with him unbearable?

Cora Flood had no answers to this dilemma and could only assume there was some flaw deep within her that she must take great care to cover up. Sometimes when she thought about it she could hear her mother's voice echoing in her brain, 'Dirty, dirty, dirty!' Dirty. Anything to do with her private parts. 'Dirty, dirty, dirty!' or 'Disgusting, disgusting, disgusting!' Her mother had never allowed her to touch herself, except when she went to the lavatory. 'Then you must *clean* it, dear. *Clean* your dirty place.'

Cora ran a bath and scooped sweet-smelling salts into it. from the crystal jar on the shelf. She sank into it gratefully and proceeded to wash away the fluids her body had secreted during the night.

'Dirty, dirty, dirty!'

Well, she was clean and sweet-smelling now.

Chapter Two

❧ ❧

Fidelma Flood was also awake early. She had a very big decision to make today. She'd promised herself she'd talk to Harry about when they would marry. Her mother had advised her to hurry up, as, she said, 'There are a lot of fish in the sea, Fidelma, and you don't want the most eligible boy in Ireland to escape and swim somewhere else, now do you? Men are fickle, Fidelma, very different from us, and a wily, scheming female can work a spell on any man if she so chooses. I've kept my eye on your father . . .' Then, seeing her daughter's surprise, 'Oh yes! There are ruthless women, Fidelma, who'll stop at nothing when it comes to men with money and looks.' And Cora sighed and added ruefully, 'And sometimes even that's not necessary. They'll pursue men who have nothing, neither looks nor money, simply to get hold of a man, for, darling, without a man a woman doesn't amount to a hill of beans!'

Fidelma had tossed and turned all night, grappling with the pros and cons. The list of reasons why she should marry Harry was long and formidable. The list of reasons why she should *not* was very short. It consisted of only one item: she was not sure whether she loved him or not.

Fidelma looked on the question of whether she married Harry Devereau as if she was entering a business contract, which was what her mother had advised her to do, and therefore the lone reason for refusal did not seem as important as it otherwise might have.

'Work out the advantages, dear, and the disadvantages. Like a balance sheet.' Fidelma didn't know what a balance sheet actually was, but she was sharp enough to get her mother's drift. 'And whichever column has the longest number of entries, then there's your answer. Though,'

Cora added, 'it's going to be difficult finding anything on the debit side if it's Harry Devereau you're assessing.'

'What about being in love?' Decla had muttered, and Cora, glancing at her second daughter, had smiled. 'Don't be silly, dear,' she'd said dismissively. 'That sort of thing is for fairy-tales, not real life.'

'Didn't you love Dadda?' Decla persisted.

'Of course I loved him. I *liked* him a lot when I met him. I respected him. Then I grew to love him. But as for that silly feeling – moon in June, stars in your eyes – such nonsense! Your grandmother would never have allowed such insanity to enter the most important decision of my life. It would be a most dangerous foundation for a life-time partnership. And make no mistake, that's what marriage is.'

Harry Devereau had been at Fidelma's side since the day she was born. Marcus Devereau had the estate adjoining Rossbeg and when his wife, who was a delicate flower indeed, died giving birth to Harry, Marcus had turned to Cora Flood for help. Cora had just had Fidelma and the nurse had taken care of both infants, until they were old enough for Fusty, Rossbeg's housekeeper, to take over. They had grown up together and everyone talked about them as a couple, almost as if they were already betrothed. But Harry hadn't declared himself and Cora had begun to hustle Fidelma.

'He'll escape,' she said. 'You've got to decide.'

'But, Mother, he's never said a word about marriage,' Fidelma protested.

And Cora had cast her eyes to heaven. 'Men don't!' she told her daughter in no uncertain terms. 'They need prompting. Manoeuvring. Have you ever seen Harry look at another woman? Have you ever seen him show the slightest interest?'

'No, Mother. I haven't.'

'Then what are you waiting for?' Cora's voice was calm. She never raised her voice. She thought to do so was uncultivated. But Fidelma could nevertheless detect her impatience. 'If you decide he'll make a suitable companion for life, put it to him that you are willing to be his wife.'

'All right, Mother.'

'You'll find the right moment. When it's moonlight. Men are more manageable then. I think he'll be thrilled.'

But it was not that easy. It had proved impossible to be businesslike and objective in the night when the bedclothes fought her, the pillow threatened to smother her, her feet stuck out and got icy cold and she developed a headache. So she got up early that June morning, pulled on her jodhpurs, a fresh shirt and a light cashmere pullover and saddled Ransome to go for an early morning ride.

As she rode she again listed the advantages to herself. One, Harry was handsome as sin. Two, he was richer than her father, or he would be eventually. Three, he was sweet-tempered, and four, she could manage him. At least she thought so. Harry often took the line of least resistance. And he would certainly give her what she wanted. What did she want? She frowned, gripping the reins, urging Ransome forward. She wanted a beautiful house. Well, Montpellier, behind Rossbeg, in Dalkey was magnificent. She wanted beautiful clothes. Harry could dress her like a queen. She wanted happy, healthy children. That was in God's hands, but the prognosis was good. She wanted to see exotic places. Now that the world was recovering from war, foreign travel was becoming popular – and, she had decided long ago, she wanted to go first-class. Harry would give her all those things and more.

And on the down side? She rode cross-country towards Wicklow, her hair blowing back from her hot cheeks. The mountains rose crimson in the morning sun, dark patches, black where the sun did not reach and golden where the gorse and broom bloomed. On her right the sea sushed and heaved and sparkled, azure patched with emerald where the currents ran deep. The sky was soft grey in the damp dawning and every leaf and blade of grass was heavy with dew. The birds sang their dawn chorus as Fidelma rode and pondered this most important decision.

She kept hearing Decla's voice. 'And what about being in love?' What about it? Fidelma did not know what it meant. She had never felt even the faintest stirrings of romance and doubted it existed outside the pages of books. She was an intelligent rational female and she could not understand the excesses of *La Bohème* or *Manon Lescaut* and was not sure she *wanted* to. When the whole audience wept around her she would sit still and wonder impatiently why they didn't just get on with it. 'They' being the characters on the stage, 'it' being life. To become fixated on one person seemed to her childish and silly and very, very uncomfortable. And yet . . . and yet . . .

She suddenly realised that Ransome was flagging. She had ridden him harder than she intended. She ran her hand over his damp neck and patted his forehead and then turned his head towards home.

She had reached her decision. She'd tell Harry tonight, or tomorrow – whenever the time seemed right – that she'd marry him. She was used to Harry. She was comfortable with him. They were good companions. She smiled to herself. Who needed love anyway?

Chapter Three

∽ ๑๑

Eamonn Flood saw his sister canter slowly to the stables. She must have ridden hard, he mused, dodging behind the chestnut tree so she wouldn't see him, for Ransome was steaming. He did not want to talk to her just then. She'd corral him into helping rub Ransome down and he didn't see why he should have to do that. The trouble with having sisters and brothers a lot older than you was that they thought of you as slave labour. Fidelma was very autocratic and just ordered a fellow to do this and that like he was at her beck and call, and he resented it. He tried to explain to her or Ossian or their mother and they simply did not understand. They actually did not *hear* him. He had only realised that fact recently. They did not listen to him.

He did his own tasks without complaining, but he just didn't see why he should help Fidelma do hers as well.

One of Eamonn's jobs was to collect the eggs from the coop and bring them to Fusty before breakfast while the dew was still heavy on the grass. He did this every morning. Then taking Rusty, their dog, with him he went into the woods to gather mushrooms. He was an expert on fungi of both the poisonous and edible variety.

He rose at the first streak of dawn, and in the breathless awakening of the world brought home to Fusty the fresh eggs and the mushrooms. She gave him a hug, a glass of milk and a cookie. After that he usually collapsed into his bed where he slept until breakfast.

This fine June morning he had had a shock.

The woods behind the apple orchard were thick and dark and Eamonn loved their mystery. He liked to scare himself. He enjoyed the rush of excitement he felt when he imagined all sorts of horrors deep within the darkening

11

gloom of the trees and yet went bravely into the shifting depths. It thrilled him to pierce the shadowy mystery even though he was terrified and expected at any moment some primeval beast to lurch out at him, or a dragon to breathe fire from some impenetrable cave-mouth, a giant to terrorise him from the tops of the incessantly moving trees, or a wolfman to materialise from the bowels of the pungent earth, jump out at him and eat him all up. While he was there, picking his mushrooms, he was constantly alert, for danger seemed to threaten from every shrub and tree. His head was full of stories about knights in shining armour, about Cuchullain and the Tain, all mixed up with the fairy-tales of the brothers Grimm.

These ancient woods at Rossbeg, he knew, had been there since medieval times, perhaps before. Anything could happen here. It was like a cathedral – the hush, the muted noise, the changes in emphasis of sound, the shadows and shafts of light when the sun pierced the thatch of overlapping leaves and played like a spotlight on the pungent, needle-strewn earth where the mushrooms grew. Owls lived there, and foxes. Badgers dug their sets and the whole place was alive with subterranean life, hidden and secret. Eamonn loved and yet was scared by the rustlings and murmurings, the whisperings and sibilant scurryings. With his nerves taut, his ears alert, the wood embraced him, held him in her leafy arms, yet subtly threatened him. A cacophony of sound surrounded him, secret and sudden movements made him catch his breath, and it was with relief that he realised it was only the shrill quarrelling of birds. Terrified, he daily challenged himself.

Eamonn had gathered his mushrooms this morning and piled them in the trug he had collected from the kitchen garden. He was picking his last few, whistling through his teeth, when he became aware of a strange presence in the place. How he knew there was *something* or *someone* there, out of place, unusual, he was not sure, but the skin on the back of his neck seemed gripped with icy terror, the hairs on his arms stood up and his heart lurched to somewhere near his bowels.

He froze. Everything remained the same. There was no sign to indicate that anything untoward had happened, yet

12

Eamonn knew that there was something there, waiting, staring at him but invisible. It could be a beast, a magic presence, or another person. Of the three choices the last one was the one he wanted least. He remained motionless, unable to think what to do next. Having prepared himself hundreds of times to face the unbelievable he now knew his preparation was not going to be of any use whatsoever. He stood gnawing his knuckles, held petrified in the grip of terror.

Then suddenly, with no warning, someone dropped out of one of the trees and stood before him.

It was a lumbering thing, a huge hulk, dark and menacing, looming over the boy. Eamonn could not make out the face or features of the apparition and he was too scared and shocked to scream. His heart beat so hard against his chest that he knew it must be visible and his knees nearly gave under him. He staggered backwards, tripping over a fallen log and landing on his back among the ferns, scattering the mushrooms.

The apparition came slowly forwards, stood over him and looked down. Eamonn could see him now for he had moved into a shaft of glimmering sunlight that had sifted through the interlocked branches.

He was a young man, younger, Eamonn decided, than Ossian who was twenty-one. He looked rough and was built square and strong, and he smelled like the wood, pungent and ripe, earthy.

'You a poacher?' Eamonn stammered. 'I won't tell. Honest.'

The man laughed. 'Hey, don't be scared,' he said and his voice, like his build, was flat and hard.

'I'm *not*!' Eamonn protested, picking himself up, ignoring the hand the stranger held out to him. He set about retrieving the mushrooms, glancing under his lashes every now and then at the young man who stood before him. He had a sort of swaggering way about him and Eamonn sensed that he had enjoyed scaring him.

By now Eamonn had recovered some of his equilibrium, and, squinting up at the stranger, he told him, 'This is private property. What you doin' here?' His courage surprised him and he decided that a real live threat was better after all than the monsters in his mind.

'Oh, I don't think anyone will mind.' The stranger began to help pick up the mushrooms and replace them in the trug.

'Don't do that!' Eamonn cried angrily. 'They're for breakfast an' I must make sure none of 'em are poisonous.'

'You an expert?' The young man was smiling a superior sort of grin and it irritated Eamonn.

'Yes,' he said confidently. 'As a matter of fact I am! That one in your hand is not one of mine. It would kill you.'

He had the satisfaction of seeing the young man drop the fungus hastily and wipe his hand on his jacket.

'Brendan O'Brien is my uncle,' the stranger said and Eamonn stared at him in surprise. 'Shannon O'Brien is my name.'

Brendan O'Brien was Eamonn's father's best friend.

'I didn't know he had a . . .'

'Nephew.'

'Umm.'

'I'm from Liverpool,' the stranger said by way of explanation and added, 'I'm on a visit with my Uncle Brendan.' He grinned sardonically. 'We're the poor side of the family.'

'Well, what are you doing here?' Eamonn persisted. 'The O'Briens don't live here. They're on the other side of the hill.'

'God, you're a right little ferret! I was just exploring.' Then the stranger turned his head as if he'd heard something. His face had a startled, alert look. Eamonn listened too but could hear nothing except the usual sounds. Shannon O'Brien nodded to him, his face serious and suddenly remote.

'I'm off then. Sorry I frightened you.' Then as Eamonn started to protest he held up his hand. 'Sorry I wandered here by mistake. I'll see you again, I suppose. Bye.'

And he was gone. It was like the wood swallowed him into its verdant shadows, sucked him into the darkness of its heart.

Eamonn shivered. He felt the chill of the morning damp on his skin. He hastily gathered the rest of the mushrooms and, putting them into the trug, he ran out of the ancient wood and into the sun.

Chapter Four

✧

Decla Flood that morning felt the first stirrings of consciousness as the shaft of sunlight through a chink in the curtains danced on to her tight-shut eyelids. She moved slowly, coming to life under its spotlight.

The sun was warm against her skin, and somewhere out of the slow surrealism of her dreams came the realisation that it was June, holidays, Saturday, her favourite day, that life was good and it all lay before her.

What would today bring? Anything was possible. She might even awaken beautiful as Fidelma, changed by some fairy godmother into a carbon copy of her sister. And then to complete the unimaginable delight of that thought, Harry Devereau would have a twin brother. Every morning the thought came and every morning she pushed it away. She opened her eyes, blinked, kicked down her eiderdown and sat up, stretching and yawning.

Decla Flood was the apple of her father's eye. She was a pretty girl with wild red hair, laughing eyes and a body that curved deliciously. She hated those curves with a passion and ached to take after her mother or her sister who were tall and slim and straight as reeds, with figures like the bulrushes down by the lake. Ossian and Fidelma had inherited their mother's lithe, rangy frame and perfect features and Decla, encumbered with breasts like fat little tennis balls and hips that gave her walk a lilt, ate her heart out with longing for their spare perfection. Why, why, why was she the odd one out, looking like Dadda instead of her mother? Only her little brother Eamonn had, like their father and her, what she decided was a chunky figure.

'Short fat legs, hips like an ocean-liner, and horrible, horrible *things* sticking out of my chest,' she told Mac

McNiece at the tennis club, exaggerating somewhat, and with theatrical abandon pulling at her jumper, pushing her fists into the front of it and shoving it out grotesquely.

'Don't talk daft!' Mac had said a little crossly, but laughing, not believing she really meant it, thinking perhaps she was fishing. 'Your legs are like Betty Grable's and your hips are nice and curvy. Honest, Decla.' Then he blushed, for how could he mention her breasts? To be so forward would be both sinful and insulting. It would mean you didn't respect her and if you didn't respect a girl it made her no better than a whore. 'You're lovely,' he finished a little lamely and Decla sighed and didn't believe him. Sadly she pined to be like Katherine Hepburn or Greta Garbo, whose clothes hung on them like they were hangers and for whom only the tiniest protuberances indicated there was a figure underneath, while her body ruthlessly took on its own shape and lodged her firmly in the category of Jean Harlow and Silvana Mangano. She thought these ladies common and obvious and loathed the messages her body seemed to send out without her permission. 'I'm not *like* that,' she told Mac. 'I'm not sexy inside. I don't *feel* sexy. I hate sex!' Mac blushed again and changed the subject. It was not a thing talked about in Dublin in the Fifties, not at all.

Actually Decla knew nothing at all about sex. She had been given a brief and clinical description of the 'facts of life', as they were called. But her experience was nil, as was to be expected of a young girl at that time and in that place. She expected to explore the sexual when she married, certainly not before. No one except very fast women, girls that boys would *never* marry, did 'it' before they had a ring safely on their finger.

Decla jumped out of bed, slipped out of her nightdress and looked in the full-length mirror. No. She had not grown rake-thin overnight as she so passionately desired. Her breasts, like milky globes, still proudly protruded. Her hips swelled. Her calves curved into long slim ankles and every line of her was gently rounded. Sloping shoulders, upper arms and thighs circled like a Roman or Greek statue, dimpled at knee and elbow. She grimaced and whispered, 'Damn, damn, damn,' then hurried into the bathroom.

It was as neat as Fusty had left it after cleaning it yesterday, yet Decla knew Fidelma had been in there already. It was the smell and the warm feel. Fidelma had gone riding, Decla decided. She was making up her mind whether to accept Harry Devereau. Decla shrugged as she ran the bath. Why should she care who Fidelma married? And just because Harry was the most wonderful, beautiful boy in the world, why should she mind? If Fidelma didn't marry him she'd be mad. They were such a glamorous pair, like two film stars, and it would be a mortal sin if they didn't end up together. Decla's eyes became remote and unfocused as she thought of Harry, visualising his tall evening-dress-clad figure dancing a slow fox-trot (*I'll be seeing you, In all the old familiar places*) not with her sister, but with *her*.

She shook her head. It was silly to dwell on that picture even for a minute. He was so far above her. A prince deserved a princess; the fairest of them all, and that was Fidelma.

She had forgotten to turn on the cold tap as she pondered these facts and the yell she let out when she stepped into the scalding water reverberated through the house and stopped her mother in her tracks.

Cora Flood was on her way down to breakfast when she was arrested by the roars coming from the bathroom between Fidelma's and Decla's bedrooms. She knew it was Decla. Those raucous cries could not come from her eldest daughter. She hurried to the bathroom door.

'Are you all right, Decla?' She was not too anxious. There was too much noise for the situation to be serious and Decla was always inclined to be rowdy.

'Yes, Mother,' Decla called back. 'I didn't put the cold in and I stepped in the scalding water.'

'Well, that will teach you a lesson. Be more careful in the future,' Cora told her tranquilly. 'The salve is in the medicine chest,' she added. She sighed and shook her head. Decla was the difficult one, the one that did not automatically conform. Cora expected a tidy, disciplined way of life in Rossbeg and all the others behaved with quiet grace and calm control, except Decla. Well, Decla and Eamonn, she amended, but Eamonn was, after all, only nine years old and could not be counted. They took after their father, and Roddy, though thoroughly conditioned after twenty-odd years of marriage, still had, she thought, coarser instincts and a slightly raucous vitality that was – well – ill-bred.

Cora passed Cecie's room. She turned, a little hesitant at first, then knocked gently on the door. There was no answer so she opened it a crack and looked in. The room was foggy with shadows and there was no sound from the bed. She moved softly through the pearly light and stared down at her sleeping daughter. The small waif-like face was without life. Cecie would look like this when she died. Cora shivered. Cecie's skin, as fine as the membrane of an egg, clung to her bones. Cora could see their shape beneath the transparent covering, the dents low in the nose, the sharp curve where the cheekbone ended and the hinge of the jaw began.

Tears sprang to her eyes and she touched her daughter's cheek with feather-light fingers. The girl's face was coldly damp, her forehead hot. She did not move but lay in her unconscious state like the Sleeping Beauty.

What did she think of, lying there, Cora wondered? Did she dream of the normal life her sisters would have, the life that was forbidden to her?

Cora sighed. She'd never know. She could not bear to have such a conversation with her child. It would distress the mother too much. No, best to be brisk, cheerful. Above all, not to acknowledge that Cecie was dying, to pretend that tomorrow, next month, next year everything would have miraculously changed. They all knew it would not, but best to deny the fact ruthlessly.

Cora kissed the hot, damp forehead of her child and tiptoed out, closing the door gently behind her.

She finally made her way downstairs to the breakfast room. Dixie, the maid, had left the mail addressed to her on her plate and Cora saw to her surprise as she sat down that on the top of the pile was a letter postmarked London. She turned it over in her hand, idly curious. It would be from her sister-in-law. She knew no one else would write to her from London. A postcard maybe, but not a letter. She sighed again. She did not like Roddy's brother and his wife. Even to talk about them set her teeth on edge.

She slit it open with the silver letter-blade. When she'd

read the contents she put the pages beside her plate and glanced up as her family came in one by one.

Eamonn was round and rosy, his face glowing from his early morning activities. Decla rose like a lark and sang through the morning hours and Cora winced at her cheerfully loud greeting. Decla did not miss her mother's fleeting expression of disapproval and she immediately slowed her pace and walked in a more decorous fashion to the sideboard to help herself to breakfast.

Fidelma glided into the room and her mother's face lit up. Her daughters' beauty was a source of constant joy to Cora and her eldest daughter's graceful demeanour always gave her pleasure. There seemed no peaks or troughs for Fidelma, just calm decision. Unless she was talking to Decla, when, for some reason Cora Flood could not fathom, she became acerbic and irritable, quite unlike her usual self. Cora had decided long ago that Decla and Fidelma did not get on. 'She takes after me and Decla after Roddy,' she said and never saw the irony in her conclusion.

Her husband, freshly shaved, kissed his daughters and Eamonn – who wriggled hastily away from his embrace, not because he didn't love his dadda, but because he hated anyone, except Fusty, to show him any overt affection.

'Good morning, Dadda,' Eamonn said, as if to make up for his rejection, and smiled up at his father.

The breakfast-room was large and airy, a framework of wood and glass panels. Roddy had built it on to the house meaning it to be a conservatory. Rossbeg, formerly called Wellington Manor, was a Georgian building facing the bay and harbour, girdled by beech trees with an orchard at the back and the wood behind that. Roddy had added the glass conservatory at the rear of the house, which faced west, and so, because the sun shone there of a morning, it became the breakfast-room.

It was Decla's favourite room. She loved the feeling of almost being outside, almost sitting on the lawn, separated only by the glass, but being warm. She loved the green and white décor, cool colours predominant. She loved the smell of the plants, the warm, moist atmosphere. She often came here to do her homework, read or write. She would sit and gently touch the leaves of the plants around her and stroke

19

the cold marble columns while she hid from the family. She loved the cool, remote gaze of the stone and marble statues, half-hidden in greenery, liked the soft comfort of the alcove seats with their bright-flowered pink, white and green chintz cushions. She loved the privacy. Everywhere else in the house there was always someone to interfere, ask her what she was doing, chide her for some lack in her. Here she could curl up and dream in the warm green shadows.

As it was Saturday they were having a bacon and egg breakfast. They lunched on Saturdays at the tennis club and it would be a light buffet affair, so they started the day with plenty of fodder. That was what Fusty said. It was the only day they could dawdle over a meal, for weekdays everyone was busy and Sunday it was Mass. So the Saturday breakfast was a sort of ritual when the Flood family relaxed and savoured the delicious food. The bacon was best back, the eggs from their own hen coop, via Eamonn. The sausages were Hafner's best. There was black and white pudding, grilled tomatoes and kidneys and Eamonn's mushrooms, coddled. The grill was followed by griddle cakes and toast, brown soda bread, jams, jellies and Fusty's marmalade. This latter was a fairly new innovation as oranges had been impossible to get until recently.

Decla didn't like marmalade. Her father and mother had rhapsodised about it during the war, when you couldn't get lemons, oranges, or, for that matter, sugar but when Fusty finally made it, Decla, used to her sweet currant and berry jams and jellies, found it too bitter.

'But that's exactly why I love it,' Cora had said when Decla wrinkled up her face at the first mouthful. 'It's lovely and sharp.'

'No, Mother, it's dire!' Decla took a quick gulp of tea and shook her head.

'Don't use slang, dear,' Cora said mildly. 'Really, Decla, you should try to be more like your sister. Fidelma never uses slang and she *likes* marmalade.' She would, Decla thought bitterly.

She didn't like bananas either when they eventually hit the shops. In her opinion they tasted squashy and bland, like baby food, but she didn't say so. She had learned not to after the marmalade episode.

Decla adored pineapples, though – their tough skin, intricate design, their stylish cock's comb of leaves on top and sweet-scented fruit inside. But she didn't remark on this either for fear of being put down.

When the family were seated around the table, when they had served themselves from the silver-covered salvers and coddling dishes on the sideboard, when their initial hunger and thirst had been satisfied, Cora looked around the table.

'Sylvie Flood is coming to stay,' she told them. They all stared at her. Sylvie was their English cousin, but that side of the family had not been mentioned for many a year.

Decla admired her immensely, though she had not seen her since they were children and the war had come. Cora pitied her, but Decla envied the fact that her cousin, her exact age, lived in that grand city where the Tower of London was and where Queen Elizabeth and the King George lived in Buckingham Palace with their two daughters, Elizabeth and Margaret Rose. Decla had seen the princesses in the newsreels being brave on bomb-sites. Her mother said the Royal family insisted on remaining in the war-torn city when they could have gone anywhere in the world. 'Anywhere at all!' Cora whispered enviously.

Decla thought it must have been wonderful to live there in the middle of all the excitement and to be a princess living in a palace. She had seen them on *Pathe Gazette* news films standing on the balcony waving and behind them Decla could see all those rooms. The Royal family would disappear inside with a last glance over their individual shoulders. Did someone tell the little princesses to do that? 'Glance sweetly over your shoulder, dear, it looks delightful.'

Yes, London would be exciting. Bustle and fuss. Lights flashing and glittering now that the war was over. Altogether smart.

Not like Dalkey, that was certain. Dalkey was small and quiet and crowdless. The suburb on the outskirts of Dublin where the Floods lived would, Decla thought, bore a sophisticated Londoner to death. Yes, Sylvie would be bored stiff. And so would the princesses, if they came here.

'Janey Mac, nothing happens here,' Decla muttered as her mother turned the pages of the letter over with one

21

hand and held her toast and marmalade askew in the other as she read. The marmalade was gathering itself to drop off the toast on to the white damask tablecloth and Decla watched it, fascinated.

'Maybe that's why she wants to come here and stay awhile; because nothing happens here,' Roddy Flood remarked mildly. 'They've had enough excitement over there to last them a lifetime.'

'The war, you mean?' Eamonn's eyes lit up. He loved war films. 'Bubb, bubb, bubb, bubb' – he made the noise films used for gunfire. 'Oh boy, oh boy, wish I'd been old enough.'

'Don't be silly, Eamonn. Some of those men came back without their legs or arms. You should be grateful.' Eamonn gulped and Cora turned her attention back to the letter. 'Her mother says here . . . I think you might be right, Roddy – her mother says, let me see, um, yes, here it is. "To recover her spirits."' She lowered the letter and glanced at her husband. 'Whatever can she mean by that?' Her clear delphinium-blue eyes returned to the page. She scanned it, her eyes darting back and forth, and murmured, 'Recover her spirits . . .'

'Mother, the marmalade . . .' Decla cried. Too late. The marmalade chunk fell with a sticky plop on to the immaculate table-cloth and Cora Flood clicked her tongue.

'Fusty will be furious,' she muttered, staring at it but not looking too put out. 'It's only fresh.'

The table-cloth was supposed to last until Monday, wash day, when Fusty boiled the whites in the big boiler on the range in the kitchen below. In the holidays Decla liked to help her, much to Cora's disgust. 'Ladies should not even *know* what happens in the kitchen. We are not expected to understand how it all *works*. Ladies *supervise*, not participate,' she told Decla, who ignored the advice. She loved the steam, the blue-bag dip, the starch and the mangling. Most of all she loved the sight of the washing hanging outside on the line near the apple trees, flapping like schooner-sails in the wind.

'Where'll we put her?' Roddy asked. They had six bedrooms, all of them occupied.

'The whole place will have to be spring-cleaned, attic to cellars,' Cora said, not hearing him.

Fidelma, who sat opposite Decla reading *Film Fan Magazine*, asked, 'Why?' in a detached sort of way. Her mother gave her a glance of total exasperation and did not deign to answer.

'Mother cleans the whole house, attic to cellar, when someone comes to *tea*!' Decla said. 'You must have noticed.'

'You mean *Fusty* cleans the house. Mamma tells her what to do,' said Eamonn with a grin.

'Yes, where *will* you put her?' Fidelma asked, looking up from her perusal of the latest Hollywood scandal. 'I hope she's not going to be anywhere near me!'

'Decla can go to the attic,' Cora said, eyeing her second daughter hopefully.

Decla could be difficult and stubborn if she did not want to do something, but she could also be generous and unselfish. Cora was lucky that morning. Decla loved the attic-room, under the eaves with its sloping roof and doll's-house daintiness. Like the breakfast-room it appealed to her imagination, and up there she could pretend. She could be Heidi, or Katie, or Anne of Green Gables.

'Okay,' she said cheerfully. She liked the feeling too, like holidays, of going to a different room, out of the routine.

'Sylvie can have Decla's room,' Cora said, more confident now that thunder-clouds had not descended upon her daughter's brow.

'As long as it's not mine,' Fidelma murmured, returning to her magazine. 'That's all I ask. No one goes in my room 'less I say so.'

Fidelma was still in her jodhpurs. She was not sweating after her ride. She had pulled off her cashmere and her white shirt was open at the neck. There was no dark patch under her arms. Decla could see the shadow of her nipples through the fine cotton of the shirt. How lucky she was, her sister thought, staring at her enviously, that she was flat and didn't sweat. Her cloud of dark hair framed the oval face and her ivory skin was pearly and glowing. It is simply not fair, Decla decided.

'No one will, dear,' Cora reassured Fidelma, who nodded, satisfied. Her room always looked like a picture from *House and Garden* magazine and Decla resented its tidiness. Her own room often looked as if a tornado had just blown through. But Fidelma's room was never a mess, oh no! Everything there was always in perfect order. The clothes in her closets were in pristine condition, always just laundered or cleaned, ironed and starched, every button secure, every pleat knife-edged. Shoes to match were placed neatly underneath each suit or dress or coat, and over each outfit the appropriate accessories lay tidily on the shelf above; scarf, belt, gloves, everything just so. On her dressing-table her matching silver-backed brushes and hand mirror and comb set were perfectly polished and arranged, and never a stray hair sullied the Limerick lace dressing-table cover set. No face-powder spilled from the Coty box and the swansdown powderpuff was immaculate in its pale pink chiffon square.

'Go into your room? God'n we wouldn't *dare*!' Decla exclaimed.

Fidelma raised one perfectly arched eyebrow and gave her sister a hard stare and Eamonn sniggered. She rose slowly and gracefully from the table, shaking her magazine closed.

'Know something, Decla, Eamonn?' she asked softly, looking from one to the other. 'You are both deeply, deeply unpleasant little worms. How Mother and Dadda managed to produce two such ugly little idiots is baffling! Will you excuse me Mother, Dadda? I'm going to change.' And she pushed back her wicker chair and went to the door.

Cora, used to the constant bickering, nodded absently, while Roddy muttered, 'That's uncalled for, Fidelma.'

Fidelma turned at the door. 'You're such a *child*, Decla. One day you'll get the hang of being grown-up. Until then I suppose I'll have to put up with your grossly *juvenile* behaviour.' And she left the room in quiet triumph. She'd known exactly the hit to make. She'd said nothing so bad that Roddy could really object and her mother, she knew, was far too lazy to get involved unless the arrows were far more stinging. But she knew that what she'd said to Decla was the most hurtful thing in the world to her younger sister. Only Fidelma knew how badly Decla wanted to be considered grown-up and sophisticated. Poor Decla. Plump and good-humoured, friendly as a puppy-dog. Sophisticated? Never!

24

Decla smarted under the words, all confidence gone. She bit her lip and squeezed her eyes shut to keep the tears out. Eamonn put his tongue out at her and she threw down her napkin and asked to be excused.

'Are you going with Fidelma to Ballyorin?' her mother asked mildly. Ballyorin was the tennis club and Decla swallowed silently and implored the Lord for patience. Fidelma wouldn't be seen *dead* with her seventeen-year-old sister. Decla wanted to hang around the eighteen- and nineteen-year-olds, her sister's crowd, but they ignored her, treating her with blithe contempt and condescension. Most of Fidelma's crowd were boys. Fidelma had more boyfriends than anyone in the world, and Decla felt she surely wouldn't miss just *one* of the crowd that followed her about everywhere she went. Decla would have given anything she possessed for a boyfriend. Just someone, anyone, who preferred her, who wanted her around, who just might be in love with her. She had never had an admirer and despaired now that she ever would, whereas Fidelma had *hundreds*! But Fidelma always ignored Decla when they accidentally met in the locker-room or on the courts. The only time she spoke to her sister was when they were at meals together and then usually to insult her. It wasn't fair, and Decla quivered with rage and humiliation under her sister's lofty disdain.

Decla glanced at her mother to see if she'd registered how impossible her question was but her mother was oblivious to her hurt.

Cora's attention was now concentrated on the impending visit of their cousin and not on Decla's and Fidelma's squabbles. Besides, Decla thought, Ossian and Fidelma were her favourites and nothing they did was ever wrong. Decla glanced at Eamonn, but he was doing disgusting things with his porridge and she looked quickly away. Her father was engrossed in his paper. No one was paying her any attention and while that was what she wanted, contrarily it infuriated her. The cloud her mother dreaded was descending on to her brow. 'I'm off!' she announced and pushed her chair back roughly, hoping in a way to be rebuked. But no one said anything. Eamonn continued messing with his food, Cora was fixated on the letter and Roddy on his newspaper. In disgust Decla stomped from the room.

When she reached the hall where the staircase curved gracefully upwards she kicked the bottom step, clenched her fists and plonked herself down on the second step, her knuckles in her mouth.

She sighed. She had to learn, she decided, to accept that she'd be an old maid. A spinster. That much was certain. She would live and die a virgin. Well, she supposed Queen Elizabeth of England, the great queen, lived and died a virgin, but, Decla amended, she *had* had admirers. Decla's problem seemed to be that she had none. It was okay not getting married, remaining a virgin even, but to have no admirers, no boyfriends, that was appalling! It was the most humiliating thing that could happen to a girl. Worst thing of all. Even if, God forbid, you got pregnant before you were married and had an illegitimate child, though society rejected you, though you were beyond the pale, at least it proved that at some time, even for five minutes, some male had found you attractive.

Well, the die was cast for her. At her age Fidelma had had *millions* of men slavering over her and, to date, she, Decla, had not had even one. Not even a crush from the ugliest boy in the school. Nothing.

She stood up and with drooping shoulders she climbed the stairs. She would put on her tennis clothes and go to the club. She'd put a brave face on the woeful situation she found herself in. After all, the day was bright and beautiful, and you never knew, did you? Anything might happen.

When Decla left the room Cora glanced first at her husband reading his *Irish Times* and then at her youngest son.

'Eamonn, isn't there something you should be doing?' she asked mildly.

Eamonn had been biting a design around his piece of toast, then dipping it in his porridge and jam, and at his mother's question he stuffed what remained of the soggy bread into his mouth, then, muttering something about Rugby practice he fled the room.

'There was a scuffle down O'Connell Street last night,' Roddy said, glancing up from his paper at his wife, then back again. 'Says here . . . at the Pillar, some youths with IRA banners. Seems some chaps objected. Ended in violence.'

'Violence is never the way out,' Cora said, shaking her

head. 'It's never acceptable, Roddy. It turns us into animals and it solves nothing.'

'I'm sure you're right, dear,' Roddy replied absent-mindedly and returned to his paper.

'There's something funny here, Roddy,' Cora said.

'What, dear?' Roddy looked up briefly from the paper but his eyes were drawn irresistibly back again to the printed page. 'About Angela's letter. There's something funny. Do listen to me, dear.'

Roddy sighed, rested his newspaper on the table and gave her his attention.

'She says here, er, where is it.' Cora's eyes raked the pages of the letter. 'Ah yes, "Sylvie has been down in the dumps."' She looked up at her husband. 'Funny expression! The letter is littered with expressions like that. What's it supposed to mean? And, um, let me see, all that about recovering her spirits.' She looked again at Roddy, then back to the page in her hand. '"She's been *unwell* and we hope a trip to Ireland might buck her up."' Again Cora shook her head and glanced over at Roddy. 'Appalling phrase! Why on earth doesn't she say what she means? Do you think she's being deliberately ambiguous? All these veiled phrases . . . they could mean anything! Is the girl sick? And if so, what with? Will we be entertaining an invalid?'

'Dear, I don't know, I really don't. I hardly know the woman.'

Angela was married to Sean Flood, Roddy's youngest brother. Sean had left Ireland when he was very young, running away from the family boat-building business as if from the plague, which was why when their father died he left the whole firm and all its assets to Roddy. Sean was a musician, a pianist. He had wanted to shake off the yoke he felt being the son of a successful businessman placed on his shoulders. He was also heartily tired of his father lecturing him about Roddy's superiority and his own uselessness.

'Tinkling keys is for ladies and queers,' Flood Senior told him with withering contempt. 'Pianist! Why not put on skirts and dance! All that stuff is for nancy boys.'

So Sean Flood ran away to England where he got a job as a pianist with The George Peabody Swing Band. However, war came and he was precipitated into the British Army. He had to leave his wife and daughter to fend for themselves in London during the Blitz. He was shipped to France and won himself a commendation for bravery.

'Madness! Madness!' Cora had muttered when Roddy told her of the honour. 'Insanity! War is a game mindless children play. No one mature or wise resorts to violence.'

The letters the Floods received from their London relations were few and far between and those they did get during the war were censored. Why this should be Angela was never sure, but there were hints that the powers-that-be, who were understandably paranoid at the time, were suspicious of Sean Flood and his Irish background. They thought he might be spying for the Germans via Dublin so they paid particular attention to the letters sent there by him and his wife. Their handiwork usually rendered the letters quite unintelligible. Big black quarter-inch lines obliterated the sense and left Cora confused as to what exactly her brother-in-law was telling them.

They had not seen Sylvie, who was the same age as Decla, since she was a child of five. Sean, then a working musician, had brought the family over to meet his relations. The meeting was not a very happy one. Cora did not approve. She thought Angela common, deplored her taste. Just after that visit the war broke out and Cora, relieved, hoped there would be no more such meetings.

Ireland remained neutral. Torn asunder for hundreds of years by her own exhausting struggle for freedom, she rested. Many of her sons went to fight against Hitler side by side with their former enemy, and many died. Cora gave thanks that Roddy did not seem inclined to offer himself up for sacrifice. She was well aware that the fight was between the powers of good and evil but selfishly she desired no part of it. Above everything she wanted to keep her family intact. It was her family, a perfect family, and nothing was going to interfere with its stability.

As she had not heard from her brother-in-law since the war ended except for greeting cards, she was very surprised to receive the letter from Angela. She was even more taken aback by the announcement that Sylvie was coming to stay. It unsettled Cora that her ordered, disciplined existence was going to be disrupted by the arrival of her niece, someone not invited by her. She did not like visitors unless she had chosen them. She disliked the slightest change in the even tenor of her routine and only had people to stay who she considered fitted in. Shrugging, she supposed there was nothing she could do about it. Sylvie would simply have to adapt to life in Rossbeg.

'I hope she's not sick,' she murmured, glancing at those ambiguous phrases again, then she sighed and put the letter away.

Decla burst back into the room. She had been reading the film magazine. 'Mother, can I go see Shirley Temple in the Adelphi? It's a great film, called *Pride of Kentucky* with Barry Fitzgerald.'

'That sounds great. I love Barry Fitzgerald.' Roddy looked up from his paper.

'It's *may* I, not can I, and I just don't know, Decla,' Cora frowned. 'It depends on your cousin. She may have seen it in London.'

'And she may not.' Roddy's voice was crisp. He glanced at his wife and began hastily to read from the paper. 'Says here, dear, says Fynnon Salts is ideal laxative for rheumatic sufferers. It would suit your mother, wouldn't it? She's a martyr to rheumatism, poor woman.' Cora stared at her husband suspiciously. Roddy hated her mother. But Roddy continued undaunted. 'It increases the fluid outflow from the kidneys, so freeing the bloodstream of poisons which would encourage rheumatic aches and pains if allowed to remain in circulation. It says here. It's one and sixpence.' Finishing, he returned her look with one as innocent as a baby's. 'Brendan says he prefers De Witts pills. At least with those you don't have to sit on the bog all day.'

Cora compressed her lips. 'That vulgarity is typical of Brendan,' she said cryptically. 'And don't think you've distracted me from Decla's idea of going to see the Shirley Temple film.' Decla and her father exchanged a glance. 'All right, Decla, you and Sylvie can go if she hasn't seen it already.'

'Oh, thank you, Mother, thank you a ton.'

'Pass me the *Independent*, dear,' Cora asked Roddy, putting the letter away. 'Who won the Sweepstake?' And with these words she put the coming visit of her niece firmly out of her mind.

Chapter Five

⁖ ✿ ⁘

Her admirers, and there were many, both male and female, said that Cora Flood was unflappable. They marvelled at her serene beauty, envied her tranquillity, basked in her relaxed good nature and fought to be invited to her lunches, dinners and parties or the Flood table at Ballyorin. What they took for discipline and an iron control of character-defects such as impatience, intolerance and bad temper was in fact laziness. Cora Flood could not be bothered to be disagreeable. She loathed scenes, had not the energy for emotional turmoil. All her life she had so arranged things that she would not be upset. She had married a man who would keep her in comfort and protect her from adversity when possible. Life's slings and arrows had passed her by and nothing dramatic had ever had the temerity to trouble her or her family. Earthquakes, tornados, floods and volcanos happened elsewhere. Death did not darken her door. Her family *behaved* themselves. And when Cecie, her third daughter, got tuberculosis she relegated her to the small room over the conservatory, did what she could medically for her, was lightly kind and considerate, and pretended it was not really happening. Cecie was an inconvenience in an otherwise perfect world. Cora loved her daughter and in all conscience did what she thought best for her. After all, most families would not have kept a TB patient at home, would have put her in hospital. So Cecie fared better than most, and Cora was not cruel, simply incapable of dealing with the problem any other way.

Her children learned early to go to their father when anything untoward happened. Not that much did. For childhood miseries they went to Roddy for advice or Fusty for comfort. Fusty's arms enfolded them when they hurt

31

themselves and her huge bosom was a pillow for their tears. Their mother did not have a bosom and her stylish dresses did not invite tears or hugs.

They loved and admired their mother and gave her the kind of respect normally accorded to the Blessed Virgin Mary, but they were not close to her.

So Cecie lay in a small room over the conservatory, on her bed of suffering, as Cora called it, and, some said, aspired to sainthood.

Sometimes Cecie was better than at others. She lay in bed and was allowed to traverse her room, leaning heavily on Fusty's arm, twice daily. She never left the room, never ran in the tall grass or played on the swing in the apple orchard. She had been incarcerated for eighteen months now on the narrow bed, surrounded by her dolls, coughing up blood, weak as a kitten, large-eyed and fretful.

Cora was exasperated by the illness. She had expected it to take its course, had been patient at first, but as time passed she became irritated that nothing they or the doctor did seemed to make Cecie better. She wanted Cecie to get on with it, fight the damn sickness and get back to normal, but Cecie hovered. Some days she appeared to be on the mend, then she'd relapse. And so it went on, and the family walked softly past her door. They were kept away from her for fear of contagion and Cecie grew more and more self-obsessed within the confines of her room.

The room, which was part of the extension, was built over the conservatory and had long floor-to-ceiling windows that looked out over the lawn and the rose-garden. The heat was supposed to be good for TB patients, so Dr Sutton said. Cecie's bed had been placed beside the windows where, in the morning, the sun blazed mercilessly on to the hot little girl in her hot little bed and in the evening the glass was cold and blurred by condensation so that she felt she was in the tropics. The windows were never opened. The doctor considered it too dangerous. 'She might catch a chill,' he warned, 'and that would be a death sentence.'

Suffering had made a stoic of Cecie and she shut her eyes against the glare of the noon-day sun and put up with a couple of hours of torture, then shivered in the evening and wished her bed was nearer the fire which blazed far over on the other side of the room, casting dancing demons across the ceiling.

'Our cousin Sylvie is comin' to stay, Cecie. Can you hear, Cecie?' Decla whispered through the keyhole. 'And Mother says I can go to *Pride of Kentucky* with her. She'll be in my room, so she will.'

The door was not locked and there was no key there but Decla was forbidden to enter.

Cecie pulled herself up. It was one of her better days and her cheeks were pale and cool and not brightly hot with fever. Nevertheless she was weak and coughed nervously, in little scales of short barks, like a puppy.

'Who's coming?' she whispered.

'Our cousin Sylvie, from London. You know, Auntie Angela and Uncle Sean's little girl.'

'Oh her! What age is she, Dec?'

'Same as me.'

'Oh Dec, she'll be the grand one! D'ye think she'll have gorgeous dresses? All glam? Still, I expect they'll not let her near me . . .'

'Oh hush, Cecie!' Decla quieted her sister. 'You won't be neglected. I'll see you're not.'

'You're a great one, Dec. They'll forget me, but not you!'

'Don't say that, Cecie. Da'll not forget you.'

'Oh, I'm not complaining! I'd be the same myself an' I was well. It'll be so exciting. Mam'll be thrilled with someone new and sophisticated from London to talk to, to entertain.'

'Oh, I don't think so, Cecie. You know Mam. She doesn't really want her here.'

'But it'll be great! Why wouldn't she want her?'

'Mother hates anything that disturbs her routine. No,' Decla sighed. 'I'll be lumbered with her, see if I'm not. God! I'm not looking forward to it, I can tell you.'

Cecie sighed and looked at the ceiling. She didn't understand at all. The longer she stayed in this room the more incomprehensible she found the reasoning of the rest of her family.

'Well, I think you're lucky to be lumbered with her, as you call it. I'd just *adore* to go out, even with someone who gave me a pain. Oh Dec, you don't know how *bored* I get.

33

I'm stuck in here in the heat of a morning, and I cough and cough till I think my lungs will burst. And Mam and Fusty say I can't read or I'll strain my eyes. They say I have to rest and they say I have to stay in the dark 'cause the electric light is bad for me. But I can't rest in the dark *all* the time, Dec. And I'm lonely. You all go off and I'm left to stare at the ceiling.'

Decla, squatting near the keyhole, sighed heavily for the umpteenth time. Poor Cecie! It must be awful for her. Lying in bed all day must be the most boring thing in the universe! But what could she do? She wished she had a magic wand to wave and Cecie would be cured. Could run and jump again. And dance. Imagine not being able to dance! Decla felt guilty and frustrated though she did not know why. Cecie made everyone feel guilty, though she didn't mean to.

'Don't let it get you down,' Decla whispered through the door. Then she rose, feeling the tingle in her legs where they had lost feeling. 'I've gotta go now.'

'Where? Where are you going?' There was a note of eagerness in Cecie's voice as if by knowing where her sister would be she could savour some sort of vicarious pleasure.

'Ballyorin for tennis,' Decla volunteered reluctantly.

'Gosh, lucky! I'll think of you playing.'

Cecie had been very good at tennis but Decla didn't want her sister thinking about her while she was playing. That too made her feel guilty. She knew that in the middle of her enjoyment she'd remember Cecie's pale little face and somehow her game would suffer. Decla hated herself for feeling like this and she shook her head as if to rid herself of unpleasant thoughts.

'And if Mam *didn't* have visitors, how could she show off that she has the perfect family?' Cecie asked.

'True, true.' Decla hadn't thought of that. Her mother certainly hated visitors but she adored showing off. 'Bye, Cecie,' she whispered.

'Bye, Dec.' Cecie's voice faded fast, like water running down a drain into silence, and Decla, feeling there was something she had not said, some comfort she should have given her sister, turned reluctantly and went to her room to change for tennis.

Fusty was there, bustling about. 'Your mam wants me to

make a start immediately,' she grumbled. 'Think there was Royalty comin'. Honest.' She hugged a pillow to her vast bosom and looked at Decla through her pebble glasses. Her eyes were small, like currants. She was the only servant who had remained in Rossbeg for any length of time. Most left, unable to cope with Cora's standards. Fusty largely ignored her mistress and got on with the essentials at her own pace. She was an incredibly hard worker, her only ambition in life to look after the Flood family. 'Do ye mind?' she asked Decla.

'No, Fusty,' Decla said, smiling. 'I like the attic. I can get away up there.'

Fusty returned to her work murmuring, 'I'm glad, miss. Otherwise it wouldn't be fair.'

'Oh, Sylvie's welcome to stay here,' Decla said and began to rummage in her wardrobe for her shorts and polo shirt. I hope she's happy here, this English cousin, she thought. 'She's going to find it dull after London,' she said aloud. 'Nothing happens here. It's all so boring!'

'Well now, miss, I wouldn't say that!' Fusty smiled, echoing Roddy's words. 'Boring is sometimes a very good thing, you ask me. They had enough excitement in London, God help them, to make anyone long for a bit of boring.' And with that she left the room.

Chapter Six

∽ ∾

Roddy opened the door very softly. Cecie was, to him, a fragile and most precious object. He was awed by her courage, unmanned by her suffering and utterly frustrated by the illness and his helplessness. He felt that as master of the house, he should be able to protect her from all harm. That he could not cure her was a constant source of irritation to him. He had had many a row with Dr Sutton over her treatment, but in the end obeyed the doctor even though he disagreed with him. He had to admit he had no medical knowledge and the doctor obviously must know what was best for Cecie.

'Come in, Dadda,' Cecie called. Though her voice was feeble Roddy could tell that she was in better spirits than she had been the past week.

'You all right, pet?' he asked, tiptoeing in.

'Why does everyone get so quiet around me?' she asked irritably.

'Because they don't wish to upset you, my love,' Roddy replied. 'See, a lot of noise would excite you. Dr Sutton said you needed quiet and rest. Above all rest.'

'When will I be better, Dadda?' Cecie asked. 'I try so hard. I don't want to be impatient, but I am. So often I am.'

'You're not, baby. You're a veritable little saint, so you are.' Roddy could feel the tears prick his eyes. He blinked them back. His little girl, showing such bravery, criticising herself. He touched her forehead with gentle fingers, massaging her temples.

'That's nice, Dadda,' she said softly. 'Don't worry about me.' She looked up at him, her eyes bright, but whether with fever or health he could not tell. 'I know you do and I wish you wouldn't. I know you and Mother are doing everything

36

to help me. It's God's will, Dadda, and I must be as good as I can. That's what Father Mulligan told me.'

Roddy could feel his blood pressure rise. It made him angry to hear the good priest pontificate so arrogantly about things he had no experience of. He talked so glibly about pain and death, about sex and marriage, yet the man himself had no knowledge of such feelings and experiences.

'Father Mulligan needs a little more humility, Cecie,' Roddy said tightly. 'Now, my little pet, you be good and rest. Can I get you a book? I'm sure a little look at the pictures in *National Geographic* would do you no harm.'

'Oh Dadda, I'd love that. The pictures are wonderful. I can imagine all those places and pretend I'm there, in the photographs.'

'Well, here you are, my dear. Let me fix your pillows. There, that better?' She nodded, gladly taking the book from his hands.

Roddy left her there, absorbed in the illustrations of magic, foreign lands.

Chapter Seven

୬ ୭

The tennis clubhouse in Ballyorin was not imposing. A pretty manor-house had been added to indiscriminately over the years. Bits were tacked on as they were needed, without thought of style or form. Most of the work was sanctioned by committee and governed by financial considerations. In other words, the cheapest tender rather than the most attractive won the contract.

Not that the club was poor; far from it. But its money was invested in the grounds. After all, the courts were the most important feature, and they were kept groomed and impeccable.

Ballyorin was *the* most popular place to go. It was the place the nicest and best people in the area gathered to socialise, catch up on gossip and chat, do deals, fall in love and, incidentally, play tennis.

An Englishman called Peck had deplored the haphazard buildings, the ramshackle changing rooms, the whole unstylish atmosphere and had bought a very beautiful manor-house the other side of Dalkey. He spent a fortune on it, absolutely certain of its ultimate success, and opened it as a tennis- and golf-club in competition with Ballyorin. Its aspects were much more charming, its facilities faultless, but it didn't catch on. No one patronised it and Mr Peck went broke. The poor man, left on his own in deserted grandeur took to the bottle and was to be seen often at midnight staggering about the golf course cursing all things Irish. A hopeless race who didn't know the difference between the first-class and the mediocre, he called them. 'You'll never be a great nation, chaps,' he lectured his small circle of sycophants who drank with him of an evening and then sniggered behind his back, not letting him in on the secret. They *knew* that Ireland would never be a super-power. They knew that the Irish were too wise to have such aspirations. They did not *want* their country to become a bullying, war-mongering power in the world, rich and feared and fearful of losing that power. They and Ireland were quite content to be comfortable rather than wealthy, safe in peaceful obscurity rather than continually on the defensive. 'Comfort, that's what we aim for. Comfort, not wealth. Sure, who wants more than they need? But the British and the Americans will never understand that.'

Ballyorin was crowded that Saturday, but then it always was. The ugly old building radiated the assurance of the familiar. Young girls with firm thighs screamed greetings at each other and flashed about in whites on the courts. Boys, awkward and knobbly-kneed, watched them avidly, hoping to partner the prettiest, for desperation to win was not their driving force. To win the loveliest was the name of the game, and who cared if you won or lost if you had a girl like Fidelma Flood on your arm?

The older men propped up the bar and relished the flavour of a Paddy or a pint while they talked of the runners in the two-thirty or the going at Leopardstown while their wives clustered around the umbrella-shaded tables outside on the terrace. They gossiped about their children and the newest fashions, sipping a pre-lunch gin and It.

Cora sank into a wicker chair at a table under the lime tree at the end of the terrace. It was the table the Floods always sat at. No one ever tried to usurp their right to it and if by some chance they were away on holidays or not able to come to the club, anyone else who sat there felt the chill wind of discomfort and a guilty feeling that they were in the wrong place.

Because of her remote air, her lofty indifference to others' opinions, because she did not seek adulation Cora Flood elicited passionate admiration from most of the people there. At the Ballyorin Club she was courted and cultivated as *the* person, whose briefest nod signalled acceptance and whose beckoning white fingers might mean an invitation to join the Flood table and bask in favouritism.

This Saturday Cora sat at the table, then, spying Fidelma, waved to her. Her daughter was chatting with Harry Devereau near the rose-covered arch that led to the courts. She did not notice her mother's salute. At that moment Dr Sutton hove into view.

'Ah, Mrs Flood, and how is our little invalid?' The doctor, a florid, well-padded man smiled down at Cora.

Cora shaded her eyes with her hand. 'Well now, Doctor, our little invalid, as you call her, is *not* doing at all well.'

The good doctor wrinkled his forehead, which was beaded with sweat, and wiped it with a large handkerchief. 'Dear lady—'

'And what's more I feel that you are *not* giving dear Cecie your best shot,' Cora interrupted him, firmly but with a sweet smile on her face. 'Not your best shot at all! There *must* be something more that you can do. So, Doctor, I urge you to find a cure for my daughter, or something to ease her pain and discomfort, or I shall have to look for a doctor who'll do a little better.'

She smiled more widely now at him, the tone of her voice mild all the while.

The doctor blinked, wiped his red forehead again and, murmuring something about it being Saturday and himself off-duty, left her to it, hurrying over to the bar.

Cora turned to her husband, who made as if to follow Dr Sutton. 'Sit beside me, Roddy,' she instructed, waving a waiter over with a languid hand. 'Brendan is joining us for lunch today. I asked him in spite of the rude remarks you told me he made about De Witts pills.' Her tone expected approval and she got it.

'How nice of you, dear,' he replied, glancing enviously at the bar. He could see it through the glass partition that cut the terrace off from the clubhouse, but he obeyed his wife immediately. He would have enjoyed sharing racing tips with his friends but he knew better than to upset Cora. It was not that she would quarrel with him; that was not Cora's way; he would be cast out into an ice-cold region where he would languish, neither seen nor heard by her until she 'forgave him' in her own good time. He never knew why the barriers went down – whether Cora had some secret way of judging his contrition – all he knew was that in Cora's own good time and when his discomfort had reached a peak, suddenly everything would revert to normal.

The terrace faced the courts and they were full. The pock-pock of balls sounded a gentle rhythm underneath the chorus of murmured conversation. The white-clad figures weaved and bobbed on the grass courts and the groups at the tables on the terrace idly followed the games or waved to a friend or clapped a winner. There was an occasional shout of 'Well done!' over the voices of the umpires calling out the scores. It all added to the general buzz and hum, as did the odd burst of laughter – sometimes the treble of women, like birds, and sometimes the deep bass of the men, oiled by numerous libations.

If the clubhouse was ugly the scenery in which it was set was not. Trees circled the courts – beech, pine, oak and ash – and their leaves shuddered and shivered in the merest whisper of a breeze from the sea. In the distance the lake lay like a dark mirror, and on it, almost motionless, there was a pair of black swans. The swans had lived there as long as anyone could remember, and some people thought they were magic, like Odile, the spirit of evil in an evil place. For the lake was a mysterious place, a wide, darkly heaving pool of brackish water. People were not comfortable near it. No one knew how deep it was and it was said its black mirrored surface concealed a depth unfathomable in its vastness. Moving tendrils of weeds could sometimes be discerned near its surface and only the swans seemed comfortable in its vicinity.

Cora contemplated the swans with pleasure. She liked their slow, tranquil movements and identified with them. She felt serene today, more so than usual. Everything was exactly as it should be. Everything was as near perfect as it was possible to be in this world. She shaded her eyes with her hand and looked over the courts to where Fidelma hit the ball with fierce, strong strokes. Decla was opposite her, defending herself from the onslaught. That was nice, Cora thought, her daughters playing in the same match. Usually they didn't and it was good to see them choosing each other like that. Cora smiled.

But they had not chosen to play opposite each other in the mixed doubles. Fidelma had been forced, to her annoyance, to incorporate Decla into her foursome. Brendan O'Brien told Fidelma briskly that there was not another girl or a

41

spare court available and if Harry Devereau and she wanted a game she'd have to play against her sister and Justin O'Brien, Brendan's son and the only other available male that day. Cora had come along and no one was going to argue with her there. She had asked Brendan and Justin to join them for lunch.

Justin was a nice boy, if a bit weedy. He would, Cora knew, eventually grow out of his acne and be a suitable escort in the future for Decla, who was nothing if not awkward with boys. Justin was a deeply embarrassed seventeen. He was constantly overcome by the certainty of his own insignificance and unattractiveness. Sometimes he did not go out at all but stayed in the house all day, staring at his blotched face in the mirror. And sometimes he forgot the problem and then he enjoyed himself, wondering afterwards why it wasn't always like that. Usually he would not have been anywhere *near* Fidelma Flood but his father insisted as all the courts were engaged and Brendan O'Brien was the club secretary.

Decla had muttered to Justin, 'Fidelma's mad as a hornets' nest, but she'll not let on. We're in Justin, we'll get a game.' Then she'd glanced at him and realised she'd boobed. He was looking at Fidelma with that stupid wounded-deer stare most of the boys seemed to acquire around her; all soppy and slack. Decla did not fancy Justin O'Brien one little bit but he was her partner, the only one she could find, and a partner you did not fancy was better than none at all. Decla felt that while he was with her he should at least pay her the attention a partner deserved and not gawp at her sister in such an obvious gormless fashion. Decla's thunderous mood descended and drove her to excess as it usually did. Justin hated her for making that remark, she could see that. Both boys, Justin and Harry, were worshipping at the shrine of her beautiful sister and Decla slammed the ball back at her in a fury.

But Cora was unaware of all this as she sat on the terrace smiling down on the foursome battling it out on the court below. What she did see and what troubled her slightly was the fact that the battle was fierce and concentrated between her daughters. The young men, neither of whom had their heart in the game, were feebly batting the ball when it came their way, but were not, she could see, being allowed to participate in the intense and savage competition between the girls. Fidelma and Decla hit the balls viciously across at each other as if each ball was an arrow aimed to kill. Cora shook her head. She was being fanciful. Her daughters were not capable of such emotion. No. She smiled again.

Decla and Justin O'Brien were now beating Fidelma and Harry. It was Fidelma's fault. She had suddenly changed her tactics. It was amazing to watch. Only Decla saw the exact moment that the change came. There was Fidelma, teeth gritted in effort, slashing her racquet in the air, when suddenly she became aware of what she was doing, how she *looked*. In an instant she altered. She modified her game. She glanced at her partner and smiled. She became more feminine, less aggressive.

'Oh gosh, I'm sorry, Harry,' she cried, and he returned her smile.

'You're playing brilliantly, Fidelma,' he shouted, but she stumbled and allowed him a quite spectacular shot.

'Sorry Harry. You play so well and I'm a glunk!'

'No you're not, Fidelma. You're terrific.'

'Girls just aren't as strong as fellas,' Justin cried. ''Cept Decla, of course.'

'You bet,' Decla muttered audibly and whammed the ball viciously back, hitting Harry on the shoulder and causing Justin to cry out, 'Gosh, take it easy, Decla! Steady on!'

'Ouch!'

'Sorry, Harry. Sorry. I'm a glunk!' Decla imitated her sister precisely and received a lethally withering glance from Fidelma for her pains. 'Oh Justin,' she then berated her partner, 'pull your socks up and *try* you idiot, *try*!'

Justin's face flooded red as a beet and his top lip trembled alarmingly.

'Oh janey, you're not going to *cry*! Talk about *wet*!' Decla sounded exasperated and served a top-spin with ferocity. Then she remembered how she felt when Fidelma spoke to her like that and she winced inwardly at her cruelty.

'Don't mind her, Justin,' Fidelma was calling across the court. 'She's a fiend, my sister. We'll have to get Father Mulligan to exorcise her. You pay no attention to her, you hear me? I think you're wonderful.' Justin nodded, flattered that the beautiful Fidelma had even acknowledged his presence, and he perked up. Being offered sympathy like that by the prettiest girl in the club – damn it, in Dublin – made the insults of his partner worthwhile.

They won, Decla and Justin, and Decla was aware that there was no virtue in her success for with every coy mistake her sister made she was declaring her power over the two men. And Decla's failure. The game over, Fidelma ran impulsively to Justin, patted him on the shoulder and gave him a hug. 'Well done, Justin,' she breathed softly, leaning near him, letting him get a waft of her *Je Reviens* and dabbing her face with a towel. 'Golly, you're a first-class player. Pity my ghastly sister was so *demonic*! Still, you won in the end. Well done!' And she linked her arm through Harry's. 'Did I let you down?' she asked him innocently.

He patted her hand on his arm. 'Golly, no!'

They turned towards the clubhouse. 'Mother's beckoning' Fidelma cried over his protests. 'Lunch must be up. Better hurry, little sister.'

Harry disentangled himself, paused a moment then watched Fidelma, legs flying, run up to the clubhouse. He looked at Decla, his handsome face concerned. 'I think you played brilliantly,' he said and smiled his marvellous smile at her. 'I'd love to partner you some time, Decla.'

'Come *on*, Harry,' Fidelma cried over her shoulder as she hurried back. 'Mother is waiting.'

Harry called, 'Coming!' then looked back at Decla. 'She can't help it, Decla,' he said softly, taking her by surprise. 'We've made her like that.' And he was gone, leaving her puzzled and not a little confused.

Chapter Eight

❧ ❧

Cora watched her daughters hurry back from the courts. She called out 'Decla!' when her second daughter paused and stood still staring up at her. 'Hurry up, pet,' her mother cried but still Decla stood, staring.

Decla had the power to make her mother uncomfortable. Cora and Fidelma were of one mind. Cora hoped that Fidelma would marry Harry, but even if she didn't she'd choose a suitable husband, being, as she was, sensible. She loved her comfort and would not settle for poverty no matter how potent the romance.

Yes, Cora had every reason to be pleased with her eldest daughter. Ossian too. He was doing superbly well. His Father Superior had told her only last week that her son had the makings of a cardinal. She was delighted that Ossian had chosen the priesthood. It was a feather in any mother's cap, both morally and socially. 'Her eldest's a *priest*!' was a phrase to conjure up an impeccable upbringing by a sainted mother. A proof of her integrity and a guaranteed entrance to Heaven. She thought about it now, a dreamy expression on her face. 'Her eldest's a Cardinal!' would be even more impressive.

'He's bright and ambitious,' Monsignor Maguire, her friend and mentor, had told her, the sun throwing a gleaming bracket around his handsome profile. It was during one of their weekly talks and he had told her Ossian might be picked as one of a working party of young priests soon going to Rome.

Cora was duly flattered. Of all the people she knew it was the Monsignor's opinion that she most respected. She was inordinately fond of their chats. She had excluded herself from the crowd in her religion as in all other things.

She was different. Not for her the line in the church to the confessional on a Saturday morning, then the whispered exchange with the voice behind the grille, everything shrouded in darkness. Not for her the breathing in of the used-up air in the small enclosure. Not for her the stale smells others left behind, the mixed odours of the masses. She chose instead a quiet chat with Monsignor Maguire in his sunny library once a week on a Friday, an exchange of views over a cup of tea rather than the act of penance and mortification the sacrament was supposed to be.

'Ossian is bound for great things,' the Monsignor told her. 'He will go to Rome and meet some of the right people.' He laced his fingers and stared out of the French windows at the peaceful cloisters. 'Rome is once more accessible to us, Cora, now that the war is over. It will do him a power of good. I only wish I were in his shoes. I would love to visit the Eternal City again.' The Monsignor shrugged. 'But there you are. The working party is going to the English College there. Ossian will fit in brilliantly.'

'And he'll meet the Pope,' Cora murmured.

'Indeed. Indeed.' The Monsignor's lips were drawn back in a line. He did not like Pius. He did not dare *say* it aloud, but he thought it in the secret places of his heart. He thought the Pontiff bigoted and old-fashioned, out of touch with the modern post-war world. To admit that would be an act of heresy. The Pope was infallible, and unless one believed that one was not truly a Roman Catholic. The Monsignor shuddered. Such a thought was alarming, and the more such disreputable thoughts plagued him the more he fought them. In the dark recesses of his soul he struggled against the constant argument. He pushed away the overwhelming tide of his disapproval, his non-acceptance, and struggled to remain afloat. Convinced that the church of Christ was the only path for him, besotted with the words of the Son of Man, he was nevertheless horrified by how the hierarchy interpreted those words. It was an unending struggle that exhausted him, made him lose heart. It also made him nervous, for if he once succumbed to his subconscious reasoning he would lose everything. The thought appalled him. How could he obey, as was demanded, when he had such reservations? When he did not agree with a lot of the Church's teachings? Not Christ's, oh no. He agreed with every word the Saviour uttered – no, it was man's interpretation he sometimes could not stomach. The Monsignor took refuge in prayer and rebuked himself for his sinful pride.

'I'm getting more like the Prods every day,' he told himself, and put heretical thoughts firmly aside. Freedom of thought or interpretation had never been encouraged in the Holy Roman Catholic Church and he'd simply have to school himself to accept that fact.

He stared at the woman before him. How calm she was, how tranquil. *She* accepted everything without question – how wonderful that must be. And she had passed her serene beauty on to her son Ossian. Like her he was tall and graceful, willow-slim with wild blue-black Irish hair, and they both had light, piercing blue eyes. They each had an other-world remoteness that beguiled and mystified and kept others slightly in awe of them, a quality that should stand Ossian in great stead in his chosen profession. There was about them both a fairy-tale enchantment that caused those who met them to fall instantly under their spell. Monsignor Maguire knew this gift, if such it was, would guarantee Ossian a difficult but probably wildly successful pathway in the priesthood. There would be jealousy and favouritism and it would not be an easy passage. He wondered at the mother's calm and thought to himself that she seemed, for a married woman of thirty-nine with five children, curiously unawakened. She gave him the impression that she dreamed, that she was only half-awake, that she was imprisoned behind glass and did not know that she was.

'Yes,' he told her that day, 'Ossian is destined for great things.'

Cora Flood recalled with complacency her last conversation with the Monsignor as she sat now in the tennis club and sipped the gin and It the waiter had brought. Roddy took a gulp of his Guinness, put it down on the table and began to drum his fingers, glancing wistfully over his shoulder at the men, his friends, propping up the bar. Cora put a gentle hand over his and he stopped.

Suddenly the terrace was invaded by waiters who shook pink linen cloths over the tables and began to set them for

47

lunch. There would be a buffet with salads, cold meats and fruit laid out inside on the long table in the room next to the bar and the guests were expected to help themselves. The waiters placed the knives and forks carefully, then the spoons and the wine-glasses, and Cora squinted her eyes and watched her daughter Decla hesitate in the middle distance.

Decla had been planning hideous fates for her sister as she walked up to the clubhouse. She could push her into the black lake below and let her drown. Slowly, so that her lungs filled up like balloons and burst. Floating like Ophelia on the surface of the lake Fidelma would be beautiful in death but she would never bother Decla again. That was when she looked towards the pavilion. Her mother was leaning over the wooden parapet waving her towards them. Harry and Fidelma were disappearing into the changing-rooms. Justin had forgotten her and was gazing longingly after Fidelma, probably nursing a hopeless passion after her encouraging words. 'I think you're wonderful', indeed!

Decla sighed, shading her eyes from the glare of the sun, and noticed as she did so a stranger watching her. Behind her mother, leaning against the corner of the clubhouse building. A tall youth, and from here a good-looking youth. Staring at *her*. Not her sister. Yet he must have seen Fidelma. Most boys, and men, when they looked at Fidelma, didn't stop looking until after she had dissappeared. But this boy was not even glancing in her sister's direction. He was staring at Decla, his arrow-glances cutting through the very air about them, meant for her, sending her a message. The sun disappeared behind a dark cloud and she could not see his face any more. Her heart did a little flip, then a somersault, and as she hurried up to the clubhouse to change she blinked the sun out of her eyes and wondered if she had imagined it.

Chapter Nine

❧ ❧

Cora, wondering what Decla was looking at, slowly became aware of the young man leaning against the wooden wall behind her. She could not see him and did not want to look over her shoulder, but she could *feel* his presence. It irritated her, his being silently behind her, and she wished he'd go away. However, what could she do about him? Nothing. He was entitled to stand there, looming. But she would not turn around.

'Roddy, there's someone near my right shoulder. Who is it?' She cast him a pleading look.

'What, my love?' he asked loudly so that whoever it was must hear. She looked at him with intense irritation. She did not want the stranger to know she was aware of him.

'Someone behind me,' she told her husband softly, but either he did not understand what she wanted or *would* not understand and kept his voice at the same loud level.

'Where, my dear?' he asked, looking around. It was in ways such as these that he got his own back on her for not allowing him to spend time with the lads at the bar.

'What, dear? Who is where?' he enquired.

'Never mind,' she murmured impatiently. She was *not* going to turn around and her husband was *not* going to upset her. At that moment the sun was blocked by a fleet of cirrus clouds and it was as if the lights were suddenly switched off. Cora shivered. Roddy, ashamed of his little game of pretended ignorance, took the cashmere wrap off the back of the chair and draped it over his wife's shoulders. 'There, my dear. Don't want you to get cold.' She acknowledged his gesture with a brief nod of thanks. The presence behind her still bothered her. She wanted to shoo whoever it was away. They were too near for comfort, yet not near enough for

49

her to enquire if they wanted something. It could be no one they knew or the person would have greeted her and that in itself was odd, for they knew everyone.

It was Justin O'Brien who put her out of her uneasy state of unknowing. Decla arrived, hair wet and limp from the showers, wearing a summer dress which, her mother saw, was sadly creased. She sat beside her father. She was followed by Fidelma, immaculate, hair tied up in a pony-tail, her white voile dress with blue embroidered forget-me-nots fresh and uncreased, and she sat gracefully beside her mother. She was accompanied by Harry Devereau and Justin O'Brien trundling hopefully behind. He jostled Harry for a seat on Fidelma's other side but Harry sat calmly down, bending his head to listen to something Fidelma was saying. Then to Cora's surprise Justin was hailed by the mysterious presence behind her.

'Hello, Justin. Thought you'd be here. I just arrived.'

The accent struck Cora harshly. Irish voices were, in general, soft, but this was flat Belfast mixed with cadenceless English.

'Shannon!' Justin, who had been too preoccupied trying to snaffle the seat beside Fidelma to notice the person leaning against the clubhouse wall, turned now and greeted whoever it was enthusiastically. 'Shannon! You got here! Great!'

'I told you I was coming.'

'I thought you only said might. This is my ... you see I ... I'd like you to meet ...' Justin, in an agony of self-consciousness, stumbled in embarrassment over his words and it was the arrival on the scene of his father that rescued him from his misery. Brendan laid a hand on his son's shoulder and with the other at last drew the stranger into view.

Cora instantly disliked him. He was a young man, not more than eighteen or nineteen. His face was strong and serious and somehow bitter. He had an attractive smile that he did not use as often as he should and there was something disturbing and dangerous about him, in Cora's opinion. He wore a tweed jacket and looked hot and uncomfortable in the sun but Cora knew he would not take it off. How or why, she did not know, but she was sure that she was right.

50

'My young nephew from England,' Brendan told them. 'Shannon O'Brien, my brother's son.'

'How odd,' Decla cried, wondering at the coincidence. 'We've got a cousin coming from England next week.' She smiled at the stranger from where she was sitting beside her father and he smiled back.

'Mr and Mrs Flood,' Brendan introduced. 'And Justin you of course know. Harry Devereau, and this is Fidelma Flood.' Wonder of wonders, Decla noted, his jaw didn't drop, he didn't gawp at the sight of her sister's beauty as most men were wont to do but turned his attention to her, Decla, as Brendan said her name, his eyes alight with interest. She couldn't believe it. Was she imagining it? Had she finally gone barmy?

But no. The young man went on smiling at her, an intimate smile, and she felt as if she was melting under the charm of it.

'Do join us,' Cora was saying. 'Do sit yourself down and tell us, are you on a visit? Decla is right. Our niece from London is arriving next week.' Gracious as ever, Cora did not let her dislike show and indicated a vacant chair.

'It's certainly a coincidence,' Shannon answered her politely if a little stiffly. 'May I?' he asked Decla, indicating the chair beside her and she nodded delightedly. She was blushing, she knew, and in an agony of excitement and hope she prayed that the terrible red would not stain her neck and cheeks and reveal to this stranger the depth of her insecurity. Sophisticated people didn't blush.

'Decla's bright red!' Fidelma said lightly. She's cross because he didn't flip, Decla thought, in torment at both the remark and the attention it provoked.

'I think it's delightful,' Shannon O'Brien said gallantly. 'Girls today are so *brash*. It's nice to meet someone so feminine.'

The compliment sounded more like a statement in that flat accent but Fidelma looked put out. She was not used to rebuffs. Decla squirmed with delight.

'I'm not from London, I'm from Liverpool,' Shannon was saying in answer to Roddy's daft query as to whether he knew their niece Sylvie Flood.

'Don't be ridiculous, man,' Brendan O'Brien remarked. 'London's not like Dalkey. Sure it's a vast place.'

'Well, you never know. Truth is stranger—' Roddy protested.

'It's thirty miles across, they tell me. Can ye beat that? Wide as the Sahara Desert!'

Eamonn and his little friend Martin Metcalf arrived with Rusty. They came dashing and bumbling up to the table, but as they came close Eamonn, suddenly catching sight of the stranger, stopped and clapped his hand to his mouth. Decla noticed this strange reaction but none of the others was looking. She saw Shannon, still smiling, shake his head almost imperceptibly at her little brother who gazed back as if mesmerised.

'Eamonn, you can't bring Rusty to the table. Tie him up outside,' Fidelma said.

'That's cruel!' Eamonn cried.

'Well, it's the rules!' Fidelma persisted. 'Dadda, tell him.' She looked at Roddy with large blue eyes. Eamonn ran to his mother. This, Decla knew, was unusual. He normally avoided public displays of affection like the plague.

'Come here, darling.' Cora put an arm lightly around him and Decla glanced back at Shannon O'Brien, but he was sipping a beer and now seemed indifferent to the child.

'Fidelma is right, pet,' Cora said. 'You'll have to put Rusty outside. Now run along.' She sighed as she looked at him, for he almost defied description. His hair stuck up like a shoe-brush, brown and bristly, his face was streaked with mud and what looked like dried blood. His hands were filthy and his knees scabby, coated with unmentionable substances. His socks were at half-mast and his short-sleeved white shirt was filthy.

'Darling, you are a terrible mess,' Cora tutted. He and Martin had been dissecting worms behind the tin shed used for storage. They had come directly from Rugger practice to test out the veracity of a fascinating theory. Another boy in Eamonn's Rugby side had told him that if you cut a worm in half the halves lived and each automatically became a whole – if smaller – worm. Buster McFee had also said that if you severed enough of them you could cover the globe with worms and there would be no room for people. The idea

52

appealed and Eamonn and Martin had decided to give it a go, but no matter how hard they tried the worms, when cut, disastrously died. They swelled up and atrophied and dried up in the sun, then lay there, two little hard lifeless tubes where before a pink wriggling worm had been. Eamonn and Martin were disgusted.

'Go and wash, you two,' Roddy instructed, glancing at his wife's stricken face. 'Go quickly and take Rusty or you're for it!'

Shannon stared at them and Fidelma wrinkled up her nose.

The boys scampered off. Lorcan Metcalf, Martin's big brother, loped up to the table. He was number-two man on Fidelma's list of suitors, a big rugged guy whose father was a judge.

'Hope Martin hasn't been a nuisance, Mrs Flood,' he said and Cora shook her head.

'No indeed, Lorcan, not at all. Oh, by the way, this is Shannon O'Brien.' Everyone turned towards the stranger again. 'Lorcan Metcalf,' Cora finished.

Shannon appeared perfectly at ease, grinning in a wolf-like way which irritated Cora. She did not know what to make of him, this hard-faced youth in the tweed jacket, but she had perforce to be nice to him. He was sitting back, eyes half closed, looking somewhere into the middle distance with that grin on his face. He had tilted his chair backwards and it was balancing precariously on its two hind legs. Cora looked at him with sharp disapproval. 'Don't do that!' she cried before she could monitor the sharpness of the command. His eyes flew open and he looked at her suddenly with such an expression of fierce fury that she was taken aback.

Lorcan Metcalf dispelled the sudden awkwardness by saying, 'Fidelma, are you free Tuesday? We're going to the Metropole dance ... are you ... could you join us? Maybe?' He looked nervously around and Cora asked, 'Why don't you join us? Pull up a chair.'

'Well, well, I believe congratulations are in order?' Roddy chimed in and turned to the others. 'Lorcan did very well, it appears, in his exams.'

Lorcan looked embarrassed. 'I think I did, sir. I don't know.'

'Well, your pa said you did and he's never wrong, your pa.' It was something Judge Metcalf often stated himself and they all laughed.

'You took the bar exam?' Brendan O'Brien asked a trifle nervously. He was not too sure of himself when it came to professions, being himself a bookie. But Brendan was not envious. He was happy with his position in the scheme of things. If, as he guessed, Cora Flood and Lanie Metcalf thought of bookies in the same bracket as band leaders and publicans, well, they were entitled to their opinion. It was a free country at last, thank God.

Brendan was not mad about Lorcan. He thought him old beyond his years and heavily serious. But then who wouldn't be with Judge Metcalf for a father? People said he *enjoyed* passing the death sentence.

If truth be known, Brendan was not crazy about Cora Flood either. However, she was his best friend's wife and therefore had to be cultivated unless he wanted to lose Roddy as his mate. She was too stuffily correct. Never let her hair down, and Brendan doubted that Roddy had much fun in the marital bed. Probably it was a twin arrangement like in the movies. Myrna Loy and William Powell, the most socially correct Hollywood pair, had twin beds in the kind of room he imagined the Floods shared in Rossbeg. He was sure it would be an antiseptic class of a room, new-pin tidy, constantly in perfect order.

He looked around the table. Fidelma was saying something to Harry about the prospective visit of her cousin.

'She'll have all the latest fashions and we'll look like country bumpkins, no less!'

Harry threw back his head and laughed and Fidelma looked put out.

Lorcan shook his head and said seriously, 'No one could ever think you were a country bumpkin, Fidelma.'

'No, *never*. Never!' Justin assured her.

'Don't be daft,' Decla sniped. 'They've been at war. Everything's rationed. They haven't got the material, not like we have.'

Harry looked over, his dark eyes smiling. 'Decla's right,' he said.

Brendan too looked at Decla. He liked the girl, thought

54

her spunky and more fun than her beautiful sister would ever be. And he saw her staring at his nephew, the bold Shannon. He felt an inexplicable chill of fear slither down his back, but shook himself, rose and announced, 'I'm going to have one more before we eat. What can I get you all?'

Cora watched him, eyes squinting against the sun as he made his way into the clubhouse. He's a little cock-o'-the-walk, she thought, a bantam strutting and crowing with satisfaction. He had a little man's swagger, and for a moment she thought how exciting he was, how he generated energy, then quickly cut off such an inappropriate line of speculation and turned to her husband. 'We'll eat soon,' she said and, to the gathering around her table 'Everyone hungry?'

'I'm *starving*,' Shannon O'Brien said.

The sun was hot now and Roddy waved a fly away and rose. 'Then let's get lunch,' he said decisively. As he turned towards the clubhouse his face lit up and he cried, 'Ossian!'

There, striding towards them in his long black robe, their eldest son arrived on the scene like a good angel. Everyone smiled. Everyone turned eagerly to him and greeted him and he responded with hugs and kisses and handshakes. Everyone was glad to see him. Charm oozed from him like honey.

'Darling!' Cora held out her arms to him, the joy of her life. 'Oh my dear, how good to see you. But what a pleasant surprise. How did you know we were here?'

'And where else would you be, Mother, the Floods on a Saturday, but in the Ballyorin club holding sway at your usual table, looking devastatingly beautiful as you always do? Eh?' She laughed delightedly. 'Yes, they let me out and I knew you'd be here. Thought I'd join you. Treat myself.'

'Treat us, you mean.' Cora touched his cheek tenderly.

'Food here is so much better than the stuff I get at home,' Ossian remarked. They made room for him. All malice and worry left them and they turned to Father Flood as if to the sun.

'Fidelma, you look wonderful,' he was saying. 'Still breaking all the lads' hearts?' Then as Eamonn and Martin came hurrying up to the table, 'Eamonn, you little devil, what have you been up to? How they won the war in Europe without your help I'll never know.' Eamonn squirmed delightedly and Fidelma smiled and glanced at Harry. 'Decla, you get prettier every day,' Ossian continued and greeted them all until he came to Shannon.

'It's my nephew from England, Shannon,' Brendan O'Brien said, returning with the drinks. 'Ah sure it's good to see you, boy.' Brendan's face was wreathed in smiles as he watched Ossian collapse his rangy body into the seat beside his mother where his father had been sitting and Decla and the others moved one down accordingly to accommodate him. No one minded. It was Ossian.

The priest pulled Eamonn on to his knee and the youngster stared up in awed delight at his big brother. Ossian smiled benevolently around the table, his handsome face full of sparkling life, and if in the depths of his eyes there lurked a calculation, a shrewdness, no one there saw it.

'How are you, poppet?' he asked Decla, gently touching her cheek.

'Smashing, Ossian,' she replied, looking up at him with glad eyes.

'And you, you gorgeous creature?' he asked Fidelma.

'I'm fine, Ossian.' Fidelma's face was unselfconscious since her brother's arrival. She'd stopped posing and her beauty glowed. She doesn't realise how she spoils her looks when she's aware of them, Cora thought, how much prettier she is when she forgets. Cora sighed. She knew they were all to blame for that; the family, the O'Briens, all their friends, everyone at the club, for they all talked to Fidelma as if she were not like other people, and who could blame her if she reacted to such admiration?

Ossian was glancing at her now and she smiled at him tenderly.

'Oh come on. Let's eat.' Roddy beckoned them to follow him and they trooped inside, filled their plates from the laden buffet. Cold salmon and beef. Ham and scallions. Radishes, lettuce and cucumber. Tomatoes and beetroot. Dublin Bay prawns and shrimp cocktails. Roddy ordered the wine and the beers and they meandered back to the table, chatting and laughing. A waiter had opened the umbrella over it and Cora thanked him, grateful for the shade. She

56

glanced distastefully at Shannon O'Brien's excessively full plate. Bad manners, she decided, mentally tutting. He had piled everything he could possibly have without it spilling off on to the largest plate he could find.

'Cor! Wish I could do that!' Eamonn whispered to Martin, whose eyes were popping out of his head at the quantity on the stranger's plate and the dexterity it required to get it all on and keep it there.

'Mam would never let me,' Eamonn whispered.

'Ah well, see, you're not growed up!' Martin replied. 'You can do it when you're growed.'

'Grown ups don't seem to *want* to!' Eamonn remarked. ''Cept him.'

'There's plenty more where that came from,' Roddy reassured Shannon.

'The war's over, lad,' Brendan added.

Cora said nothing and decided her first impression of unease in this young man's presence had been right. She did not like or trust him.

They sat around the shaded table, eating, drinking, laughing, sharing confidences and flirting in the warm drowsy afternoon.

Then Eamonn saw the gun. They were, of course, he and Martin, smaller than the rest and so their line of vision was lower down. They had been seated with the stranger, their backs to the view, and as the youngsters hungrily tucked into their food, Eamonn, mouth full, squinted up at the chockfull plate, still amazed at the immense quantity and mixture on it and wondering enviously how the stranger was going to down it all without being sick. Shannon O'Brien was eating swiftly, shovelling food down him like he'd been starving.

'You seem very hungry, Shannon,' Roddy remarked.

Brendan O'Brien looked uncomfortable. 'He's been with us overnight and we fed him good,' he said almost apologetically.

Cora wrinkled her nose in distaste at this inappropriate conversation, but Brendan continued undaunted. 'He's wolfed down more food these twenty-four hours than I normally do in a week.'

'Food's short in England,' Shannon said, his mouth full, indifferent, it seemed, to their opinion of him.

'War's been over a long time,' Lorcan Metcalf volunteered, glancing at Shannon as if he was an interesting specimen in a zoo.

'But they still have rationing. Right, Shannon?' Ossian said kindly.

Shannon nodded, still shoving food into his mouth.

'It's *amazing*!' Eamonn had whispered to Martin, staring in stunned admiration at the stranger beside him, riveted by his performance.

Then Shannon picked up his wine and threw back his head to drain it. As he did so his tweed jacket fell outward and Eamonn saw the gun. Stuck in the waist of Shannon's trousers, it was, just like in a movie. Eamonn was about to draw Martin's attention to it when he thought better of it. Martin would be sure to exclaim, fall off his chair, behave like an eejit, and then Shannon would know he knew. And in that split-second Eamonn decided that would not be a good thing. There was adventure here, a mystery, and Eamonn was not yet sure how he was going to tackle the situation. A gun. A real gun stuck in this guy's trousers.

He'd never even *seen* a real gun before. No one here, no one in Dalkey had any use for guns. When he went into Grafton Street in Dublin with his mother or father they passed a shop with gold lettering above it saying *J. Taggart, Gunsmith.* There were beautiful old-fashioned matched pistols in the window and those were the only guns Eamonn had ever seen. Until now. Oh, he'd seen the rifle old Peck kept over at his failed club but it hung on the wall behind glass. No one ever used it. It was cold and sort of ancient, while the gun in Shannon O'Brien's belt looked warm and smooth and cared for. Small and lethal.

Eamonn knew that guns were necessary for some people, but why for Shannon O'Brien? Policemen and soldiers carried guns and people in the movies in America, but Shannon wasn't a policeman or a soldier. And he wasn't a movie star either.

Eamonn decided there was something peculiar about Shannon O'Brien and he decided to watch him. Secretly. It would be like Bulldog Drummond. An exciting thing to do. He debated with himself whether to include Martin in his plans and decided against it. Martin might blab and spoil everything. A gun! It was certainly unusual.

There were men in and out of *J. Taggart, Gunsmith* in Dublin, but Roddy had told Eamonn they were country folk. 'You can tell by the way they dress son,' he said. The men going into the gunshop wore tweeds and cavalry twill trousers. Shannon's trousers were gabardine, not twill, but his jacket was tweed. Maybe Shannon was a hunting man, but Eamonn seriously doubted it. He did not think there was much hunting in Liverpool.

They were all eating now, the white-jacketed waiters moving in and out of the tables collecting used plates and cutlery. Shannon had finished before any of the others and was gently sucking his teeth. Cora decided he'd never be asked to join them again. Even if Brendan O'Brien was Roddy's best friend. She noticed then, as the waiters poured the coffee, that Ossian was going to tell her something. She knew suddenly, as if by divine inspiration, that she was going to hear something she did not want to hear. She almost left the table, then realised that would simply be putting off the evil moment. She turned to her son. 'Yes, Ossian?'

'Mother, I'm off to Rome on Tuesday,' he told her.

She had expected that, was glad and excited for him. That news did not upset her in the least. She was about to decide that her premonition had been false when Ossian added, his eyes bright, 'Guess who is coming with me?'

'Who, dearest?' she enquired innocently. But she knew already. With a sinking heart and an inner rage, she knew.

'Monsignor Maguire. Your friend. Isn't that wonderful?'

She froze. Sitting there in the sun her blood ran cold.

'He told you, didn't he?' Ossian asked.

'No,' she replied.

'I expect he didn't think you'd be interested. After all, he's only your confessor.'

She picked up her straw hat and fanned herself with it even though she felt icy cold.

The Monsignor gone! Not in Wicklow any more. Not available any more, to sustain her, give her courage. What would she do without him? He had no business going to Rome, none at all. He had not warned her. He should at least have warned her. That was the predominant thought among all the others, all the words swirling around in her head, the tumbling sentences and questions drowning reason and logic.

'What will I do without him?' she cried and they all looked at her, surprised by the anguish in her voice.

Only Ossian knew to whom she referred. 'Mother, he's simply your confessor,' he said softly, wiping his mouth with his napkin, an edge to his voice.

'Who's that?' Roddy asked. Fidelma turned back to Harry and Decla gazed soulfully at Shannon. Eamonn was still preoccupied with the gun.

'Mother, you're not such a great sinner that you need anyone all the time.' Ossian stared at her puzzled. 'You'll find another priest soon enough.'

Brendan O'Brien looked at Cora, a twinkle in his eye. 'Another priest? Did I hear ye say? Another priest! Why, Ireland is riddled with priests! They're ten a penny in this part of the world,' he grinned.

She looked at him, eyes cold, almost hostile. 'I've . . . we've . . .' She could not finish the sentence and she suddenly rose and left the table, excusing herself with mumbled words.

Ossian shook his head. 'What's the matter, Dadda?' he asked. 'Why's she like that? I only told her Monsignor Maguire was coming to Rome with me . . . I thought she knew. There's no reason for her to take on so.'

'She's very close to the Monsignor, 'Roddy said. 'Go after your mother, Fidelma.'

Fidelma was deep in conversation with Harry Devereau and did not seem to hear her father.

'I'll go, Dadda,' Decla suggested and hurried into the clubhouse after her mother.

'He's been Cora's confidant and spiritual adviser for a long time,' Roddy said to Ossian.

'Bit extreme, if you ask me,' Ossian mused. 'Over a priest.'

'Another glass of wine, Roddy?' Brendan asked and poured the ruby liquid into Roddy's glass without waiting for a reply.

The Monsignor had remarked casually to Ossian, 'I'll miss your mother, Ossian. I'll miss our talks. Still, it's all in the family and it will be nice to get to know you better. She's talked a lot about you.'

Ossian suddenly felt sorry for his mother. She had no real friends, he realised, and Monsignor Maguire had been someone she relied on. Oh, she had a million acquaintances and people she *said* were her friends. But she confided in none of them. She did not trust any one of them. Only the Monsignor. Still, it was not like her to show emotion like that.

There was nothing, however, that he could do. The powers had decreed that Monsignor Maguire, who spoke fluent Italian and was therefore eminently suitable, would be put in charge of the small group of five priests chosen to go to the Vatican. Such instructions often came without warning, without consultation, and obedience was a prerequisite for a priest. In any event, Ossian was quite sure it would never occur to Monsignor Maguire even to think of refusing to go. He wanted to go. Ossian had caught the excitement in his voice.

'My mother is Italian,' he had told Ossian. 'She is very beautiful. I've always had a great love of Italy.'

And if he was honest with himself, Ossian wanted the Monsignor to take them. Monsignor Maguire was an influential man, he had friends in high places, and Ossian Flood was ambitious. He knew his mother relied on the Monsignor and it now seemed to her son that the dependence was more complete than he had understood. He remembered now her telling him about it long ago, before he had been ordained.

'He explains things to me, Ossian, makes things clear,' she'd said. 'Your father, I'm afraid, is not really interested in spiritual matters.' This was true. Roddy believed religion should be left to priests and women. Cora, Ossian decided, would miss the Monsignor much more than he'd miss her.

Chapter Ten

❧ ❧

The first meeting between the Monsignor and Cora had been at afternoon tea in the Shelbourne. Cora was pregnant with Eamonn at the time and the Monsignor did not know it but he was being interviewed by her as a prospective spiritual adviser. She had had tea with countless clerics, searching restlessly for someone upon whom to lay the burden of her problems. Someone to talk to about spiritual matters, a confidant and a guide. None of the young clerics passed muster. Either they were too hidebound by rules and dogma, too narrow-minded, or, worse still for Cora, some were too *broad*-minded for her exacting taste. Some were fools and some knaves, some obviously drank too much and some, with tight lips and severe, ill-humoured faces, did not drink at all. Some were so sharp they could cut through any debate with Jesuitical skill and, she felt, would leave her floundering far behind them. The Monsignor, on that first meeting and ever since, astonished and delighted her. He met her every requirement with flying colours. He was sensitive, erudite, obviously ascetic and disciplined, yet he had a lively sense of humour combined with a knowledge and appreciation of worldly things and real compassion for the struggling masses. He was also personable, an attractive man approximately her own age with a lean Italianate face and bright eyes. And his manners were impeccable.

There were people in the Shelbourne that day at the next table, she remembered, who laughed a lot and spoke loudly, a little too loudly for comfort. She had said reprovingly, glancing in their direction, 'It's difficult to make oneself heard. Some people are very inconsiderate!' And he had smiled and replied charitably, 'Perhaps they are deaf!' She was delighted at his tolerance, his magnanimity. And after that first meeting he was chosen.

Since then he had guided her, advised her, seen her through Eamonn's First Communion and the others' Confirmation. He had officiated at Ossian's ordination. He would, she confidently planned, conduct Decla's and Fidelma's weddings and he would eventually (she shivered at the thought, but facts had to be faced) bury Cecie.

She often found herself thinking of him. The thought of his noble ascetic face, his sensitive mobile mouth so quick to smile in understanding, brought reassurance and comfort to her soul.

Roddy did not understand the spiritual side of life at all. He was a very worldly man. She had done her duty by him, given him two sons, three daughters, managed his house impeccably, was, in every way in her opinion, the perfect wife.

And she loved Roddy. She told Monsignor Maguire she would give her life to save his, although subconsciously she felt it should, by rights, be the other way around.

'He is a *simple* man, Monsignor, and I am complicated.'

'Well, we have to make allowances for that,' he had said. 'It was the simple folk, Cora, that Jesus loved.'

'I know, Monsignor, I know, but I cannot help myself.'

So they met every Friday. She would arrive at the Monsignor's appartments in the Abbey and he would receive her in his library. It was a beautiful room, wood panelled and tranquil, looking out over quiet cloisters and a splashing fountain. A plump housekeeper called Mrs Dumphy would bring in a silver tray with tea and Cora would pour. There was always a plate of digestive biscuits and Cora always ate one though she did not really want it, and the Monsignor always glanced at them distastefully and refused. Their talks had sometimes been serious, sometimes touching on dogma. Sometimes their conversations were light-hearted, and sometimes they laughed, but whatever the topic or her problem she always came away from their meetings reassured and at peace and with some new concept she could ponder through the week.

The Monsignor often joined the Floods for Sunday

lunch and he was always present at Cora's select entertainments.

Now he was leaving. Going away, just like that, and without telling her. Carelessly withdrawing from the tapestry of their lives, leaving a ragged torn place behind. It was a shattering piece of information and Cora knew she'd lost her head in receiving it without preparation, so cruelly, so suddenly. Her serenity had abandoned her, her tranquil façade had slipped. She felt unprotected, horrendously exposed and vulnerable.

The ladies' room in the tennis club was usually awash underfoot. The showers used by the heedless young sprayed water on every surface and it was no wonder Decla and most of the female clientele emerged from the place damp and dishevelled. The miracle was that Fidelma managed to make an exit so well groomed. Cora seldom used it, preferring to wait until she got home if at all possible. It was not an ideal place to find solace and she ran some cold water into a cracked white basin in a row of such basins in front of the showers and, dampening her handkerchief, pressed it to her temples.

How *dare* he! How dare he do this to her! How could he up and go to Rome and not give a thought to her feelings? Outraged, she shivered in fury and struggled to control herself.

Losing control was unseemly and she did not remember ever before in her life doing so. It was not allowed. She did not remember ever before feeling as she did now. She wanted to scream and yell and throw a tantrum. She who deplored any excessive show of emotion wanted to go berserk.

I'll stop him, she thought, knowing she couldn't, I'll kill him first. Then, horrified at the violence in her, she looked around, terrified someone might see and divine her feelings, but there was no one there. They were all at lunch. After lunch there would be a run on the ghastly place, but for the moment it was deserted and she was safe.

She filled her palm with water from the tap and lapped it, like a puppy, from her hand, trying desperately to get a hold on herself. What was the matter with her? She hated the overwhelming storm that raged within her but she seemed to have no control any more.

Then she caught sight of herself in the long mirror, also cracked, above the basins. She looked, to her vast surprise, the same as ever, quite calm. Only her eyes betrayed some of her inner turmoil.

What was wrong with her? She looked at her reflection, puzzled. Why should she feel this wild fury simply because a family friend, her spiritual adviser, was taking her son to Rome? She wanted to cry, wanted to sob helplessly as she'd seen Garbo do but had never had cause to herself. Gulping, she looked at her hands. She thought of his face, the grave concern he showed for all her problems.

'I'm afraid, dear Monsignor, that I'm developing arthritis, or rheumatism in my hands,' she had told him.

The Monsignor glanced at her. 'You get pain?' he asked, instantly sympathetic.

She nodded. 'I'm getting old,' she told him ruefully.

'Not only the old get arthritis,' he said. 'Children get it too. But it's very painful.'

'I thought only the old suffered from such illnesses,' she said quietly. They always spoke quietly. There was never any need to raise their voices.

'My mother suffers badly. She is only in her forties,' he said.

'I'm not there yet,' she told him. Why did she tell him that? As if it mattered what age she was. And she *was* thirty-nine. Why had she said that? Vanity?

'My mother misses Italy. She misses the sun,' he said, his eyes thoughtful. 'She blames the dampness here in Ireland for her pain.'

The sun shone through the heavy velvet drapes and butterflies danced in the lilac outside the open French window. 'Come here,' he said, standing and moving to the window. She obeyed. Her throat was dry and her heart beat in her breast. He led her on to the patio outside. The library gave on to a cloistered walk surrounding a green square with the fountain splashing in the middle and four little rose bushes at each corner. It had a medieval flavour and an atmosphere of tranquillity and peace, as if all the prayers murmured by the nuns and monks strolling around that place had laden the air with spirituality. Cora loved the atmosphere. Sometimes they talked there, ambling around the square of grass under the stone arches, chatting, intently discussing some theological question, or silent, listening to the fountain.

But that day, talking about arthritis, he had led her to a stone bench beside the green square. She followed. He sat down, his hands pressing her shoulders so that she sat too. Then he took her hands in his long brown fingers. She drew in her breath sharply, staring up at him, hardly daring to breathe.

He was looking at her hands, examining them, staring curiously at her long pale fingers, her nails, filed round and short and covered with clear colourless nail gloss.

She held her breath. What was this feeling of suffocation that made her think her heart had stopped?

He was laying her hands on the bench, on the warm stone in the sun. He put them palm down, arranged each finger separately until her hands, like star-fish, lay spread-eagled in the sun.

'There now,' he said softly in a satisfied tone of voice. 'That's what I used to do with my mother's hands. She said it helped. Letting the sun shine on her poor painful hands.' He looked into her eyes. 'The sun heals, you see.' Then his eyes suddenly changed and he took his hands abruptly away from hers as if he had seen something in her eyes that gave him pause for thought. 'The sun heals,' he said, and walked away.

She thought of that now, remembering, and saw Decla behind her.

'You startled me, dear,' she said.

'Are you all right, Mother?' Decla sounded anxious. Cora was always all right.

'Of course I am, dear. It was hot out there.'

'Yes, Mother.'

'That young man is quite beyond the pale,' she told her daughter matter-of-factly. She examined her face in the mirror but did not really see it. Nor did she see the expression on her daughter's face.

For Decla's heart had sunk. That young man could only be Shannon O'Brien. She pretended to misunderstand.

'Oh, Justin will be okay. He's a bit gauche but he'll grow up one day,' she said.

66

To her surprise Cora did not bother to correct her or pursue the conversation. She handed the damp handkerchief to Decla and said, 'Let's go out again, dear. It really is horrible in here and I'm tired. Let's go home.'

'Would you mind if I stayed behind, Mother?' Decla asked, wondering what to do with the damp handkerchief.

'No, of course not.'

Cora wanted desperately to go home. She wanted to be alone. She did not even want Ossian near her at this time. She returned to the table.

'I think I'll go home now, Roddy. The sun is hot and I'm tired. If everyone will excuse me.'

Roddy looked at her, surprised. Cora rarely if ever said she was tired.

'Of course, my dear. I'll take you,' he told her, heart sinking, knowing that by driving her home he forfeited the chance to hang around the bar with his friends and while away the afternoon sipping a few drinks.

'No, Dadda, I'll take her.' Ossian leapt to his feet.

'Ossian, no. Let Roddy,' Cora said but Ossian, sweeping away her protests and to Roddy's great relief, guided his mother out of the club to where he'd parked his car. Cora had no option but to follow his lead.

Chapter Eleven

೦ಾ ௸

It was the last thing she wanted. She tried, sitting in the small black Ford, to collect herself but to the very core of her being she was in turmoil and needed to be alone to sort it out.

She could not understand herself. All her life she had tried to do the right thing. She had slavishly obeyed social, moral and national laws. By-laws even. Any instruction from Church or State found a willing slave in her. Unspoken do's and don't's had been uncritically followed. She had never protested, rebelled; it was not in her nature, yet here she was, utterly unstrung, and she did not know where she had gone wrong; she whose whole way of life was bound up in doing the right thing found herself floundering helplessly in a morass of untidy emotion.

'The difficulty is, Cora, deciphering what is right and what we would *like* to be right,' he had told her. He always called her Cora and she called him Monsignor. It made her feel young, somehow, like a student. 'You see, thirsting for justice can easily mask a thirst for revenge, and if I decide this would be *good* for me, the right thing for me, examined more closely, it can simply be a selfish *I want my own way*.'

'But if you don't *know*, if you believe your heart is pure . . .' she ventured.

'There *is* only one prayer,' he told her. She gazed at him wide-eyed. She had thought there were so many.

'Thy will be done,' he said.

'Thy will be done,' she murmured now and Ossian glanced at her.

'What is it, Mother? You haven't been yourself today.'

She looked at him, his pure profile turned from her, intent on his driving.

68

'Is it my going away?'

She felt suddenly ashamed. No, unnaturally, it was not her beloved son's absence that was upsetting her, it was another. God damn it, what kind of a woman was she?

He pulled the car off the road, turned it towards the coast and drew to a halt facing the sea. It shimmered like a blue velvet cloak strewn with diamonds. Boats made small and toy-like by the distance bobbed gently against the sky. The headland jutted aggressively into the blue waters, and if she narrowed her eyes she could just make out their house nestling peacefully in its cluster of trees and dappled sunshine.

Ossian turned to her. 'What is it, Mother? I don't understand what's wrong. I know there's something . . .'

She shook her head.

'Don't do that, Mother. You know it's not the truth.'

She had always told the truth. She bit her lip. What could she say? How could she explain something she did not understand herself?

She stared out at the dancing sea and blinked her eyes rapidly to stop the tears she felt behind them. The earth seemed to her in that moment so alive and heart-breakingly beautiful. The colour of the sea, a constantly moving depthless indigo, the purple and mauve and gold and amber of the mountains, the sky, becoming pink at the edges over the horizon, the vivid verdancy of grass and tree, the lacy decoration of the blossoms shivering and shaking in the breeze, all seemed to her unbearably moving.

She looked at her son, his handsome face, his troubled eyes.

'I don't know what's the matter with me, Ossian,' she said truthfully. 'I think it's a lot of things.' She frowned. 'That young man with the ridiculous name, the O'Brien boy . . . Shannon . . . I do hate it when people call their children after *places*. It's so *banal*. Still, I suppose, Liverpool! Parents homesick for Ireland. It's understandable.' Why must she sound so trite? How did she manage to trivialise everything?

'You didn't like him?'

'He . . . well, I know it sounds silly but he *frightened* me, Ossian, and I don't know why.' Her large eyes were turned to her son. Trying to make sense. Trying so hard.

'He was arrogant,' Ossian agreed. 'His manners are deplorable. But *frightening*, Mother?' He thought for a moment, trying to understand, then added, 'I think perhaps it's because you are not used to such coarse behaviour and it shocked you. *You* would certainly feel alarmed by anyone that brash. But that's not the whole of it, Mother, is it?'

She stared out at the sunshine on the water. The sea looked silver now, a pavement of glittering platinum. 'He disturbed our usual peaceful gathering. He was an *intruder*! Then you came along and, well, dear, I'm really happy you're going to Rome, I know how much it means to you . . .'

His eyes narrowed. She was not looking at him or she might have been surprised by the fanatic gleam in his eyes.

'It means everything to me.'

'And yes, I will miss you, Ossian, you know that too, and hearing you say it, knowing it is so soon, a fact, not just an idea . . .' She laid a delicate hand on his arm. He covered her hand with his. 'And I'll lose Monsignor Maguire at the same time. I'll miss him more than you can imagine.'

He glanced at her sharply. She was staring out of the windscreen, her eyes far away. She seemed unaware of his presence. He did not know what to make of it all and an awful idea fought to be born within him, but he squashed it ruthlessly and turned to her. She seemed to have lost control of her face muscles and her mouth pulled up one side in a nervous twitch. She covered it with her hand.

'This piece of news, Ossian, has disturbed me more than was warranted,' she said. 'Darling, I've been comfortably cocooned in my disciplined way of life, protected from all agitation, and I simply do not like change.'

Ossian turned the car, his expression remote. As he began to drive home she was grappling with the realisation that everything *had* changed. She did not know how or why but nothing, she knew with certainty, would ever be the same again.

She tried to recall whether Monsignor Maguire had ever advised her about emotional turmoil but all she could remember was something he had said about placing one's problems in the strong hands of God.

70

'Mother, you won't say anything to the Monsignor, will you?'

'What do you mean, Ossian?'

Her son's voice was anxious, his hands clenched tightly on the wheel as he drove. 'I mean you won't try to dissuade him from going to Rome, will you?'

She looked at him, surprised at the vehemence of his tone.

'See, Mother, I want this more than *anything*. It's very very important to me. If I didn't go I think I'd . . .' His profile was frightening in its intensity.

'Ossian!'

'I mean it, Mother.' He glanced sideways at her, his blue eyes dark as coals. 'I'd go to any lengths to go on that journey to Rome. It will launch me on the road I'm determined to travel.'

'But, Ossian, your vows? You promise to obey. Monsignor Maguire has often talked about his obligation to subject his will to the will of God, and that means the will of the Church.'

'Well well well, you *are* close to the good father, are you not?' She had never heard him talk this way before and she hated the sound of his voice.

'What do you mean to imply, Ossian?' she asked, tight-lipped.

She heard him draw in his breath. He shook his head.

'Oh, never mind. I didn't mean anything, Mother. Just don't jeopardise this chance for me, using your influence with the good Monsignor. Please.'

'I'll not stand in your way, Ossian,' she reassured him. 'Never fear.'

Why had the conversation turned this way? Why was Ossian so intent on warning her not to interfere? What possible influence could she have? She was not that important to the Monsignor.

Yet she remembered everything the Monsignor said, everything he had told her. She had pondered his words, analysed them, come to the conclusion that he was a wise man. But that was then, when she was still her own mistress and not, as she seemed to be now, at the whim of every and any emotion. She leaned back in the car and tried to shut her brain up. She was tired of thinking, tired of reasoning, tired most of all of *feeling*. She concentrated on the cottonwool clouds scudding past the window up there in the madonna-blue sky. She stared out of that window until Ossian turned up the driveway into Rossbeg, then sighed as the record in her head clicked on again.

Chapter Twelve

꿍 꿍

Cora sat alone at last in her bedroom. The room was feminine and light, with bowls of roses, lace pillows and chiffon curtains. Roddy felt distinctly ill-at-ease there so he simply *slept* in what he thought of as Cora's domain. He did not enter the room a moment too soon nor stay in it a moment longer than necessary. If he'd had the nerve he would have suggested one of the other rooms – his study or the music room – be converted for himself, indeed he would have preferred that, but he knew such a proposition would outrage Cora and go against her religion. It would not be worth making the suggestion and it would probably land him in hot water. Her objections would fundamentally consist of what she thought other people would say or think. And what the children would think. He knew she too would prefer separate rooms but outside opinion weighed more heavily than what suited them. So Cora and Roddy had perforce to be tolerant of the other's presence in this most intimate of rooms, Roddy being the one who suffered most.

Untrammelled now by the presence of family and friends, Cora let fly for the first time in her life. She burst into a storm of tears, pent-up emotion erupting in volcanic suddenness and fury, and, picking up her beautiful Venetian vase full of her favourite yellow tea-roses she hurled it against the primrose damask wall with unnatural abandon. Aghast, she stared at the mess, the sacrilege, her carpet blighted, her vase in smithereens. Staring, she realised she did not regret it at all.

She collapsed on her bed, an outburst of hysterical sobbing overwhelming her. Giving herself over to this new self-indulgence, she let her feelings rip and for a long time allowed the waves of fear, frustration and fury to break over her in mindless tides.

Eventually it was over, the outburst finished. It passed as quickly as it had come. Exhausted, she rose and went slowly, hiccupping, to the dressing-table and sat down, surveying the ruins of her face.

Her mascara had run. Her skin was blotched, her lipstick smeared. She looked like one of those women she so despised, a drunk or a whore from the slums; careless and undisciplined.

What shall I do? she asked herself helplessly, her shoulders drooping. How had this happened? She tried to clear her brain. The truth, she wondered, what is the real truth? This had nothing to do with Ossian. It had nothing to do either with that dreadful Shannon boy though she tried to tell herself it had. She was pleased with Ossian's success and had to admit that the absence of any of her children would not devastate her. And Shannon was worthy only of a wrinkled nose and a frown of disapproval.

Fighting to extract reality from her tempestuously mud-dled thoughts, she endeavoured to unearth the knowledge deep inside her that she wanted so badly to keep hidden.

The root cause of her turmoil, she realised, was Monsignor Maguire. She did not want him to go away; it was as simple as that. The cause of all her unruly emotion and bewilderment could, must be laid at that door. She did not want Monsignor Maguire to go to Italy with her son and leave her here, alone, without him. It was an astounding thought, a worrying one. Why should she be so selfish as to not want him to go? Then the next thought came: what could she do about it? Nothing! Nothing at all.

She sighed and went to the bathroom off the bedroom. She shared it with Roddy, but, like the bedroom, it revealed little evidence of her husband's presence. A small mirrored cabinet concealed his shaving stick, brush, the lethal-looking cut-throat razor he used and the leather strop he honed the blade with. There was little else of Roddy's in the bathroom.

She filled the basin with water and washed her face. She towelled it dry, rubbing her skin roughly as if to scrub away this terrible knowledge.

She had faced it now, here in this room, but she wondered how long she'd really known, how long the truth had lurked in her subconscious while she led her calm and tranquil life. When had she decided that the Monsignor was the most precious thing in her life? It had happened without her knowing or realising, for it had been buried there inside her all along. It had grown and grown, this dependency, and now, today, she realised it engulfed her.

When had it happened? she asked herself. She remembered the last time they met. No talk then of leaving, of going to Rome.

They had been in the cloister. It was a beautiful day, the sun shimmering, the light like crystal. The birds were singing and the lilac was in bloom. The water was splashing melodiously under their words.

She had been thinking of him putting her hands into the shaft of sunlight, remembering that moment. They were sitting on the same bench.

'She gets weaker and weaker, Monsignor.' They were talking of Cecie.

'She'll be in God's hands soon,' he said, sighing. 'You must prepare yourself.'

She realised then, to her horror, that she was not concerned with Cecie's death, but with his involvement in it. Dear God, what kind of a mother was she? She was *looking forward* to being consoled by him. She had risen quickly, pushing the dreadful thought away, brushing the crumbs from the digestive biscuit off the skirt of her floral dress. 'I must go!' Why? She'd done nothing and the Monsignor had told her never to be afraid of her emotions.

'It's how you *act* on them,' he had said. 'What you actually *do*. If someone harms you you obviously will feel anger. It is only wrong if you decide to harm that person back, or if you allow a growing resentment to overwhelm you so that you become obsessed. Emotion is not intrinsically wrong, even powerful emotion. It is, as I say, how you deal with it that separates the grown-ups from the children.'

She believed that. It was the foundation of her life. But now, she had done nothing wrong. She was innocent.

She had forgotten Cecie then and came back to the moment. It was so still in the cloister. She could feel his presence beside her and felt, because of it, complete.

'I find it difficult, Monsignor, to really love people,' she told him as she sat back down, thinking of Cecie, of Roddy. 'I keep everyone at arm's length.' Except you, she thought, except you.

He said to her, his brown eyes wandering over the silver-grey stone, 'To attain real intimacy with another you have to have true peace within yourself.'

At that moment she had felt suddenly within herself a surge of such peace, such content that time seemed to stop. It was as if the whole earth held its breath and even the birds were stilled and the leaves on the trees stopped trembling and everything waited. This moment is perfect, she thought. Everything around me is harmonious. The cool cloister, the ivy-draped walls, the heavy clusters of lilac beset by bees, the fat sparrows and the white doves cooing on the roof. The sweet splashing of the fountain and the motes dancing in the sunbeams. And the Monsignor beside her, his hair dappled with grey. When had that happened? It had been raven-black that afternoon in the Shelbourne when she had first met him. She wanted to run her fingers over the soft hair and enchant away the grey. She looked quickly back at the birds.

She had known then. Must have.

What had she known? Her mind shrank away from the question, ran away like mercury spilled. She had not wanted to face the truth.

She looked around her now as if her surroundings were foreign and she sighed a long shuddering sigh. Oh, this was indeed a pretty pickle!

She undressed and slipped into a peach satin *robe-de-chambre*, wrestling with what she *could* think about; what was allowable and what had to be shelved.

She picked up her silver-backed brush and began to brush her hair. Suddenly she smiled. An enormous sense of relief flooded her. She knew the answer. Simple. So simple.

She'd go to the Monsignor and confide in him, tell him her confusion. She glanced at the broken glass, the disintegrated roses, scattered petals, water soaking the carpet. What a fool she had been. What an idiot. He was her spiritual adviser, he would tell her what to do. He'd helped her through everything, everything else in her life up to now. He'd guided her safely and painlessly through all and any

76

vicissitudes so surely he would get her out of this whirlpool of emotional unbalance she was floundering in.

She'd go and see him tomorrow. Oh, it was so simple. Mind made up, she felt the relief of decision remove all tension and, still smiling to herself, she began to repair the damage to her face.

Chapter Thirteen

❦ ❦

Decla was hardly aware of her mother's departure. Roddy and Brendan repaired to the bar like kangaroos to their mother's pouch. Diving into the packed smoky den, they breathed in the tainted air greedily and ordered two large ones.

Outside at the debris-strewn table Decla sat frozen, waiting with baited breath for what would happen next.

Fidelma rose and tapped Harry on the shoulder. 'Come on, Harry,' she commanded, 'I've booked us for a game. And don't you try to muscle in on this one, Decla, understand?'

Decla didn't hear her. She was aware of her sister and Harry leaving the table. Harry touched her shoulder as he passed and said, 'Don't pay any attention, Decla,' and she looked up at him vaguely. He was smiling at her, his gentle, reassuring smile, and she nodded, not really bothered about Fidelma, not since Shannon O'Brien had appeared on the scene. Justin was hovering uncertainly nearby. She held her breath, willing him not to settle near her, not to try to make conversation, but he was staring after Fidelma and seemed unaware of her presence.

Shannon glanced at her every now and then, giving her a covert and intensely personal smile, a slow communication that made her heart stop.

'Want to take a walk?'

He was asking *her*, inviting *her*, Decla! He had shown no interest whatsoever in Fidelma but was making overtures to her, the plain little sister. It was, Decla decided breathlessly, phenomenal.

'Sure.' She gazed at him, eyes wide and as starry as the sea.

He walked a little ahead of her and then turned and held

out his hand. She took it, fingers trembling, feeling his fist close around it, envelope it.

They walked past the courts, then down the grassy incline to the lake. The trees were old and tall there. They stretched their branches over the brackish water so that the sun never reached it.

A chill rose damply from the dark mirror of the lake and the black swans floated in stately pavane across the glassy surface.

'It's scary, this lake,' Decla said, feeling safe, her hand confidently in his. 'No one knows how deep it is. Seaneen Kavanagh was asked by the committee, you know' – she glanced up at him – 'up in the club, to cut back the trees so maybe the sun could reach the water, make it a little less spooky, y'know?' He nodded, saying nothing. She looked back at the lake, its opaque and sinister surface seeming impenetrable. 'He must have fallen in,' she whispered. 'Him and his ladder were never found. Men cast down lines, couldn't reach the bottom. They dragged it but the nets disappeared too and everyone was afraid. They say it goes to the centre of the earth.'

They were standing a couple of feet from the edge and she was a little behind him, nervous now of the lake's depthless mystery. He let her hand fall, then moved forward until he stood perilously on the brink. Looking down just under the surface weeds that swayed in a slow ballet, the water as dark as sin.

'Do you trust me, Decla?' he asked.

'Of course,' she replied nervously.

'Then come here and take my hand.'

'But it's . . .'

'I'll keep you safe.'

She moved forward. She hated the dark and mysterious place, hated the smell of decaying vegetation, the sinuously moving water, the dank gloom. But she went to him, hand out, trusting him, believing him. Like a pledge.

He gripped her hand. 'Good,' he said. 'Now we're one. We're together, Decla, you and me. Against the world.' It was thrilling. Nothing like this had ever happened to her before. It was like something out of the films.

She didn't know about the last bit, though. Against the

world. But she nodded passionately to the import of what he said. They were one. A pair.

They stood together at the edge of the glowering pool and suddenly he pulled her away. 'Come into Dublin with me. Let's go have some coffee.'

She would have gone anywhere with him. A slow boat to China. Outer Mongolia.

'I'll tell Fidelma so Mother and Dadda won't worry,' she said.

He had a serious face, she thought, deciding without hesitation that she loved him. He was the one. She did not ask herself whether they had anything in common. She did not enquire into his status, what he did or thought or felt. She simply dived headlong into love as her father had dived into the cosy womb of the bar.

She told her father on the way out, opening the bar door, calling in to him. He'd never stop her in front of his pals. She couldn't help crowing a little at Fidelma in the locker-room.

'Shannon's asked me to go have coffee in the Italian place in O'Connell Street.' But Fidelma glanced at her absent-mindedly and said okay. Decla decided she was preoccupied with Harry. It would be great when Fidelma got married and left the house, then she wouldn't have to deal with her sister any more.

'Could you take my tennis stuff back to the house?' she asked her tentatively. To her surprise Fidelma nodded. Decla pushed her skirt and polo shirt into her sister's bag before she could change her mind.

Shannon was waiting for her in front of the club. 'I've no car,' he said.

'We can walk.' She didn't care what happened as long as she was with him.

'To Dublin?' he laughed. It changed his face, made him look less serious, sort of carefree and boyish.

'No. To the tram.'

They walked down the boreen to the main road. They could see the twinkling lights from the small terraced houses bordering the woods. Then into Dalkey town.

The tram started at the church there and there was one waiting with DUBLIN on it. They went upstairs.

They sat on the top deck. It was open to the skies and the seats were damp from long exposure to the warm, moist air.

'It's great up here,' Decla said. 'You can see everything.'

The world lay spread before them; the sea, the mountains in the distance, the coves, the harbour, Dalkey town, then Dun Laoghaire, then Blackrock and the houses of Dublin. The people seemed smaller from here. Soon the tram filled up, with mainly the young upstairs. Old bones did not find the climb easy nor the damp air conducive to their comfort. Couples were in their Saturday best, dressed up for dances or the Saturday flicks in the city.

There were a lot of people in the town when they got there and Shannon steered Decla over to the coffee bar. It was very brightly lit inside. Chrome everywhere. High stools around the bar and Mr Pachelli behind it wearing a white coat and a small white chef's hat. He told people he had come over from Italy to escape the war.

'I don' hol' wi' it,' he said. 'Don' hol' wi' violence, no way!' And with a huge grin he'd add, 'Is a coward, is what. A yella coward.' He'd ramble on about Mussolini and the *faschisti*, but no one listened. It was the most popular place. Everyone went to Luigi Pachelli's. It was full morning, noon and night. Luigi served coffee, ice-cream, milk-shakes and snacks. If you wanted a soda, an ice-cream or a milk-shake you sat at the counter on the high seats that twirled. For coffee or snacks you sat in one of the little booths at the side or at a marble-topped table at the back. The neon lights were very bright and the juke-box music very loud. They played Frankie Lane, Sinatra, Chuck Berry and Elvis Presley.

Shannon slid into a booth. The juke-box was playing 'Mule Train'.

'You've been here before,' she told him, sliding in opposite him. She had thought of him as a stranger. He nodded but did not elucidate. A girl with fuzzy hair dented in the middle by her waitress cap asked what they wanted and Shannon looked enquiringly at Decla.

'Oh, um, a coffee'd be okay.' It was not what she wanted but it was the cheapest thing on the menu. It was her first date with a boy and she was not sure exactly what to do. A thousand questions trembled on her lips and tumbled about in her brain. Did he have any money? Could he afford to pay? Would he go right off her if she had to? They were in a booth but did he know they rarely served ice-cream here? Would he think her awful if she ordered some cake? Who would pay? She had money and he had invited her. She hoped he knew that when you invited someone you paid, otherwise how would she cope with the embarrassment? *What was the right thing to do?* Her mother was absolutely adamant that behaving correctly was the most important thing in the world. But what was correct?

Shannon was ordering spaghetti. Spaghetti Bolognese. 'But we just had lunch!' Decla heard herself say.

'Rabbit food,' Shannon replied briefly. When it came he wolfed down the hot pasta. It was not a dish she was familiar with. Since the war a Chinese and an Indian restaurant had opened recently in Dublin, but Luigi's Italian place had been there before that. However, Cora did not think it a suitable place for her family to dine, favouring mainly English or Irish eating houses where steaks, lobster, Dublin Bay prawns, and fish in all its different guises were served. She bowed to French cuisine, though mainly to the language and not the cooking. *Pommes de terre, chou-fleur au gratin*, and *filet de boeuf* were simply charming titles for pots, cauliflower cheese and steak. Or, as Roddy put it, steak and chips with veg.

Decla thought the spaghetti in its meat sauce looked lovely and would have liked to try it but she was hampered by her shyness and inability to be unselfconscious. She censored everything she said in case it was wrong.

Shannon, however, cleared his plate, wiping it clean with bits of bread, and she thought of him stuffing himself at the club. Instead of it putting her off she decided he must have starved in England.

'What you lookin' at?' he asked her, not unkindly. He smiled again at her, wiping his mouth on his napkin.

'You,' she said simply, her heart in her eyes.

'Funny kid!' he said and chucked her under her chin, like in the movies. Humphrey Bogart called his women 'kid'. She squirmed with pleasure.

'You said . . .' She hesitated, then took a breath and repeated, 'You said we were . . . you asked me . . .'

'Listen, Decla, I like you. I like you a lot. You know

that. You can tell.' She nodded eagerly. She wanted some reassurance from him. He said, 'Don't ask me for promises, kid. I'm just here on a visit.'

'But you're my, my boyfriend?' she asked. Her heart was in her mouth as she looked at him, eyes wide and scared. She couldn't think why she was pressing the point. She wanted to be with him even if it was only for an hour, but she *had* to know.

He nodded. 'Whatever you want,' he said. 'Yeah.'

It was not what she wanted him to say but it was better than nothing. She moved her hand cautiously across the table and tentatively touched his. For a second he froze and she had the sinking feeling she had made a mistake. But then he responded, covering it with his, weaving his fingers through hers. She breathed freely again and wallowed in the delight of his possession of her hand. The hand represented her, everything about her. Her soul, her body, her heart.

'What now?' she asked.

He glanced at the big clock over the bar. 'Sorry, got to go. Can you get back to Dalkey okay?' Her heart plummeted and she suddenly wanted to cry. But he took her other hand across the table. 'Let's go to the pictures tomorrow evening, okay? I meet you here, say four? We have a cup of coffee and we go see Montgomery Clift?'

She heaved a sigh of relief and happiness flooded her whole being. 'Yes. Oh yes,' she breathed.

'Okay.' Then to her amazement he took out his wallet and pulled some bills from what appeared to be a substantial wad. Where did he get money from? Had he a job? Did he work and if so what at? And why didn't he talk about it? She realised there was so much she did not know about him. Ah well, she'd find out tomorrow. He pulled some change from the bottom of his pocket and threw it on the table. She'd only seen that done in films too. Her father and the men she knew counted it out carefully or paid by cheque. She smiled joyously at him now she knew she could admire him. She did not have anything to apologise for about him.

'Let's go,' he said, leading the way out of the place.

Outside dusk had fallen. People surged around them on their way to dances in the Gresham or to the Gate Theatre or to the Savoy or Carlton Cinemas. Fidelma and Harry would be at the Gresham now, dancing a slow foxtrot or a quickstep, indifferent to the admiration they aroused in the crowd on the floor. There was a sliver of a pale moon hanging over the Pillar.

Shannon took her elbow and walked her towards the Column where the tram stop was. There was a tram waiting. They stood a moment beside a paper-seller and she looked up at him.

'Well, then,' he said. 'This your tram?' She was staring at him as if she expected something. He bent his head and kissed her on her lips, softly and sweetly.

It was like a benediction. She opened her eyes, feeling the fleeting pressure his lips had made, like a tender bruise – so warm, so thrilling on her mouth.

'Bye,' he said and he turned and disappeared into the crowd.

In a trance she got on the tram, went upstairs and sat in the exact same seat where she had sat with Shannon on the way into town. Bemused she looked out over the city, the lights beginning to twinkle on in the thickening dusk.

'Yiz'll be petrified up here,' the conductor chided her. 'What would yer mammy say? God's sakes go downstairs wit' ye.'

She shook her head, smiling at him, infinitely wise and tolerant. Didn't he realise she didn't feel the cold? She was impervious to the mundane feelings of mere mortals.

In Blackrock a couple got on a little the worse for wear. They were in the middle of a row, verbal fireworks and bad language tossed back and forth with abandon. Normally Decla would have been frozen with fear and distaste. She never heard loud voices at home except her own or Fidelma's and that didn't count, and she certainly never heard bad language or saw drunkenness. Her father sometimes came home a little tiddly but he was always gentle as a lamb. But when these raucous voices unpleasantly pierced the peaceful night air, insulting the other travellers' ears with foul-mouthed obscenity, Decla did not panic. Some of the other passengers left the top to descend to the lower deck. After all, drunks were unpredictable. But Decla sat cocooned in the protective shawl of her love. Nothing, no one could harm her or upset her. They could not shake her out of the magic overcoat of her thoughts of Shannon. She felt his presence envelope her even though he was not there and she was too preoccupied thinking about what he had said to her, but most of all how he had looked at her, and how he had kissed her. She, Decla Flood, had been kissed by her very own boyfriend.

He was enamoured of her, that was for sure. Otherwise why would he bother with her? She could tell he was struck by the look in his eyes. She squirmed in her seat, blissfully unaware that the male drunk had passed out and the woman had been sick over the side of the tram.

The conductor returned. 'Some people!' he remarked contemptuously. 'Listen, miss, I really think yid be better off downstairs in the warm. Outta the reach of this scum.'

She smiled up at him seraphically. 'No. I want to sit here,' she told him. 'You wouldn't understand.' How could he understand great love? How could anyone but the stupendous lovers of old know what she was feeling? Juliet, Desdemona, Helen of Troy, Deirdre of the Sorrows.

She was loved. She, Decla Flood, bathed in a rosy glow on the top deck of the Dalkey tram, was loved. She, like one of the stars twinkling above her, was inviolate.

She was madly in love.

Chapter Fourteen

❦ ❧

'I'm going to see the Monsignor tomorrow,' Cora announced calmly that night at dinner.

The dining-room was a dark and austere room, its walls covered in crimson damask, its furnishings heavy Victorian.

'I thought you saw him Friday as usual,' Roddy replied mildly.

It was very strange for Cora to disturb routine, but Roddy had knocked back a few in the club that afternoon and was feeling relaxed. His responses were slowed up and he was not at all as surprised as he would have been had he been stone-cold sober.

Actually, as he thought about it, Roddy's heart bounded joyfully. Another unsupervised afternoon when he could do as he wanted, have a few jars with the boys, spend more money than he was supposed to, and maybe, just maybe spend an hour with Rosie Daly on the way back to Dalkey. You never knew your luck.

'Yes, I saw him yesterday,' Cora was saying. 'I *always* see him Friday. But he is going with Ossian to Rome and I want to check with him about clothes and so on.'

If Roddy had been looking at her he would have seen the rare phenomenon of his wife blushing, but he was thinking about Rosie and how he could swing it. Then suddenly he was afraid Cora would change her mind, think he minded her proposed visit. In the elaborate and deceptive pavane of their lives they often talked themselves out of what suited them both. 'Of course you must talk to him, dear,' he said swiftly. 'You must have a lot to discuss.'

'Yes,' she nodded, confused again. What would she, could

she say to him? What would they discuss? Oh, she told herself, never mind that now. The Monsignor was wise, so wise. He would figure out something.

What? Dear God, what could he do about her tangled emotions, the disorder of her mind?

That was his job, wasn't it? Straightening people out? That was what the Church was for. To sort people out when they were confused, when they felt like doing things they were not supposed to. Forbidden things. That's what priests were for.

She stopped her train of thought sharply. She did not want to think further than that. To pursue such ideas was to plunge into the darkness and fear of the unknown. She'd leave it until tomorrow.

'Where's Decla?' she asked.

'She went off with that disgusting Shannon,' Fidelma said and Roddy glanced at her with distaste. How could anyone so beautiful be so mean-spirited? he wondered.

'Oh no! Where?' Cora was shaken out of her preoccupation. Decla needed supervision. She was at a very vulnerable stage in her life.

'They said they were going to a coffee bar in O'Connell Street,' Fidelma supplied.

'That Italian place,' Cora murmured. Italy, Italy, Italy! All she seemed to hear about today was Italy. 'And you let them?' she asked so sharply that Roddy glanced at her, surprised. She who was always so controlled, so calm, sounded distinctly scratchy this evening.

None of them had eaten much. The delicious lemon sole Fusty had cooked had been played with, pecked at, but not finished. Roddy was too high to want to eat, Eamonn too tired – and he'd found a bone which quite put him off – Cora was too preoccupied to notice his behaviour or to eat, and Fidelma too excited. She was going to talk to Harry tonight.

'I'm going to the dance in the Gresham tonight, Mother,' she said now. 'I'm going to talk to Harry tonight.'

'Oh darling, that's lovely.' Cora's reply had not the enthusiasm Fidelma expected.

'You said I should,' she told her mother. 'You told me to. I thought you'd be pleased.'

'He'll make a perfect husband for you,' her mother said as if that was that. 'He's comfortably off. Good family. He's our sort.'

'Does she love him?' Roddy asked. 'Does Fidelma love him?'

They both looked at him blankly for a moment. Then Cora smiled at her daughter. 'Darling, I think your father had a few too many down at the club today.'

Roddy gave up.

'Where is big brother?' Fidelma asked, eyes alight. 'Why didn't he stay to dinner?'

'He had to get back to St Jude's. He's got a lot to do before leaving.'

'I'd love to go too,' Fidelma said. 'Italy! Maybe Harry and I'll go there for our honeymoon. Wouldn't that be wonderful?'

Wouldn't it, though. Cora gasped at the thought, then Roddy killed the idea dead. 'You've forgotten Sylvie. She'll be here on Monday.'

Sylvie arriving! She had completely forgotten about her niece. Oh damn and blast, a visitor.

'I hope we won't have to entertain her all the time,' Fidelma muttered.

'You'll behave with courtesy and kindness to our visitor, miss. You understand?' Roddy commanded and Fidelma looked at him, surprised at the sharpness of his tone.

It had been, Fidelma thought, a funny old day. Everyone behaving out of character. Her mother in a state. She'd lost control in the club and Fidelma had never seen her do that before, and she'd been crying. Any fool could see that. Fidelma had never seen her mother cry and it alarmed her. Then there was her father talking out of turn, talking back. Brendan O'Brien making her play with Decla. That terrible boy preferring Decla to her. The world had gone barmy. A distinctly odd day. She hoped tomorrow they'd all be back to normal.

And she was going to broach the subject of marriage to Harry Devereau. He'd be a good choice for her. She could manage him easy, wind him around her little finger. He had money and would eventually inherit Montpellier next to Rossbeg. Yes, she had thought very seriously about it all and decided that as he'd said nothing, she would. Tonight. Boys needed gingering up sometimes. She sighed and asked to be excused.

Chapter Fifteen

❧ ❧

Fidelma drifted in the darkness towards the oak tree at the bottom of the lawn. There was an old iron seat circling its wide hippopotamus-rough girth and she sat there. She was a little worried about the back of her peach satin evening dress but pushed her worry away. Harry loafed near her in his dinner-jacket and white tie. They had been dancing and he had driven her back from the Gresham in his Humber. He'd wanted to go straight home but she'd told him she wanted to talk to him. They'd strolled across the lawn and came to rest under the oak, she a little breathless with excitement. After all, she'd made up her mind.

She *knew* that Harry wanted to marry her although he'd never actually *said* so. He'd *implied* it often enough when they talked of the future. Things like 'when we are old and grey, Fidelma' and suchlike.

He was jumping up now to pull at the higher branches of the oak tree, leaping, stretching his hand up, his lithe young body taut with the effort, gripping a leaf, pulling it off. It irritated her. She wanted his full attention.

The moon spilled on to the lawn and spangled it with quivering shadows. It was such a small slice of moon, like the curve of a nail, yet it bathed the world in silver. She sighed and Harry turned to her. 'You okay?' he asked, smiling. He was so good-looking that she thought, for a moment, I must be insane not to be madly, passionately in love with this man.

'I'm fine, Harry,' she said, then, taking a deep breath added, 'Don't you think it's, well, time that you ...' She was stammering. Now that she was actually talking about it, *out loud*, it was not nearly as easy as she'd thought it would be. It was all very well for her mother to say, oh so comfortably, 'Talk to him, darling.' *She* wasn't doing it. And face to face with Harry now she suddenly felt awkward and shy. Almost embarrassed.

'Time I what?' He was back jumping up at the leaves again.

'Oh, stop that please!'

He looked at her, surprised at the vehemence of her tone.

'I say, Fidelma, I only . . .'

'Sorry. It's just, I'm *trying* to say something to you, Harry. Something *important*. Something *you* should've said to me *ages* ago.'

He looked at her, innocent-eyed. Seemingly he had no idea what she was talking about.

'What?'

'Oh, you are an eejit!' she cried petulantly, then clapped her hand to her mouth. 'Oops! Mother would never forgive me if she heard me say that!'

Harry laughed.

'It's not funny.' Fidelma looked at him seriously.

'Yes it is,' he replied. 'It doesn't matter what you *say*, Fidelma, it matters what you *are*!' He stared up at the moon. 'Don't you know that yet?'

'I don't know what you're talking about, Harry, I really don't.'

'What did you want to say, Fidelma? Oh, do spit it out. You're rabbiting on and I don't know what you're getting at.'

She hesitated, squeezing her eyes shut, then blurted out, 'Well, isn't it time you proposed, Harry? Asked me to marry you?'

There was a silence. She waited, but nothing happened. She opened her eyes slowly and his face swam into view.

She gulped when she saw the expression there, not at all the expression she expected – one of excitement and joy. What she saw in his eyes was startled confusion.

'I mean, I mean everyone is *expecting* us to . . .' she cried swiftly. 'It's understood, isn't it? And I . . .' She stammered to a halt. She had obviously taken him by surprise. Yes, that was it. That was why he looked so strange. He needed a moment to get used to the idea. Cora had always said that men were

91

terrified of marriage. Fidelma had been so accustomed to
thinking about it, her family talking about it, that it seemed
almost a reality. It had not occurred to her that maybe the
concept was new to him. Maybe the thought of marriage
had not entered his head.

She could not see his face now. It was turned away from
her. Suddenly the curve of his cheek, the soft wing of his
hair, the line of his neck were infinitely precious to her.
She leaned over and touched him just behind his ear, gently
brushing his neck with her fingertips.

At her touch he jerked away violently, taking her by
surprise. The gesture was abrupt and irritated, reminding
Fidelma of how her mother brushed away the midges and
mosquitoes that gathered in small clouds beneath the trees in
summer. 'What is it, Harry?' she asked, unable to understand
his reaction, not believing he could possibly be as appalled at
her suggestion as he was appearing. After all, she was by far
the most beautiful girl in Ireland. So everyone told her.

'Oh God, Fidelma, I never thought . . .'

'I took you by surprise?' she asked, then said, 'You must
think about it . . .'

'I don't *have* to think about it, Fidelma. I'm sorry . . .' He
shook his head and turned to her. His face was apologetic
and worried. He looked *worried*! Aghast at the thought of
marrying her!

'Oh my God!' she cried, anguished, and turned to run
away from him but he caught her arm.

'Listen, Fidelma, it's not that I don't care. I do! I love
you very much. But like a *sister*. It would be like – *incest*.'

'All *right*, Harry. I don't want to *talk* about it any more.
I'm embarrassed enough as it is. Let me go!'

'No. I want you to understand. Oh God, this is awful! I
care about you *so* much, but, dear one, not in that way.'

'Oh, I understand. I understand it all right.' Her voice was
very sarcastic. 'All those kisses, they were just—'

'Brotherly! I *never* never once kissed you on the lips,
Fidelma. You've gotta admit that.'

'Oh, what? Now you're blaming me . . .' Angry tears sprang
to her eyes. He took his hand from her arm.

'Listen, Fidelma, we've been like brother and sister since
the cradle. We've been so close . . . too close. I want to

92

keep your friendship. Don't let this spoil things for us. Please.'

But she knew without a doubt that everything would be different from now on. It would be unrealistic to imagine otherwise. It was different already. He was looking at her anxiously, but deep in his eyes was the guarded expression of a man whose favourite dog has turned against him. The spontaneous trust always there before when he looked at her was gone, to be replaced by caution.

'I'm not going to *eat* you, Harry,' she said, then, remembering her upbringing, recalling what her mother would want and determined to salvage what was left of her pride, she looked at him squarely. 'I made a mistake, Harry,' she said, tight-lipped. 'I wasn't all that serious. It just popped out. It seemed a good idea.' She sounded very calm, considering her whole world was in ruins.

She hoped he'd catch on to what she was trying to do, pick up his cue, play the game. And to her everlasting relief he did. ''Course, Fidelma. It was a good idea. Tell you what,' he said lightly, 'if we don't find the right one, each of us, in the next five years, say, then we'll give it some serious thought. Okay?'

She nodded. 'Okay,' she said.

He was edging away from her, moving from the tree, as if, she thought, he's nervous I might pounce on him. The moonlight hit his face full-on, like a spotlight, and she felt a huge tide of anger within her. God damn him! How *dare* he not be in love with her?

'Yes, you're right. It's getting cold. Let's go,' she said and ran up the moonlit lawn, away, away from him. I'm fleeing, she thought, running, and looked over her shoulder at him.

But he had turned his back and was pulling on those leaves again.

Chapter Sixteen

❧ ❧

Marcus Devereau stood in the library window and stared out at the moonlit lawn. His eyes were not taking in what they looked at.

Montpellier had been in the Devereau family since they'd fled from France as the first of their kind were rounded up for Madame Guillotine. His ancestors had seen what so many other aristocrats were too self-centred to visualise and had escaped just in time.

The family felt no shame for this act of desertion; too many of their friends died purposelessly in the blood-bath that followed the capture of the king. The Devereau motto was 'We will survive by the Grace of God', and that was more important to the family than pride of position in a tottering social upheaval. If those Devereau ancestors had not fled in order to survive there would be no Devereau today. The family would, like the Dodo, be extinct.

'We will survive,' Marcus Devereau muttered, staring out of the window, thinking of his only son.

All Marcus's hopes rested in his son. He loved Montpellier. He loved the river, the sloping fields, the mountains in the distance, but most of all he loved Harry.

He had fallen in love with Melanie Duvall at first sight on a visit to Paris and had married her *tout de suite.* He had brought her home to the house and land he loved in the country he felt was his native land and they had enjoyed five blissful years together. Melanie loved him with a passion and he her, and when she became pregnant their cup of joy ran over. Suspicious of such happiness, superstitiously he guarded her, sought the best advice, the most expensive help, but to no avail. Melanie died giving birth to Harry and in doing so broke her husband's heart and spirit. From then on he was marking time until he could join her in the grave.

He had only one desire: to see his son grow to manhood, marry and produce an heir for Montpellier. In this way the name would continue and the sacrifice his ancestors had made would not be wasted. And he could let go of a life he had grown weary of.

So far Harry had been indifferent to the girls he met at the dances and parties he attended. He was much in demand, having inherited his mother's good looks and his father's debonair manner, but so far none of the females had quickened his pulse or generated any passion in him, and Marcus was hard put to conceal his impatience.

Marcus had thought at first his son might be serious about Fidelma Flood. He personally did not warm to the girl, though he had to admit she was incredibly beautiful and had all the social graces in abundance. However, it became obvious to him that his son felt only a deep friendship and a brotherly love for the girl he had grown up with. It was convenient to partner her but marriage was certainly not on his mind.

Marcus sat down at his desk. He wished he did not have to worry about the succession but it was something he felt strongly about.

Why did it matter? If the name died out who would really care? No one at all. Yet there was, deep in his soul, in his blood, this drive for continuance, this fierce necessity for an heir before he died.

And there was another thing. His own life-span was now predictable. Dr Sutton had diagnosed terminal cancer.

Marcus was not half as upset as the doctor was and his only anxiety was to see Harry settled before he passed on.

The boy came into the study now, bringing that whiff of nature with him; a scent of the sea and saltweed, of the grass and the trees. It was a thrusting, vibrant smell of youth and vitality and Marcus felt old and diseased. Harry looked so handsome in his dinner-jacket and Marcus pushed aside a memory of himself at his son's age, deep in love with Melanie. They fell hard when they loved, the Devereau men, and Harry was so like him it hurt.

'Hello, Papa. You're up late. Saw the light on my way in.'

Marcus nodded. 'The old need little sleep, Harry. The young even less, I suppose. It's the middle years, the worry years, when it's necessary.'

Harry nodded, not really listening. He was staring at a spot on the ceiling. The room, full of books and shadows and dancing firelight, was warmly beautiful. Marcus felt cold all the time these days and needed the fire even in summer. Marcus saw that Harry's mind was elsewhere. He waited.

'Father, Fidelma Flood proposed to me just now,' he said eventually and tapped his forehead. 'I still can't believe it. I never gave her any cause to think . . .'

'It's the mother, Harry. It's Cora Flood arranging things to her satisfaction. Or trying to.' He glanced at his son. 'I take it you're not interested?' he said.

Harry shook his head. 'Heaven's, no! I told her, I think of her as a sister, no more, no less.'

Marcus grinned. 'That must have pleased her! I quite approve of Fidelma Flood's nose being put out of joint.'

'Oh Papa, don't! She's fun, you know. People spoil her so. But if you get her alone she can be . . .'

'But you're not interested!' Marcus said with finality.

'I told you, no!' Harry looked intently at his father. 'You all right? You sound tired. Why are you so curious? It's not like you.'

'I'm not. Only I thought . . .'

'You thought I'd be fixed up with Fidelma Flood and you could stop worrying about the Devereau name.' Harry grinned. 'Think I don't know what you're up to, Pa!'

'I'm sure I don't know what you're talking about, Harry.'

'Don't snarl! It doesn't work with me. Dear old Papa. I'll try to accommodate you as soon as possible, but you must give me leave to take my time and choose my love when she touches my heart and not before. After all, Papa, you chose Mother very carefully.'

'Your Mother came like a bolt from heaven, Harry.'

Harry nodded. He'd heard the story of his father's love so often he knew it by heart. It was a tale he loved to hear, a treasured saga about a woman he'd never known, a woman whose portrait hung in the great hall and whom he'd talked (or rather whispered) to when he was a little boy and felt sad and missed her. He loved the stories his father told and he hoped one day he too would find a woman like his mother to love.

Living in an all-male household he had idealised the opposite sex. His mother was sanctified by his father and by Mulcahy, the old retainer, who loved her almost as much as his master, so Harry revered women with a chivalrous and ardent awe. He worried his father, who was well aware of this trait in his son and hoped against hope he would find this awesome love, though doubted very much that he would. After all, the likes of Queen Maeve, Deirdre of the Sorrows, Marguerite Gautier or Juliet hardly existed any more, so he prayed that Harry would grow more accommodating as he matured, lower his standards – a little at any rate.

Harry, he knew, loved him. How could he hustle him without sharing the reason for his haste? He'd known for a long time, suspected rather, that he was ill. He'd lost that drive, that passion for life he once had the day Melanie died and try as he might (mostly for Harry's sake) he could not rekindle his enthusiasm. He'd always known that life dealt unkindly with non-participation and indifference and was good only to those who accepted her gifts eagerly, and so when the pain struck he was not surprised. Recently, when it became severe, he'd gone to Dr Sutton who told him what he had already guessed. But he did not want to worry his son. Harry would find out soon enough, and if he knew his father was dying the boy would never be open to romance.

Marcus glanced up now at the clear pure profile and sighed. The pain had begun again and was stabbing him with ferocious savagery.

'Go to bed, my boy,' he told Harry. 'It's late.' He'd missed his injection earlier and soon it would become a necessity.

'I think I'll lie low for a day or two,' Harry muttered.

'You mean with regard to the Floods?' The pain hit on target again and he choked back a grunt.

'You okay, Papa?' Harry saw his face twist and Marcus now wanted him out of the room as he could not trust himself to hide the pain much longer.

'I'm fine, son. Just a little tired is all. Off you go now.'

'Okay, Papa. You come up soon, won't you? If you're

tired there's no reason to stay down here messing about with those papers.'

He dropped a kiss on his father's head then left the room.

A wave of agony gripped Marcus and he clutched his arms around his chest. 'Oh God help me!' he murmured, opening the drawer, groping for the syringe. He pumped the morphine into his body, injecting a little more than Dr Sutton had prescribed. But that was becoming a habit, and each day the pain got worse and the dosage higher.

The drug was beginning to work and Marcus rose wearily. He glanced at the beautiful painting of the *Pietà* as he left the room. 'And find a girl for Harry soon,' he asked the sad face of the virgin. 'He'll be lost without me and he has so much love to give. Find him someone, please.' He crossed himself reverently and made his way slowly up to bed.

Chapter Seventeen

ை ஒ

Cora, rising that Sunday morning exhausted and horrified, blessed herself and prayed that no one, not ever, would find out what she had dreamed the night before.

She ordered the trap to take her after lunch to the Monsignor's. Every time she thought of him she blushed like a schoolgirl. Every time she remembered her dream she went pale as death and bit her lip till there was a small swelling there.

There was no doubt she would never tell the Monsignor her dream. She would have to go anonymously to confession in Clarendon Street in Dublin and whisper her shame to some priest she did not know. For it certainly was sinful.

Where had those images come from? No, no, no! She must not remember. In her bath she felt voluptuous, like a passionate woman after a night with her lover. Yet she had been alone; Roddy didn't count. She caressed her legs delighting in the elegant ankles, the smooth curve of her thighs, admiring her slim and lovely body, enjoying the feel of it. She had never done that in her life before. Her body was functional and she groomed it only in order that it would be as perfect as all her other possessions.

She thought of the dream. She knew it had not been real, a dream, and yet . . . and yet . . .

She remembered the feel of the satin on her body, the folds of her nightdress between her legs. Roddy had lain inert and snoring beside her. Alcohol always made him snore.

The door had opened and the Monsignor stood there. Only he was naked. She had not been surprised. His tall body was beautiful and she had held out her arms to him, not minding Roddy at all. He had walked towards her and she could see the movement of his sinews beneath his bronzed skin. And she could see his manhood, there between his legs. She had never looked at Roddy like that, never really seen him, yet now, unabashed, she drank in the beauty of the Monsignor's maleness.

He had lain on her, covering her, his masculinity not alarming her or offending her as Roddy's did, but exciting her in a way she had never felt before.

She had caressed him, run her hands over those long brown limbs, over that part of him she had never touched on any man before. She who had fastidiously refused to put her hands anywhere on her husband now greedily explored the priest.

And she felt herself melting into him, her body suddenly alive, throbbing and needy. He had entered her as Roddy had done hundreds of times but, ah, this was different. She had sucked him into her, her whole being desperate for him there inside her. And she could feel him taking pleasure from her and her body responding in the most lascivious and shocking way.

And not only could she feel, she could *see* them both as if she floated above their intertwined bodies. She felt, deep in her body, the crescendo of waves of pleasure coming to a climax, something she had never felt before. She had often wondered what was so great that Roddy, when he cried out his release, said over and over, 'thank you, thank you, thank you'. She knew now.

Then suddenly she was alone, her body wet, shivering with wonderment. Terrified too. Ashamed, yet defiantly content.

She felt odd now though – wonderful while bathing then aghast as she dressed, realising where she was going, wondering what she should do. How she could face him after that night? How could she face God?

Mass. She was going to mass and communion.

She was going to receive communion with her family and she was supposed to be in a state of grace in order to do that. Never before in her whole life had she been in any doubt as to her preparedness to do so. This morning she knew herself to be unworthy. To go to the altar after what had happened last night would be a sacrilege. She was not pure, not in a state of grace, but in sin, deep in lascivious sinfulness.

Horrified, she looked at herself in the mirror. Roddy had awakened, obviously feeling awful, and staggered into the bathroom she had just vacated, rubbing his eyes and clearing his throat. She hated that sound. She listened and could hear him slapping the razor up and down the strop. But she looked fine. No mark of sin marred her serene beauty or turned her into a witch. She glowed. Her eyes sparkled, her lips looked full and red, her skin seemed ripe and satin-smooth.

She could not understand it. Did sin make you prettier, younger-looking instead of making you ugly as she had been led to believe? Did impurity enhance one's appearance? Oh, what was it all about, what was the meaning of it all?

She rubbed her forehead, dipped her finger into her jar of Pond's Vanishing Cream, dabbed her brow, cheeks and nose, then blended it over her skin.

'I'll ask the Monsignor,' she decided blithely, suddenly very happy. 'I'll ask the Monsignor. He'll know.'

Chapter Eighteen

❧ ❧

The family assembled in the hall for mass. Cora insisted on a check-up: stocking-seams straight, hands clean, missal marked on the correct page, shoes polished, gloves fresh, dress modest. Wearing the correct clothes was very important to Cora. Everything had to be just right; then, like the model family they were, they piled into the Daimler and drove to the church in Dalkey.

Except that this morning Cora did not check the children. For the first time in their lives together she did not perform the ritual. She simply wandered into the hall, then out of the door and into the car, leaving Roddy, Fidelma, Decla and Eamonn staring after her.

They quickly pulled themselves together and hurried after her.

'Mother, it's raining!' Fidelma cried. She had a face like thunder this morning, Decla noted, keeping out of her sister's way. Her mother had no raincoat or umbrella.

'She can share my umbrella,' Roddy said and got into the front seat. He was bewildered. She had not waited for him to open the front passenger car door. She *always* waited for him to open it for her, but today, there she was, installed in the front seat, eyes fixed in the middle distance as if she were in a trance. Roddy felt distinctly odd. This was very peculiar indeed.

He knew he'd got himself the *crème de la crème* in Cora. He had pursued her with diligence and single-mindedness until he'd won her. Only thing was, when he got her he didn't quite know what to do with her.

They came from different spheres. He was the eldest child in a huge family; eight brothers and sisters now scattered across the face of the globe, whose parents were happy-go-

102

lucky, enjoyed their hard-earned money and worried not at all about position or power or the niceties. The do's and don't's did not influence their behaviour, and except for a kindly consideration for their fellow men their main interest by and large was to live as happily and healthily as was possible while keeping the commandments. Within reason.

His wife's family was the exact opposite. Cora was an only child, her father obsessed by power and position and his wife with retaining her place as a leader of the society she then moved in. When her husband died all those so-called friends dropped her, never having liked her very much in the first place, and the poor lady suffered from a burning desire to have her daughter lodged in an unassailable position so that the same thing would not happen to her.

Cora was a carbon copy of her mother, and Roddy, when they married, looking only for the fun they could have together, was to be sadly disappointed. Cora was so hidebound by rules and regulations that all real pleasure was eschewed in favour of the 'right' thing or the 'wrong' thing.

When drinking tea or coffee the little finger *had* to be *bent*. Straight out was the sign of atrocious breeding. So was pronouncing 'garage' to rhyme with marriage. It had to rhyme with *ménage*. Oh no, no, these little mistakes placed you, showed where you had come from, how you had been educated. The head must *never* be touched in public, nor the nose, no matter how urgent the itch. Elbows must *never* rest on the dining-table. Knives and forks must be placed side by side on the plate, turned downwards when eating, upwards when finished. The napkin must be picked up in the right hand, shaken out, then laid across the knee, in one movement if possible, if the waiter did not do it for one. Make-up must *never* be repaired in public. Men must *always* stand back for a lady. Open the door for her. Cora would stand outside a door waiting until the Angel Gabriel blew the last post, Roddy said, rather than open a door for herself.

The rules about cigarettes would fill a book. Smoke must never be blown near a lady's hair, or into her face. Upwards if possible. Cigarettes should be held between the first and second finger of the right hand, *never* cupped. That was for gurriers and corner-boys. You knew a gentleman by these things. Like always walking on the outside, the street side, of a lady when accompanying her down the road. Never smoking in the street, except a pipe, which was permissible.

The burden of these rules tired Roddy out. It was daunting to try to remember them all but he had no choice if he wanted a peaceful existence, even though they interfered with every aspect of their lives together.

'Roddy, please wait until you go to the bathroom to clear your throat like that. It sounds revolting!'

'And I don't want to find your nail clippings on the bathroom floor, you understand?' Her tone never aggressive, simply plaintive.

'Roddy, please put on your dressing-gown until you actually get *into* bed. What do you think it is *for*?'

'Roddy dear, don't *ever, ever* belch like that in my presence. It's terribly rude!'

'Roddy, *always* wash yourself after *it*. There is a bidet in the bathroom.'

He didn't know what a bidet was until he married Cora and she'd installed one. It was not a normal fixture in Irish houses and he'd been confused. But he soon learned what its function was. She called sex 'it' and insisted on his washing both before and after. Depending on the circumstances she often did ditto. 'It's so insanitary!' she'd say. 'So unhygienic!' And that was that. Roddy, a good-humoured sexual man, was doomed to years of unrequited passion and sex with a wife who found the whole procedure distasteful.

Then he found Rosie Daly.

It had happened quite by accident. He met Rosie just about the time his wife met Monsignor Maguire. She was expecting Eamonn and, naturally for Cora, any suggestion of sex while she was pregnant was greeted with incredulity and shocked disgust. Roddy would also be regaled with the repetition of a lot of old wives' tales. Roddy was a very frustrated man. But he was also a good Catholic. It had never occurred to him to be unfaithful to Cora. His upbringing, despite its relaxed lack of discipline was nevertheless rigidly RC.

104

He'd met Rosie Daly in a bar. When in Dublin, away from Cora's rigid supervision, he often escaped into one of the brass and polished wood establishments the city abounded in, met up with pals, supped a pint.

He liked the Shelbourne best. It was one of his favourite hang-outs. His office was on the Green and around eleven he would stroll down through the park, have a lean over the little bridge and a look at the ducks, envying their carefree existence, then meander into the Shelbourne bar and order himself a large Paddy. He never had more. Or rarely. Perhaps he might if friends popped in. He would sit in the pleasant gloom with its peaceful ambience, and let his troubles drift away.

One or two of his pals usually wandered in; he often passed the time of day with Brendan O'Brien, who had similar troubles to his own.

Both of them had difficult wives, or rather, both of them found their wives difficult. Brendan divined that Cora must be a sergeant major to live with and Roddy understood that Delores O'Brien was best left at home. Both men were loyal to their wives and would not have dreamt of complaining openly about them. They talked around the subject and were very glad of each other's company.

Delores O'Brien was a working-class woman from the slums of Dublin who had no desire to improve herself or even try to keep up with her husband's social progress. She did not lack enthusiasm in bed but was incapable of running Brendan's rather large household. In fact, she was the exact opposite of Cora Flood. Where Cora succeeded Delores failed and *vice versa*.

Now Roddy prepared to drive the family to mass, conscience clear; he'd been to confession the evening before, confessed his adultery and done his penance; three Our Fathers, three Hail Marys and three Glorias, and received absolution, so that he would be able to go to communion this morning. This was his habit. His conscience winced a bit at the technical advantage he was taking of the rules and regulations of the Church. How he hated rules and regulations; Cora's, the Church's, the Government's. When he confessed he had to promise not to commit the same sin again. The requirement was obviously necessary. How could he show true contrition if he planned to repeat the same offence over and over? So Roddy had come up with a way out, Jesuitical in its adroitness. It could not be faulted *technically*, but it still made Roddy shift uncomfortably whenever he examined his conscience, which was as seldom as possible.

What he did, with Rosie's heartfelt co-operation, was never to have sex *in exactly the same way*, therefore designating the sins as different.

So he'd met her in the Shelbourne bar. Women were seldom there at eleven o'clock in the morning. Except Lady Mabel Campbell-Whyte. She was an alcoholic chorus-girl from the Tiller-girl line-up in the Royal Theatre who had married the cranky old Lord Campbell-Whyte. Oddly enough they were a devoted pair, although they were the butt of public derision, and when he had died Lady Mabel took to the sauce in a very big way and proceeded to get stoned all day, every day, in the Shelbourne bar. The staff were tolerant – she was no trouble. A quiet drunk, she talked to herself a little, hat askew, and sometimes sang one of the songs she used to kick her legs up to and that her husband had adored. 'California Here I Come.' 'Ragtime Cowboy Joe.' 'Do, Do, Do What You Done, Done Done Before, Baby.'

Other than Lady Mabel women were not usually to be found in the bar until cocktail time. So when Rosie Daly, a complete stranger to him then, entered confidently, with no hesitation, into the heart of the all-male dominion, sauntered up to the counter and sat on the high stool beside Roddy, he was stunned with admiration for her aplomb.

'What'll ye have?' he asked her, astonishing himself with *his* aplomb.

'A large brandy,' she told him unhesitatingly. She gave him a brilliant smile. 'I've just buried my husband,' she said. 'I'm celebrating.'

He was shocked for a moment but she giggled, a very infectious sound, and he could not help but laugh a little too. It was then he noticed that she was all in black.

She was plump, a soft womanly woman, not spare and lean like Cora, and about the same age. She had big dimples in her cheeks and chin and bright hazel eyes round as pennies. She removed the hat she was wearing and shook out a mane of shiny mahogany curls.

He liked her immediately, warming to her, finding her extremely attractive and sexy. As she sipped her brandy she told him that her husband had been, in her words, 'hell on wheels'. He was a demon, a layabout, a messer. And to round things out on the debit side he was a drunk, a lush, a constant imbiber.

'Now as ye can see, I like a drink,' she told Roddy. 'I'm not at all averse to alcohol. But my ould fella drowned in it. 'Twas the ruin of him an' me an' our marriage and in the end it killed him.' She looked at him, her lashes batting up and down over her eyes like fans, and he reckoned she was fighting tears. 'He ruined my life so he did, an' this day I buried him. I can't believe it's all over. I can't believe I'm free. I feel like doing the cha-cha-cha down O'Connell Street in me bathin' suit!' She smiled and her hazel eyes danced like the sun on the sea and those dimples ducked and dived in her cheeks and around her mouth and he thought her the most seductive woman ever.

'I was standing there in Glasnevin beside the grave an' you know what I thought?' He shook his head, staring at her, fascinated. She wore a black knitted top that clung to two of the most perfectly rounded, voluptuous breasts he had ever seen. Every woman he had ever known wore a brassière, but he would swear she did not. To his horror, sitting there on his stool in the Shelbourne bar, he was seized with an almost uncontrollable desire to squeeze and knead those soft round thrusting globes, to hold them in his hands and . . . and . . .

'I thought, this is the happiest day of my life since my weddin' day. I *thought* that day was happy but it was ruined by yer man gettin' himself maggoty drunk and letting me down in all departments.' There was no doubt what she meant and he blushed. She took a sip of her drink. 'My weddin' day was the end for me. And today I thought, standin' there watchin' them sling the sods on to poor ould Peadar, I thought, this is the beginnin' for me.'

She licked her raspberry-coloured lips, plump as her breasts were plump. 'Earth to earth crap an' me cryin' Hallelujah inside!' Roddy blinked his eyes. No woman he had ever known used such language, was so explicit. It was, as Cora would have said, not done. But more, it was a sin!

The priests were very hard on foul language and yet here was this well-dressed woman, her fox tippets brushing the floor of the bar, using a word like crap, cool as a cucumber. It thrilled him for some strange reason and he squirmed on his seat in an agony of expectation. What would she do or say next?

She hoisted her fur tippets up over her shoulders and said with a sweet and vulnerable smile, dimples at play again, 'Now ye must let me return the compliment.' And she raised her fingers and beckoned the bartender over, saying, 'Same again please!' and Roddy gulped. Her nails were long and red. Cora said red nail varnish was tarty. Well, if it was tarty he loved it. And she'd ordered him a drink and was paying for it! Ladies didn't do that. Order drinks. Buy a man a drink. He held his breath. It was past his time here and he should be back at the office – he had a pile of papers to sign, invoices to check and initial – but he heard himself ask, 'Will you let me take you to lunch?'

'Ashes to ashes, dust to dust, yeah! He can't hurt me any more. What? I must celebrate, not mourn. I thought, I'll go for a brandy in the Shelbourne, that's what I'll do.'

She glanced at him, sipping her brandy and he wondered whether he'd imagined her acceptance.

'Is that a yes?' he asked.

'I said that'd be lovely. You want me to faint?'

She was grinning at him, her grin infectious and he found himself laughing with her.

'I don't know your name.'

'Rosie Daly,' she said. 'You are Mr Flood. I heard the barman.'

'Roddy to you.'

'You married, Roddy?' she asked lightly and he immediately felt uncomfortable. For a moment he was tempted to lie.

'Yes,' he said.

'Just my luck. Well, don't let it bother you. I won't.'

They'd had lunch there in the Shelbourne, bold as brass, all the world to see. They'd laughed a lot together then went for a stroll in the Green, her in her widow's weeds, his hand under her elbow. She'd squeeze it every so often, pressing his hand against her body so that he

108

felt what must be the soft curve of those magnificent breasts.

They had said goodbye and she sighed at their parting and kissed him tenderly on the cheek. 'Goodbye, Roddy. Thank you for sharing this day of celebration with me.' She smelled of jasmine and lemon and he wanted so badly to kiss her, to hold her, to fondle her, something he not only had never been allowed to do with Cora, but something he did not *want* to do with Cora.

He thought of Rosie Daly constantly after that. She invaded his life completely. The thought of her sat with him always. When he had his once a week 'it' with Cora he thought of Rosie Daly and Cora said he was being unnecessarily enthusiastic. 'Almost *brutal*, Roddy, if I may say so, and there's no necessity for that, dear.'

Months passed. Then one Monday he had walked into the Shelbourne for his morning large one and there she was. Sitting on the same stool she'd sat on the previous time, smiling broadly at him. His heart leapt with pure joy at the sight of her.

'I gave in,' she told him. 'I surrender, Roddy. I *knew* you were thinking about me. Like someone singing in my ear. So here I am.'

Thinking of her now, Roddy, reversing the car out of the drive, nearly hit one of the rocks that bordered it.

'Sorry, dear,' he said, but to his amazement Cora was silent and did not rebuke him in that oh-so-gentle voice. She must be sickening for something, he decided. Well, whatever it was, please God let her go to Melrose Abbey and see the Monsignor so he could go to Molesworth Street and make love to his Rosie.

Please God.

Chapter Nineteen

❦ ❦

They knelt in a row in the church. Second row from the front. Front would be pretentious, Cora said. Second row was just right. There was Roddy, Cora, Fidelma, Decla and Eamonn at the end. Eamonn spent most of the mass under the seat in communication with Martin Metcalf in the pew behind them. They had snails in matchboxes and were comparing size.

None of the Floods was thinking of spiritual things that morning. Roddy was preoccupied by lustful thoughts of Rosie Daly and the afternoon with her if it could be arranged. Cora was consumed by thoughts of the Monsignor, rehearsing what she should say to him, how to explain her dilemma, trying desperately to exorcise thoughts of her dreams. Fidelma was trying to contain the rage and humiliation that seethed inside her, boiling up in her head at the memory of Harry's reaction to her talk of marriage. And Decla was in a starry-eyed daze over Shannon.

The priest was saying mass. No one was paying a blind bit of notice. It was the jovial Father Bannister and his sermon was all about loving thy neighbour, which suited Roddy down to the ground. Father Doherty, the fiery young curate, always gave sermons about mortifying the flesh, which, on this overcast and drizzling morning, would not have suited any member of the Flood clan at all.

When it came to the elevation of the host Cora was seized by terror. To receive communion after her lascivious dreams, those churning voluptuous feelings of the previous night, was unthinkable. To walk up the aisle to receive the body and blood of her Saviour after *that* would truly be sacrilege. She would go to hell.

But *not* to go would be worse. *Not* to go would announce to the whole church, *and* to her family that she was in mortal sin and *could* not receive the sacrament. They would wonder what she'd done and who knew what conclusions they'd jump to? She'd never, never in her whole life *not* received communion before. What had happened? Her mother had assured her that if she followed the rules, the social and moral rules laid down by law, the Church and society, she would be safe in this world and the next. The rules were an insurance policy. But she had been betrayed. Her mother had lied.

'*Domino Gloria.*'

'*Et cum spirito tuo.*'

It was coming nearer and nearer. '*Agnus dei, qui tollis peccáta mundi.*' '*Dominus vobiscum.*'

As Father Bannister raised the host a fit of coughing shook her. She spluttered, barked, fumbled for her handkerchief, and finally, as most of the congregation flooded towards the altar, she headed in the other direction, to the back of the church where the layabouts hovered in the doorway, barely fulfilling their sabbatical duty. The crowd parted to let her pass, giving her sympathetic glances as she hurried to the rear. They thought she was unwell.

She went out into the air, taking deep breaths, wondering what had made her cough, grateful it had saved her. She gulped in draughts of the sweet breeze, tasting the salt from the sea and smelling the rain-soaked apple trees.

In a moment or two she hurried back into the church. No one noticed, or seemed to, that she had not received the sacrament. They took it for granted that she was returning from the altar rails. She sighed with relief. Then she realised she had broken a rule, practised a deception, and nothing at all had happened. Except that she felt much better.

'Your cough all right, dear?' Roddy asked and she nodded. He asked her again in the car going home and again she nodded, but made no comment and no one referred to the incident again.

The rain drizzled on the glass of the breakfast-room. It gave Decla a secure and protected feeling to see it gather force and pour down while she was warm and safe inside.

''Twon't last long,' Roddy said, worried in case plans would have to be cancelled. He wanted Cora to take the

111

trap to the Abbey whilst he had the car. The car gave him freedom of movement.

'Where we going, Dadda?' Eamonn asked.

'To the races. Leopardstown,' he said, glancing sideways at Cora, expecting a protest because of the weather. But none came.

'Be great in the rain, 'Eamonn said, and Roddy suddenly wanted to murder his own son.

'Oh, it will soon pass,' he said hastily.

'But Dadda, it's *pouring*!' Eamonn persisted. Then, catching his father's eye, realised the threat. 'But I love it,' he said placatingly. 'It'll be great fun in the rain.'

'Oh, don't be stupid, Eamonn.' Fidelma pursed her lips. 'You'd get soaked and then kick up a stink because you were wet.'

'No I wouldn't, no I wouldn't.'

'You're not going, dear,' Cora interjected. 'You stay home with Fusty and Cecie.'

'Oh no, Mother, no, no, no!'

'Don't contradict, dear. Fusty says she'll make fudge.'

Eamonn's face cleared.

'Well, I'm not going unless it clears,' Fidelma announced. 'I'm not ruining my clothes.'

'You could wear a raincoat,' Cora said mildly.

Everyone looked at her, surprised and puzzled by her unusual response. Normally she would, like Fidelma, worry about how smart, how well-groomed they could remain in the rain, but Cora did not want them at home where something, anything, might happen to stop her visit to the Monsignor.

'We won't have to worry about that, dear,' Roddy told her, scanning the *Sunday Independent*. 'It's due to clear up by lunch-time. I thought we'd start out about two-thirty.'

'And miss the first race?' Decla asked.

'Perfect time,' Cora told him, smiling. She had decided to go to the Abbey at three o'clock.

'Mother, you look beautiful today,' Fidelma said suddenly, staring at her mother's pink cheeks, her shining eyes, the glow that emanated from her like a mystic aura.

'Your mother always looks beautiful,' Roddy said without looking up from his paper.

Decla, beside her father, judged this a good time to whisper, 'Is it okay if Shannon comes with us to the races, Dadda? He telephoned me this morning an' I told him he could if Mother isn't. We *were* going to go to the cinema.

'I'm not sitting in the car with that oaf!' Fidelma said loudly.

'What's the matter with *her*?' Eamonn cried. 'She's been real mean to *everyone*. She pinched me in church, Dadda.'

'She's mean to everyone all the time!' Decla muttered, wincing, and glanced apprehensively at her mother, but Cora's thoughts were elsewhere and Roddy patted Decla's hand reassuringly.

'Of course, pet. 'Course he may. Fidelma, be nice to your little brother, you hear me? I won't tolerate unkindness in this family. Understand?'

Eamonn looked at Fidelma and pulled a hideous face which she loftily ignored.

'Only I told him to come after lunch. Is that okay?' Decla said to Roddy urgently. She wanted to have everything worked out, nothing to go wrong.

'Mother, aren't you going to stop her?' Fidelma shrilled.

Cora didn't reply and Roddy reiterated, 'Of course, pet. That's fine.'

Cora rose. 'Well, enjoy yourselves this afternoon,' she instructed, to Fidelma's vast astonishment. 'Brush your hair, Eamonn – it's like a haystack. And be good with Fusty. I'll ask. And do your homework.' Eamonn groaned loudly. 'Girls, the suits you are wearing are perfect. But you'd better take umbrellas.'

'I told you, dear, the weather forecast . . .'

'Just in case, Roddy. Just in case. I don't want my girls looking like drowned rats.'

And she left the room.

Chapter Twenty

ↂ ↂ

'Did you make contact?'

The rain beat steadily on the roof of the Nissen hut at
the bottom of Angus O'Laughlin's vegetable patch. It was
quite a large hut, having been built as a bomb shelter for
the families on Rothmere Terrace during the war in case
the Germans took it into their heads to break the neutrality
agreement and invade Ireland. 'On their way to America!'
Maggie Doyle was fond of saying. 'If they get this far there'll
be no stoppin' them!' And Des, her husband, looked to
heaven in amazement. 'They want America, the Nazis do.
Dominate the world. I'm sure of it. Sure who wouldn't? An'
isn't Ireland a steppin' stone to the USA?'

'It's a steppin' stone, all right. Into the bloody Atlantic!'
Des said dryly. 'Don't be thick, girl. The Nazis'll steer clear
of Ireland.'

But the families who lived on the little terrace that
bordered the Devereau and Flood land and stood with its
back to the woods decided between them that it was better
to be sure than sorry and they built the shelter. The Germans
didn't, however, get the option to invade and after the war
was over the Nissen hut had sort of settled into the landscape
at the bottom of the row of gardens. So it remained. The
residents found it useful and it was used as a storage place
for garden tools, lawn-mowers, tricycles and bicycles, bags
of fertiliser, ladders and tins of paint and such.

Then Angus O'Laughlin started to have his meetings
there. It was safer than his house on Rothmere Terrace.
A fiery fellow, Angus. Very hot on Irish unity.

Most of the inhabitants of the terrace couldn't give a
toss about Irish unity. They were too busy discovering what
being independent from Britain meant to them, and that, to

most of them, primarily meant financially. As none of them was exactly solvent and every penny counted, they felt the idealists could go screw themselves.

Angus O'Laughlin was an idealist. So was Shannon O'Brien and some of the others, but most of them were simply angry men, frustrated and jobless, and 'The Cause', as they called it, provided them with the perfect outlet for their rage. Another would have done as well.

They were gathered now on this rainy morning in the hut. The place was cold and smelled of mould even in the middle of summer. It was lit by a fat beeswax church candle which cast flickering shadows over the walls and the faces of the men around the table set against one side of the place. There were four tiny windows in the hut but almost no light got through them, so it looked like the middle of winter in there.

Behind the table was the blue flag with the gold harp at its centre which was to be the flag of a United Ireland, when the six counties in the North, still occupied by the British, were handed over. On that great day the blue flag would fly over Dublin Castle and the Dail. Till then the tricolour – green (Eire), white (peace), and orange (the North) – would have to suffice.

At the table sat Angus, with his head of thick red hair and full beard that would make Red Hugh O'Donnell jealous in his grave. He was a huge man, a man with a burning passion to see Ireland whole, a man who was not satisfied while the rich six counties remained in the hands of the enemy.

Beside him sat Hugh Bassett and Seamus O'Sullivan, two veterans of the '16 rising, old bitter men seeing their task as only half done. They had resisted the peace offered, the partial freedom of their land. They had caused trouble, protesting their dissatisfaction at the division of Ireland, what they saw as the carving up of that body, and they had been vociferous about what they saw as the betrayal of their aims by fellow countrymen, fellow patriots who by accepting this partition were selling out to the enemy.

Half a loaf, some said, was better than no bread, but Angus, Hugh and Seamus, purists and fundamentalists all, were very angry at the capitulation of their fellow patriots and their acceptance of a divided Ireland.

115

They were not quiet in their dissent. They had protested loudly, and so when the papers were all signed and the new government formed their names were conspicuously absent. They had been deliberately overlooked in the formation of the Dail, the new Irish Parliament, passed over because of their extreme views, their inability to accept compromise. They saw their comrades-in-arms elevated to prestigious positions in the corridors of power. They were left behind.

They were the last of the disbanded Irish Republican Brotherhood and they would not give up the fight, would not lay down their arms.

'As long as one British soldier treads the soil of Ireland, as long as the English Union Jack flies from an Irish building in any part of our country, we will fight. We will win.' So Angus O'Laughlin and the members of the IRB pledged.

They had sympathisers in all sorts of places. In Liverpool and New York. In France and Spain. In Germany and Chicago, but only a few in the newly formed Irish Republic. It was a small band there, for the rest of the population were far too excited about their new freedom and far too busy assessing their ability to rule themselves and remain economically afloat to bother about the secret societies which were, in any event, banned by the new Irish Government.

Shannon O'Brien stood in front of the seated Angus to report the progress of his mission.

'I've made contact, sir. I've met the girl.'

'Well done.'

'What next, sir?'

'You'll keep the relationship going till I tell you. Understood?'

'Okay, sir.'

'We can get at our target through her,' Angus said, tight lips pursed.

Shannon looked at the man he hero-worshipped. Everyone in Ireland admired Angus Rudh, as he was called. Red Angus. He'd braved the British, been the hero of many a skirmish, and look at him now. Shannon's heart beat angrily. Reduced to giving orders to a motley band of stragglers, most of whose motives were highly suspect, and in secret, acting outside the law while Ireland lay bleeding, severed at the neck, a Loyalist flag at her head and a makeshift one on her body while the traitors, ex IRB members, sat in comfortable seats and sipped drinks with their enemies.

'Who is the target, sir?' Shannon ventured.

Angus's amber eyes glittered in the dark. He cleared his throat. 'I can't tell you that, boy. Not yet. He's the enemy. Not the British, at the moment, not here. We'll attend to the British soon enough. Divide and rule, eh? Jasus! No. There's some here, our own, have to be made examples of. What right have they to agree to a severed Ireland? We'll tell you in good time, but remember, you'll get him through the girl. Remember that.'

Shannon nodded and Angus smiled. This was the kind of lad he liked; uncompromising and with no humour about the Cause. The trouble with the Irish temperament, Angus decided, was that they tended to trivialise everything. The Northerners did not do that. The Protestant ethic prevented that. The bloody Southerners made a joke out of everything and it was the undoing of them.

'Ye've done good, boy. Ye've done as we asked. When do ye see her again?'

'This afternoon, sir. We're supposed to go to the races at Leopardstown.'

Angus Rudh rubbed his hands together. 'Better and better. From now on you love racing. You're passionate about it. Understand?'

'Yes, sir.'

Shannon wanted to remain in the hut with the veterans. He would have loved to hear Seamus O'Sullivan speak, the dry man of the group, the powerful one, the killer. But Angus gave him a nod and jerked his head towards the door and Shannon knew he was dismissed. Reluctantly he took his leave.

He turned up the collar of his mackintosh against the rain outside and pushed away his reluctance. It was not what he'd hoped to engage in when he'd joined the secret society in Liverpool. He could, after all, face a firing squad or be hanged for the tasks he was engaged in. Treason was a serious affair. But to become friends with a girl! Jeez, it was not what he had in mind at all. Especially when they'd asked him if he was prepared to shoot to kill. He'd said yes, of course, and imagined himself, dead of night, setting

117

bombs. Shooting the enemy. Executing traitors. But Angus told him, 'Make friends with the girl. Court her if you have to. It's vital.' And there he was, soppy as a film star, messing about with Decla Flood.

He hated her and her stupid family, their total unconcern for Ireland's freedom. He resented hanging around them when there was, in his opinion, serious spying work to be done.

But Angus Rudh was his hero, his god, and Angus was the leader. If you wanted to remain a member of this organisation you toed the line. Obedience was as exacting here as it was in the Church. You were expected to obey blindly.

Shannon lit a cigarette. Strands. You're never alone with a Strand, the advertisements said. He shrugged and pulled the brim of his hat down over his eyes and walked away from the backs of the houses and up into the wood.

Poor Decla Flood, he thought. She didn't know it but she was being led up the garden path. He laughed mirthlessly to himself, not liking what he had to do but resigned to it.

Poor Decla.

Chapter Twenty-one

&?&?&

Ruth O'Grady hated Roddy Flood. She knew all about his carry-on with Rosie Daly. She felt deeply the outrage to her daughter, and her own pride was hurt.

Her daughter Cora was perfect. No man should *dare* to be unfaithful to her or feel the remotest need to be. She was the prize of prizes, the Academy Award of women, and any man lucky enough to get her should not even *think* of another woman, let alone mess with one.

Ruth had invested all her creative ability in producing the lady her daughter was. She had taught her everything she knew, all the do's and don't's. She'd sent her to the finest convent school in Ireland and augmented this with every extra instruction available: piano and ballet lessons, dancing, singing, elocution and drawing lessons. She sent her to the Adare School of Cooking (for social rather than culinary skills), to learn about *placements*, table arrangements, elegant French menus. She sent her for a course in artistic home decoration, and to Jessica Devane's Charm School to learn polish, perfect her manner, and how to conduct herself in the highest society.

The result, Ruth felt, was perfection, and when Cora brought home Roddy Flood of the Boatyard Floods she was very disappointed. Ruth dreamed of a prince, a millionaire or a film star and Roddy Flood was none of these. Cora asked her mother where she hoped Cora would find a prince, a millionaire or a film star, they not being thick on the ground in Ireland, and her mother, seeing the point, began to look more favourably on Roddy's suit.

He may not have been a millionaire but he had real money, old money. Roddy's grandfather had started the boat-building business in Dalkey. His father doubled it.

Roddy trebled. His grandfather had employed only the most talented craftsmen and Roddy and his father had kept the quality of their product high so that Flood boats were renowned worldwide for their excellence. They built, to specifications, small boats of all sorts and exquisite yachts, but never felt impelled to take orders for larger vessels, for the huge luxury yachts and military ships built in the shipyards of Belfast. They stuck to smaller craft, pleasure boats and elegant schooners, sail-boats, and relied on their perfectionism and their reputation for excellence rather than having a priority of money. It was a sore point with Ruth, who would rather Roddy and his father sacrificed excellence to economy.

However, Cora had decided Roddy was what she wanted. He came of good family and Ruth realised he could provide her daughter with a lovely home and a social background suitable to Cora's upbringing.

Ruth would always be disappointed her daughter had not done better, but Roddy sufficed. He had bought Rossbeg for Cora. It was a jewel in a setting perfect for her daughter. He gave Cora all she needed, was generous in the extreme, and he had bought his mother-in-law a charming little cottage near Rossbeg and gave her an allowance. Ruth was in fact coming to terms with him and beginning to feel quite pleased at having placed her daughter so perfectly, when this terrible burden had been placed upon her shoulders: she found out about Rosie Daly.

After years of marriage, after Eamonn's birth, when at last Ruth was beginning to count her blessings, her dear friend Cilla McCrae confided in her, 'I'm *sure* you would want to know, I felt I *had* to tell you, Lady Mabel Campbell-Whyte says that Roddy Flood is seeing Rosie Daly, Peadar Daly's widow.'

'What do you mean, "seeing"?'

'He meets her almost daily in the back bar of the Shelbourne. As bold as brass for everyone to see. Unbelievable! She's a loose woman, is Rosie Daly. A loose woman, Ruth.'

Ruth was incensed, her security threatened and her pride dented. How *dare* he? How *dare* that man so demean her daughter – how dare he?

At first Ruth tried to convince herself (and Cilla) that it was a mistake. After all, everyone knew Mabel Campbell-Whyte was a drunk and she could easily make a mistake in the alcoholic haze she permanently dwelt in, couldn't she? But Cilla said, 'They're there *every* day, Ruth. Not hiding or anything. I saw them myself. I asked Alf' (her husband) 'but you know men. He wouldn't commit himself or say diddly-squat about it. Said it was the chap's own business. As if it didn't affect Cora. Shameful!'

Ruth decided to take a leaf out of Cilla's book and went to the Shelbourne herself. She half hid behind a pillar in the foyer, pretending to read a newspaper, when, lo and behold, her son-in-law arrived, puffing on a cigar, something Cora discouraged in Rossbeg. He went around the corner into the back bar just as Cilla had reported. Minutes later Rosie Daly had appeared in a glamorous and sexy suit of powder-blue wool and an angora sweater tight over her generous breasts, with, Ruth assured herself, no brassière underneath. That, if anything, provided Ruth with all the proof she needed that Rosie Daly was indeed a hussy. No lady would ever, ever go without her brassière. It simply wasn't done. Why, even swimwear had brassières built into the top. Automatically.

Making her way to the Ladies she cautiously passed the bar, only to see Roddy, head back, laughing at something Ruth was sure was *rude*. His laugh had that lascivious tone. Obviously Rosie had made some lewd remark and she, leaning near him, smiling at him provocatively, was, Ruth decided, a disgrace to her sex.

Ruth went home absolutely furious. There was fear mixed up in her fury, fear born of doubt as to Cora's future if Roddy, God forbid, decided to go off with this Rosie Daly. Ruth contemplated with horror a Roddyless world for Cora. An allowance? Could she keep the house? She was hardly likely to be as well off as she was now. Then there was *her* monthly cheque. Roddy was unlikely to continue her own generous allowance if he and Cora were separated. Ruth had come to rely on it and would miss it dreadfully if it were stopped.

There was no divorce in Ireland, thank God. Ruth knew how unpleasant it was in America and England but it was out of the question in Dalkey. But there *was* separation and the man just *leaving* and living with another woman. It happened all the time. It made Ruth's blood run cold just to think about it. And there was desertion, although, to give him his due, she could not envision Roddy doing that. And the judiciary in Ireland, predominantly male, never really took the woman's part or felt her interests should be looked after.

Yes. The man had it every which way. Roddy could leave Cora, dump her and simply go and live with this floozie. Oh, people would disapprove, the Church would tut-tut, but no one would *do* anything, and Cora would be dropped and Roddy and the floozie become a couple out and about in the town. Ruth was in a quandary. What she wanted to do and what she *should* do were two different things entirely. What she *wanted* was to go to Cora and tell her all, watch her trounce the blackguard who had done this to her, watch Roddy squirm. But then what? Cora was very fastidious. Ruth had always told her daughter to steer clear of men who had been – who knows where? Messing around with a back-street whore. Well, maybe not. Rosie Daly could not be described in that way, exactly, but hussy, certainly. Ruth knew her daughter and what her daughter would do was either leave Roddy or throw him out, and both would be bad news. Perhaps, she thought, *she* should do something. Maybe she should have a very strict, calm word with Roddy as his mother-in-law, letting him know she knew. And threatening . . . what? She had no hostage, no weapon.

What she must not do was precipitate a rift that might be detrimental to Cora, weaken her position. But how on earth could she know what would and what wouldn't?

After due and careful consideration she decided to do nothing, simply bide her time. And now, seven years later, she had been waiting a long, long time. She had told herself that at some point it would be a valuable piece of information to have, the knowledge that Roddy had a fancy woman. But when, oh when would an opportunity arise for her to use it to Cora's advantage?

Little did she guess that Sunday afternoon as she sat staring out of the window of her pretty little bungalow, the one Roddy had bought for her, little did she guess that her long wait was nearly over.

Chapter Twenty-two

☙ ❧

Ruth and her fellow gossips were in fact incorrect at first. Roddy and Rosie were innocent of any wrong-doing. They had their drinks and that was that. For a long time that was that. But inevitably it changed.

One day, having their usual drink in the Shelbourne, sitting side by side on the high bar-stools, Rosie Daly, looking very fetching in a pearl-grey suit trimmed with silver fox, turned her large eyes on Roddy and said, 'Why not let's go back to my place?' She didn't add anything, just looked at him.

He knew what it meant if he did. They both knew.

They'd known each other now for six months, had been having drinks together for all that time. Roddy felt his stomach gripped in a sudden fierce twist and he gulped, then nodded. He did not hesitate.

They stood to leave, Roddy, suddenly overwhelmed by guilt, glancing around him. He had faced the world confidently before, aware of his innocence. He was just having a drink with her, God's sakes! Now, in the sure knowledge that he was about to commit adultery, he was seized with terror. Besides, he'd never been with another woman. Cora, his wife, was the only woman he'd ever *known*, in the biblical sense. How would he be with anyone else? Would he make a fool of himself? He was not very skilled in the art of love-making. Cora would not allow him more than a few minutes for the dirty deed. How would he be with Rosie? Would he be adequate? Would he be up to the event? He was, frankly, scared silly.

She saw his confusion, his terror, and read him aright. She'd guessed he'd never made love in the fullest sense of the word and she smiled at him reassuringly and they left the bar.

They took a taxi to her apartment in Molesworth Street. All the way there Roddy looked around, sure everyone was staring, condemning.

'Don't be so worried,' she whispered, and tucked her arm in his. Once again he could feel the soft outline of her breast against him but he remained rigid, gripped by terrible doubts and fears, his mind a whirlpool of confusion.

Of course he'd thought of her 'that way', but when he had he'd always pushed such thoughts aside. They were not seemly and he was wicked to entertain them even for a minute. Until that day.

He would never forget that day. Rosie Daly had opened a door for him into a sweet garden of sensuality and love. He learned that love was generous and fulfilling and sex an expression of that warmth.

She had taken him directly to her bedroom and she had undressed before him. She had taken her time and she was not coy. She had revealed her dimpled body to him as she would unwrap a gift of love, trusting him. And he had sat enthralled before her, like a gormless schoolboy. Then she had undressed him and he had felt utterly helpless, his body weak with pleasure, melting under her fingers.

She had caressed him everywhere, places he had never been touched before, and she encouraged him to do the same to her.

At first some of the things she did shocked him, but sensation took hold and he could only moan and hope for more. And more. And more.

He was ready for a long time before she opened her legs and told him to come home. Those were the words she used. 'Come home, into me, darling, come home,' she said. He had not known he could feel so strong, so big, so hard, and entering her, plunging into her, taking his time, drowning in the sensation, he realised that this was what they talked about, this was what men killed for.

And she, legs around his waist, straining to him, fully his partner in sensuality, she was reaching the same kind of orgasmic release that he was. He could feel the excitement within her, her opening and closing on him. She shouted out too when they came. She had heightened his orgasm by her own gasps, her sharp intakes of breath, her 'Now, now, now, oh God, oh God, oh God, now!'

He could not believe what had happened. He'd never known until that day that a woman could feel that too. He'd never known that sex could be like that and not simply an arid release. He had to make love to her again and again and again before he was assured that this was what sex was all about. This was what the Church forbade. What he did with his wife was what the Church recommended. Roddy felt the Church had made a terrible mistake and that what he did with Cora was a sin and what he did with Rosie Daly was sublime. What he did with his wife was like rape, what he did with Rosie was like love.

He had read the gospels from cover to cover to find out what Jesus said about it and could find nothing specific. Jesus was curiously silent about orgasms while the clergy were amazingly eloquent.

She became necessary to him. Like sunlight and rain, like the food he ate, she was essential. Full of gratitude, he wanted to move her into a larger apartment or a house, but she would not hear of it.

'No, my love. I'm quite content here.'

He bought her jewellery in the generous desire to express his gratitude but she never wore it. It lay in a velvet box on her dressing-table. But she wore the diamond band he gave her, on the third finger of her left hand beside the wedding ring Peadar had put on her finger when they married. He wanted her to take that off, but she wouldn't. 'No,' she said. 'He was a big part of my life and I don't want to forget. He taught me a lot.'

Roddy wondered if she meant about sex, if she'd learned all that wonderful stuff from Peadar, and one day, driven by jealousy, he asked her and she laughed aloud at his tragic little-boy concern with a dead man.

'No, my darlin', never, not at all. Peadar Daly taught me how not to do it. How I'd least like it done. I knew by the way he did it how not to do it and so I learned the opposite, what I wanted was the opposite. I'm a novice just like you.'

She explained that what she meant was that Peadar had taught her the qualities that had stood her in good stead.

'Oh, he didn't know he was teaching me patience, tolerance and understanding. He didn't know he was teaching me how to value you, my dearest one.'

They became, over time, very comfortable with each other. They experimented with sex, life, food, everything. They enjoyed each other, laughed a lot together and built a store of joint memories. And Rosie had no rules. When he was with her there were no do's and don't's.

And Roddy was easier with Cora. After the first guilt had been dealt with (there was no way he was going to give up Rosie so it *had* to be dealt with), he was a much more amenable husband and father.

He'd wanted to leave Cora but Rosie would not hear of it. 'We'll talk about it when the children are grown,' she'd say. 'Darlin', the cup's not broken, why try to mend it?'

She was a relaxed, undemanding and generous woman, was Rosie Daly, rounded and warm and good-humoured, the exact opposite of Cora, and as time passed Roddy counted himself the luckiest man in Ireland.

Chapter Twenty-three

꼭 꼭

Cora was not at all sure what the family were doing, whether they were going to the races or not. And she didn't care. She knew she'd had a conversation about it but had no recollection of what was said. She seemed to be acting in a dream.

Normally there were no races on a Sunday, but a special dispensation had been granted for the Aga Khan who was visiting Ireland and whom the Irish wanted to please so that he left his considerable stable in the country. The powers that be had come to realise that horse-breeding and training was an industry they could excel at and were anxious for his patronage and his vast investment. The Church's permission was sought. And, always interested in investment, not averse to the riches of the Muslim potentate, the Church gave its permission.

The rain cleared up and the sky turned a pale washed blue and the sun, a cowslip-yellow, peeped shyly out from behind the wispiest of pearl-grey clouds as Cora prepared herself for her visit to the Monsignor. She anointed herself as if preparing for an important event. She wore a beige silk suit and a white blouse with a tie bow at the neck. She wore white cotton gloves and high-heeled beige suede shoes. Her small hat, perched on her wayward hair, had a veil to her nose and she had a cashmere throw over her knees.

She knew she looked beautiful yet she felt afraid. She could not imagine what she was afraid of. Monsignor Maguire had been her friend now for years and she had always gone to him with her problems. Well, she had a problem now and so where more natural to take it than to the Monsignor?

But this was different, she realised that. Nevertheless,

it would all be worked out. *He* would work it out for her.

The pony and trap, driven by old Vinny Healy, jogged along under the trees. Cora felt herself nodding off, then jerked her body into a rigidly upright position as she saw the Monsignor standing naked and beautiful just down the road under the weeping trees. He stood near her favourite beeches, his body the colour of the bark, a golden mahogany.

She blinked her eyes and looked again. The vision was still there, the naked Monsignor revealed in all his splendid manhood standing beside the beech trees just as he had appeared to her last night, only now the leaves half hid his nudity and the dappled light played over his body as if caressing it.

Then he vanished. In an instant he was gone, and there was nothing but the swaying branches tossing raindrops off their leaves.

Cora blinked again and glanced apprehensively at Vinny's back, but the jarvey was hunched over his crop and had obviously noticed nothing. He was clicking his tongue at the pony, and the trap jogged along the country lane at a dignified pace. The fuchsia stained the hedgerows like blood, diminishing the delicate flowering cow-parsley and wild iris, the hawthorn and meadowsweet with its vibrant colour. The whole countryside was now bathed after the rain, washed clean, the air fresh as a baby's breath. It was a mild and gentle scene and she was horrified at the lewdness of her vision. But it was *not* lewd, she told herself. No, no, it was not!

The Monsignor simply had no clothes on. He looked like a Michelangelo statue breathed warmly to life. What was she thinking of? She shook her head, straightened her veil and tried to pull herself together.

What *was* the problem that she hoped to confide to the Monsignor? That he came to her as if in a vision, gloriously naked, proud and joyful, arms outstretched? How could she tell him that? Yet if she didn't how could she ever understand what was wrong with her? How could she ever go to holy communion again? This morning had been pure farce. She could not pretend to have something in her throat every Sunday.

128

She decided not to think about it until she saw the Monsignor. It would come out obliquely, she supposed, and best not to decide what to say beforehand. It was not the kind of stuff one could prepare.

They jogged along and she admired the purple hills in the distance, the smoky-grey bosoms of the Wicklow mountains.

It began to drizzle as the pony and trap turned into the Abbey driveway. Salty tossed his head in excited anticipation. There would be a rub-down and a nose-bag to munch at. He'd done this trip many times and knew the score.

Vinny reined Salty in as the trap swung around in front of the Abbey and drew to a halt. 'There ye are, safe an' sound.' Vinny always said the same thing in the same triumphant tones as if they had just successfully crossed the Alps.

Cora descended. Her heart was beating fiercely yet she felt curiously calm. A feeling of happiness seemed to flood her being and she turned an eager face towards the Abbey and climbed the short flight of steps to the thick oaken door.

She rang the bell. She could hear the ringing echoing through the house. She waited. And waited, perplexed at the delay in answering it. She thought, it's Sunday. Of course. She always came on Friday and they expected her. Nevertheless, they were certainly taking their time.

Salty and Vinny had disappeared around the side of the building and she could feel a heavy irritability descend upon her. Where were they all? She had been tranquil when she arrived and now she'd lost that sense of being in charge. She tapped her foot and rang again. Still nothing.

She looked around and caught sight of Paulie the Abbey gardener in the distance. He was slow-witted, poor lad, but a wonderfully gifted gardener and she had often taken cuttings from him. She raced down the steps and hurried after him, over to where the vegetable garden began, through an arbour of climbing roses bridging a gap in a white wall.

Paulie had bent down and gone through the arbour just ahead of her. The drizzle was light but penetrating and she could feel the fine material of her jacket absorbing it. She knew there was a dark patch on each shoulder and that bothered her. A week ago she would have returned home at once but it did not even occur to her to do that now.

'Paulie! Paulie!' she called out and the young man turned in the slow way he had and looked at her.

'Yeah, missus?'

'I'm looking for the Monsignor,' she said.

He shook his head and spread his hands.

'Do you know where he is?' she asked as patiently as she could manage. She wanted to shake him but she kept her voice calm. Paulie shook his head. 'Gone,' he said, then, carefully, 'Gone out.'

Her knees went weak, she felt faint for a moment and her lips began to tremble. It had never for a moment occurred to her that the Monsignor might not be there. He was, she subconsciously believed, a fixture of the Abbey, atrophied between her visits. Of course she knew that he said mass, ate, slept, but that he might detach himself from the Abbey, perhaps be entertained by someone else, have a separate life of his own, had not entered her head and to think about it made her angry.

'Gone? Where?' she asked.

'Dunno.' The boy shook his head and bent over his bed of scallions. She was dismissed.

She turned and went back to the Abbey. She pulled the bell again but nothing happened for a long time. Then there were slow footsteps that stretched her nerves to breaking-point, an even slower pulling of bolts and chains and the huge door swung open.

The tiny Sister Benedict, who hardly looked strong enough to open a tin of sardines, peered up at her through pebble glasses. 'Yes? Yes?' Then recognition dawned. 'Oh, 'tis you, Mrs Flood. Sure 'tisn't Friday, now is it?'

'No, Sister, no, it's not. But I wondered if I might see the Monsignor?'

The door swung a little wider, the sister with it, her frail body hanging on to it, and Cora stepped into the hall. She loved that hall, the wide space, the huge biblical paintings on the wall; Christ walking on the water, feeding the five thousand, the Last Supper. The oak panelling glowed and the parquet floor was polished to a high gloss by earnest postulants in the service of God, with Pure Beeswax Mansion High Shine. She loved the stained-glass window and the beams of jewel-coloured light the sun cast, shining through it.

130

'Oh no, ye can't! He's out, see.' The little sister was emphatic, eyes blinking rapidly behind her spectacles as the door swung her backwards and forwards, carrying her with it willy-nilly.

'Could I wait?' Cora asked. She wouldn't mind sitting here in the gloom fragrant with the scent of incense from the chapel just off the hall. She could be quiet here in the peaceful shadows, waiting for him.

'Ah well now, that wouldn't be a good idea at all, Mrs ... Mrs Flood.' The tiny sister peered up at her, insistent in her certainty. Cora wanted to cry like a baby. Why? Why? 'No. The Monsignor won't be back till late,' the little sister was telling her. 'He's out to dinner, Mrs ...'

'Oh!' Cora gulped. 'Oh!' she cried in disbelief and fled.

She hurried out, down the steps, around the corner to the stables, angry, humiliated, miserable. Out to dinner! How could he when she needed him so? Damn him, damn him, *damn* him!

The sister was calling after her. 'What'll I tell him, Mrs ...?' and Cora looked over her shoulder and called back, 'Tell him I'll see him tomorrow. The afternoon.'

She ran around to the stables, her high heels catching in the gravel, tripping as she ran. She had to unearth Vinny, much to his disgust, from the kitchens where he was enjoying tea and homemade scones with Sister Philomena, then wait while he harnessed Salty, both of them disgruntled by the haste, trying all the time to curb her impatience.

The family were probably at Leopardstown. Not that she would have liked any one of them around. She didn't however want to go home to an empty house with all this bottled up inside her.

When Salty was hitched up and Vinny had turned the trap he asked her, 'Where to, Missus? Home?'

She suddenly decided to make another visit. 'No, Vinny. But on the way. My mother's, please.'

131

Chapter Twenty-four

∽ ✑

When she saw Cora's face Ruth was perfectly certain she knew what had happened. Cora had found out! Her daughter had discovered the truth of the terrible secret that she, Ruth O'Grady, had sat on all these years. Cora had found out about Rosie Daly.

Cora came up the short garden path to the cottage from the trap and her mother watched her through the window. She could see at once that something was badly wrong and she jumped instantly to her conclusion. What else could make Cora look so shocked, so distraught?

Cora did not have time to ring the bell this time before the door was yanked open straight away, in sharp contrast to the Abbey, and Ruth was hugging her daughter and urging her inside, commiserating with her, sympathetically soothing her with tones and gestures of extreme consolation. Cora was confused to say the least. She knew she could rely on her mother's support, but *before* anything was said? She allowed herself to be hustled and bustled, clucked over and seated in the cosy little front room, all chintz and silver photo-frames, flowers and cushions. But she was taken aback when her mother sat down opposite her and stared at her with what Cora thought of as her avid look and asked, 'How did you find out?'

'About what, Mother?'

'About Roddy, of course. Don't try to pretend to me, Cora. I'm your mother after all. I know you like the back of my hand. As soon as I saw you, damp and soggy, face white as a sheet, I knew you'd found out at last.' Ruth lit a cigarette. She would have denied with her last breath that she was enjoying the situation, but she would have been lying. 'Oh my dear, if only you knew how I longed to tell you before.

132

How I ached to put you straight about that man. But I held my tongue. I was thinking of you. I did not let you know by as much as a glance that I knew all about Roddy Flood and his fancy woman.'

Cora looked at her mother with wide, blank, uncomprehending eyes. She could not imagine what her mother was talking about and sat in bewildered silence.

'I went to see the Monsignor, to ask him about a problem . . .'

Ruth's eyes lit up. 'What a splendid idea!' she breathed, looking at her daughter, head cocked to one side. 'Brilliant! I couldn't think what to advise you to do. But the Monsignor would know. Although he's probably tough on adultery.' Her lips narrowed. 'I never had any problems with your father. He was beautifully behaved, dear, as you know, and remained faithful to me until the day he died.' Her eyes misted over. 'He was a beautiful corpse,' she sighed dreamily.

Cora had difficulty remembering her father at all. He was a foggy unreality in her mind, always had been, even when he was alive. A shadowy presence in the background, a sort of back-up for her mother, forever behind a newspaper. Her mother, however, had enough personality for two and Cora often felt that, like a vampire, she had sucked her husband dry as a husk.

What was her mother on about? Cora did not understand. She felt remote and untouchable, as if she'd been anaesthetised and all this was happening to someone else. As she put two and two slowly together, making a picture from her mother's words, she came up with Roddy and adultery. A frown creased her forehead. As the idea permeated her brain she felt she was going to laugh. It was a thoroughly ridiculous idea. Utterly fanciful and silly. As if Roddy would! He was such a good, considerate husband, so loving, so generous. And he was a terrific father, a better father, she often thought, than she was a mother. No, it was a daft idea.

Then she thought of the clincher. She *knew* Roddy was not unfaithful to her, that her mother's idea was baloney. Roddy could not be unfaithful for he went to communion every Sunday morning. He certainly would not risk going to Hell by receiving the sacrament whilst in mortal sin.

So he said firmly, 'Nonsense!'

Ruth stopped in full flow: '. . . Cilla said he was drunk all the time, Peadar Daly, and beat her. No sooner was she a widow-woman than she lit on Roddy, got her mitts on him . . . what, dear?'

'What woman?' Cora asked, curious.

'Rosie Daly, of course, who did you think? Didn't you know it was Rosie Daly?' Her mother's eyes narrowed. 'She's the tart Roddy is playing around with.'

Cora suddenly believed the story. A strange sick feeling seized her stomach and she knew it was true. Despite all the signs to the contrary, it was a fact. The name Rosie Daly did it for her.

She knew Rosie Daly slightly, an obvious woman, she always thought, overblown, in Cora's humble opinion, but then, as Roddy often said, anyone not stick-insect thin was overblown to Cora. She'd met Rosie Daly at a few social gatherings, seen her photograph in the newspaper and generally looked down her nose at the widow-woman.

But what made her suddenly sure that what her mother was saying was true was the memory of her own unease in the presence of the widow and Roddy's attitude to her. He would not hear a word against her. She remembered being astonished when Roddy, usually the mildest of men, told her to shut up when she'd made some derogatory remark about Rosie Daly. She remembered the white look around his mouth when Brendan O'Brien had said something facetious at the Curragh races about Rosie being the kind of woman any red-blooded male might, in his words, 'enjoy a tumble in the hay with'. 'Those boobs . . .' Brendan had enthused, rubbing his hands together and licking his lips and Roddy had surprised them all with his white-lipped rage, his blistering stricture, 'Don't ever, ever speak like that in front of me. Not ever, y'hear?'

The moment had passed and Cora had thought no more about it, but it came back to her now. Then at the Gaiety one night about three years ago, at the first night of a melodrama called *Pink String and Ceiling Wax*, the leading lady was playing a blatant hussy of a girl, Pearl Bond, who had been causing havoc in a Victorian family, and someone, it *must* have been Cilla McCrae, a woman whose main talent was causing trouble, whispered audibly, 'Isn't she the spit of Rosie Daly now?' And Roddy, again white-lipped, leaned around the pillar that divided their box from Cilla's and hissed, 'I did not pay to come here and listen to your vicious comments, Mrs McCrae.'

And she had suspected nothing. Was she a half-wit? Was she a total and complacent fool that when Roddy told her Cilla McCrae was not welcome in their home or at their table any more she thought nothing of it, did not question the reason underlying the command, accepted in blind trust that all it was was Cilla being a vicious trouble-maker whom Roddy, with his pure mind, decided to drop. Pure mind? Dear God, how stupid could she get?

Had she been sleepwalking, blind and deaf to what was going on under her very nose? *Did everyone know except her?*

Or had she subconsciously known all along and kept it well and truly buried to protect herself from having to face up to it? She didn't know and now, sitting opposite her mother, who, she decided, was not much better than Cilla McCrae with her obvious relish in the troublesome situation, she decided that she would really have preferred to remain in ignorance. She thought about that, then seemed to see the Monsignor's fine and noble head, recalled his wise and compassionate smile and stood up.

'Sorry, Mother. I've got to go.'

'But, my dear, we've got to decide what to do. How to proceed. How to punish that bastard but still keep ahold of what's rightfully yours ... dear ... don't you understand ... ?'

But Cora had turned swiftly and left the cottage, her mother spluttering behind her.

Chapter Twenty-five

᪐ ᪑

Leopardstown races were crowded in spite of the weather. People milled about, curling race-cards in their hands, the tic-tac men waved their arms and umbrellas proliferated. The Aga Khan, short and fat, was so surrounded by people he was impossible to see. The betting was fierce, the champion, Rust Red, was running in the three-thirty and the going was tough.

To Roddy's and Decla's surprise Lorcan Metcalf was waiting for them just inside the gates. Father and daughter exchanged glances and Fidelma greeted him enthusiastically. Lorcan's face was anxious, searching the crowd as they pushed into the race-course. Roddy pondered mildly what Fidelma was up to, and why Harry Devereau wasn't there. Lorcan was obviously her date. He was wearing Wellington boots and there was a drop of rain on his nose.

'You shouldn't have waited here for me, Lorcan,' Fidelma said. 'You're soaked!'

Lorcan shook his head and put up his umbrella to protect her. 'Come on, get under, Fidelma. I've reserved a nice place on the stands for us all. Ye'll be dry there.'

Decla was searching the crowd for Shannon. He had not come to the house and she was sick with disappointment.

'Where's Harry?' Roddy asked his eldest daughter.

'Harry who?' she snorted and he exchanged a pregnant look with Decla, who shrugged and cast her eyes up to heaven. She was sure she was going to burst into tears and was doing her level best to retain her control.

'You looking for someone?' Lorcan quizzed her.

She glanced at him sideways, hoping not to sound as tense as she felt. She nodded. 'I sort of expected Shannon

O'Brien to come with us. He said he'd be at the house . . .' she petered out feebly.

Lorcan grinned. 'He's on the stand. Waitin',' he told her. 'With Brendan. I said I'd meet you and take you over.'

Decla gasped with relief.

'That's nice of you, Lorcan.' Roddy smiled at the young man. It was heart-breaking, Roddy thought, to see such a pathetic desire to please. He hoped Fidelma wouldn't hurt the young man too much and wondered again where Harry Devereau was. 'I'm very cold and very wet, Lorcan,' he said briskly. 'Can I leave you in charge? I'm not going to enjoy myself here very much, I'm afraid. Too old. It's fine for you young ones.' He saw the young man's eyes flicker before he had time to disguise his expression, and realised with a sickening lurch that Lorcan knew about Rosie. He probably knew exactly what Roddy was up to.

Overcome with a sudden sense of shame, nevertheless Roddy brazened it out. 'So can I leave the girls with you? I'll take off.'

He'd been going to elaborate on his excuses, but changed his mind in the face of Lorcan's expression of eagerness to play the game with him. Lorcan looked at Roddy as if to say, you can count on me to back you up, even if you say you're Jack the Ripper. He'd pay lip-service to any ploy Roddy asked him to because he wanted Fidelma.

Lorcan was nodding eagerly. 'We'll take care of them, Mr Flood,' he said confidently. 'I have Pa's car so we're all right for transport.'

Roddy left them. Decla was already making her way to the stands and Fidelma had tucked her arm into Lorcan's and was cuddling up to him under the umbrella which he held attentively over her head. He looked down at her protectively, an expression of abject adoration on his face as he gazed at her, and at that moment Fidelma was a carbon copy of her mother. Roddy was reminded sharply of himself and Cora as they were twenty years ago and he shivered. He turned away and left them and drove straight to Rosie Daly.

Chapter Twenty-six

❧ ❧

Decla ran to him. Shannon, sitting under the Nissen roof of the stands, hearing exactly the same sound the rain made beating on the tin awning as he had in the garden shelter in Rothmere Terrace, like Roddy shivered as he saw the expression of devotion in someone's eyes. As she came running towards him Decla's face glowed with an inner light that burned so fiercely, so brightly for him. He felt awkward and embarrassed as he tried to smile while his uncle nudged and winked. 'Yiv made a conquest there,' Brendan said.

'Shannon, oh Shannon, I thought you'd forgotten!' She was out of breath, panting as she sat beside him, shaking the rain out of her hair, tucking her arm through his.

'Sure how could I do that?' he asked, trying to keep his smile in place as it slipped ever away.

'But you said the house,' she frowned. 'I thought you said you'd come to the house.' Then she shrugged. What did it matter? He was here waiting for her and now they were together. Everything inside her, the turmoil died down and became calm.

'Where's your ma and da?' Brendan asked.

He got no reply from Decla who was too absorbed in Shannon, but Fidelma replied, 'Dadda's gone home and Mother's gone to see the Monsignor. Lorcan is taking care of Decla and me.'

'Is your Dadda sick?' Brendan queried, a little puzzled as to why Roddy would miss the crack of a day at the races, then he caught Lorcan's eye and realised he might be putting his big foot in it. ''Course it's a lousy day,' he said hastily. 'Only good for lunatics like me.' Then he rose. 'I'm putting five guineas on Bull Run, Shannon. Suppose

I put a half-crown each way for you and your young lady? The odds are smashing.'

'Dadda gave me some money,' Fidelma said.

'You can use that later,' Brendan cried and hurried away. He was dying for a jar after he put the bets on but at the same time didn't want to miss the race. There was no time to stand around talking. He left the stand, his binoculars round his neck, and, having given the bookies his five pounds, five shillings and the half-crowns, he downed a quick jar in the bar, then hurried out into the drizzle, put the binoculars to his eyes and focussed on the race-course. He could smell the horseflesh, a warm satisfactory odour that he loved. The horses were still in the paddock and, reassured, he returned to the bar. He hurried to the counter and ordered himself another large Paddy.

'Have it on me, Brendan,' a voice said behind him.

He turned and found himself looking up into the face of Monsignor Maguire.

'Oh God bless us, Monsignor . . .'

'He will, Brendan, he will.'

'Ye gave me a terrible fright. Put the heart across me, so ye did. Well, well, well, out to enjoy yourself, are you?' Brendan smiled up at the tall cleric.

'Indeed I am, Brendan. I've put two bob on Bull Run in the next race, but I'm holding off on Rust Red, the odds are too high.'

'Yeah,' Brendan agreed. 'An' the going is rough. She likes the going sweet, does Rust Red.'

'Sure even if she won she'd only pay a few coppers. Not worth it.' The Monsignor had a small brandy before him and he tossed it off and clapped Brendan on the shoulder. 'Nice seeing you, Brendan. Enjoy yourself.'

'Have another, Monsignor.'

The tall man shook his head. 'No. No, thank you, Brendan. I won't. One is enough to warm me in the damp.'

Brendan held his arm as he turned to move away. 'Er, I think, I'm almost sure that Cora Flood went to see you today.'

'Oh?' The Monsignor raised his eyebrows. They were thick, as if drawn with charcoal. His skin was tanned – touch of the tar-brush, Cilla McCrae said – his face austere, his direct gaze making Brendan uncomfortable, as if he could see all his secrets, those thoughts Brendan hoped no one would ever find out about.

The Monsignor smiled at him. The smile was sweet and tender and melted that austere face. It banished Brendan's fears.

'You must have made a mistake, Brendan. I saw her Friday.'

Brendan shook his head. 'No. Fidelma said her mother had gone to see you today.'

'Are the family all right? Nothing wrong?'

'Oh yes. No worries on that score,' Brendan reassured him.

'I thought it might be trouble with Cecie.'

No, Roddy would never have gone to see Rosie Daly if Cecie had been bad. Brendan knew that. 'No,' he told the Monsignor, 'Fidelma would have said.' Brendan adjusted his face from its natural light-hearted look to the serious and grieving expression people wore when they spoke of Cecie Flood. It was an automatic adjustment and curiously similar in everyone.

'All right. Well, thank you, Brendan. I'm sure if it's important Cora will telephone me.'

'No, thank *you*, Monsignor. For the drink.'

Brendan hurried back to the stand. The race had started and, caught up in the excitement, he forgot about the Monsignor and Cora Flood. Bull Run won at twenty to one. His luck was in.

Chapter Twenty-seven

❧ ❧

Eamonn knelt in front of the door to Cecie's bedroom. His face was sticky with fudge and on a level with the keyhole.

'You okay, Cecie?'

'You're always asking that! Everyone comes to that door an' asks that. 'Course I'm not!'

Eamonn thought. It was what he figured. No one would be okay spending their time in one room. In bed. Running about was the thing.

'Martin says you look like the Phantom of the Opera. Your face all scary and horrid. He says that's why you stay in there. He says you've not got consumption, not really. That's what Martin says.'

'Martin's a *dope*! Doesn't he know *anything*? I stay here because consumption is contagious. But Martin doesn't know big words, does he—'

'Yes he does!'

'—so he wouldn't know what contagious *meant*!'

'Cecie, I'm sorry.'

'So'm I.'

'Gotta go now.'

'Oh, all right.'

She heard his feet patter down the corridor. She wished he'd stay. Talk. But she couldn't think of what to say to keep him there.

She was so lonely. In *What Katie Did* Katie had been strong and brave in suffering but she'd had people around her. She'd been nasty at first and Cecie had never been nasty. She wondered if it would have helped if she had.

She stared at the ceiling. She knew every crack and cranny, every shadow and smudge and stain, and she hated it. She hated the room that Fusty tried so hard to make pretty for her.

She often wished she was in hospital. Most people with consumption were put in isolation wards but they had each other to talk to, to complain to if they felt like it. Only Dr Sutton said the chances of recovery in hospital were not as great as the chances at home and her mother *would* insist on doing what she thought was the right thing. Dr Sutton had agreed that if certain rules were kept to Cecie could remain at home.

Cecie had said she'd like to go to hospital but no one would listen to her. Even Monsignor Maguire told her she was very lucky to be with her family. She didn't tell him she never *saw* them. They were voices outside her door, voices she desperately wanted to hear, but she could never think what to say to them. Oh, her mother and father came in to chat to her once a day, but it was peculiar talk, not natural. They asked how she was and she told them. Then they listed things she shouldn't do. 'Not if you want to get better, sweetheart.'

She was dying, she knew that. 'Not long for this world,' Sister Agnes, who often came to nurse her, give Fusty a break, would say. 'Aren't you the lucky little girl, Cecie?' she would ask, smiling. 'You'll be in the arms of Our Blessed Lord in no time at all.' Cecie wasn't at all sure that she wanted to be in the arms of Our Blessed Lord. Not just yet. How could she know whether she'd like it or not?

'What'll it be like?' she'd ask.

'Well, they say, "Eye has not seen nor ear heard the glory of Heaven",' Sister Agnes told her fervently. 'It's marvellous! Like a wondrous garden where the sun always shines and it rains only at night. Where there are fountains of silver and birds so exotic the eye is astonished at their beauty. And their song is a symphony. And people who get there, the holy ones, and sure aren't you one of those, Cecie, my dear, and you a child still as innocent as the day you were born, stainless and pure . . .'

Cecie wanted to interrupt, contradict the good sister, tell her that no, she was bad, bad, bad, confess to her the terrible rages she was shaken by, the unkind and vicious thoughts she sometimes nursed, but Sister Agnes gave her no chance and

142

nipped any confession she started to make by telling her she didn't know what she was talking about. She would continue relentlessly, 'You'll be so happy, my dear, you don't know the meaning of sin. And you will see God. Long before I do. Isn't that great? Seeing your Saviour will fill you with heavenly joy, you can't imagine.'

She was so enthusiastic about the after-life that Cecie always felt quite resigned to be on her way there for quite some time after she left. But it didn't last.

She would like to live. Heaven, she felt, could be here on earth if she could swim in the cove with Decla, play tennis with Fidelma and have picnics with Eamonn. Or go punting down the river under the willows. Or feel the sand between her toes. Or make a snowman in the winter, her face ice-cold and her scalp hot under her fur-lined hood. Or go to the races on a wet day. Or join Fusty and Eamonn making fudge in the kitchen, the warm and cosy kitchen with all its gorgeous smells of coffee and bacon, of baking bread and stock on simmer, onions and strawberries, oranges and roasting meat.

Cecie had read *The Phantom of the Opera*, Mary Shelley's *Frankenstein* and Bram Stoker's *Dracula*. She'd read the complete works of Edgar Allan Poe. She read a great deal, under her sheets though she was not supposed to, mostly her taste running to Gothic horror. Her one great fear was that she would be buried alive. That they would think her dead and they'd bury her and she would wake up in the coffin six foot under. Her blood ran cold thinking about it. But Cecie was afraid of a lot of things. She was afraid of the judgement she would have to go through in order to enter the blissful Heaven that Sister Agnes spoke of. You couldn't just walk in when you were dead; you had to do a sort of moral Entrance Examination. She was afraid too of the pain she suffered and of it getting worse. And she was afraid of actually dying. The darkness. Would the darkness go on forever? Suppose Sister Agnes was wrong and there was nothing, only emptiness afterwards? But no, Sister Agnes was quite sure. She called it Cecie's 'heavenly reward'. Cecie hoped that what came before was not too bad.

They talked about death in front of her all the time.

Fusty, Sister Agnes, Sutton. Only Monsignor Maguire hadn't talked about it at all until she asked. Then he was very consoling. Reassuring.

It was coming very soon, she knew that. She dreaded it but that would not stop it coming. Then she would be no more. Imagine, Fidelma would still play tennis. She'd marry and have children. Decla would marry too and Eamonn would go to college and there would be no Cecie. She would have ceased to exist. Would she wander, a pale wraith around Rossbeg? Could she do that? Be a ghost?

She loved life. Even though she spent most of it in this small room behind a closed door, she liked being alive. Did the others realise how lucky they were? Did they know how wonderful it was to wake up well, able to eat, to walk and to smell the air? The gift of energy was so precious they should guard it like a thing of great price, but they didn't.

Ossian worried all the time about how he was doing in his climb to sainthood. Fidelma thought all people cared about were her looks. Decla thought she was plain Jane, undesirable, yet she was, as far as Cecie was concerned, a regular pin-up. Why worry? Anyhow, people liked Decla, couldn't she see that?

And Eamonn? Well, maybe Eamonn was content, but did he really appreciate how lucky he was? Of course not. Why should he? He took it all for granted just as she had long, long ago.

Hot tears scorched her cheeks and slid down her neck, lodging in the crevice there. She was tired, oh so tired.

She pushed back the bedclothes. She sat up. The room spun around, then righted itself. She tried to stand up but her legs were too weak. She strained and strained until a cold sweat covered her body and her head felt on fire and she began to cough.

Then she heard Fusty on the stairs. Fusty wheezed at every step. Oh, why couldn't Fusty be the one who was going to die? No, that wasn't fair. She'd never get into her heavenly bliss thinking thoughts such as that.

She fell backwards on to the bed and pulled the covers up to her chin. She turned her head to the wall. I'm exhausted, she thought, and hoped Sister Agnes was right and that Heaven was indeed more wonderful than this earth. But she doubted it. She really doubted it.

Chapter Twenty-eight

❧ ❧

Roddy had his key to the apartment in Molesworth Street. However, he rang the bell of her door in case she had company. To warn her. He rang their secret code – short, short, short, long, then two more short rings. She never did have company but he was a considerate man and his years with Cora had taught him never to burst in on a woman unannounced. Besides, he had the delicacy to let her see that he did not take her for granted.

She opened the door, a smile of glad surprise on her face. 'Darling Roddy. How lovely to see you.' She always made him feel as if he'd lightened up her day. The smile on her face glowed, her joy at his unexpected visit obvious. She led him inside, then took his raincoat, kissed his cheek and took his jacket. Cora would never let him do without his jacket in the house and it delighted him when Rosie divested him of it. Then she kissed his mouth, slowly, running her hands over his shirt, there in the hallway, then slipping the buttons open and her hands over his back and chest and kissing all the time, soft butterfly kisses that melted his bones and made them feel like butter. She drew him inside and kicked the door shut behind them.

He wanted her instantly in a lovely exciting familiar way. The thing with Rosie was, and he never ceased to marvel at it, that she was a passionate woman who loved sex. He'd never heard the like! Women weren't supposed to enjoy sex at all. They went through a phase of being in love and during that time and when they were first married they responded to their husbands, but more out of duty than passion. So he'd been led to understand. His friends all agreed about this, nodding their heads sagely as they discussed that strange phenomenon, the female. But after the babbies they went

146

off sex. Maybe Rosie hadn't gone off it because she had no children. He didn't know and didn't care. She was a marvel and never ceased to amaze and delight him.

He would not have minded if Rosie *had* gone off sex. Well, not too much, although it would have been a shame. But their relationship had gone much further than that. She was his friend, his lover and his soulmate. He was besotted with her. He thanked God, who must surely condemn him, Cora being such a good wife, so holy and all, for Rosie's presence in his life.

She led him to the bedroom and, as she had done that first time all those years ago, undressed before him. And he was just as excited by her now as he had been then.

They took their time making love. She made it fun for him and their orgasms were shattering. He always had to restrain himself with Cora, but with Rosie the sensuality she brought into their coupling, the skill they had acquired in knowing each other's bodies, and most of all their passionate love for each other, acted as a spur to their climax and made it soul- and body-shaking.

They lay in each other's arms afterwards, he planting kisses in her hair every now and again and she kissing his shoulder and chest. They were content. The soft rain pattered on the window-pane, the air was laden with the smell of sex and they were utterly happy.

After a while she glanced up at him and asked, 'What happened?' Then rolling over said, 'It's so good to have you here, my love, but how'd you get away?'

He shrugged. 'Well, the races . . . Cora suddenly decided she had to see the Monsignor.'

Rosie frowned. 'That's unusual.' She knew the routine of the house by now, the personalities of the family, their habits and preoccupations.

He nodded. 'Weird,' he agreed. 'She always goes Fridays, but suddenly she says she's going today.'

Rosie raised herself on her elbow. 'But she never changes plans, does she? You don't suppose she suspects anything?'

'No, honey. She was her normal self.' He stopped suddenly and said, 'Come to think of it, she wasn't! She was peculiar. Sort of excited, like she'd been . . .' he searched for the word '. . . released.'

147

Rosie giggled. 'Maybe she's found a lover.'

He looked at her and cast his eyes to the ceiling. 'Jasus, don't be daft, girl! Not Cora. Cold fish, is my wife. And she doesn't know about us. I don't exist except as that nice man who provides for her, who meanders around at the edge of her life. I'm blotting paper. There to mop us the messes.'

Rosie was surprised by the bitterness in his voice. Marriages, she knew, were rarely perfect. Couples were often in love but sadly mis-matched and when the love wore off they were left face to face with disillusionment.

'Marriage is an odd institution,' she told him. 'Girls get married to have security. Men to have a housekeeper and a family. We veil it in passion and love and romance but often it is simply a convenient contract, and people living together will clash.' Then she laughed. 'I'm glad mine is over. This arrangement suits me much better.' Then, glancing at him, 'Maybe Cora *does* have a lover. That would make you unreal to her.'

'Wishful thinking, Rosie my love. And wouldn't it be great if she did? But as I say, Cora is a cold fish. No, far more like she has a plan in mind for one of the children. For their social advancement.' He could not keep the sarcasm from his voice and she laid a finger on his lips.

'Hush!' She did not like him saying unkind things about Cora to her, even if they were true. She did not want to encourage any animosity.

'Anyhow, I don't care if she finds out about us. I'll be relieved. All the deception over and you and me walking together in the full sight of everyone. Oh, that'd be grand.'

She looked at him seriously. 'You know I don't want that until the children are grown. I don't want it on my conscience, pet.'

'The children *are* grown. They're adults.'

'All but little Eamonn.'

'Yes. Though a more heedless youngster would be hard to find. I don't think it would bother him in the least.'

'Well, we're not going to find out,' Rosie said firmly.

'Until when?'

'Until he is eighteen.'

'That's ages. Years! I can't be without you for that long, my love.'

'You're *never* without me, me darlin'. I'm here for you night and day, whenever you can be with me.'

'It's not enough. It's never enough. Don't you understand, Rosie, I want to acknowledge you publicly? I want you to hang on my arm in sight of all men.'

'Roddy, I'm grateful for what I've got. You are my world and I don't want to see you hurt and torn apart, and hating me because your children hate me.'

He sat up and folded her tenderly in his arms, holding her as if she was infinitely precious. 'Oh my darling, I'd never hate you. I couldn't. I don't think you know how much I love you, how important you are to me. You've given me love in a way I never expected to receive it, Rosie.' He let her go, looking at her with pleasure. 'Oh, we were a happy family, as families go. I never saw my father. He was never at home. He was so enamoured of his boats that he was hardly ever there.'

'But that was considered normal in those days,' Rosie said. 'You can't blame him.'

'Oh, I don't. I don't,' he assured her. 'And Mammy loved us indiscriminately. She let us do what we liked, more or less. No. There was lots of love in our house, careless taken-for-granted love, but I was the eldest and expected to follow in my father's footsteps and I never felt any deep love focussed on me. Everybody got a bit but no one got the lot. Then I married Cora!' It was said bitterly and again she laid a finger on his mouth. 'No darling, don't you see what I'm saying? *You've* been my love,' he told her. 'You've been the height and the breadth of it, the light and the shade. You've brightened my life, lit it up. You've shown me the glory of this world – so how could I ever hate you?'

'But you'll wait. We're happy. Why be greedy?'

'I don't like the deception, is one reason. And I'm proud of you, of our love. It completes me. I want to live with you exclusively and be your love.'

She knew he was being unrealistic. She also knew he did not see the pitfalls. He really thought he'd be happier with her. But she knew he'd miss Rossbeg. She knew he'd miss the role of Father, Master of the house. She knew he'd miss his mates and having his drink with his comrades in the Shelbourne bar. He would not take easily to the role of outcast, she knew that. Roddy was a gregarious bloke and being ostracised would appal him. And they would, in this Catholic community, be outcasts. They would have broken the rules, and no one was allowed to get away with that. You had to be seen to pay. Otherwise society collapsed.

'Maybe if you did you'd tire of me. That's what happens, they say.'

He grabbed her by the arms and shook her gently. 'Haven't you heard me, woman?' he asked intensely. 'I'm not kidding. I love you. Oh God, I'll always love you. There is nothing in God's world you could do to stop me. Don't you understand?' He wrapped his arms around her, holding her fiercely now, burying his face in her hair.

'All right, dearest, all right,' she soothed him. 'But you'll not tell Cora yet. Promise?'

'You'll make me wait years?' he asked anxiously.

'Maybe not,' she whispered, drawing back her head, looking at him with smiling eyes. 'We'll see.'

And with that he had to be content.

Chapter Twenty-nine

❧ ❧

Sunday evening was set aside for the family at Rossbeg. They gathered in the drawing-room and Cora played the piano and Roddy would sing. 'My Lagan Love' and 'Mother Macree'.

Ossian always tried to be there but often these days had to miss out. Fidelma and Decla also sang, nowadays reluctantly; they were both more interested in the music of Elvis Presley at the moment.

Up in her room Cecie lay and listened, staring at the ceiling in the dusk, and cried as the music came faintly to her ears, heralding some romantic bliss she'd never know. There was something so wistful about the Irish songs her father sang that tugged at the heart-strings and brought tears to the eyes. They seemed to whisper to Cecie of excitements and dreams that would never happen to her, that she would always remain apart from. She felt, listening to that music, as if she was a ghost already.

Eamonn sat on a stool at his mother's side and fidgeted.

The drawing-room faced the mountains and the light was marvellous to see these summer evenings, changing from gold to emerald, shining ochre to amber, brilliant purple to vermilion and then to ripe raspberry and raging scarlet.

They did not draw the curtains against the dazzling view, but always, winter and summer, gave it importance in their evenings. A soft breeze blew in and shadows fell between Roddy and Cora, Fidelma and Decla, Ossian and Eamonn. Everybody was separate. They sat around, each lost in their own thoughts, Cora working on her tapestry when she was finished playing the piano.

The tapestry was going to be a cushion cover and this evening she worked on it feverishly, a hectic flush on

151

her cheeks that made Roddy decide she was sickening for something.

'Fusty's been busy,' Fidelma said suddenly, breaking the silence. She sat with her chin cupped in her hand, her elbow resting on her knee, a frown on her forehead. 'The house has been done over even though it's Sunday.'

'Sylvie is arriving.' Cora darted a critical glance at her husband, as if it was his fault his niece was going to stay with them. 'She did a lot yesterday.' She looked at Fidelma, cross at the implied criticism of her servant working on the Sabbath. Roddy realised that they were both cross as hell and he wondered why. They were a perfect family sitting around on Sunday evening yet the undercurrents swirled and bubbled beneath everything.

'Vinny helped her with the heavy stuff,' Cora continued, 'and she had Mary Mac.' Mary Mac was Vinny's sturdy wife and was sent for by Fusty for heavy-duty times like Christmas and Easter. Or when a visitor came.

'She'll be here tomorrow? This cousin Sylvie?' Fidelma asked, making a face.

'You do that with your face, you'll get stuck!' Eamonn taunted. 'Then you won't be beautiful any more, then what'll you do?'

'Oh, shut up, you little twerp.'

'Now, now children. Think of your mother,' Roddy reprimanded gently. He always said that and he didn't know why. He didn't know what it meant. Think of your mother. Why should thoughts of Cora change their natures? She was so remote. Like a shadow.

He looked at her now. She was like an exquisite effigy, a statue by da Vinci, a painting by Raphael. That tint in her cheeks, that perfect nose, that curve to her jaw. Did passion ever stir her small round breasts, tighten her nipples, moisten her thighs? He doubted it. He had never known it to. The pure lines and bones of her face were virgin-like and her calm eyes innocent. He could not see them now for her lashes were lowered on her rosy cheeks. He marvelled at her unflappable tranquillity, her ability to live her life cocooned from emotional turmoil, safe in her self-contained world. How did she escape what others suffered?

Suddenly she looked up and startled him, for her eyes

152

were restless as a wild beast's on the prowl, hungry and fierce. In a second the look vanished and he decided he'd imagined it, that it had been a trick of the light.

Still, she surprised him again. 'I don't feel like staying up this evening,' she said. 'I think I'll go to bed early tonight.'

Everyone looked at her, startled. They *always* spent Sunday evening together. A change of routine astonished them. However, Fidelma and Decla, Ossian and Eamonn were relieved. They were all individually preoccupied. They watched their mother as if she was changing shape. She let the tapestry she had been stitching fall. 'Sylvie,' she said and sighed. 'What a nuisance!' So that was it. She was worried about their cousin's stay.

She rose and looked around the room. Their faces were like silvered masks looking up at her. She wondered for a moment who they were, then thought, oh yes, my children. She could not bear to remain in the room much longer.

'Ossian, can you drive us tomorrow, to the station? Or will I order the trap?' she asked. 'I know Roddy wants the Daimler for the office.'

'Best the trap, Mother. I've got to be in Dublin tomorrow. I'm meeting Monsignor Maguire for breakfast in the Gresham.'

There could have been no statement better calculated to stupefy her. She stared at her son, her heart suffocating her. 'What?' The question was sharper than she'd meant.

'We've got to discuss plans for Italy and he's saying mass in the Pro Cathedral. So he suggested we meet in the Gresham after.'

'Why didn't you tell me?' she demanded, her voice unusually harsh.

'Mother's going bonkers!' Fidelma whispered to Decla, who did not hear her, being at the moment in another world.

'She's away with the fairies,' Eamonn murmured back to Fidelma.

'Shut up you,' Fidelma ordered.

'Why should I, Mother?' Ossian sounded doubtful. 'It can't interest you.'

'I've got to see Monsignor Maguire tomorrow afternoon.'

'I thought you saw him today?' Roddy said mildly.

153

'No. I did not. He was out.' Roddy looked at her and saw a stranger. Eyes blazing, hands twitching violently, breaking the thread she held. Who was this woman?

'Where were you then?' he asked.

'I was with my mother,' Cora told him. 'She told me some very extraordinary things.' Cora bit her lip. She did not want to go into that now. She'd accepted the *fact* of it, but did not want to dwell on the implications. Besides, who knew if it was really true? Roddy! Mild little man, middle-aged. Dull, dull, dull. Who'd want him? Not a sex-pot like Rosie Daly for sure. She tried to imagine them together and almost laughed. Then a vision of the Monsignor naked as she'd seen him in her dreams flashed into her head and she drew a sharp breath.

'He was at the races today,' Fidelma announced.

'Who?' It was out before Roddy could stop himself. He had not told Cora he'd left the races almost as soon as they arrived.

'Monsignor Maguire, Dadda.'

Cora was frowning, her face thunderous. 'That's ridiculous!' she said and Fidelma innocently persisted, 'No. I *saw* him. Brendan O'Brien talked to him in the bar. I saw him after Dadda left. He was with the Aga Khan's party.'

'What would a Catholic priest be doing with a heathen, I ask you? And where were you, Roddy?'

'I left. Lorcan Metcalf was in charge and they were with Brendan O'Brien and Shannon.'

'That ghastly boy!' Cora exclaimed.

Her head was buzzing. She felt as if she might faint. She had to get out of the room.

'I'm going to bed,' she said, her voice, if not her eyes, under control. 'I want you, Fidelma and Decla, to accompany me to the station tomorrow.'

'I can't, Mother,' Fidelma told her.

'Why not, Fidelma?' Cora turned her attention to her daughter. 'By the way, have you any news for me, dear?'

She sounds more like a headmistress than a mother, Roddy mused.

Fidelma turned to look out of the window. The darkness was gathering fast, getting denser by the minute now. 'No, Mother,' she replied absently.

154

The last thing she wanted to do was enlighten her mother as to the true state of affairs between herself and Harry Devereau. She was still smouldering under his rejection of her. She'd lit on Lorcan Metcalf so quickly that the poor fellow was not quite sure how it had happened. Or why. Fidelma, bruised and chastened, was licking her wounds and wondering where she'd gone wrong. Her mother had brought her up to believe that if she did certain things, followed certain rules, everything would happen according to plan. Well, she had discovered on Saturday night that this was not necessarily so.

'Well, you then, Decla?' To Fidelma's relief her mother turned to her sister.

Decla was engrossed in a dream. She was standing beside the black lake with Shannon and he was saying that they were a pair. A couple.

'Decla.'

She glanced up, surprised at the loudness of her mother's voice.

'Yes, Mother?'

'You'll come with me in the trap tomorrow to the station. If it's not raining. If it is, your father will have to drive us in the car.'

'But, Cora—' Roddy began to protest but Cora had left the room.

They watched her go. In the purple gloom of the drawing-room they could see the crescent moon hanging over the mountains. It was casting silver beams on their faces.

Each of them had a secret that engrossed them to the exclusion of all else. Fidelma, staring into the grate, frowning, worried and agonised over Harry Devereau, wondering what she'd done wrong, dreading her mother's and Decla's discovery of the fact that she'd been rejected. Oh, how Decla would tease her, how she'd gloat and how her mother would criticise.

Decla ached and ached for Shannon, yearned for him, sickly conscious all the time that her mother did not approve. There was something elusive about Shannon and she dreaded waking up to the world and finding him gone. She tried and tried to visualise a future for them but could not imagine it. She felt like crying all the time, as if there was too much emotion bottled up within her.

And Ossian burned for Rome. No one knew, no one must know how he burned with ambition. No one must ever find out how lacking in acceptance he was, how he would ruthlessly pursue his aims. If they ever did he would be thrown out of the priesthood. And now, to his horror, an awful doubt had entered his mind. He had become conscious that his mother was pursuing Monsignor Maguire. Ossian was close to his mother, he could guess her thoughts sometimes and intuitively knew her feelings. There was something going on, he could not guess what, between his mother and Monsignor Maguire, and Ossian felt threatened. If anything happened to stop his visit to Rome he'd . . . But no. He'd not speculate on that eventuality. It would be unbearable.

The piano lay open still. Ossian closed it gently. He had, Roddy thought, a noble head. He too looked like a Raphael. And Fidelma sitting on the floor in front of the empty fireplace, she resembled her brother so much they could be twins. The French windows were open and the smell of the dew and the grass, the sleeping roses and the gardenias had invaded the room. Roddy smiled at Decla. Decla was dearest to his heart. He felt her feelings. He too had known all about inferiority and insecurity, the sense of not being good enough. Cora had inculcated that in him and in Decla. Because they were different. They were not like her and Ossian and Fidelma. Her eldest children were flesh of her flesh and familiar to her. They had her beauty and her grace. Awkward Roddy and Decla puzzled her.

He sighed. Roddy had the biggest secret of all. He ached, even now, sitting here in the bosom of his family, to have Rosie at his side. Here, or at her own place, or in a place of their own that they had created together. He longed to take her out of hiding, show her off, flaunt her, and he sat in the twilight dreaming of her. And so the perfect family sat together as darkness fell.

Roddy glanced around the room at his children. Ossian was yawning, thinking no doubt of his trip to Italy. Not because he looked forward to seeing the ancient city, its treasure-trove of art and antiquities, but because it would push his career forward. That's it, thought Roddy, he does not think of the priesthood as a vocation, he thinks of it as a career. *He* certainly does not need me.

And Fidelma, wondering if she should marry Harry, weighing up the boy's prospects, what she would get out of the alliance, what she would lose. She was thinking about it carefully, so Roddy thought, and he despised her caution. Fidelma would not grieve for Roddy except in so far as it affected her social status.

Decla. He'd miss Decla, but he could see her often. Like a date. He'd meet her in the Gresham for breakfast, like Ossian and Monsignor Maguire. That would be sophisticated and they'd be friends. Chat together. Exchange confidences. His eyes rested fondly on his favourite. This evening, her father knew she had fire in her head and was drowning in love for this Shannon boy. Roddy believed no good would come of it, but he knew interference would not solve anything or protect his daughter. He knew enough about love to know that. She would not die of it. She would think she was going to, but eventually she would not.

Cecie, however, would die. That was certain. And Eamonn would grow up and go his own imaginative, heedless way, playing Rugger and drinking pints and making lewd jokes about women with the lads, his pals at the tennis club, Martin and Gary. Who would miss him, their father, if he went? No one.

He sighed, thought of Rosie and smiled.

Chapter Thirty

❧ ❧

'So? Ye went to the races?'

'Yeah!'

'Who was there?'

'The girl. The father, for a while. The sister. Her boyfriend. My uncle.'

'Who else?'

'The Aga Khan. People from the State Department. Big nobs.'

'Aha!' There was relief in the voice and Shannon knew he'd pleased Angus Rudh.

'Who else?' The dapper Seamus O'Sullivan spoke quietly.

'The Taoiseach. With the Aga Khan.'

Angus Rudh let out a long contented sigh as he sat back from the table he'd been leaning across in the damp little hut. They were alone today, Angus and Seamus with the boy. Angus's red hair was wet and his clothes were steaming. It was pissing down, Angus said, angry at the rainy Monday morning. There was a small electric fire with one bar glowing. Its heat encouraged the smell of rotting vegetation, coaxing scents from the ground that would have better remained dormant. Who knew what was in the corners in those ripely scented piles of rubbish?

But Angus smelled more pungently than the trash. He exuded odours that unsettled Shannon's stomach and made him want to cough. But he didn't dare and was very careful not to show his discomposure. However, every time Angus Rudh leaned forward across the table a blast of scorching dragon-breath laden with the stink of bad teeth and stale tobacco seared his sensibilities. It made it extremely difficult to keep his attention on what was being said.

Seamus O'Sullivan on the other hand was perfectly groomed.

He smelled of carbolic and toothpaste. Shannon veered towards him as much as possible.

'Who's my target, sir?' Shannon asked timidly.

'That's not your concern yet,' Angus said coldly. 'You'll know more when the time comes. You just keep up the good work.'

Shannon hesitated. 'Is it fair though, sir? She's ...' He stopped, then added, 'She's, well, gettin' sort of *intense*.'

'All's fair in love and war, eh, Shannon?' Angus drew his lips back over his discoloured teeth. He looked like a large red fox, and the man had power and magnetism. He seemed rooted in the earth. When he said, 'I am the soil of Ireland, its clay, its peat,' you believed him. His eyes had a fanatic's glow while Seamus O'Sullivan's were cold and hard and determined. A professional soldier's eyes.

'Don't get too fond of her, boy,' Seamus said. His voice was not unfriendly.

A rat scuttled across the floor. It stopped a moment, unafraid, gimlet-eyed, and looked at them. Shannon blanched. He kept quite still, but his insides shrank. Neither of the other men moved or showed any interest.

'No, sir.'

'You're going to have to shoot someone. Coldly. Without hesitation,' Seamus said softly.

'Yes, sir.'

'I hope you are the right man for the job.' He looked intently at Shannon, who met his unflinching gaze full on.

'Oh, I am, sir.'

'Just remember it. We are not playing here.'

'Yes, sir.'

Seamus had turned towards Shannon as he spoke and he now turned away, his face still as if carved of stone.

'Ireland is a beautiful land, a golden land,' he said softly. 'It's like the Garden of Eden, boy. Those who betray it are less than the dirt and must be made examples of. We can have no pity for them.' He spoke quietly, in contrast to Angus's bark.

'The bloody British lordin' it over us, it's not over!' Angus cried. 'Slicin' us apart like that. Dividin' our land to suit their tastes. Turnin' us against each other. That's what they're doin', the bastards. The British are predators and thieves, they take what is not theirs.'

Seamus O'Sullivan waved a hand. It was well cared for, nails cut short, a competent, strong hand. 'At the moment it is not the British we are concerned with.' He said it softly, glancing reprovingly at his hirsute friend. 'Curb your ardour, friend; for the moment the British can sleep sweet in their beds. Their day is over, their Empire spent, though they don't see it yet. Power swings both ways and they are on the way out.' He looked at Shannon, his gaze level, his voice unemotional. 'We don't want, Erin has never wanted power over other lands, other peoples. We want simply to be left in peace, whole and healthy. We'll deal with the British in the North, never fear, Shannon, in the fullness of time, and hopefully you'll be part of that fight. But first' – his eyes narrowed, slits that glittered icy-cold – 'what preoccupies us at the moment, Shannon, and keeps us awake at night are the traitors of our own blood. The Irishmen and women who sold us out. They, and one in particular, must be made an example of.'

'Yes, sir.' This was more the talk Shannon was used to in Liverpool, the talk that fired his blood and inspired him, making him a candidate for this undertaking.

'So that all the world can see, particularly the Americans, that we mean what we say. That we will not tolerate traitors.' Seamus O'Sullivan, this hero, this giant of the Cause, stirred Shannon's heart. They talked about him in hushed tones in Liverpool, and here he was, confiding in Shannon. His heart beat strong in courage within him. He felt he could rise to any order.

'So, while you are cultivating the girl, remember that, Shannon. We are not playing a game.' He stared at the boy. 'Got the message?'

'Loud and clear, sir.'

'All right. You may go.'

Shannon left. He was going to telephone Decla. The two men in the hut remained quiet. They were opposites; the one emotional, impulsive, passionate, the other professional, bitter and dedicated. Seamus had been horrified that his comrades had accepted a half-measure freedom to self-govern. He had one aim in life: to see Ireland united and free. The division of North and South nagged at him like a throbbing tooth. There would be unrest among the people of Ireland until this was resolved. He had no doubt that the British knew this. And there would be terrible discontent among the downtrodden Catholics in the North. No people deprived of jobs, education, opportunity for self-advancement were going to be happy for long and there would be work to do there. It would be easy to galvanise them into action. He was well aware that passion for a cause is often simply anger finding an outlet, but that did not worry him. It could be utilised, channelled.

No, it was the betrayal here, in the now free South, that concerned him, the traitors who had accepted the partition of the new formed Free State, the ones who talked of prison for the freedom-fighters and still had the audacity to say they were patriotic Irishmen and women.

He sighed. It would be a long hard battle, but then, that was nothing new. Since Henry VIII had cast an eye across the water, Ireland had been engaged in a violent struggle. That was why the rotten apples, the compromisers, had to be taught a lesson.

And the British were providing a fertile battleground in Derry and Belfast. By keeping the Catholics in bondage they provided the brotherhood with fodder. They were guaranteeing dissention.

'Ye think he'll be all right?' Angus asked, lighting a Woodbine.

Seamus O'Sullivan wrinkled his nose in distaste as the smoke drifted past him. He was a fastidious man.

'Yes,' he said, rising. 'He's still young. He has no experience of the real thing, but he'll do.'

'I hope to Jasus he won't go all soppy on us.'

'No. He won't. He's a cold bastard. He's like his da. He'll not let us down. He's committed.'

Angus nodded, satisfied. 'Then let's get out of this cesspit. Jeez, when can we get a dacent room te meet in, Seamus? Eh? As befits us, eh?'

'Soon, Angus. Soon. This place is very safe. Extremely so, and that is the important thing, you'll agree?'

161

Angus nodded, drawing on his cigarette, shivering in the gloom.

'Hold yer horses, man. Everything will work out in the end. You'll see.'

Chapter Thirty-one

❧ ❧

It was cosy and welcoming in the Gresham restaurant at breakfast-time. Guests, bathed and fresh, greeted each other, moaning about the weather (it was raining), but laughing, content. Their breakfast was at hand and the aromas of bacon and coffee, fresh bread and blackberry jam teased their nostrils and excited their palates. Waiters in white jackets hurried to see each guest was satisfied and the waitresses served expertly with twinkling automatic smiles.

The two men sat in a secluded corner. The Monsignor, wearing a touch of the purple, looked distinguished and learned and commanded respect. The young priest, ridiculously handsome, talking earnestly while he scoffed bacon and eggs, sausages, tea and toast, prompted admiration and sighs from the waitresses who, seeing his collar, felt it was a terrible waste. The older man ate more sparingly. He had scrambled eggs and coffee and he did not finish those.

They had been discussing their forthcoming trip, what Ossian should pack, and Ossian was listening eagerly. It would be the first time he had left the shores of his native land and excitement welled up within him.

'It's going to be hot in Rome,' Monsignor Maguire told him. 'Very hot. You'll need a light jacket, Ossian. I'll give a list to your mother.' He smiled at the boy's eager, flushed face. 'It seems she's coming to see me today.' He looked at Ossian enquiringly. 'No trouble at home, I hope?'

'No, Monsignor. Except Cecie. There's always Cecie. Sometimes I wonder at God's will.'

'Don't even try, my boy.' The Monsignor sighed and continued, 'It's the nub of it, isn't it? In itself it is our biggest stumbling block; trying in our human way to make sense of God's plan. We can't, you see, because we *are* human and

163

He is divine. So what we are really saying is, why can't God do what would suit *me*? Now, if He did that, what would become of us? Where would we draw the line?'

Ossian nodded, thinking, I'd like that. If God did what would suit me, I'd like that fine. 'But Cecie did nothing wrong,' he said. 'She's innocent.'

'That has nothing to do with it. Cecie is not being punished. Perhaps God wants her with Him too much. He cannot bear to leave her here. She is one of His favourites. See, Ossian, if we believe in the resurrection and the hereafter, and our religion hinges on that, then Cecie is blessed. She gets there sooner than we do.'

'Do you really believe that, Monsignor?' Ossian asked him.

The Monsignor spread his hands. 'I don't know, Ossian, is the honest answer, but I have faith. I love this life. I don't want to die, but' – he shrugged – 'who knows how I'll feel when the time comes?' He watched as the waitress refilled his cup from a silver coffee-pot. She was flirting with Ossian but the boy seemed unaware of it. He was too intent on their conversation. The Monsignor gave him a mental congratulatory salute for his lack of response.

'I've seen a lot of deaths, Ossian,' he said. 'And they all, all those people at the end, seemed resigned. As if they accepted death. God, I believe, gives us that ability at the end.'

They were silent a moment and the waitress left. Ossian stirred his tea, the Monsignor his coffee.

'How do we go?' Ossian asked.

'We fly from Collinstown to Rome.'

Ossian whistled. No one travelled by air. Only the military or dignitaries or the very rich.

'Wow!'

'Nothing, Ossian, is too good for the clergy in Ireland or Rome. Long may it last.'

Ossian laughed. 'I like that. It's good for the status quo.'

The Monsignor frowned. 'Ossian, be careful. The Vatican is a hive of intrigue. Jesus would find it just like home. Jerusalem then and Rome now. I think it might anger Him. So remember, you have to be careful.'

'Oh, I will, never fear.'

'Some of the, well, right-wing views I have heard you

express are a little extreme. They may find favour there, initially. But there are always the left-wingers too, and they too are powerful. Be careful not to antagonise anyone. You are inclined to wax eloquent, you know. So don't be indiscreet. Eh?' He smiled at the boy to take the sting out of his words. He touched the corners of his mouth with his napkin, then laid it on the table and raised his hand for the bill.

'Don't underestimate me, Monsignor,' Ossian said, blushing. He hated to be criticised. 'I'll be very discreet.'

'I must say though, Ossian' – the Monsignor laid some notes on the table – 'that your views are most unusual for an Irishman. You are the first Irish Conservative I've ever met.'

'I'd rather be considered British,' the boy said stubbornly. 'After all, I was born British, under their rule here.'

'No. I don't think so.'

The young priest nodded his head fiercely. 'Yes. I checked. Anyone born before 1946 is technically British.'

The waitress, picking up the coins, snorted in disgust. The Monsignor gave her his most beguiling smile. 'Keep the change,' he said. She was too well-trained to say anything but she made how she felt perfectly plain and shot daggers from her eyes now at the young priest.

'That's what I mean, Ossian,' the Monsignor told him, glancing at the waitress's retreating back. He leaned across the table, his face very serious. 'The powers that be gave you to me,' he said. 'Don't let me down. And get this. I will not feel it my duty to clean up after you if you are tactless. You are a good boy, Ossian, and have the makings of a wonderful priest. But God is *not* selective. No matter what you may think. He told us to love *all* His people. All. Not some. The disciples, just like you, tried to squirm out of that one, though the ones they wanted to exclude were the Greeks, the Pharisees and the heathen, and incidentally the prostitutes. Jesus, however, made it quite clear that God created *everyone* in His own image. *Everyone* had His love. *Everyone* was His child.' He nodded to the people around. 'See that man over there, picking his teeth? He is made in the image and likeness of God. That old woman spilling her porridge? God's beloved, and she therefore must be beloved by you. You are God's representative on this earth. Not just for the beautiful people here, Ossian, but for the least attractive, and it would be well for you to remember that.'

Ossian nodded. He disliked sermons, especially those aimed at himself. He knew he had his faults and failings. Didn't everyone? But it was hard to swallow when the Monsignor criticised what everyone knew to be self-evident. There were people God did not love, Ossian was sure of it. Murderers and child molesters. Members of the banned IRB. They were outlawed by the Irish Government, Fianna Fáil. Naturally God did not love those outside the law. Ossian felt very badly about the IRB. It was a disgrace what they were doing, what they were up to. Sowing discord, revving people up. Using poverty and want to entice people to violence and murder. They were terrorists and Ossian was sure that God did not love terrorists.

Ossian knew the Monsignor did not agree with violence. He knew the Monsignor was of a mind with him about the IRB. But the Monsignor drew the line at publicly denouncing them as Ossian had done. He did not believe the clergy should become involved in politics, while Ossian felt it was imperative.

He would keep a low profile in Rome. He would be in a strange land, unfamiliar with the language. Oh, he had the essential smattering but until he learned the nuances he'd be discreet.

Later though. Later. He'd be up to his neck in it later. He'd work to have all terrorists banned by the Church. Banned by Rome, that would give them something to think about. He had discussed this often in the seminary, preached about it when he covered for priests who were on holidays or sick. It would be something he could be proud of.

'I better get back,' the Monsignor told him. 'I appreciate your feelings, Ossian. I've known you all your life and I've heard the talk in the seminary. Your feelings are leading you and you must learn to control them. You must lead them. We all abhor violence, but this . . . this . . . *confronting* it aggressively is not the way. You must see that.'

If not that way then how? In the dark? With this lot? No, no, no. But he'd taken on board enough of Monsignor's advice to remain silent and not cavil.

The Monsignor rose. 'I must go. I've got quite a few visits to make, and then I'm seeing your mother this afternoon.'

Ossian rose too, wondering again at the reason for his mother's anxiety to see the Monsignor.

'God bless you, my son, and think on what I said.'

'I will, Monsignor.'

'A little more discretion.'

'Yes, Monsignor.'

'All right. Let's go!' And the two men went out into the rain.

Chapter Thirty-two

❧ ❧

Nothing had happened. Nothing had actually happened. Her feverish dreams, wet-bodied, languorous-limbed, filled with wild yet drowsy sensation, had been in her own head and no one else was privy to them. She had to remember that.

Cora had thought about nothing else. She had decided she was going to devote herself to the Monsignor – utterly, entirely. Like Sister Clare to St Francis she would be his slave, his servant, his minion. In God. Always, she would tell him, in God. She would wash his clothes, prepare his meals, cook for him, tidy up after him. How, she did not trouble herself to ask. The fact that she'd never cooked a meal in her life nor cleaned up did not enter her mind. It would happen.

She groomed herself as if in a dream, hardly noticing Roddy, his presence but a mild irritation. She smiled at him, thinking her mother must be hallucinating. Dear old Roddy unfaithful? Rubbish!

Roddy said he would take her to the station as it was raining. They could not go in the trap. She nodded and went to the phone in the hall.

'I'll just telephone to make sure Monsignor Maguire will be there this afternoon,' she told Roddy. 'I made the mistake yesterday of forgetting to do that.' Then she added, 'Won't keep you a moment, dear.'

'Won't the visitor, my young niece, need you here, Cora?' Roddy asked mildly.

'Sylvie is not going to disrupt my routine,' Cora told him lightly but firmly. He forbore to remind her that going to see the Monsignor on a Monday was not routine.

She had a brief conversation on the phone, nodding and saying 'That's fine' every now and then, and Roddy assumed the Monsignor would be there. As she put the phone down it rang again, making her jump. She picked it up, listened, and asked, 'Who?' Then she frowned. 'Shannon? No. No you can't. She's busy!'

Roddy grabbed the phone from his wife as she was about to replace the receiver. He said into it, 'Hold on, Shannon, she'll be with you in a moment.' He shouted upstairs, 'Decla, Shannon for you!' Cora had her hands to her ears, murmuring, 'Don't shout please.'

Decla came running down the stairs, face flushed with excitement. She took the phone from her father, thanking him with her eyes. Cora looked irritated and Roddy shook his head.

'You must not do things like that, Cora,' he said to her and her eyes widened innocently. 'It was a lie,' he said.

'For her own good,' she hissed back. 'Hurry up, Decla, we haven't got all day.'

Roddy wondered, as he often did, about her pronouncements. Decla had no intention of spending all day on the phone. And she *did* have all day, come to that. Sylvie would need to settle in. She would feel strange in a strange place in a strange land, meeting new people. Decla's meeting her would make little difference in the overall scheme of things. But he said nothing. Decla was only on the phone for seconds.

'Yep. Yep. Yep, Shannon. See you then. Okay.' And she put the phone down.

'You're not going *anywhere* with that boy, Decla. You've got to be hostess to your cousin.' Cora's lips were tight.

Decla too said nothing. She too knew better. She'd work something out. She smiled at her father and he winked at her. She winked back.

He realised with sudden optimism for her future that Decla had inherited or learned his own trick of peaceful non co-operation. She went her own way unnoticed, with quiet determination, agreeing, or rather not disagreeing, with her mother then doing precisely what she wanted.

They drove in the teeming rain to the station. The Daimler was cosy and smelled of leather and wood. Roddy liked driving. It relaxed him. He felt as his daughter always did, warm and safe in this mobile cavern of a car moving through the bad weather.

The railway station was small and the train from the newly named Dun Laoghaire (Roddy still called it Kingstown) the only one due. It chuntered up, right on time, and disgorged one small, solitary figure.

They were standing in a group, Cora, Roddy and Decla, under Roddy's big black umbrella and the small person on the platform looked at them hopefully, then took a few tentative steps towards them.

'Auntie Cora? Uncle Roddy?'

She had an elfin face, huge anxious eyes and a bright smile. Her hair was pale as a fairy-tale princess's.

'Sylvie, my dear,' Cora greeted her, keeping her at arm's length although the small girl showed every inclination to embrace her aunt. 'Roddy, get her bag. Is that all you've got with you, dear?' She pointed in astonishment to the holdall Sylvie was clutching. The girl nodded. She bit her lip and Roddy drew her to him and hugged her. She looked so forlorn, so small and fragile, anxiously standing there in the rain and his heart was touched. She looked so much younger than Decla yet Roddy knew she was the same age.

'Come along, dear. A nice cup of tea will warm you. We have the car outside.'

Roddy took the bag from her with difficulty. He had to prize open her fingers which clutched the tattered old handle as if *rigor mortis* had set in. There was a nerve in the corner of her mouth that twitched ever so slightly and he realised that she was terrified. He longed in that moment for Rosie's ability to soothe away fear and make others feel comfortable, a quality that Cora lacked.

'Don't be scared, my dear,' he whispered. But Cora heard.

'She's not scared,' she announced. 'Are you, Sylvie? Don't be silly, Roddy. Why would she be scared?'

Sylvie shook her head. Roddy wanted to kill his wife. He put the girl into the front seat, much to Cora's chagrin. 'Start as you mean to go on,' she hissed at him.

He tucked the cashmere throw over Sylvie's legs and found that she was trembling. He smiled encouragingly. 'It's all right, Sylvie, promise,' he said.

She looked back at him gratefully. Cora was getting into

the back of the car with Decla, who seemed at a loss to know what to say.

They drove to Rossbeg in comparative silence. Cora made a couple of efforts at bright social chat but the girl answered too softly for Cora to hear so she gave up. The rain surged on to the bonnet and windshield of the Daimler, making a whooshing noise, and Roddy had to concentrate on his driving.

Decla's mind was full of Shannon. She too found it hard to concentrate on her cousin. All she could think about was her boyfriend, his eyes staring at her so piercingly, the way the skin beside them was creased from squinting. How wonderful he was, the way his lips curved and ended in a little crease that she wanted to kiss. His fingers – tobacco-stained, nails broken, skin calloused on his knuckles – those things, normally repulsive to her, made her knees weak. What did he *do*? She was afraid to ask in case it was something that would give her mother the right to ban their meeting. Suppose for instance that he was a labourer? Or a street sweeper? Who knew what he did in Liverpool. And her mother said Brendan O'Brien was very common. Dadda had asked her what she meant by "common". Common, he said, meant "one of the people" and her mother shook her shining hair and stretched the muscles in her neat little nose the way she always did when she talked of something or someone distasteful to her and said, 'You know perfectly well what I mean. He's not well bred. He's not top drawer.' And Dadda sighed and muttered that he was no wiser.

He'd said to her mother, who set store by what people *did*, who set the rules? Why was it okay to be a chemist but not a publican? Would Sean Flood, his brother, Sylvie's father, be considered more the thing if he played in a symphony orchestra rather than in a swing band, and she'd glared at him. Then he remarked that it took just as much talent and hours of practice to play jazz as it did to play the classics and Cora had tightened her lips and changed the conversation. Now her Uncle Sean's child sat in the front seat next to her father and Decla wished profoundly that she wasn't there. She knew as sure as God made little apples that the burden of entertaining Sylvie would fall on her shoulders. She was the same age as her cousin and her mother would delegate responsibility to her. Well, Decla decided, she'd have to find a way to see that Sylvie was otherwise occupied and that she was free to see Shannon.

Her cheeks burned at the thought of him. He'd said on the phone that his Uncle Brendan was going to the club after lunch and he would be there and maybe she could meet him at the lake.

She'd agreed, of course, but she knew, just *knew* that her mother was going to ask her to look after her cousin, and sure enough, as the Daimler purred carefully along the country road, the windscreen wipers battling against the onslaught, Cora turned to her daughter and said, 'You'll take care of Sylvie, dear, won't you? She's bound to be homesick and feeling a bit awkward and I have to go to the Abbey and Dadda is going to work, so I'm leaving her in your hands, dear. I know you'll do your best.'

Decla caught her father's eye in the rear-view mirror. His glance was reassuring. She thought, he knows, he understands, and hope surged. She said nothing and her mother relapsed into silence beside her as Roddy steered the Daimler through the deluge and Sylvie wondered if it always rained this much in Ireland.

Chapter Thirty-three

෯ ௧

Decla showed the visitor her room. She'd been moved up under the eaves and all her things with her and her mother had had Fusty do over the dainty bedroom for Sylvie.

Sylvie gasped when she was led in. Her eyes widened at the sheer prettiness of the place. The bed and windows were curtained in pale yellow muslin. There were soft sheepskins on the floor and floral pictures on the walls. The furniture was cream and a bowl of yellow tulips graced the mantelpiece. Her pale little face lit up and her big brown eyes widened as she said, 'This is *mine*? This? It's *beautiful*!'

'Oh, it's nothing.' Decla preferred her room upstairs with its nooks and crannies. Besides, she was not really paying attention, she wanted so badly to escape. 'I'm glad you like it.' Then she said hurriedly, whispering, afraid someone would hear, 'Listen, Sylvie, I know my mother said to look after you this afternoon, but, see I have a date.'

Sylvie stared at her in admiration. 'Wow!' she breathed.

Decla smiled complacently. It was wonderful how much kudos having a boyfriend gave one. 'And I'm not going to be here,' she added. 'Could you . . . do you think you could sort of entertain yourself? And not let Mother know?'

Sylvie smiled at her. 'Oh, that's all right,' she said eagerly. 'I'm sure Uncle Roddy and Auntie Cora . . .'

'No, no, I'd rather Mother didn't know. She's not going to be home so she needn't find out.' She sat beside Sylvie on what had been her bed. 'Mother's going to the Abbey to see Monsignor Maguire. He's going to Rome with my brother the priest . . .'

Sylvie nodded eagerly, 'Yes, yes I know, Ossian.'

'Yes. And Dadda, well, Dadda wouldn't mind as much as

173

Mother, but he's going to work so that's all right. He took the morning off to meet your train and . . .'

'Oh, I don't want to be a bother,' Sylvie assured her. 'I want to, well, just fit in if I can.' A worried frown creased her forehead. 'I don't want to be a nuisance.'

'You are not that, Sylvie,' Decla assured her.

'Besides, this room is so pretty I would be happy just being here.' She glanced around her, then looked confidingly at Decla. 'Truth to tell, I'm a bit scared of all this . . .'

Decla looked around, puzzled. 'What?'

'This . . . space. I'm used to crowds and small spaces with street signs and everything obvious and visible. Like where the kitchen and the bathroom are. I've no idea . . .'

'I'll show you,' Decla said. 'Don't worry.'

Sylvie seemed so nervous that Decla felt sorry for her. Nevertheless her priority prevented her from being as sympathetic as she would normally have been. 'Fusty'll be in the kitchen. She's our housekeeper,' Decla told her. 'So she'll be there if you want anything.' She grimaced. 'Eamonn's not going to be any use to you, I'm afraid. He's our—'

'Little brother, I know,' Sylvie put in.

'Look I'll introduce you to . . .' Who? Decla couldn't think. Apart from Fusty there was no one. Mary Mac would confuse the girl. Her accent was indecipherable even for a native Irish person and strangers from Dublin or Limerick, never mind London, found her incomprehensible. She smiled at her cousin, suddenly contrite. 'I'm sorry, I really am, Sylvie, that I've got to go.'

Sylvie smiled back at her but her lower lip trembled and Decla saw her clearly for the first time.

She had obviously slept on the train for there was a mark on her pale cheek left by her fingers. Her eyes pleaded to be accepted, a puppy-dog look, Decla thought. She looked helpless and lonely.

Decla had an idea. 'There's Cecie. My sister. She's sick. She's got consumption. You mustn't actually go near her 'cause she's contagious. But you can talk to her. Through the door if you don't want to go in, if you're nervous.'

'Oh, I don't mind. In the war . . .' Sylvie hesitated. 'Well, we met all sorts. TB wasn't the worst. I've talked to lots of people with TB.'

Decla stood up. 'Well.' She went to the door. 'Lunch is any sec. I'll take you down. Don't say a word to Mother about my date.'

Sylvie shook her head vehemently. Decla looked around the room. 'I suppose this afternoon you could unpack . . .' She looked doubtfully at the small bag. 'This all? Or you could rest,' she added hopefully.

Sylvie nodded eagerly. 'Of course,' she said. Her eyes, big, like wet pansies, made Decla feel guilty. But there was no way she was going to miss seeing Shannon. There was a hard little core of determination within her, daring Sylvie or her mother to try to thwart her.

'I'll be back in a mo',' she said, waving at her cousin, and ran upstairs to change for Shannon.

Chapter Thirty-four

❧ ❧

Sylvie looked around the room. It was without doubt the loveliest room she had ever slept in. She pressed her cheek against the counterpane. It was white and various shades of yellow, soft to her skin. One of the tulips shed a leaf, then another, and she could see its dark heart.

She went to the dressing-table and opened the drawers. They were lined with pretty patterned paper and there was a frilled lavender sachet in each one. The wardrobe too had a sweet smelling heart-shaped sachet pinned to the back of the door.

She had nothing to put in the wardrobe or in the drawers. Or almost nothing. She had the dress she was wearing, her very best, and her everyday one in her bag. It was grey wool, serviceable and not in the least pretty. Certainly not pretty enough to deserve sachets.

She hoped no one would examine her underwear. She had two well-worn chill-proof vests, a Liberty bodice, a couple of pairs of knickers, and a pair of lisle stockings. She had taken the lisle stockings off in the lavatory in the train because they felt too hot and looked so awful.

This was the most beautiful place she had ever been and she knew she was so lucky to be here, yet she wanted desperately to cry. She didn't know why. She should be grateful, she knew. She should be down on her knees thanking God, yet all she could feel was misery.

'Oh, forgive me please,' she murmured, looking heavenwards.

At that moment Fusty came in, making her jump. The old woman took the situation in at a glance.

'This your bag?' She pointed to the small tattered grip on the floor.

Sylvie nodded, gulping, hoping that there would not be another humiliating reference to its size and meagre contents.

'Don't look so woebegone, Miss Sylvie. I expect you lost your case on the boat.' It was not a question, it was a statement. Sylvie stared at her, bewildered. 'Now, I'll tell you what I'll do. I'll unpack this and get you some of Miss Decla's and Miss Fidelma's things that they've grown out of, for you're very small indeed, and you can use them for the time being. All right?'

Sylvie didn't know what to say. The formidable woman stood over her, hands on hips, and Sylvie decided it would be foolish to argue with her. 'My name's Fusty,' the large woman continued, 'short for Florence Fussell, but Father Ossian when he was a wee boy shortened it to Fusty an' Fusty I've stayed. Now you wash yer hands an' face an' Miss Decla'll be here directly to tek ye down to lunch.'

The sadness left Sylvie's face and quite suddenly she felt cheerful. Perhaps, after all, things might be different this time. Perhaps she might fit in. She smiled and nodded at Fusty and went obediently into the bathroom.

Chapter Thirty-five

❧ ❧

Brendan O'Brien was feeling uncomfortable. He could not seem to get a hook on his nephew from Liverpool. Like Decla, he wondered what exactly he did for a living, what job he held down, or whether he was, in fact, unemployed, but all his efforts to find out came to nothing. A man, in Brendan's view, was what he *did*. His occupation defined him. It earned him respect. It was how you assessed people and if you were unemployed, you were, in Brendan's opinion, unworthy to breathe the same air as the rest of the male sex.

As far as he was concerned he felt he was in the right niche. Being a bookie was, in his view, a noble and fun profession. He thought of bookies as the salt of the earth. He had no desire to be a professional man. He paid respect to those of his friends who were but he did not wish to be one of their company.

His work was easy now. He made a lot of money and he could be around the horses he loved, the racing crowd. He did not have to be a role model for anyone and he could enjoy himself.

He had a string of betting shops across the country that kept him, he said jokingly, in pin money. Actually he was making a fortune. The bookie never lost. At least not so far.

Every morning he checked unexpectedly on one or two branches. They never knew which one he'd choose. Sometimes he'd revisit a branch he'd done the day before; the staff never knew when he'd pounce so they had to keep on the alert. They knew that Brendan O'Brien was merciless with malingerers. And one attempted fiddle and you were out. Reputation gone. When a spiv called Peadar Prunty had been foolhardy enough to try to double-cross Brendan

O'Brien he had been not only sacked but prosecuted and clapped in jail. Brendan was famous for being utterly ruthless with anyone who tried to screw him or take advantage of him, so no one did. People knew where they stood with him, worked hard for him and were rewarded by him. He was very successful.

Otherwise he was affable and pleasure-loving, a kindly and temperate man who was popular with everyone – friends, colleagues and work-force alike. He liked seeing BRENDAN O'BRIEN TURF ACCOUNTANT over his shop doors. On any journey he would admire his name printed large and stare in admiration at where he had got to. Chomping his cigar he would grunt with satisfaction. He was proud of his success and was known to affirm that his business was built on the foolish extravagance of others. 'Anyone who bets is throwing their money away,' he'd say, laughing. 'And it usually ends up in my pants pocket. In the end, ye can't win!'

Brendan led a pleasant, untroubled life, though Delores, his wife, was a disappointment to him. She couldn't seem to climb with him, didn't seem to want to.

Brendan was not interested in high society, however. The Floods were his best friends – well, Roddy was – but Brendan had no ambition to march side by side with Cora in her desire to be thought of as a leader of fashion, a society doyenne. All he wanted was to be accepted and feel comfortable with the people who, like himself, had money and wanted to spend it agreeably.

Delores was only comfortable in a two up, two down little shebeen, tea in the kitchen, dinner at one p.m. dressing-gown preferred, a sloppy lackadaisical class of existence favoured greatly in the slums where she grew up. He couldn't change her, didn't try any more. She further disappointed him by producing their one child Justin and refusing point-blank to try for another. 'Anyone who'd go through that more'n once is daft!' she told him. 'I done my duty, Brendan; Justin nearly split me in half. You think I'm goin' through that again, you're crazy!' Brendan would have liked lots of kids, would have been a good father, but it seemed it was not to be. Justin was all he was going to get and unfortunately his awkward, shy son only baffled him.

He envied Roddy his set-up. Wife, just the right number of children (though it was a shame about Cecie), and a sexy mistress – Roddy had it all. Mind you, he wouldn't take Cora on a plate, not for all the money in the world. Not Cora Flood. That woman, Brendan thought, was sharp enough to castrate a man. At least Delores was soft. He could relax with her. She didn't bother him much, he had to say that for her, and if his only sexual release was a quick job with a floozie from the Quays on a Saturday night, well, he couldn't complain. Life on the whole was very good, and show him a man in Ireland, except perhaps Roddy Flood, who was sexually fulfilled, and he'd show you the Holy Grail!

Brendan had a full social agenda and if people thought it strange that his wife was rarely at his side they'd long since give up speculation about it. It had become, in time, the accepted thing. He was a good fellow, a convivial man, nice to have around, and that was that.

He had hoped his young nephew and he would hit it off. As far as his son was concerned, when he tried to have a conversation with Justin he might as well have been talking double Dutch. So he had hoped that Shannon might be a companion, the son and mate he longed for, someone he could chat to, brag to a little about his business, do fatherly things with, but no.

Shannon was slippery and non-committal. Brendan could not even get a straight answer about how long he intended to stay. To make it more confusing, Shannon had money. People who didn't work rarely had money. And Brendan's brother Dec, Shannon's father, was a drunkard, a layabout, a stereotypical class of Irishman, despised by the rest of the world and an embarrassment to his fellow citizens. He couldn't have staked his own son, not in a million years.

And Shannon was curiously busy. For a stranger in town he seemed to know people and Brendan wondered how. He had appointments and often left the house purposefully, as if he had a mission, only to return late. Very late. What, Brendan wondered, was he up to?

He seemed to like Decla Flood, though, and that was great. Brendan was devoted to Roddy Flood and he admired Decla enormously. She was so friendly and gorgeous and much more approachable than her mother or Fidelma. They'd make a great couple, Shannon and Decla, Brendan decided. He'd give Shannon a shop, set him up in Dublin. Shannon would be able to look after Decla and she would be the daughter Brendan never had. He'd shower them with good things. If they married. If Shannon shaped up.

But what did he *do*? Brendan aimed to find out. He had his ways.

Chapter Thirty-six

✥ ✥

Sylvie opened the door of her room very cautiously and looked right and left. There was no one about. The house seemed deserted, a strange suspended hush hanging over it. It seemed huge and mysterious and daunting to the stranger and not at all welcoming.

Most of the places Sylvie had lived were small and overcrowded and the size of Rossbeg alarmed her.

Lunch had been odd. Auntie Cora had seemed preoccupied, hardly aware of her presence. Uncle Roddy too. In fact, everyone's minds seemed elsewhere and she'd felt superfluous, almost invisible, and that frightened her. But she had to admit she was used to being ignored.

Did they see her, she wondered, did they notice that she was a presence in their midst? She had minded her manners as instructed by her mother. 'They're toffs. If you don't mind your manners they'll pack you back on the next boat and I don't want that, y'hear? Especially Cora. Watch out for your Auntie Cora. Sharp as a knife, Cora Flood.'

Her mother had been rubbing the rouge into her pale cheeks as she spoke, her eyes glittering behind mascara'd lashes. She'd puffed on her cigarette as she unloaded her daughter once again. The smoke made Sylvie cough. And her mother always made her cry.

Well, she'd minded her manners but the Floods didn't seem to notice. Maybe they'd have noticed if she *hadn't*.

After lunch Auntie Cora had gone off in the pony and trap. Sylvie would have loved a ride in it but she was afraid to ask, Auntie Cora looked so remote, so unapproachable.

Fidelma came down to lunch in her tennis clothes. She was so beautiful that Sylvie hadn't the courage to speak to her at all. Her cousin seemed in a very bad temper. Uncle

Roddy introduced her and Eamonn, both of whom ignored her. *Their* manners, she decided, weren't so terrific, but they were in the bosom of their family and acceptance did not depend on their behaviour. She was probably so low-down on their scale of importance that they felt they had no need to exert themselves for her sake.

After lunch, Decla, at her mother's bidding, took her to her room. They watched at the window as Cora was carried off in the trap. Roddy drove the Daimler down the drive and a boy called Lorcan Metcalf called for Fidelma in his MG roadster and she jumped into it without the door being opened, all tanned legs and flying hair. Sylvie thought she'd never seen anything so sophisticated in her life. But Decla muttered 'Bitch!' and that made Sylvie's eyes widen in surprise. Then Eamonn ran down the drive and into the woods with another little boy who Decla told her was Martin Metcalf, Lorcan's little brother, and who was, according to Decla, dubbed "the horror".

Decla then asked Sylvie, 'Do you mind if I scram?' and Sylvie shook her head. In a way she was glad to be left alone. It would give her time to explore her new surroundings, relax and learn her way around. She was naturally nervous and shy and life had done nothing to reassure her.

When she tiptoed into the corridor after Decla had gone her heart was beating fast and her breathing was ragged. There was no one there. She knocked at the door of the room next to hers but there was no answer so she opened it.

It had to be Fidelma's room. It was perfect. The room the Floods had given Sylvie she had thought of as perfect, but it was nothing compared to this.

The spotless cream blinds were drawn halfway down the wide bay windows against the sun. White muslin curtains billowed in the breeze and the heavier blue velvet ones were looped back with gold ropes. The bed was a four-poster with an immaculate and totally uncreased blue and gold cover. There was not a stray sock or stocking anywhere, not a hair on the dressing-table and for some reason Sylvie wanted to cry. It was perfection and she was only too aware that she was very far from perfect. The room seemed to emphasise her human frailty. She tiptoed out of it and closed the door quietly behind her as if in the presence of death.

She jumped as a voice called out 'Hello? Hello?' It came from a room opposite and Sylvie knew at once that it must be Cecie. She turned to the door and knocked.

'Cecie?'

'Yes?' The voice was faint but clear. 'Don't come in. I'm contagious.'

'Oh . . . fiddle!' Sylvie pushed open the door and stood peering in. The girl in the bed stared at her, small pale face drawn and white. She wore a white lawn nightdress and she looked very hot.

'Let me open the window a crack,' Sylvie said.

'Oh no!' the girl protested. 'I might catch a chill. It's not allowed.'

Sylvie was used to illness, to using her common sense, and she went to the glass wall that shut Cecie in.

'Nonsense! There must be a window I can open. Here . . . yes!'

The catch was easily turned, the pane slid back and a whiff of sweet scented air blew like a benediction into the room.

'Oh no!' Cecie cried but the conviction had gone and she pulled herself up in bed, sniffing at the fresh air like an alert little animal.

'I'm your cousin Sylvie,' Sylvie told her, sitting on the end of the bed while Cecie sniffed avidly.

'It won't do you any harm, honestly. How could *air* harm you? It's what we breathe, God's sakes. Honestly, Cecie, all that went out with the nineteenth century. Keeping you shut up, no air, it's so old-fashioned. Like Henry the Eighth or something.'

'It smells so good,' Cecie said wistfully.

Sylvie saw now that her face was pale and bony, the yellowish skin stretched across it and her eyes ringed with dark circles like a silent movie star or a racoon.

'Let me make you comfortable,' Sylvie offered and fetched a cloth from the basin in the room and moistened it from the cold tap which she first left running. She bathed Cecie's hot face and neck. She turned the pillows. She changed the top sheet, getting a fresh one from a cupboard next to the bed.

'I'll bring in some flowers later,' she told Cecie. 'There are masses of flowers here. I've never seen so many.'

'Mother says flowers eat the oxygen and are bad for the sick.'

'Well, that's as may be but they'll cheer you up. They'll give you pleasure,' Sylvie said decisively

'Mother said I'd get an allergy. It might affect my chest.'

Sylvie sat on the bed, the fresh linen smelling of lavender and starch. 'Listen, Cecie, all I've heard since I came here is that . . .' She hesitated.

'Is that I'm not long for this world,' Cecie finished for her.

'Well that's nonsense. I've seen people dying of TB and you are not one of them. Oh, I'm not saying you are not ill. But if you actually are not long for this world, why not enjoy the time you have left?'

The young girl's precocious acceptance of death made Sylvie uncomfortable.

'Why can't you do what you want, if it is true and you are . . . are . . .'

'Dying?' Cecie smiled. She looked much happier now, pillows plumped up behind her, face bathed, cool. 'Yes, why not?' she asked. 'I never thought of that before. Why can't I see the sun, breathe the air? Why not?'

'They could put you in a room with a balcony, couldn't they?' Sylvie asked.

'Well . . .'

'Like Fidelma's. You could sit there, all wrapped up. Shout to them down below.'

'Oh no! Fidelma wouldn't hear of it. She's the eldest. Her room, Decla says, is *perfect*.'

'So much the better. Muss it up!'

'Oh no, no, no!' Cecie's horror gave way to mirth and she began to giggle.

Sylvie continued, 'That room is dead but you are alive. It looks as if no one lives there. Like a picture arranged for a magazine.'

'Oh gosh, I . . .'

'Listen, Cecie, why can't you go outside? Someone could carry you downstairs. If you can't have Fidelma's balcony, why can't you go to the garden?' Cecie's head was swirling with all the novel ideas planted there by her cousin.

Sylvie said, 'Listen, Cecie, I'm going to come and see you

185

lots. No one here likes me or wants me.' Cecie opened her mouth to protest but Sylvie waved her silent. 'Oh, I'm used to it. I've never really been wanted anywhere.' She said it quite matter-of-factly.

'Oh Sylvie, I'm sure that's not true . . .'

Sylvie's wide brown-pansy eyes rested on Cecie's frail little face. 'Your skin is like an eggshell,' she said, then, shaking her head, added, 'It is true, Cecie. Mum and Dad racketed around when I was a kid and I was sent to five foster homes to get me out of London. They said it was because of the war, but it went on after the war was over. My parents really don't want me.'

Cecie stared at her aghast. Not to be wanted was worse than being sick. Worse than anything. And Sylvie was so unemotional about it, so calm. 'Three of the places I went were in London. So that'll show you. There was my mother saying, you have to go, darling, you have to get out of London, and there I am in Pimlico. I ask you.' She shook her head briskly. 'I'm always superfluous.' She stared out of the windows. 'It's so beautiful here, Cecie, but I'm still not wanted. I know that. Your mum doesn't want me. Fidelma doesn't even know I'm alive. Neither does Eamonn. Not that I'd expect them to. And Decla was terrified I'd need her to stay in with me.' She met Cecie's sympathetic gaze. 'I don't mind, Cecie. Really I don't. I'm used to it.' She got a chair and put it at the foot of the bed where Cecie could see her easily and sat on it. 'So let's be friends, Cecie. You and me? I've no one else.'

'You've got me,' Cecie said in delight.

'Yes, Cecie, I've got you,' Sylvie said and smiled.

They spent a quiet afternoon, Cecie chatting to her cousin about the family, Sylvie telling her about her life in London. The room was full of pleasant scented air, air sweetened by the sea and the trees and the flowers it had brushed against on the way to the house. Sylvie discovered that Cecie really didn't know much about her own family. Nobody talked, it seemed. Or they chatted and swapped pleasantries but they did not exchange confidences. Her Auntie Cora was perfect. So was Fidelma. So was Ossian, Cecie was sure about that. Decla was the only slightly imperfect soul, it seemed, and it was obvious that Uncle Roddy and Decla were the ones

Cecie was fondest of and talked to most. Not that anyone really bothered about her, or so it seemed to Sylvie, and this formed a bond between the cousins.

'No one bothered with me either,' she said. 'It's funny how you can be there and yet no one really sees you. But we mustn't be depressing,' she added, smiling suddenly. She leaned forward and patted Cecie's little hand which lay like a bird on the counterpane. Cecie instinctively recoiled at the touch, but her cousin held the hand firmly in her own.

'I'm not used . . . people don't touch me,' Cecie said.

'Well, phooey! I'll wash,' Sylvie said, smiling. 'With carbolic,' she added, giggling, pleased that once more she had succeeded in bringing a smile to her cousin's face.

'Will you be here for a while?' Cecie asked her hopefully. She'd fallen in love with her cousin. She was enamoured of her friendliness, her unconcern about contagion, the excitement of having a friend actually in the room with her. She loved the change in the room, being able to take long draughts of sweet air.

'We'll have lots of secrets, Cecie,' Sylvie said, nodding. 'And we'll get things changed. I really think you could go outside.'

Cecie gasped, nearly said 'Mother won't like that', but bit it back in time.

'I'll stay here as long as you want me,' Sylvie went on. 'See, Mum doesn't want me back at all really and who knows where my father is? In Soho maybe, or on the Left Bank in Paris. Those are his haunts. But he'd not be somewhere I could join him, and if I did he'd ditch me anyhow. He's more interested in jazz than in me. Mother hopes she'll be shot of me. She's got a new fella and when that happens she takes off.'

'But . . . but . . . what do you mean?'

'It means she runs away from me. Leaves me like a package wherever we've been living and disappears. Then they get a foster home for me. The authorities.'

'Oh golly, Sylvie, that's awful!'

'Not any more. I'm a big girl now and I'm trying to make a life for myself.' Sylvie looked wistfully out of the window. 'I got Mother to write to Rossbeg. It was my idea. I want to talk Uncle Roddy into giving me a job. That's my aim, but don't tell anyone. I did shorthand and typing in London and I'd make a very good secretary.'

'I'm sure he will help you. Dadda is a pet. But it must have been awful for you, growing up an' your mam dumping you.'

Sylvie stared out of the window at the majestic view. At the eternal mountains and the peaceful blue sky. The rain had stopped and the whole world was washed fresh and clean.

It looked wonderful to Sylvie and she promised herself a new life here. She did not like to look back. It was too painful. 'Yes, it was awful,' she said to Cecie, her voice light. 'When I was a little girl, well, I was scared all the time.'

Fusty opened the door. She had a tray of tea with scones and three cups and saucers on it.

'I heard ye talkin', an' right glad I am that ye got a friend, Miss Cecie.' She looked at Sylvie. 'Yer very welcome here,' she said. 'I've always said if she was that contagious then why amant I sick with the consumption too?' She bustled about the room. 'I've brought ye some tay an' we'll sit here, quiet like, an' keep ye company, missy, until ye get sleepy, which would be, I reckon, in about an hour. Five o'clock. An' not a word about this to yer Auntie Cora, y'hear?'

Cecie's eyes lit up. 'You don't mind, Fusty? You don't mind me being here? The windows open?'

'Ye know, miss, I've often said, I've *said* an' *said* to the missus that shuttin' ye up in a room, sealed in, is no good for man or beast, sick or well.' She shrugged. 'But no one would listen. Sure who am I? Only a servant is all, an' why should anyone pay any attention to me? I ask ye!'

'You're right, Fusty,' Sylvie said. Fusty smiled at her.

'Yer welcome, *alanna*, an' if ye can get Miss Cecie outta here into God's own world, then the blessings of the saints be on ye.'

Sylvie nodded. Cecie smiled. She'd never felt so happy. Not since she became ill. She prayed silently, fervently, that this wonderful cousin would stay at Rossbeg, and stay, and stay.

Chapter Thirty-seven

❧ ❧

Cora sat in the chair she called 'her' chair, across the mahogany desk from the Monsignor. Outside the open French windows the rain had stopped and every leaf nursed iridescent, trembling drops. They fell occasionally with a tiny plop when their weight proved too much for the delicate petal they shimmered on. The sun, out after the downpour, steamed the vegetation, and trees, grass and flowers were all refreshed and Technicolor bright. The fountain in the cloister splashed gently and the music of the water, the birdsong and the ticking of the clock in the Monsignor's room were the only sounds. Paulie was out in the cloister, weeding. He was bending down, his body curled over, working peacefully, slowly and with concentration. Under the stone arches around the walkway the shade brooded dark and mysterious, for the rich gold sunlight never reached there. A monk paced in the shadows, telling his beads. They were under his cassock and his hands were folded over them but she could see the wooden rosary and its large crucifix swinging as he walked.

Cora contemplated the scene and the Monsignor remained silent, giving her time to collect her thoughts. She had told herself that when she saw the Monsignor all would be well. She had depended upon that. Now that she was actually here in his presence, his calm eyes upon her, waiting for her to speak, she felt confused and terrified, emotions foreign to her, and a terrible tight tension clenched her stomach.

At last he spoke. 'What is it, Cora? Don't be afraid. That's not like you.'

'I'm . . . it's difficult, Monsignor.'

'That's your pride, my dear. We hate to admit wrong-doing, it sticks in our throat. But the love of Christ transcends

189

all sin. He does not condemn. He is forgiving.' He wondered idly what Cora Flood could have to tell him that was causing her such acute embarrassment. She was an open book to him by now and this behaviour was not at all normal. One of the things he most liked about her was her directness. She had never been coy. But now she sat twisting her fingers, blushing a little, looking across at him under her lashes. He suddenly felt the first stirrings of apprehension.

'But I haven't sinned,' she said, then bit her lip. 'Well, that is I *have*, but, oh, I don't know!'

'Why don't you explain, Cora? Take your time,' he told her gently. He sighed. It was going to be one of those, the kind he dreaded most – having to coax the penitent, prize the confession out of them. It was always an ordeal. But the Monsignor was a patient man, a kindly man and he took a deep breath to relax himself, help him to settle back and wait. Listening to the catalogues of sins in the confessional bored him to distraction. He was appalled by the pettiness of human nature, the smallness, the grubbiness of sin. People did not usually bring great sins of passion to the box; he could have dealt with that. No, his penitents did not commit great crimes that often. Mostly their sins were puny and nasty. Backbiting, tittle-tattle that damaged, little cruelties that hurt, petty crimes; the catalogue depressed him, wore him out. He felt he could grapple with Don Juan, Othello, Medea or Clytemnestra. Even Faust. His intellect would enjoy the cut and thrust of persuasive logic pitted against unreasoning emotion, but the skinny little everyday sins, the fleshless grey misdemeanours, so mean-spirited, so venal, stretched his tolerance and made him tired.

Now he watched Cora with eyes that carefully concealed his impatience.

He enjoyed his Friday afternoon sessions with Cora and his involvement with the family. She had a bright, sharp mind and his inclusion in all their celebrations flattered him. He never tired of hearing her talk of the children's development and progress. He enjoyed her intelligence, their discussions on theology and spiritual matters. He could affirm his beliefs to her and sharing his faith confirmed it to himself. He was amused by her assumptions about Roddy and her oblique complaints about her husband, who

190

seemed to the Monsignor a good and kindly man. He too had heard about Roddy's alliance – or misalliance – with Rosie Daly. Cora's dismissive attitude vis-à-vis Roddy he often rebuked. She obviously thought no other woman could possibly be interested in her husband, a staggeringly arrogant assumption that nevertheless the Monsignor understood. He worried what would happen when she found out about the other woman. Her pride was in for a terrible fall.

The Monsignor had jumped to the conclusion that this flurry of unusual activity, her rushing about trying to see him yesterday without an appointment, her coming to see him today, had to do either with Ossian's visit to Rome or else she'd found out about Roddy's liaison with Rosie Daly. Either way the Monsignor was prepared. He was very good at dealing with such situations and had his answers ready. So he was relaxed and calm on her arrival, but what she said now, after that long pause, shocked him out of his complacency into an animal alertness.

'You see ... I love you, Monsignor.' She was plucking at her skirt, not looking at him. 'I love you with all my soul, all my being,' she was saying. 'Oh, it is a pure and holy love ...' She stammered to a halt, remembering her vision, her dream of him in her bedroom, in the boreen. She looked at him now, eyes feverish and ardent. 'Oh, how I love you,' she breathed.

He froze, his back to the cloister, not moving a muscle, immobile with shock. Her eyes were wide and joyous now that he had said nothing. She was looking at him with relief. It was out. She was giving him this precious gift. She went on, 'You must understand, Monsignor, this is not easy for me. I've thought of nothing else since I realised the truth about us. I've been blind, I've been deaf to my heart.' She paused, looking out at Paulie bending over the rosebush.

Does she know what she is saying? Does she realise? Is the woman mad? he wondered.

'All these years *you've* been my husband. You have, dear Monsignor, you know you have. You've guarded me and the children. Roddy's done nothing.' She flicked her fingers as if brushing away a fly. 'He's been useless. You've stood by me, given me what other women get from their husbands; the strength, the support ...'

His eyes, fierce as an eagle's, were fixed on the book on his desk. *The Confessions of Saint Augustine.* Help me, O Lord. Help me not to murder her.

He wanted to shout at her to shut up. This was blasphemy and he did not want to hear it. It was distasteful to him. The stupid woman was tearing up a friendship, a relationship with the family. She was demolishing in a few minutes a sunny and bright spiritual pleasure that innocently lit up his life and that he had come to rely on.

'I don't expect this to come as such a surprise to you. You've always given me to understand that you cared for me, that we were soulmates, and that is most important, surely?'

She *was* mad. How could he have misjudged her so? She'd seemed to him so sane, so detached. He remembered thinking that she was sleeping through life. Well, now she had awakened with a vengeance.

'. . . Protestant clergy get married. I remember you saying once that the only difference between Protestants and Catholics was that they didn't believe in the Virgin Mary and transubstantiation, and we do. It's a small technicality.'

The Devil quoting scripture. Was she suggesting that he become a Protestant? Name of God, she was insane. Quite unhinged. The Monsignor winced. She sat there drivelling rubbish, her slim legs crossed, and calmly talked to him, or, he amended, *at* him, as if he were a prospective mate, as if her proposals could actually become a reality.

'. . . All I want is to be with you. Every day and night for the rest of my life.' She said it simply. 'I don't mind in what capacity. I'll become a nun if you want as long as I can worship at your feet.'

The Reverend Mother might have something to say about that, he thought bitterly, feeling his disgust rise.

'I want to serve you, be near you all the time. Worship you, adore you.'

He wanted to cry, shut up, shut up, you bitch, but he pressed his lips closed and did not allow his anger to come roiling out, demean him, bring the conversation down to her level. The last appropriate thing would be argument. He kept his mouth shut tight until he could be sure of control. She continued, 'I said prayers of gratitude when I realised, Monsignor, when I knew. Dear God, I said, dear God, thank you for this moment of perfect happiness, this hour of ecstasy, knowing what is right for me. Feeling his arms around me, letting me know in a dream that he is the one for me. My love. My passion. My life.'

The Monsignor closed his eyes. He was very calm now, had control.

'. . . you are the great love of my life, Monsignor, and I never noticed. I came to you with all my burdens, I laid them at your feet, loving you, trusting you, and I never thought of you as a man. Until the other day when it all became clear. So clear.' Cora's cheeks were glowing and her eyes were bright as stars. She stood up and he could feel her desire for him palpably across the room. It was like a suffocating erotic blanket that he desperately wanted to escape from. He could see a difference in her, a nervous energy he assumed was passion, a lascivious curve to her mouth, a wanton look in her eyes. He was totally alert, danger signals screaming, and as she approached him – to do what? he dared not guess – he too stood, but calmly.

Her face lit up. She thought he was going to come to her, but he retreated gracefully, swiftly into the cloister and turned his back on her. He was facing Paulie and he spoke to him, much to the gardener's surprise. 'How lovely the roses are, Paulie. You tend them well.' Then he saluted the praying monk, who suppressed a frown of irritation at the interruption, bowed his head in acknowledgement and continued his traverse around the cloister.

She had followed him, a little confused by his sudden move outdoors, into the sun, and stood shading her eyes with her hand. He turned to her, indicated a bench opposite Paulie and sat on it. It was still wet from the rain and the damp rose in clouds of steam. He was well aware of this but did not care how uncomfortable she might be. He wanted to be within hearing distance of Brother Anselm and Paulie, in sight of someone at all times. He wanted an end to this now and forever.

'Cora, my dear, you are obviously unwell,' he said in a cold, calm voice. She had never heard this freezing tone before; it was like an arctic wind. 'These things you are saying, these things I cannot hear. I will not hear. I decline to listen.'

'But why? You've been—'

He swiftly interrupted her. 'No, I've been *nothing*. Your spiritual adviser is all. What you are raving about—'

'I'm not raving . . .' And there, in front of Paulie and Brother Anselm, she put her hands on his chest and leaned forward as if to kiss him.

What halted her was not his roughly snatching her hands away, not his words, which were icy, not his standing tall and fierce like an avenging angel. No. It was the expression of loathing and contempt in his eyes that stopped Cora, shocked her out of her trance. She had never been looked at like that before, never in her whole life. She shrank inwardly, dwindling under his look of revulsion, felt his disgust and transferred it to herself. He made her, in one second, loathe herself.

'I do not want to hear another word nor see you again, Cora. I am a priest and will not mess about with a situation like this, which, I have to tell you, I find intolerable, not to say disgusting.' His voice was tranquil and unemotional, which made what he said to her worse.

'Aha . . . ah . . . no, no,' The words gurgled in her throat, strangling her.

'I do not want to see you alone again. Ever,' he told her as if she were a child or a half-wit.

'But it's all so simple. I love you!' she cried.

'It is not in the least simple. I fear you have lost your reason. You are sick. As I've said, Cora . . . Mrs Flood, I do not wish to see you again. I hope I make myself crystal-clear? Good day to you, madam.'

And he left her sitting there in the cloister, walked away, his cassock flapping around his ankles, his tall frame distancing himself from her forever.

She remained sitting, watching him vanish around the stone pillar, out of her life. Her dress was damp and uncomfortable beneath her but she did not feel it. She felt nothing. Dazed, she sat there a long time, lonely and alone. Paulie continued dead-heading the roses and Brother Anselm continued his slow pacing under the arches of the cloister. A bird sang and another joined in, then another, but she did not hear their joyous chorus. Raindrops still rolled slowly down the leaves and plopped on to the old grey flagstones, swelling the puddles cupped in their hollows. One fell on her cheek. It was warm from the sun and she licked it absently, then sighed and stood.

Something had gone. Gone forever. She didn't know what it was but she felt the absence. Like when a tooth is extracted or a limb amputated and you keep thinking that it is still there. Something was missing. She frowned, wondering what it was, then went out towards the stables where Vinny waited with Salty and the trap, aware with a sick heart that nothing would ever again be the same.

Chapter Thirty-eight

❧ ❧

Decla stood beside the black lake watching the swans, throwing bread to them. She peered down into the opaque depths and all she could see were the squirming, coiling weeds. People said there were sea-snakes down there as big as tree trunks but she didn't believe it. Sea-snakes lived in the sea and this lake was stagnant. Nothing came or went. But there *was* life down there – eyeless creatures moved, blind embryos stirred, slimy things twined themselves about each other. She shivered. She wished she was meeting Shannon somewhere else. Somewhere glamorous and sophisticated, a hotel or the Italian ice-cream parlour in O'Connell Street.

Looking up at the ugly old clubhouse from where she was she could see the people, distance-small on the terrace. Not many people today. It was only crowded on the weekend. Monday it was mainly girls. Married women out for an afternoon game of tennis; calm contented women whose lives were all mapped out for them, predictable and secure. She pitied them. What did they know of passion? Like Fidelma they had picked the most suitable mate, their future prosperity, a ticket to bourgeois respectability and comfort. Passion was uncomfortable and painful and these women did not tolerate suffering, whereas she relished hers. Feeling her heart pump at the mere thought of Shannon, the blood in her veins throb and swell hotly, she felt sorry for those who had never felt or chose to ignore this clamorous call. She could imagine Fidelma doing that; squashing the hot flood of passion, killing it dead. Well, more fool her.

She could see her sister now with a bunch of friends, laughing on the terrace in the sun. Harry wasn't there, Decla realised, and then reflected that he'd not been around since Saturday night. That was odd. Harry and Fidelma were rarely apart.

She could hear her sister's voice chattering with her entourage. Justin O'Brien was there and Lorcan Metcalf and some others. There were a few girls. Kelly Brocklehurst, Daisy O'Meara and Sheena Beardsley. They were discussing whether the courts were still too wet to play on. They all wore white shorts or pleated tennis skirts and polo sports shirts, white ankle socks on their tanned legs and tennis shoes. They looked sweetly sexy and neat. Perfectly groomed, cossetted by money.

Decla shook her head. She could foretell with accuracy what the future of any one of those girls was. They'd be here in twenty years, sitting up there, outside the clubhouse, discussing the courts, just as they were now. Their daughters would be here too in a group, chatting, flirting with their sons, and their husbands would all be prosperous locals. They'd not have had adventures, not taken risks, not felt even the merest flutter of the passion she now felt boiling in her blood. Or if they did they'd either kill it at birth or their Mammas would do it for them. Ruthlessly. For passion did not come with suitable matches. All any of them wanted was a well-to-do husband, a nice house, money enough to live comfortably with the amenities they were used to, four children and a couple of holidays a year in the Balearic Islands, or Italy (Capri was popular), a couple of weekends in London to see the shows, a small boat anchored in Lough Derg, and they'd have achieved their goal.

Oh, sometimes their souls would yearn . . . ache for something wonderful and dangerous, just out of their reach, but at the mere approach of anything remotely unexpected in their lives they'd run for cover, pull up the drawbridge and duck.

Decla was determined not to be like them, not to go down that tried and true road. That road meant an atrophied spirit, that road was dull, dull, dull.

Now, as she looked up at her sister, a shadow darkened the little light there was here in this place and Shannon was before her. She caught her breath.

'Shannon! You're here.'

'Yes. I told you I would be. Did you forget?' He was always so literal.

'Oh no. No. I'm glad, so glad to see you.'

'Me too.' Silly, he thought, silly, stupid bitch. Having to talk soppy. It did not come easy to him. He'd once seen a movie, Cary Grant or James Stewart pretending to be in love with a 'dame', as they called her, to save his life, something like that, and he did it great. Very convincing. Shannon couldn't work up the enthusiasm. He wished only to be a man of action, doing something with guns or bombs. Something manly. This shit with Decla Flood was driving him crazy. Still, he knew better than not to do as they asked. They could wipe him out, no trouble. A blot erased. You had to obey the commanders. They were gods. Once you were in you could not escape, not ever. Not that he wanted to. Angus O'Laughlin was quick-tempered but might have mercy. Seamus O'Sullivan would not. He'd make an example. He loved making examples. It was a new thing in the IRB. Since they'd been banned they'd developed a style that was becoming known, and making an example was their trademark. Shannon did not want that to happen to him.

Still, Decla was so ahead of him she made it easy. She was overwhelmingly grateful for any little bit of affection or admiration and took his smallest gestures, his most meagre and grudging compliments as tokens of a burning attraction he did not feel.

'You phoned and wanted to see me, so I knew you cared,' she told him haltingly.

'I do,' he said and nodded.

The black lake was not moving. Or barely. Swollen from this morning's heavy rain it hardly stirred. Yet it seemed to exude something dark and sinister. The black swan fixed Decla with a yellow eye, staring at the girl as if she threatened. The tangled branches of the ancient trees met overhead and creaked and sighed like old women in pain. The laughing voices of the players on the courts, the plop-plop of the tennis balls, came to them as if from very far away, and the sunlit social scene seemed like another planet. No birds sang here.

They stood awkwardly side by side, he bored, trying to do his duty, she in breathless expectation. Shannon threw a stone into the lake. It did not make a ripple but disappeared as if in oil. He turned to her, taking a deep breath, ascertained where her lips were, then planted a swift kiss on her closed mouth.

He loved her. She knew. She felt such a flood of joy she nearly coughed. He'd kissed her. It was true. He wouldn't have done that if he didn't love her.

'I gotta go,' he muttered, wanting to rub his lips with the back of his hand but restraining himself.

'But, but you just got here,' she said, disappointed.

'I know. Still, I gotta.'

'So soon!' she sighed, not looking at him, looking into the baleful eye of the black swan. 'Where?'

'I've things to do.'

'What things?'

'Business.'

'Like what? I want to know. Why can't you tell me?'

'Don't you trust me, Decla?' he asked, his tone cold.

Tears sprang to her eyes at the unkindness in his voice, but she nodded vehemently. 'Oh yes,' she protested.

'Then don't ask.'

'Your uncle was wondering what you did. He said.' She was muttering defiantly, hurt by his refusal to share everything with her.

He took a hold of her arms, over the elbow, in a fierce grip. And she, misunderstanding, held up her face, eyes closed for another kiss. He had been going to shake her, order her not to discuss him with anyone, but, looking down at her, he sighed and gave in to the inevitable. He had orders to keep her sweet. He was good at obeying orders.

He kissed her again, slower this time; the target was easier. She went limp in his hands and he took his face away. It had given him time to get a hold on himself.

What was this shit about his uncle? He'd have to be careful. Jeez, if his Uncle Brendan suspected, he'd crucify Shannon, land him in dead trouble for sure. Bring in the polis.

'What's Uncle Brendan say?' he asked her casually.

'Whaa . . .' She was bemused, still savouring his kiss. The taste of him, so hard, so soft, so sweet.

'Ah! I love you, Shannon.'

'An' I love you.' He said it glibly, but he'd said it.

She understood by now that he was shy. Diffident. 'Oh gosh, Shannon, we're doing a line. You love me. Oh gosh!'

Jeez, she was a cow. Doing a line! Like office workers from Cleary's or the bleedin' bank.

'What'd he say?'

'Who?'

How to stay patient? God give him strength!

'Uncle Brendan.'

'Oh . . . nothing much. He said, what does Shannon *do*? I haven't a clue, do you? I told him, no. I didn't know either.'

'That was it?'

'Sure.' She took his hand, kissed his fingers one by one. He did not feel her kisses; his thoughts were elsewhere.

'What *do* you do, Shannon? I'd love to know. Why keep it a secret? No matter what, I won't mind.' She glanced at him shyly. 'I mean, if it's the sort of thing my parents wouldn't approve of, it wouldn't matter to me.' She gazed at him fervently.

'No. Nothing like that. Oh, tell my uncle to mind his own business!' His tone was irritated.

'Maybe you're doing secret work, like in the war. Spying. For the government.'

She was fantasising but he jumped angrily. 'God. You could only like me if I was doin' somethin' glamorous an' excitin', that it?'

'No, no, Shannon. No. I'd love you no matter what. We won't talk about it again. I promise.'

'I gotta go,' he said and turned away.

'When will I see you?' she asked. Her eyes were starry, even he could see that.

He said, 'I'll telephone you. You'll be at home?'

She nodded.

'Then I'll call you tonight,' he said and walked away, up the incline towards the tennis club, and she watched him, her heart flooding with love for him, watched him till she could no longer see him in the glare from the sun.

Chapter Thirty-nine

Cora's face was calm but inside she seethed with rage. Her anger turned against Roddy. Refusing even to think about the Monsignor she vented her feelings of overwhelming rage against her husband. The scene in the Monsignor's library was a bad dream. It never happened. She drew a veil, quite firmly blotting it out, and nursed all the while her resentment towards Roddy.

When the trap reached Rossbeg Cora went straight to her room. She checked her appearance carefully. She was amazed at how well she looked. She *felt* as if she'd been buffeted by a storm, emotionally pulverised, but she looked serene, beautifully groomed, exquisite. Her silk dress was slightly damp at the seat but it was not noticeable and she looked elegant, her hair and face model-perfect.

She knew where she was going. Not what she would do when she got there, but exactly where she was headed.

She telephoned for a taxi. It would take half an hour, Charlie Sweeney said. He said he was on a tea-break and he'd come for her at five o'clock. Cora knew there was no shifting him so she sat down to wait.

She sat quite still. She could feel nothing, but knew that rage was simmering deep within her, like a volcano waiting to erupt. She knew that in some curious way she was husbanding her emotional turmoil and that it would be lanced, like a boil, quite soon.

She heard laughter coming from down the landing and wondered who it was, in a disinterested sort of way. It sounded like Cecie, but that couldn't be right. Another laugh sounded like Fusty, but she did not really care. Another time, terrier-like, she would have followed it to its source, found out, but not this afternoon. This particular

Monday afternoon Cora Flood was dead, yet obsessed.

When the taxi came she ran downstairs and was out of the front door and into the taxi before Charlie had time to open the car door for her. Charlie used his Ford as a taxi when a Dalkeyite wanted to go to Dublin and not take the tram. He made, as he put it, a nice few bob outta it without putting himself out. He thought Cora would ask for a hospital, so great was her hurry, and so unusual her behaviour; she was such a stickler for form, was Mrs Flood, and here she was leppin' about like a teenager . . . someone must be sick.

But it was not a hospital she was going to, or a hotel, or anything like that. The address she gave him was familiar – hadn't Mr Flood used him a few times and tipped him handsomely too to take him to and from this house in Molesworth Street? Charlie Sweeney gulped, astonishment, salacious curiosity and an unhealthy excitement fighting for ascendency in his breast.

He realised that Cora Flood was going to the house of her husband's mistress. The address she'd asked for was where Rosie Daly lived. He clicked his teeth, put in the clutch and headed for Dublin, glancing every now and then in the rear-view mirror to catch a glimpse of Mrs Flood's face. She was, he saw, impassive as usual and sat looking out of the window as they drove.

When at last they reached Molesworth Street she got out, asked him to wait and went to the same door Mr Flood was wont to slip expertly through with, Charlie guessed, his own key.

The house was let in apartments and the front door was ajar now. Cora pushed it open and vanished inside.

There were three doors facing her, a bell beside each one. The one ahead had DALY printed on a small brass plate.

Cora pressed the bell. She glanced around the landing with dispassionate appraisal. There was a half-table against the wall, imitation Chippendale, she guessed, and on it stood a ghastly green bowl of artificial flowers. If there was anything Cora despised, it was artificial flowers.

She sniffed and the door to the apartment opened and Rosie Daly stood there. Before Rosie could say anything or

202

recover from the surprise of her visitor Cora had walked past her into the apartment.

The door led directly into the living-room. It was a cosy place but to Cora's eyes appallingly untidy and decorated in atrocious taste. There were flowers, real ones this time, everywhere, some of them full-blown, some shedding petals – all, Cora thought, needing attention. The sofa, a big cumbersome piece covered in faded chintz, was sagging in the middle and faced a huge empty fireplace. Empty of a fire, that was, but used for magazines and papers which were in a big pile on the hearth and strewn over the floor in a hideously untidy manner.

Cora's eyes ran over the framed copies of Renoir, Watteau, Fragonard and Constable on the walls. Sickly sentimental chocolate-box paintings all of them, revealing, Cora thought complacently, a trivial mind.

The room was cluttered. An open door revealed the bedroom, with an enormous bed covered in a pink satin eiderdown, and an angelic framed Raphael Virgin hanging over it, dead centre. Cora hooted under her breath. Did they have no shame? Were they not embarrassed to cavort on that bed, the Virgin Mary Mother of God looking down on them? Cora's conviction that Rosie Daly was a vulgar slut was confirmed.

As Rosie closed the door she turned and faced her.

The two women knew each other casually. They had met briefly in public places, at the races and the theatre, sometimes in the houses of mutual acquaintances. They knew each other not very well and now they saw each other close to.

What Rosie saw, near to her now, was Cora's divine beauty. She gasped at the perfection. Cora looked so calm and pale and elegant in her silk dress and white gloves, a perfect face, and if it was cold and white-lipped, what mattered with such beauty? Rosie felt in that moment suddenly inferior, second-class, and she thought that if that was how Cora made Roddy feel, then it was no wonder he came to her for a boost to his ego, a bit of a laugh and a cosy feeling of relaxation.

What Cora saw was the round sensuous face and body of Roddy's mistress. A red mist swam between her and the softly pretty woman, a violent commingling of her fury at rejection, her terrible anger and frustration, and as Rosie stood admiring the goddess before her, Cora hit her full force across the face with a clenched gloved hand.

Rosie was too surprised to defend herself, and swiftly after the first stunning blow came another with Cora's other fist. Like a boxer in the ring Cora smashed into Rosie, one, two, one two, on either side of her face. She then hit Rosie's face full front, in cold fury, and again, hard as she could, brutally, savagely. Rosie still did not try to protect herself. The first blow had taken her by surprise, the second had stunned her. The attack was fierce, vicious and intense, the jabs were hard as rocks, granite-fisted. Rosie stood and took the onslaught. She was not a woman who could or would fight. By the third blow, accurately aimed, sledge-hammer hard, the pain hit her. As her nose cracked it became excruciating and the blood spurted. It overwhelmed her and deprived her of any normal reaction. She did not even try to shield her face and head with her arms but stood there swaying as blow after vicious blow pulverised her face and head.

Eventually she sank slowly to her knees, her face a bloody mass, her eyes closed and swollen, her lips cut and bruised, her cheekbones sliced by the rings under Cora's gloves, her nose purple and red, and still the beating went on, methodically, slowly, hammer blow after hammer blow, an unexcited, calm attack. It did not stop until Rosie Daly fell further, from her knees on to her face, and a pool of blood stained the pink carpet, outwards, ever outwards, as she lay there, mercifully unconscious.

Cora looked at her calmly. She felt no disgust, no horror, only relief. She peeled off her once white, blood-soaked gloves and dropped them on the inert body of her husband's mistress, then left the apartment, closing the door softly behind her.

Chapter Forty

⤫ ☙ ⤬

The O'Briens were invited to Rossbeg to dinner that Monday night. Cora had thought it a good idea, to take the edge off Sylvie's first evening and relieve the family of the sole responsibility of entertaining her. Cora's fear of outsiders contributed to her love of crowds. She shone like a star when in a group and not too much was demanded of her. One-on-one frightened her to death.

Except for Monsignor Maguire. Ah yes, except for him. But she wouldn't think about that now. That was a mistake and she'd deal with it another day, another time, somewhere in the future when she could bear to. Not yet though. Not yet, not now.

She had asked Brendan and Dolores, knowing only Brendan would come, glad of O'Brien's gregarious personality and convivial ability to keep the conversation spinning happily along.

But Brendan brought Shannon. Cora was momentarily thrown, then she bowed to the inevitable and welcomed him into her drawing-room. She was nothing if not gracious. Decla was overjoyed. Her face lit up and she took Shannon's arm in a possessive gesture that alarmed her mother.

They sat in the drawing-room, having cocktails before dinner. Mary Mac served. The light was going and the moon was out, shimmering brilliantly over the trees, a graceful curve in a deep indigo sky. A solitary owl hooted from the woods, loudly and mournfully.

Brendan talked about Comptometers, the new thing in offices. Everyone, he said, should have a Comptometer. Roddy sighed and said he hated the technology of progress. He said it was all baffling to him. 'Everyone and everything is getting faster and faster. No one can keep up or live a quiet life.'

'Life, Roddy, is not meant to be *quiet*!' Brendan protested. 'Speed is the aim.'

'Well, I can't think why,' Roddy said. 'I like the grace of slowness. I like the patience it engenders, the wisdom resulting from ponderous thought. Building a boat is a work of art, not a race against time. Love should go into it, consideration and time. Fast, in my opinion, is decidedly dodgy. Nothing great was ever achieved fast.'

'Well, but Roddy, you can build *more*. Make more money.'

Roddy nodded sagely. 'Ah, money! I have enough. Why be greedy?'

And Cora sat smiling prettily at them, her hands folded in the lap of her grey chiffon dress.

Charlie Sweeney had made no comment on her blood-stained frock. He had driven her straight back, nervously glancing at her cold, expressionless face every now and then. She had not opened her mouth until they stopped before the entrance to the house, when she'd said calmly, 'Send me the account, Charlie. Good-day and thank you.' And she'd waited this time in the back of the car till he opened the door for her. She got out gracefully, not seeming to care if her dress was blood-stained or not. It made Charlie avert his eyes, not knowing the cause, not *wanting* to know the cause, for the Floods were good customers.

At first he did not think that violence had occurred. Mrs Flood appeared so calm, so unemotional, that the thought did not enter his mind. She was not an excitable woman. She was the perfect wife and mother, so how could there be cause for alarm? Then he got to speculating where all the blood came from. He did say, 'Are you all right, Mrs Flood?' and she'd looked at him over her shoulder halfway to the front door, a surprised expression on her face. 'Of course, Charlie,' she replied, smiling faintly, then looking a bit puzzled. 'Why on earth shouldn't I be?' As if a wife called on her husband's mistress every day of the week and came out again, her dress all blood-stained.

Then a novel concept struck Charlie. Maybe the blood *was* caused by an accident. Maybe, maybe they were friends, herself and Roddy's mistress. He'd heard the Frenchies were like that. Frenchmen had mistresses and their wives knew all about them. Were chums! Charlie smacked his lips at the idea and wished Ireland were not so prudish. Well, the Church really. You'd never call Irishmen prudish, an' wouldn't he relish a Tiller-girl from the Theatre Royal on the side, now wouldn't that be a gorgeous concept? But it would cost, probably, and that sort of thing, Charlie decided, was only done by the upper classes. That kind of behaviour would never filter down to his sort, become permissible for fellas like him. No, the Church would put her foot on it, squash the mere idea of such fun. Only the well-off seemed to be able to have fun. God knew the rich, Charlie ruminated, were peculiar. They had funny ways about them, did outrageous things and were never brought to book over their actions.

He hurried home to his missus, who liked a good gossip, and they spent a very satisfactory evening speculating. But his missus curtailed his more vivid flights of fancy by saying 'For God's sake, Charlie, mebbe poor Mrs Flood got her period unexpected!'

Charlie, disappointed by this logical explanation, said, 'Not *her*! Not Mrs Flood. Something like that'd never happen to her.' And his missus pursed her lips and replied, 'Cora Flood is human too. She goes to the lav like the rest of us. An' gets periods unexpected.' And she stretched her nose in slight derision. 'And at her age, ye never know!'

Cora was her usual self at dinner that evening and she was, to Decla's vast surprise, charming to Shannon. It struck Roddy as odd. Cora did not like Shannon, thought him ill-bred, ill-mannered and uncouth, and normally she would be polite but cool. But tonight she smiled at him, asked him – without much interest in the answer, it was true – how he was enjoying his stay in Ireland. He said he was having a really nice time and glanced across the table at Decla, exchanging a look with her. Cora did not react, which amazed Roddy and Decla alike. Roddy decided to leave well enough alone and prayed this calm of hers would last a long time. Her cheeks were flushed, her eyes bright and her smile permanent. Perhaps time was mellowing his wife's insistence that everyone should strive for perfection. Perhaps she was beginning to accept life on its own terms, though she did appear a trifle absent-minded.

The evening was full of surprises. Just before dinner Fidelma and Lorcan arrived into the drawing-room and announced their engagement. Decla choked on her drink and Roddy was too surprised to speak. But Cora kissed Lorcan and welcomed him most graciously into the family. She was behaving, her husband thought, as if she had done it a thousand times before.

Roddy opened a bottle of champagne to celebrate and the evening took on a festive air. Roddy could not work up the enthusiasm he felt he should feel at the idea of his eldest daughter's forthcoming marriage to Lorcan Metcalf. It was all wrong. A day or two ago she'd been deciding whether to marry Harry Devereau and the talk tonight seemed more like a business merger than a romantic attachment. Not once did Fidelma say anything about her betrothed. She talked instead about the wedding. 'I'd like to have it in the Royal in Bray, Dadda, please,' Fidelma insisted. 'We'll have to ask so many. And I want flowers from Regan's and my dress from Paris. And I want six bridesmaids and little pages – *not* Eamonn, please. He's a pig and he'll do something unspeakable, he always does. Lorcan's father is building us a house overlooking the bay and we've decided, Dadda, we'd like you to give us a new car. You know, a Mercedes.' And on and on and on. She kept the conversation that evening firmly fixed on the forthcoming celebrations, hardly pausing for breath. Brendan O'Brien egged her on. What she said seemed to amuse him and Roddy was surprised that Cora, usually so sharply aware of such sub-texts, remained indifferent.

'Fidelma, forgive me if I'm being impertinent,' Brendan said at last, claiming her attention, 'but I always assumed you and Harry Devereau were doing a line?'

'Of course you're being awful, Mr O'Brien,' Fidelma twinkled roguishly at him and her father could glimpse a feverish glitter in her eyes. 'But you're quite wrong. Harry and me . . . we'd never marry, we're too close. Like brother and sister.'

In a flash Decla realised what had happened between Harry and her sister. Harry had turned Fidelma down with those exact words. She knew that as clearly as if she'd been there and heard him say it with her own ears.

Decla spent the evening clinging close to Shannon, indulging in the luxury of her mother's acquiescence. She hung on Shannon's words as if they were pearls of wisdom.

Then Sylvie shocked them all out of their various preoccupations by asking why Cecie couldn't come downstairs sometimes. 'For meals and outings. To the garden. You have a gorgeous garden, Auntie Cora.'

'We'd all catch poor Cecie's illness, dear, and die,' Cora said simply, forking asparagus into her mouth.

'If you were that susceptible, if she were that contagious you'd all be dead by now,' Sylvie said stubbornly. They looked at her, lost for words. The idea had never entered their heads. She stared back at them, blinking her dark brown eyes rapidly. 'I'm sorry,' she said. 'I hope you don't think me rude.'

'You have to admit she has a point, dear,' Roddy remarked mildly.

'Yes,' Sylvie added boldly. 'And it is terrible for her, up there alone, cut off, day after day all by herself. She could sit way down at the end of the table, at least be part of the family. Or in the rose garden when no one is there. The flowers are beautiful and would give her such pleasure.' Sylvie's words tumbled out in a rush.

'No, no,' Cora said lightly. 'The doctor said—'

'Well *Cecie* says if she's going to die *anyway* she might as well have a good time before she goes,' Sylvie announced, then clapped her hand to her mouth as if frightened of the consequences of what she had said. It was not what Cecie had said exactly but it had the desired effect. There was complete silence in the room. Even Fidelma had nothing to say. Everyone looked uncertainly at each other.

'As Roddy says, the little lady has a point.' Brendan O'Brien broke the spell.

Then to everyone's surprise, everyone who knew her well, that is, Cora said, 'I think that's a nice idea. I've long said that Dr Sutton is a fuddy-duddy. And Sylvie, my dear, you're right. If we were going to get it we'd have it by now. I don't want to put you or anyone else at risk though.'

'I think Sylvie's right too,' Roddy said. 'Sometimes it takes an outsider to show you the way. And it would be lovely having Cecie down here with us.'

'It will be hard work for Fusty and Mary Mac,' Cora added.

'We'll get another girl to help. Someone young and strong,' said Roddy.

'I don't mind helping,' Sylvie volunteered. 'In fact I'd love to. I want to be a nurse, eventually. I've already done some basic training at St Mary's Hospital in Paddington.'

'Cecie said you wanted a job as a secretary?' Decla asked.

'Temporary. It would just be temporary.'

True to form at last, Cora wrinkled her pale brow, saying incredulously, 'A *nurse*! A secretary! How odd. Do you really want to?'

Sylvie nodded, eyes bright.

'But you'd have to do all sorts of terribly intimate things to total strangers,' Cora said with distaste.

'Oh, I don't mind,' Sylvie laughed.

'I'm not sure it is a good idea, Mother.' Fidelma sounded doubtful. 'If she's contagious. You don't want the whole house dying, now do you?'

'*You*, you mean. You're only worried about yourself! God, you're so selfish. All you think of is yourself. What about Cecie?' Decla sounded exasperated. 'I want her down for one.'

'Well, I *don't*,' Fidelma announced firmly.

'Now you see, Lorcan, what you'll be marrying. If you get leprosy or anything catching, she'll have you out in the *garden*, so she will.'

'Don't be silly, Decla. You are so stupid. I'd rather she didn't come down until after I'm married, then you can do what you like.'

Brendan looked in surprise at Fidelma. So the lady had claws, had she? He'd long suspected it but had never really caught her at it. He sat very still, watching.

Roddy was surprised too, for he realised suddenly that Fidelma was not happy. She was *excited* about her engagement but was, for some reason he did not understand, intensely irritated. He could only suppose her bad form was in some way connected with Harry.

'Children, this is inappropriate.' Cora's voice was light and conversational but the bickering stopped instantly. 'Not at the dinner-table. We'll talk about it at breakfast,' she said, but they all knew her mind was made up and Cecie would be down next day.

Shannon, who had ploughed his way through the crown of lamb, the strawberries and cream, masticating steadily, smiling at Decla when he remembered, contributing nothing to the conversation, was not at all interested in the subjects under discussion. Brendan talked about everything under the sun, including the IRB, but Shannon did not want to listen. He firmly shut his mind and this gave him, to Decla, a very spiritual and detached air.

Cora looked at them all with benevolent eyes. She seemed that evening the most perfect of hostesses.

It was when the meal was over, when they were drinking their coffee in the drawing-room, the men smoking, that Fusty came in to say there was an urgent phone call for Mr Flood. And Roddy afterwards would search his memory for some sign, some peculiarity, some tell-tale tension or guilt in his wife's face or manner, but try as he would he could not come up with anything. Cora appeared calm and tranquil that evening. A perfect wife and mother, a beautiful woman, a fond and proud parent, utterly relaxed in the warm circle of her family.

Chapter Forty-one

❧ ❧

'What will become of us, Shannon?' Decla asked. They were
walking hand in hand in the moonlit garden. Everything was
silvered over; the roses, the bushes, the trees and the grass.
They had strolled down from the terrace after coffee. Roddy
had left the house, saying one of his employees, one of his
most brilliant craftsmen, working late to finish an order, had
been badly injured and was in hospital. Brendan shook his
head in disbelief. 'At this time of night? Janey, Roddy, none
of my men'd work so late.'

'Counting betting slips is not the same as planing wood,
whittling living substance, creating a thing of beauty,' Roddy
said with an unusual lack of diplomacy. He tried to shoot
Brendan a warning glance, but his friend was lighting
his cigar.

'Well, but can't the hospital deal with it without you going
there? We're having such a jolly time. You could visit in the
morning.' Brendan, full of good food and wine, did not want
the party to break up, but Roddy had left them abruptly,
going on the instant.

Shannon and Decla had strolled out on to the terrace and
stared at the dancing stars. 'They're like fairies doing a ballet
in the sky,' Decla said and Shannon sighed. There was going
to be more of this, he just knew it.

He took her hand. It seemed like a good idea. They
meandered over the wet lawn and he tried to think of
appropriate things to say, but couldn't, so kept silent. Up
in the house he could hear someone, he presumed Cora,
playing the piano and singing. Her voice was clear and high
and she sang an old Irish ballad.

'My young love said to me, my mother won't mind,
And my father won't chide you for your lack of kind,

212

Then she moved away from me and this she did say,
It will not be long, love, till our weddin' day.'

The song trembled on the stilly air and Decla sighed. 'It's so beautiful, the world, isn't it, Shannon?' she breathed.

'Sure is.' He did not think like that. He did not see beauty. He wished sometimes that he did. To him, at this moment, there was a crescent moon, there were stars up in the sky if you looked, and that made it bright. The grass was wet and there was an evening chill. She obviously saw things differently, colour mebbe. It irritated him. He remembered in school in Liverpool how the others seemed able to write essays about that sort of stuff, yellow daffs and blue skies, and he just couldn't. They laughed at him, made fun of him, and the teachers were acid and contemptuous. Most of what he wrote was meaningless, they said. It was just stuff he thought up. But he could never elaborate, never embroider the stuff. The sky was blue was all he could say, and anything more was of no interest to him. Now he had to spend time with a girl with poetic tendencies because they told him to.

The Cause. It was the only thing ever meant anything to him. Only thing that inspired him. The meetings. Learning to use a gun to fight for Ireland gave him a purpose, the buzz that the stars and all that shit gave *her*.

He tested his patience. Could he hold out a while before he escaped? Talk some more garbage? Do what they wanted, do a good job on this girl? He decided, yes.

He wished he was not working in the dark and hoped the guy they wanted taken out was not Roddy or Brendan. He quite liked them and they seemed harmless enough. But it didn't really matter in the end, he'd do as they asked. It wasn't up to him. He wished nevertheless they'd quit messing him around and let him get on with it, whatever it was they wanted done.

She was blethering on about her dadda going to see that guy who'd had the accident, saying her dadda was always doing what was right.

'Sometimes you have to do what is wrong though,' he found himself saying, arguing with her, tired of her assumption that what she said was true.

She looked at him with that innocent, trusting look he

hated. It made him want to hurt her, shock her. 'I don't see why,' she said defensively.

'Like soldiers at war,' he replied. 'It's wrong to do murder but it's all right to kill then.'

She shook her head. 'No,' she said decisively. That irritated him too. She had agreed with everything he said so far and now she disagreed and he didn't like it.

'What would you know?' he scoffed and saw the pain in her face at the derision in his voice. 'Girls!' he added, shrugging, hoping the word would take the sting out of his words. He did not want to have to tell Angus O'Laughlin that he'd upset her and she did not want to see him again.

'I suppose,' she acknowledged, trying to see it his way, trying so hard to identify with him, get close to him in understanding. Then she looked up at him, touching his arm with the hand he was not holding and she said, 'What will become of us, Shannon?'

'How should I know?' he shrugged, beginning to feel the chill of the dew through the soles of his light shoes, the shoulders of his jacket.

Again the pain in her face. He could see that puzzled look again like a wounded animal. He was not doing it right. Clumsily he drew to a halt. 'What would you like?' he asked.

'Oh Shannon, it's the man who . . . who . . . should . . .'

There were tears in her eyes, shining, catching the light.

'Tell me.' He felt helpless, all fingers and thumbs and awkwardness.

'I don't . . . I mean . . . like Fidelma and Lorcan,' she stammered. This was not how it should be. She should be swept into his arms in the moonlight, like Fred Astaire and Ginger Rogers. Still she ploughed on. Anything to find out, to *know*.

'Your sister? Oh sure. You mean the one who is gettin' married?' His stomach churned. Married! The mere idea gave him the screaming habdabs. Married! He thought of the terrace in Liverpool, the housewives scrubbing the steps each morning. 'Morning, Tilda, how's the babby?' Fag in mouth, both hands on the scrubbing brush. 'Oh great, Maggie, great. An' little Paddy's cough?' Married women, each a carbon copy of the others, dressing-gown all day, hair in curlers half-hidden under a scarf, ancient slippers, varicose veins, permanently pregnant or, if not, looking as if they were. And when they got all gussied up of a Saturday, too much make-up, their hair badly dyed, fluffed out in a wild frizz because of the long time in curlers, a dress a size too small (did they always buy clothes a size too small or did they just keep putting on weight? he wondered) and high heels, loud voices, shrill laughter; he found them either way equally distasteful, the idea of marriage a nightmare. Manfully he gulped. 'Sure,' he said. 'Some day. Sure. 'Course! What you think!'

'Oh Shannon. Shannon.' She was ecstatic. Her eyes shone, tears gone, and she threw herself at him as if he'd proposed, rained kisses all over his face.

He decided enough was enough, and to finish off the episode he took her arms above the elbows and kissed her mouth hard, his lips closed, his face screwed up as if he'd swallowed medicine. Then he let her go abruptly.

'There,' he said.

'Oh Shannon, I love you,' she breathed.

'Me too,' he said swiftly and she giggled.

'You mean you love *me*, don't you? Not you, silly.'

He laughed uncomfortably, not seeing what she meant.

'Well, say it,' she pleaded, anxious-eyed.

'I love you,' he said monotonously, repeating a lesson, and she had to be content with that.

Chapter Forty-two

❧ ❧

At first Roddy thought she must be lying. Hallucinating. Cora couldn't have done this. His elegant, remote, unemotional, perfect wife simply could not have done this; it was out of the question.

Rosie Daly lay on the hospital bed, bandaged, bruised and bloody. What he could see of her face under the bandages, her neck and arms, were purple and crimson. She was a mess.

'She won't tell us what happened,' the young night-nurse had told him, whispering in the sleeping ward. The place was lit only by the pinpoints of nightlights. 'Simply won't say. I'd like to find the bastard did this to her.' She looked at him as though she thought it might be him. The sister in charge hurried her away, then came back and glanced blushingly up at him. 'Oh, I do beg your pardon, sir. She didn't mean to imply . . .'

'I know,' Roddy reassured her.

'She asked for you, sir. Gave us your number. You were the only one she wanted to see. But please, Mr Flood, if she'll tell you, find out who the cad who did this to her is. His name, so that we can report it to the police.'

And Rosie, whispering through the bandages, said it was Cora. Cora! She must be mistaken. His wife couldn't, wouldn't. But he'd never known Rosie to lie and she was always nice about Cora, never a nasty word about his wife.

He sat beside the bed, holding her hand, not knowing what to do, what to say to make it better.

Eventually he decided to ask the nurse to put her into a private room. That would be the thing. Take her out of the public ward. The only times Cora had been in hospital, for the births of her children, she had insisted

216

on a private room. So Rosie should have one too. It was only right.

The sister said they'd move her in the morning and perhaps he could come back then. Mrs Daly, she told him, was getting very drowsy. The morphine was taking effect. They'd given her a shot when she'd been brought in this afternoon before they'd treated her and another just before he came, to help her sleep.

'Who brought her in?' he asked.

'Well, apparently poor Mrs Daly crawled to the hallway of the apartment house she lives in and she managed to bang on the door of a neighbour, though where she found the strength is a wonder. It must have taken enormous courage,' the sister said, shaking her head. 'The neighbour went down the street to the pub and phoned an ambulance from there. She's a frail old lady . . .'

'Yes. Mrs Earle is her name,' Roddy said. 'An elderly woman, suffers from rheumatism.'

The sister gave him a funny look and he lapsed into silence. After a moment or two she continued, 'She was afraid to go into Mrs Daly's apartment in case, she said, the maniac who did this to her was still there. So she phoned from the pub.' She pursed her lips in disapproval and shook her head. 'It's terrible, Mr Flood, isn't it? Did you ever see the like? I don't know what the world's coming to, really I don't.'

Rosie was asleep now, her mouth open slightly. She obviously couldn't breathe through her nose. Her breath made a rattling noise behind it and it upset him. It sounded like a death-rattle.

'You'll see she's moved to the best private room in this place?' he asked.

'Yes, sir, in the morning, first thing. But first she must sleep. She's out of it now, poor thing.' The sister was figuring relationships, he could see, her brain working overtime. He was Mr Flood. She was Mrs Daly, obviously not married to him, so what was the connection? 'She's my cousin,' he whispered confidentially, answering her unspoken question. 'A widow.' That much was true at any rate. 'I do what I can.' He loathed himself for the deception, for using that tone, but he did it to protect Rosie, not himself. He was beyond caring about himself. He felt at that moment only numb fury struggling with horror and uncertainty.

'Give her the best. She deserves it,' he repeated to the sister. She nodded to him benignly, having cast him now to her satisfaction – a kindly relative, looking out for a poor widow.

He bid the sister good-night. 'We'll shift her to the best room possible, sir, when she's *compos mentis*,' she again assured him. 'Good-night, Mr Flood.'

Roddy left, his emotions in turmoil. Why had Cora done this terrible thing? If indeed she had done it. He could not imagine the how or the why of it in a hundred years. It had occurred to no one in the hospital that the beating had been done by a woman and Roddy shook his head in disbelief. Did Cora really care for him, her husband, so much, so passionately, that she could brutally assault another woman and put her in hospital? If she'd found out about himself and Rosie Daly, could she do that? He could not believe she had that much fire in her. Rosie must have been tipsy or deluded. She must have had some kind of mental aberration. But if Cora hadn't done it, then who had? And why? Rosie was a very loved woman. She had no enemies.

He drove home a bewildered man. Cora was asleep when he got there. He tiptoed to the bedside and looked down at her. Her dark hair fanned out on the white pillow around her pale face and her lashes lay serenely motionless on her cheeks. She looked the picture of peace and once more Roddy decided that there must have been a terrible mistake, that Rosie must have had some kind of breakdown.

He lay with his eyes wide open beside his sleeping wife, trying not to move about and disturb her, and puzzled all through the night.

Chapter Forty-three

෧ ௯

Cora was the only one sleeping in Rossbeg. Fidelma, like her father, lay still in her bed, biting the sheet, her hands clenching and unclenching.

She had been cursed with beauty. That was what she had decided. No one saw further than the perfect façade. She was never sure whether people were admiring her face or herself. She very much doubted whether anyone in the whole world, including her mother and father, saw past her beauty to what lay behind.

The worst thought she could think, the thing she was most afraid of, was that perhaps she was wrong; perhaps, for instance, Harry Devereau *had* looked behind the façade and found nothing. Perhaps that was why he'd looked at her with such horror when she'd brought up the subject of marriage.

She had never had to nurture virtues within herself and she was aware of that lack. What she wanted was always within her grasp. It was given to her, handed to her on a plate, and was therefore worthless to her. She could see Decla developing in a way she had never had to, working on the acquisition of patience, tolerance, good humour in adversity. Everything Fidelma had ever hankered after had been thrust at her as soon as she expressed a desire for it by people intent on pleasing her, worshippers at the shrine of her beauty.

Only Harry Devereau had not played that game.

Lorcan Metcalf's proposal had come breathlessly after she had remarked casually that she intended to marry young. 'So I can have a big family like Mother.' And her acceptance of that proposal had been greeted by Lorcan with disbelief, almost dismay. How, poor Lorcan was wondering, could one man be so lucky? To obtain such perfection was slightly alarming. He had always assumed that Fidelma would marry Harry Devereau. She had always shown a preference for that dashing young man and to find himself propelled into first position in her affections was elevation beyond his wildest dreams.

Fidelma lay in bed thinking. Obviously Lorcan would feel that he didn't deserve her and he would probably feel obligated to please her in every way from now on. He would hurry to do her bidding, and it bored her that he would. What was there for her for the rest of her life but boredom?

She stared morosely at the ceiling, then, turning the bedclothes back carefully, she got up and went to the mirror. She turned on the lamp and stared at herself in the glass.

'Mirror, mirror on the wall, who is the fairest of them all? Why, you are, Fidelma, no contest.' But the face that stared back at her looked vacant, like an untenanted house.

She had everything and nothing. She wanted to break the mirror but she didn't. She hadn't got the energy.

Everything on the dressing-table was in its position. The stopper was in her bottle of Chanel No. 5. The cover was on the crystal bowl of Coty face powder and the matching one of white talcum, each with their swansdown puff inside. Not a grain of powder was spilled on the glass top. And suddenly, desperately, she wanted to smash it all. But again she did not. Something inside her, something rigid and controlled, refused to allow her.

Her gaze rested on the large solitaire diamond on the third finger of her left hand. She could have had an emerald, a ruby or a sapphire if she'd wanted, but it made no difference to her. It was a trophy, that was all.

And now what? Lorcan's father would buy the house for them. Her father would pay for the furniture and her mother would decorate it. Her mother would listen to Fidelma's suggestions but ignore them. Or counter them with 'Oh no, pet, that wouldn't be in good taste', and Fidelma would have the house her mother wanted for her. In all this she felt she hardly figured.

She'd obeyed orders from her birth, done the right thing for Mother and Dadda. Hereafter she'd do the right thing for Lorcan. His father held the purse-strings and she would play the game with a cheerful face, obedient to the format of their chosen lives. Appearances were all.

She sighed, tiptoed across the room and slipped back into bed, resuming her contemplation of the ceiling, hands once more clenching and unclenching, eyes wide open. She should be the happiest girl in the world but she was miserable. She had done all they told her to ensure happiness but it still eluded her. Where, oh where had she gone wrong?

Decla lay in her bed in the attic and dreamed while she was still awake. Stretching her arms above her head she smiled as she thought of Shannon. I'm doing a line, she thought. I've got a real live boyfriend. I'm not repulsive and gruesome like I thought I was and maybe I'll not end up a spinster virgin undesired by any man. I have a boyfriend. Me. Decla Flood. At last.

There was a mystery, though, about Shannon O'Brien. It both thrilled and frightened her. It irritated her too, not knowing what he did. She'd have to find out eventually. Her mother would probe until she knew whether to welcome or rebuff him.

Her mother didn't like him, Decla knew that. Well, too bad! Her mother was not his girlfriend. Decla frowned. Her mother also puzzled her. Her attitude had changed radically and recently she did not seem to mind about Shannon. It was very queer, but, Decla thought, snuggling down and closing her eyes with a contented yawn, it was wonderful.

Eamonn too was awake. He'd built a tent with his bedclothes, his fishing-rod holding up the sheets. Inside he had around him his poison arrows (he'd dipped the tips in a mixture of Jeyes Fluid and the pollen from the deadly nightshade in the wood), a thumbed copy of *Boy's Own*, a miniature pack of cards collected from cigarette packets and a couple of dead slugs in a matchbox. He also had his water pistol and a packet of sticky bull's-eyes, one of which he sucked noisily.

He sat cross-legged under the sheet, chewing the peppermint and cogitating what to do about Shannon O'Brien. He had *Boy's Own* open at a page which showed you how to foretell the future by reading the cards and he was

221

trying to work out what the cards he'd carefully dealt out meant.

He frowned in concentration. Shannon troubled him. He did not like him and it was just too bad that Decla did.

He'd followed Shannon through the woods after he'd left Decla. Eamonn was good at stalking and in the last few days, since his mother seemed to have taken to allowing him to do pretty much as he wanted, he'd been able to break the rules about bed-time as he pleased.

He'd tailed Shannon, just like Dick Barton, Special Agent did on the radio, and crept through the wood after him. He'd scared himself half to death several times when, in the dense darkness, Shannon had come to a sudden halt and stood listening, as if he'd heard something. Eamonn's heart had threatened to jump out of his chest and he'd pressed his lips together, squeezing them tightly as he crouched in the underbrush just behind his quarry. But Shannon had seemed satisfied he'd imagined whatever he'd heard and continued his journey until he got to the hut.

It was on the other side of the wood behind the houses on Rothmere Terrace and Eamonn, his face grimy, the scab on his knee rudely sloughed off by the undergrowth, now stood trembling on tiptoe and tried to see inside.

Were they a gang of thieves plotting to rob a bank? Eamonn wondered if he could join them. That would be a wheeze to make even William Brown from the *Just William* books look wet.

Then he remembered Shannon's gun and he shivered. He was sure now that Shannon was a gangster. He was up to no good and Decla might be shot dead and lie dying in a pool of blood, her tongue sticking out like in the movies. Eamonn shuddered, then crawled to the window near the door. Through the cracked glass he could see a big red-haired man, bearded like a giant, and the other, smart like his father, and Shannon standing before them, to attention. What was going on? He could hear nothing and it was cold and damp outside and he was suddenly alone and tired and very scared.

He'd hurried home, arriving breathless, and sneaking up the back way to his room. He made his tent and cast the runes using cigarette cards instead of the real thing in an attempt to find out what Shannon was up to.

But the cards didn't help. They silently informed him that there was a ship carrying death across the sea. That, he thought, was no use to him at all. It had nothing to do with his problem. In a temper he pulled down the fishing-rod and, clutching the matchbox in his fist, lay totally entangled in the rumpled sheets and fell suddenly and completely asleep.

Sylvie too was awake. She lay in the bed, a soft bedside light on, savouring her new-found luxury.

She had a routine. It was one of the only things constant wherever she was. It reassured her to know that wherever she found herself, in whatever strange place, she would always, without fail, brush her hair one hundred times with her old silver-backed brush. Then she would brush her teeth twenty-five times to and fro and twenty-five up and down.

In some places they'd not given her toothpaste so she'd sneaked some salt and used that. Then she'd say her prayers, kneeling beside her bed, eyes tight closed. Sometimes when she'd shared a room with other children and they'd teased her for doing this, labelling her pious and goody-goody, she'd been upset, but she'd been stubborn too and stuck to her routine.

God bless Mummy. She'd swallow hard so as not to cry. Mummy, why did you leave me? Why did you let me go? Oh, you should have kept me, held me to you, not let me racket about on my own, lonely and afraid. Dear God, bless my mother.

And my father. Tinkling his keyboard. Scott Joplin-style jazz. Smiling at me but not really seeing me. I can't see him clearly either through the cigarette smoke.

God bless Father.

Then a prayer that the good guys would win the war. Everyone knew Hitler was bad. He could not, must not win. Churchill and Montgomery were the good guys so they would triumph in the end. They did. Eventually. Still, she always said that prayer, forgetting that the war was over.

And now, in this princess's bed, luxuriously alone, wearing her old cotton nightie, patched but fresh and clean, she stretched her arms and folded her hands and added, 'And

God bless my aunt and uncle and all my cousins and Fusty and Mary Mac and *everybody* here, and thank you, thank you for giving me such a lovely new family. Especially Cecie.' Then she put her arms down, breathing in the scent of lavender. 'And please, please, dear God, let it last this time. Let them like me. Don't let them send me away from here. Please.' Snuggling against the pillow she hoped and dreamed and stared at the lovely curtains and the pictures on the wall and the flowers on the mantelpiece, enjoying the prettiness, storing it in her memory so that she could conjure it all up again if she was sent away.

'Oh please, God, don't let me be sent away,' she whispered again. 'I don't think I could bear it.'

She was so tired of being passed from place to place, from one set of people to another. So tired of smiling all the time, pretending she was grateful when all she was was bewildered. Hoping, trying to please, to *make* them like her, sometimes succeeding, sometimes failing. Scared to talk and say the wrong thing. Scared not to talk and be sent away as stubborn and uncooperative.

She had sensed Fidelma's distaste at her craven efforts to make them like her, accept her, but Fidelma had been accepted all her life, loved and cosseted, so how could she understand the anxiety that dwelt within her cousin night and day? How could she know how Sylvie felt when she arrived at a new place?

And there had been so many rejections. So much desperation, striving to fit in, being overlooked, being ignored, being shouted at. Not that she'd been abused or suffered violence at the hands of her many foster parents. They had, in the main, been honest well-meaning folks. But they had not been very sensitive or understanding to the little stranger at their door. The English tended to be brisk, with a no-nonsense attitude that led to many a tearful night.

She'd remained hopeful. Against all odds she'd kept a modicum of optimism in her struggle for survival. And now that hope had blossomed. If only she had not ruined her chances by being too forward, by suggesting that Cecie came downstairs. But how could she do otherwise? She was too familiar with loneliness and neglect not to understand her cousin. She sighed. It was difficult.

224

But things had never looked so rosy. She was here, in this enchanting bedroom in Rossbeg with a new friend, Cecie. It was more than enough. Her demands were modest. All she craved was a little love, a little continuity. It would not matter to her if it was in a palace or a cottage as long as someone loved her and let her stay with them. That was the important thing. A haven that was constant, people who remained. She was quite prepared to work at knowing them, understanding them. She'd learn to fit in with their ways, their peculiarities. What she craved was routine.

'Oh please,' she whispered. 'Oh please.'

Cecie never slept through the night, at least, not since she became sick. Tonight however she thought she might.

It had been such a wonderful day, so much fun, so much hope. And it had all been because of her cousin.

Sylvie promised she'd see the garden. The idea made her sick with excitement. See the garden! Feel the breeze on her cheeks. Did they know how stupendous that would be?

If it was going to kill her, so be it. She'd had enough of isolation and darkness. Her cousin would prize her loose and Cecie decided that she loved Sylvie.

She could see a star through a crack in the curtains. It burned with a fierce white light that beamed like a silver ribbon in the black velvet sky. She crossed her fingers and wished. Please let me be all right tomorrow. Please keep me from fainting, from being silly and coughing too much and bringing up blood. Oh, don't let that happen because if it does they'd stop me ever going out again, and I think I'd die if that happened now. I want so much to see the garden.

Heaven that night was bombarded with pleas. But the soft singing stars and the pale crescent moon and the pitchy mantle of the sky held their secrets and made no reply.

Chapter Forty-four

❧ ❧

'There'll be an Anti-Partition Rally in Lower Mount Street on the fourteenth,' Angus said.

'Want me to be there?' Shannon asked.

'Aye. But be careful.' Angus looked towards the window and thought he saw a face there. It was a pale little face, like a goblin or an elf. He blinked, looked again, but there was nothing there now. He thought he'd imagined it.

Seamus O'Sullivan cleared his throat. 'We're nearly there,' he said to Shannon. 'Nearly there. You sure you've got the balls for this, boy?'

Shannon nodded. 'Aye, sir. But what *is* this?' he asked hesitantly.

'You'll find out soon enough,' the neat little man said. 'Just so long as you can wipe out someone without question. For Ireland.'

'I can, sir.'

'You'll be honoured by the party,' Angus remarked.

'The girl believes I'm in love with her,' Shannon said.

Seamus looked at him sharply. 'And are you?' He watched the boy carefully, noting the expression in his eyes, but all he saw was an eagerness to ingratiate and please. Oh, the days had gone, he reflected sadly, when patriots' motives were pure.

'You were not followed here?' Angus asked him suddenly, thinking of the apparition at the window, wondering still if he'd imagined it.

'Quite sure, sir.' Shannon stifled the lurking suspicion that someone had indeed been behind him. But no, he assured himself, it had either been his imagination or a woodland animal, that rustling, that snapping of twigs. He looked candidly into their eyes. 'Quite sure,' he reiterated.

Following in the woods was very different from tailing in the streets of Liverpool.

'Good. Good. Then you may go. Keep up the good work.'

Shannon saluted and went to the door.

'O'Brien,' Seamus O'Sullivan called, his voice soft as usual. Shannon turned. 'Good work, boy.' He gave a twist to his lips that passed as a smile. 'There'll be a promotion in this for you.'

'Thank you, sir.' Shannon nodded and left. A promotion! He did not feel as proud and pleased as he should. What did promotion mean in a small ragged army of dissidents, their cause outlawed? The patriots of Ireland who had survived like Eamonn de Valera sat now in soft chairs in the seat of power and gave thanks for the end of hostilities as if the war was over. As if Ireland wasn't severed, head from body, with the North still under the Union Jack. Sure what kind of men were they?

There were few in the South who saw it that way and Shannon was beginning to feel the isolation of his position. Hanging around the girl and her family he could not help but hear their different views, note their indifference. He would have preferred to belong to a more popular cause, like long ago in 1916 when the whole of Ireland burned in a fever for freedom. People were tepid today, no heat any more. They were lulled by that partial freedom and did not see or suspect the bloodshed ahead that the divide and rule policy would inevitably bring in its wake.

Shannon looked right and left when he left the hut, peered in the bushes, rustled the undergrowth, but there was nothing there. He was right. He had not been followed.

Chapter Forty-five

❧ ❧

Next morning Cora was in fine fettle. She was up and about before Roddy stirred.

He had stayed awake most of the night, until his bedside clock showed four a.m. and the dawn was breaking, when he fell asleep at last. Then he slept heavily, tormented by nightmares of Rosie being beaten while he watched, helpless, his limbs treacle. Eventually he woke, feeling drugged.

Cora had been arranging flowers before breakfast and she looked out through the glass wall of the breakfast-room as he entered, glanced at him, then back out into the garden. 'The azaleas are a miracle, dear,' she remarked. 'Just look at them.' She pointed at a brilliant splash of cerise and orange near the oak tree. Her face looked childlike in its serenity. Calm and untroubled. 'How is your friend?'

Confused by her question, for a moment he couldn't think who she was talking about. Then, when realisation dawned, he said, 'Fine. Well, not so good really. But sh— he's being taken care of.'

'Good. That's as it should be. The governor has a duty to his employees.' She smiled as Decla came into the room. 'Good morning, dear.'

'Mother, Shannon and I are doing a line,' Decla exclaimed, her face wreathed in smiles. Roddy thought, that's what a face should look like when one is in love and he wondered if he had ever looked like that.

Then he saw a dash of anxiety as Decla waited for her mother to reply and both of them were surprised when all she said was, 'That's nice, dear.'

Roddy knew then for certain that Rosie Daly had made a terrible mistake. How or why this had happened he could not figure out at this precise moment, but he was sure that a rational explanation for the whole episode would be found, only he could not imagine what it could be. But he knew that no woman could perpetrate such a vicious act and then behave like this with her children. Clear-eyed, calm, dispassionate. No. She could not have done that terrible damage, she had neither the temperament nor the strength.

Sylvie greeted them and asked if Cecie could come down after breakfast. It was such a glorious day. The sun was out, the roses were in full bloom and she and Mary Mac between them would manage. 'There's not a wind that might chill her or any damp at all. It's as dry as a desert out there today and will do her good,' Sylvie said.

Cora felt full of the milk of human kindness, full of goodwill to all that morning, which was why she greeted Decla's impulsive announcement and Sylvie's proposals with no resistance at all. She was operating in a sort of cushioned daze, as if she were drugged and the world functioned in slow motion. There was a pleasant buzz in her head, a sumptuous calm within and all her nerves were at rest.

'Wrap her up well,' she told Sylvie.

'We'll cocoon her. We'll swaddle her like a babe,' Sylvie breathed.

'All right then.' Cora smiled at the girl. 'Put her in the rose garden then, it's warmest there. In the big wicker chair, wrapped up like a parcel, and I'll come and see her by and by.'

Roddy's certainty that his wife could have had nothing whatsoever to do with the attack on his mistress grew and grew.

He went to work, checked things out at the yard, then drove to the hospital around ten o'clock.

The day was glorious. The sea heaved, a huge blue cloak edged with white lace. The mountains seemed like cut-outs against the washed-blue sky. Little clouds scudded across the azure dome as if they were being chased and seagulls called raucously to each other.

In Dublin he bought some flowers from the flower-seller at the Pillar. People hurried about greeting each other, men raising their hats, smiling in the sun.

At the reception desk at the hospital the woman, grey-haired, greeted him with 'Gorgeous day, sir, isn't it?'

They'd put Rosie in a small private room, prettily decorated, and the nurse, a different one today, took the flowers
and said she'd fetch a vase. This one was pert and pretty,
a saucy Dublin girl. She looked at him with wise eyes, as if
they shared a secret, and he wondered if she'd twigged the
situation, if perhaps she knew who he was, maybe thought
he did this to Rosie. You never knew.

Rosie greeted him feebly. She was trying hard to smile and
be her sociable self but she was failing miserably. She couldn't
smile, her face was too damaged, and her pain was obvious
when she moved even a muscle. Her mouth was stiff and she
spoke through her teeth, one at the side missing.

She lay there, drugged, in acute discomfort, and one thing
was certain. *Someone* had given her a most terrible beating. It
wrenched Roddy's heart to see her and he was overcome by
a tide of loving concern.

'Darling, my darling, who did this to you?'

The nurse burst in, all efficiency, carrying a vase with his
flowers daintily arranged. Her quick eyes lit momentarily on
his hand covering Rosie's, then flickered away as she bustled
about the room.

'They're lovely, aren't they? So pretty. Pink carnations and
roses. We'll put them here where you can see them, Mrs
Daly, and they'll cheer you up no end. Now, I'll leave you
in peace. Just ring the bell if you want anything.' And she
left the room.

'I told you, Roddy. Cora did it.'

He looked at the white expanse of ceiling, then back at
her, his perplexity obvious.

'Don't tell me you don't believe me. Oh, don't tell me that!'
A tear appeared at the corner of her eye and ran down into
the bandage around her head.

'Of course I believe you, Rosie,' he said, but his voice held
no conviction. 'Only you must see . . .'

'See what? See that your wife came to my apartment and
beat the hell out of me and you think, for some bizarre
reason, that I'm lying? Why? Why would I do that, Roddy,
tell me that? What possible reason could I have to want
to . . . ?'

She was in distress now and he felt alarmed as her tears
flowed faster into the bandages. Her breath rasped harshly

and she made a little moaning noise from the pain, the hurt he was inflicting.

The sassy nurse suddenly appeared, saying, 'I thought I heard—' Then, giving Roddy a hard stare, she demanded, 'What have we here? Oh, this won't do at all.' Glancing sympathetically at Rosie, she said gently, 'Mrs Daly, rest now. There, my dear. I'll give you something to relax you.' Then, glaring at Roddy, 'You're upsetting my patient. I'm afraid I'll have to ask you to leave.'

'Please, Nurse, let him stay. Something we have to . . .' But Rosie's feeble protests did not count for anything with this nurse. She hustled Roddy out and he found himself in the corridor, furious but helpless.

He would come back this evening. He hoped that particular nurse would have gone off-duty by then. He was bewildered, anxious and angry. Everything in his life had turned topsy-turvy and he realised that before this monstrous event things had been quite perfect. It had all been arranged just as he would have wished. Now that lovely life had vanished, the happy slipping of day into pleasant day; the joy of his shipyard, his love and pride in what they produced, his beautifully run home, the adornment of a perfect wife, his fabulous, erotic and delightful mistress, he'd had everything.

Now that even tempo, the trust, had been smashed and it might never be completely mended.

He hit the wheel of the car with his fist. 'Damn! Damn! Damn!' he muttered. 'I've *got* to get to the bottom of this. Got to!' He needed to think. Needed to focus and work it all out.

Who could have beaten up poor Rosie? It could not have been Cora, he was certain of that; his Cora was not a woman given to losing her temper and whoever beat up Rosie must have been blind with rage.

But he kept coming back to the question, why would Rosie lie? 'Beats me,' he muttered and started the car. 'Beats me.'

Chapter Forty-six

లు ం

As Roddy drove along Leeson Street he decided that what
he needed to clear the muddle in his brain was a drink.
He'd go to the Shelbourne bar, his old haunt, where he'd
met Rosie. What he needed was a stiff one and that particular
place would bring back reassuring memories. He hadn't been
there in a long time. Not for years really. Oh, he'd been to
the restaurant with his family but he'd avoided the bar in case
they asked him about Rosie in front of his wife. Not that they
would have committed such a gaffe, but to be sure.

He parked the car in Dawson Street and walked into the
hotel through the lobby. Yes, what he needed was a drink.

The stool he had always sat on was occupied and he felt
a moment's intense annoyance. People were as territorial as
animals he thought, and ordered a whiskey. The barman was
new, a young bloke, rosy-faced, from the country. He was a
very pleasant young chap but Roddy hated the change as
much as he disliked finding his stool occupied. He told
himself to quit being neurotic, like a bloody woman, and
tossed off his Jameson's, then ordered another.

'You beginnin' early this fine day,' said a voice and a hand
was clapped on his shoulder.

It was Brendan O'Brien and Roddy was glad to see him,
glad of his company.

'How are ye, Brendan?' he asked, not expecting an answer,
and, glancing up at his old friend, to his horror he felt his
eyes well up.

'Jasus, man, you all right?' Brendan was instantly sympathetic. He pulled him into a booth and sat him down.

Roddy found himself confiding in Brendan, spilling his
guts, as they said in the movies. What astonished him was
Brendan's lack of surprise.

'You knew?' he asked, having told Brendan of his liaison with Rosie Daly.

'About Rosie?' Brendan smiled. ''Course! Everyone knew.'

'Oh God!'

'You didn't think it was a secret, did you, old man? Come on!'

'Yes. Funnily enough I did.'

He felt very foolish. Like he'd been half-witted. The *eejit* who thought no one knew his secret when the whole world was in on it.

'Don't worry, old friend. Tell me what happened. Why the tragic face?'

He told him. About Rosie's beating. About what Rosie said. That Cora had done it. Brendan stared at him, fascinated.

'I can't believe it, Brendan. This morning, indeed last evening, she was so calm, so serene. Last night, which would have been right after she was supposed to have . . . she was totally calm. I just don't believe . . .'

'Or don't want to?' Brendan asked and Roddy frowned and looked at his friend sharply.

'What do you mean?'

'I mean you don't want to disturb the status quo. You liked things the way they were and now something has happened to rock the boat and you don't like it.'

'I know *that*,' Roddy said. 'But about Cora . . . it just doesn't seem feasible. You don't realise how calm and cool she is. I've *never* seen her agitated, Brendan, I've hardly ever seen her lose her poise. I simply cannot imagine . . .'

'But why would Rosie lie?' Brendan asked the question Roddy could not answer. 'She's the most honest woman I know.'

Roddy shrugged. 'She sure is and the answer to your question is, I don't know, Brendan, I just don't know. There must be an explanation but I haven't worked out what it could be.'

'How'd she get to Rosie's? If she went? Cora never goes by public transport, so how'd she get there?'

'What do you mean?'

'How'd she get there?' Brendan spread his hands. 'Remember it was raining.'

'If she went into town she'd take Charlie Sweeney.'

233

''Xactly.' Brendan nodded and looked at Roddy, closed one eye, then looked back at his whiskey.

Light dawned and Roddy stared at Brendan admiringly. 'Charlie! Of course! He'da noticed if she . . . if she . . .'

''Xactly!' Brendan repeated. 'You ask him if he took Cora to Dublin or not. That way you'll find out. See what he has to say.'

'Brendan, you're a genius.'

'I'll drink to that.'

'Barman, same again.'

They settled down to a cosy chat and a few convivial drinks. Brendan puffed on a cigar and complained gently about Shannon. 'There's something not quite right about him, Roddy. Something I can't put my finger on.'

'He's going with Decla. So she says.' Roddy looked at his friend. 'I hope he's sincere. She's very smitten . . . I don't want her hurt, Brendan.'

Brendan nodded, took a sip, rolled it around his mouth, swallowed it. Then he said, 'I'll have a word with him.' He glanced at Roddy. 'It would be great though, if they made a match, him and Decla. I'd give him a shop. Outright. See them both right. I've always been fond of your Decla, you know that, Roddy.'

Roddy was frowning. 'Can't get it off my mind, Brendan. Cora couldn't have. Could she? But Rosie wouldn't . . .'

'Look, call Charlie now. Why wait? Get the girl to get the number for you . . .'

'No, I have it . . .'

'Then off you go. Settle it now.'

Roddy rose stiffly. He'd put away quite a few jars with his friend and he blinked his eyes rapidly, pulled himself together and went to the girl at reception. She sent him to a cubicle down some steps. 'Number three, sir, an' I'll put the call through when I get it.'

He went to the cubicle. It smelled of stale tobacco and there was a lot of scribbling on the instruction card. After a few moments the phone rang and he picked it up.

'Charlie?'

'Yes. Who is this?'

'Roddy Flood.'

'Oh yes, Mr Flood?'

'Did you take my wife to Dublin yesterday?'

'Yes. Yes I did, Mr Flood.' Charlie's voice sounded gleeful. The fat's in the fire now, he thought to himself.

'Where did you take her?'

'Well, um . . .' The man was hesitating. Why? 'Well, well I took her through Blackrock . . .'

'Naturally you took her through Blackrock, you were going to Dublin!' Dunderhead, what was he playing at? 'I'm asking about Dublin.'

'Yes, Mr Flood. Well, I took her to . . .' Pause, then in a rush, 'I took her to Molesworth Street.'

My God, it *was* Cora! Roddy's knees went weak and there was a sick feeling in his guts. Rosie had told the truth. And Charlie must know all about Rosie. He'd taken Roddy there and now his hesitation spoke volumes. Not wanting to tell him where he'd taken his wife meant that he knew something. Dear God, did everyone in Dublin know? And Cora . . . how could Cora . . . ?

'Sir . . . Is that all?'

'Oh yes, Charlie, yes. No, no, just a minute. Did you take her home?'

'Yes, Mr Flood. I waited. She asked me to.'

Now that he'd admitted taking Cora to Molesworth Street he seemed anxious to fill it all in for Roddy. 'I waited for her, Mr Flood, then took her home to Rossbeg.'

'Was she okay?'

There was a pause. 'What do you mean, Mr Flood?'

'I mean was she all right? Was there anything odd about her appearance?'

'Well, yes, as a matter of fact. There were blood-stains on the front of her dress. I thought it odd myself, like she had an accident. But she said she was fine.'

It *was* true. Irrefutably true. 'Thank you, Charlie, for taking care of her. Goodbye.'

He'd thought to lie to Charlie, make excuses, but he couldn't. He sat in the cubicle, his forehead on the glass-covered side, pressing against an advertisement for Cleary's July sale. *Frocks, 7½ guineas to 12 gns. Corsets, 11/9. Straw hats 29/6.* The glass was cool on his forehead.

Cora, Cora, Cora! What got into her? It was the most incomprehensible thing ever. One thing was certain, he could never go back to her. She'd shot her bolt. He'd leave her now, that was for sure. He'd always wanted to clear up the situation with Rosie, let the world know they were partners. There was only one thing he was absolutely sure of and that was that he could not be in a room alone with the person who did that terrible thing to the woman he loved and not kill her.

He shook his head.

Brendan came and collected him. 'What's up?' He took in the expression on Roddy's face. 'It was Cora, wasn't it? Somehow I'm not surprised. Wouldn't put anything past Cora. Not at all happy about people who never show their emotions.' Brendan slapped his friend on the back. 'What we need is a tincture of alcohol. Right? C'mon,' and he led his dazed friend out of the hotel and down the street to Davy Byrne's.

Chapter Forty-seven

❧ ❧

'I'm sorry, Ossian, I can't take you to Rome.'

Ossian sat very still, not a muscle in his face moved, and for a moment everything in the room seemed to hold its breath. Only the old clock ticked, wheezing a little, grunting out the minutes of their lives. Then a bee buzzed, hitting the transparent glass to the Monsignor's right, for he sat with his back to the open French windows, in his usual place. The bee attacked the glass again and again, hurling itself mindlessly against the polished transparent pane, not able to understand what impeded its flight.

Stupid bloody insect, Ossian thought, then, I'm like that bee; attacking obstacles over and over, not knowing what or who bars my way.

He had fondly imagined he had leapt forward, bounded towards a new and desirable position. Accompanying the Monsignor to Rome was a feather in the cap of a very young priest. The Vatican. The Holy See. At his age it was a very bright move. The people he could meet there, the contacts he could make. He'd been congratulating himself, thought how fortunate he was that his mother was such a good friend of the Monsignor and how kind it was that strings could be pulled on his behalf, for he had no doubt that that was what had happened.

But in the car, in the car that Saturday, something had alarmed him. What? He could not remember.

He had already made up his mind that he was not going to come back to Ireland from Rome. He'd wangle an appointment in the Holy See. He did not want to return to Ballyloch or Drimnagh or Skibbereen or Tuam to some little backward parish no one had ever heard of. No, his place was with the hierarchy, up there somewhere with the

237

high flyers. He did not want the sum of his achievements to be parish priest in some backwater. He'd charm the powers that be in the Vatican. It would be easy; he had been doing it all his life. Some eminent cleric would take him up and he would start his rise to the top. What Monsignor Maguire was saying now made no sense at all. On the eve of their departure the Monsignor was telling him that he was not going. Like that! It was absurd.

'Why?' Trying to keep his voice under control. 'Please tell me why.'

The Monsignor folded his olive-skinned hands, his fore-fingers like a church steeple, the tips touching.

'I can't tell you that, Ossian,' he said tranquilly.

'That's very unfair.' The petulance, the disappointment were perceptible.

'Your vows demand complete obedience, Ossian. You have to learn to do as you are told.'

'But for no reason. Just like that.' Ossian's voice did not conceal his fury.

'That acceptance is precisely what I'd expect of you as a priest.' The Monsignor was unmoved and he continued, 'You have my word that this does not reflect badly on you. In fact it has nothing to do with you at all. Simply my plans are changed.'

'But *you* are going to Rome?'

The Monsignor nodded. 'Sure.'

'Then why . . . ?'

'I've already told you, Ossian. Blind obedience. Now, my boy, you must excuse me.'

'This is a bitter disappointment to me, Monsignor. I'm—'

'Be careful, boy.' The Monsignor rose slowly, unfolding his tall frame, shooting Ossian a warning glance.

'I'll *not* be careful, Monsignor. It's *unfair* and you know it. You're giving me all this crap about obedience and you know perfectly well it's an excuse.'

The Monsignor sighed and sat down again. 'Ossian, Ossian, that is no way for you to speak to a superior. You have to take your disappointment on the chin.' Then, softening, 'Listen, Ossian, in a while, in a very short while I'll be going back to Rome again, and I promise you

238

next time you will come with me. In a year's time maybe.'

'That's simply not good enough.'

The Monsignor was startled by the steely look in the boy's eyes. Had he misjudged Ossian Flood too? He was not as guileless as he appeared. Oh, he'd known Ossian was ambitious, but immoderately so? Fanatically? He stared at the young man, whose jaw was clenching and whose eyes shone with a wild intensity. Where had he seen that exact look before? he wondered, then remembered. Cora Flood's face when she told him she loved him. He shivered. Perhaps he had indeed misjudged the whole Flood family.

'Ossian, I think you have gone far enough,' he said in a calm impersonal voice. 'I think you should leave before you say something you might regret.'

But the boy would not be stopped. The Monsignor could see the emotion propelling him, naked in his eyes. He could not but reflect that perhaps it was as well he was not taking this fiery and impulsive young man with him to Rome, where diplomacy was essential.

'It's my mother, isn't it?' The young priest's eyes had narrowed and he saw the instant alarmed response in Robert Maguire's own eyes. He had hit a raw nerve.

'Aha!' he said, then, like a person playing twenty questions, 'She's said something . . . ? She's done something . . . ?' He watched the prelate closely. 'Something? What?'

'I can't tell you that.' The Monsignor felt on the defensive and it was not a position he was used to. He was tired of the whole conversation. He wanted to leave, get on with other, more important things. But the boy stood and leaned across the desk and the Monsignor was once more startled by the anger and desperation he saw in the priest's eyes.

'My mother is in love with you!'

Ossian had remembered. The car. The sun. The sentence he'd thought nothing of at the time, 'I'll miss him more than you can imagine', and the way she said it. Her eyes. His mother, his perfect disciplined and beautiful mother was besotted with this man. It explained everything. He could see confirmation in the prelate's eyes, the way the lids flickered, and the Monsignor flinched openly when

239

Ossian said again, 'My mother is in love with you! And because of that you are not taking me to Rome!'

The interview had got out of hand. The Monsignor felt the first quivers of anger and his hand closed tightly over his paper-knife as he looked up at Ossian, who was now standing over him.

'I think you've said enough, Ossian. You are dismissed.' And he picked up the letter he had been reading before this distasteful interview had commenced and began to read.

But Ossian did not leave. To the Monsignor's surprise he sat down in the chair again, the chair his mother had so often sat in, and looked at the Monsignor challengingly.

'I think, Monsignor, I *will* go to Rome with you after all.'

The Monsignor looked stunned and for the first time could not conceal his emotion. 'What?' he barked.

'You heard me,' the young priest smiled. He leaned back in his chair. 'How do I know you two are not having an affair?' he asked blandly. 'How do I know you have not broken your vows of chastity? How do I know you did not seduce my mother? A married woman?'

'You are mad, Father.' The Monsignor looked at the young priest in horror. He knew exactly the way Ossian's mind had led him and thought briefly how well suited he would be to Vatican intrigue. He almost mouthed the next sentence with the young priest, so predictable was it.

'There's no smoke without fire!' Ossian said.

The Monsignor knew full well what could happen. An accusation by a young and charming priest – and Ossian could be persuasive, today's performance proved that clearly enough – and an enquiry would be unavoidable. There would *have* to be an enquiry and in the meantime his reputation would be in the mud of public speculation, with all sorts of surmisings flying about. Did the public ever restrain themselves when it came to salacious scandal? Of course not. The man in the street was not noted for restraint and the facts of such a case were usually twisted out of all recognition. He could see the headlines now: 'Priest accused of adultery', 'Monsignor in love sessions with wife of shipyard owner', 'Priest accused of seducing wife of ship owner in Abbey' and other such drivel. The newspapers would try him and even if found innocent his good name would be tarnished forever. No smoke without fire, indeed!

There would be no keeping it quiet, Ossian would see to that, and his reputation would be forever muddied. Even if Cora denied it, and he could not count on that – like mother like son – he'd forever be branded the priest who had had it off with Cora Flood, and innocent though he was his career would inevitably flounder, his life would be tarnished forever and there would be no going back.

Ossian was watching him closely. The Monsignor stood, spreading his hands. 'All right, you win,' he said mildly, conceding defeat. 'You can come with me to Rome.'

The boy was thrown. He had not expected such a quick and complete capitulation. He had no knowledge of diplomacy and compromise. He had not learned, the Monsignor smiled softly to himself, that he who fights and runs away lives to fight another day. Ah well! He'd find out in time.

'Thank you, Monsignor,' Ossian floundered, not wanting to meet the Monsignor's mild and amused stare, not knowing how to proceed. The Monsignor watched him, not helping him. 'Thank you, Monsignor', was all he could think to say. It seemed curiously inappropriate.

'But you'll not stay there, as we intended. You'll return with me at once. I'm there for a long weekend, as you know. We'll leave the rest of the party in the English College and return here on the Monday.'

Ossian was not going to argue. It suited him fine, whatever the Monsignor wanted. What he needed was to get to Rome; after that anything was possible.

'And you'll give me at least one introduction to someone who can eventually help me?' Ossian asked eagerly.

The Monsignor nodded coolly. 'Yes. Now you may go.'

'You understand I only did this because—'

'Do not presume to explain yourself. I understand you very well. It is an insult to my intelligence and yours to imagine things will ever be the same between us.'

'But, Monsignor, you would have done the same thing in my place. You too are ambitious.'

'No. Never. How very wrong you are, Ossian. And how short-sighted. I would never have behaved as you did just now. You disgust me and I would be obliged if you would leave my room now and get out of my sight.'

Ossian looked at him anxiously. 'But you will—' he began.

'I will behave appropriately, Ossian, never fear. But do not expect me to like you. Now leave me in peace.'

They both left the room. Monsignor Maguire shook himself as if to get rid of an evil. He stepped out into the cloister and breathed in the sweet-scented air in great gulps. He thought of the Floods with repugnance. Cora, her avid face, her eyes feverish with lust, and Ossian, sly and devious under that breath-takingly handsome façade. Fidelma, cold as ice, marrying for none of the noble reasons. Why, he wondered, were they like that – so heartless, so self-obsessed? Roddy wasn't like that, or Decla, or Cecie. Only the beautiful ones, the perfect ones. Did beauty have so high a price-tag? He shook his head and stopped pacing, his attention caught by a perfect pink rose. It was as near to utter beauty as it could be and the Monsignor breathed in its scent. Then he saw, beside it, another rose, a rose that had certainly been as perfect but was past its prime now, its petals curling, tipped with brown. And near its heart a darker hue, the hue of decay. Here a drunken bee feasted and, sated on its bounty, fell sideways to drop at the Monsignor's feet.

'Golden lads and girls all must,
As chimney-sweepers, come to dust.'

He took out his breviary, opened a page and, clearing his mind of worldly things, began to read.

Chapter Forty-eight

❦ ❧

Cecie sat in the big wicker chair, cocooned in soft cashmere shawls and rugs and cushions. Her face turned gratefully to the sun, she breathed in the air as if gulping champagne. She held on to Sylvie's hand. Cora was not there. She had supervised Cecie's journey from her room over the breakfast-room to the rose garden, then sat a moment on the stone bench as if in thought while her daughter and her niece watched her expectantly. She had opened her mouth a couple of times as if to speak but closed it again wordlessly, then stood up and returned to the house.

Cecie did not speak for a long time. Her face was wreathed in smiles and her eyes darted here and there constantly, drinking in the beauty all around her. Starved of nature's glories, the scent of the sea and the sweet honey-laden air, she was drunk with sensation. Her cousin let her be.

Sylvie understood how she felt. She sat beside Cecie, stroking her hand occasionally and smiling. She too was overwhelmed. To sit there in the shade of the sycamore under the shadowy interlaced branches, the cool breeze soothing her brow, the smell of the roses overpowering her, made her think she was in heaven.

For a while she need not nurse anxiety. For a short time she could feel free from restraint in this beautiful place, be herself.

Harry Devereau came upon them by accident. He felt so guilty about Fidelma that he'd done the coward's thing and kept away from the Floods, to avoid awkwardness. But he'd realised that that state of affairs could not continue. The Floods were his near neighbours, his friends, he was going to see them everywhere he went and so he had to face up to the situation eventually. Whistling through his teeth he had decided to stroll over to Rossbeg there and then and pay his respects. Besides, he'd heard that Fidelma had become engaged to Lorcan Metcalf and he guessed that she was as anxious as he to gloss over the whole awkward incident and behave as if nothing had happened.

Her engagement to Lorcan surprised him, and he had thought the announcement had come with indecent haste after his rejection of her, but, he shrugged, it was none of his business and he'd like to wish her well in any case.

So he meandered over to Rossbeg, across the fields and skirting the woods, and came upon the girls in the rose arbour.

For a moment before they saw him he was held, spell-bound, watching them. It was as if a medieval picture had come to life.

Cecie looked frail, wrapped in shawls, her skin like wax, her eyes full of an almost unbearable wonder as she gazed about her.

And the stranger with her, an ethereal creature that made his heart jump like a trout on a hook and whose gaze suddenly caught his, the eyes widening, lips quivering, startled like a fawn half-hidden in the trees.

'Who?' she breathed and he could see a faint flush rise beneath her transparent skin and an eagerness suddenly agitate her.

She stood, dropping the rose from her fingers, and took two steps towards him.

'It's Harry! Harry Devereau!' Cecie cried. 'Don't you remember me, Harry? Look, they've let me out. Isn't it wonderful!'

He turned reluctantly away from the enchanted gaze of the stranger and Cecie began to cough.

'I'm Sylvie Flood. I'm Cecie's cousin. Oh Cecie, are you all right?' Sylvie cried anxiously and he saw the concern in her eyes. She held Cecie's head while the invalid sipped some water. 'It's all right, Cecie. Maybe we ought to take you back up.'

'Not yet, Sylvie, oh please not yet.' Cecie's large eyes pleaded and Sylvie glanced at the wonderful stranger. What do you think? her look enquired. What is your view for it is valuable to me and I'd believe anything you told me.

He smiled at her then and said to Cecie, 'Stay awhile. You look so happy. It can't harm you that much.' Taking the responsibility manfully.

'We could have some tea out here?' Cecie suggested eagerly.

'How lovely,' Harry laughed. 'And then if you are good, Cecie, I'll carry you up to your bed.'

Cecie nodded again, smiling, and Harry loped out of the garden and around the house. 'I'll unearth Fusty,' he said over his shoulder.

Sylvie stared after him and Cecie, watching the bemused expression on her cousin's face, asked, 'You like him, Sylvie, don't you?'

'Oh yes!' Sylvie breathed. 'Oh yes.'

Harry made his way to the kitchens, his head full of the enchantress. She was so small, so delicate, so fragile. There was something about her that made him ache to take care of her. Her eyes were vulnerable, as if begging not to be hurt, a softness there that beguiled, and he knew he'd never recover. Her first glance had pierced his heart and he was hers forever. So he did not see Fidelma as she came running down the steps, hand in hand with Lorcan, who came to an abrupt halt on seeing Harry and stood looking sheepish.

'What is it, Lorcan?' Fidelma cried, then, catching sight of Harry, she too stopped quite still and stared.

'Oh, it's you, Harry,' she cried, very brightly. 'Come to congratulate us?'

'Matter of fact, I did,' Harry replied. 'Only I met Cecie and' – he glanced at Fidelma, then continued – 'and your cousin Sylvie.' Chalk and cheese, he thought.

'The little mouse?' Fidelma giggled. There were two spots of red on her cheeks and she spoke breathlessly. She looked, Harry thought, exquisite, standing there on one foot, the other curled around her ankle, in her cool tennis whites. Exquisite and cold. The little mouse, as she had called Sylvie, was warm and soft and trusting.

'No,' he said firmly. 'I'd call her, rather, a dove.' He saw her eyes widen in surprise and he thought, to your hawk, madam.

'Oh ho, ho,' Fidelma hooted. 'She's made a conquest! The little mouse has won our hero's admiration.'

245

'Don't be silly, Fidelma.' Harry's voice was gruff. Lorcan looked acutely embarrassed, as if he might at any moment apologise.

'Congrats, old friend, the best man won,' Harry said generously, clapping Lorcan on the shoulder. Fidelma looked cross. She pulled at Lorcan's pullover which hung over his shoulders.

'Come on, Lorcan. We'll be late,' she cried, nodding at Harry in dismissal and walking purposefully away, her back firmly to him.

'Have a happy life,' he called after her but she did not stop or acknowledge that she had heard.

He made his way to the kitchens at the back of the house and found Fusty dozing by the empty range. He put the kettle on, not wanting to disturb her, but she heard him and jumped appalled to her feet. 'Oh, Mr Harry! I didn't see you there! It'll be a cup of tay ye'll be wantin'.'

'Outside in the garden, Fusty please,' he said, hugging her.

'Now, now, Mr Harry, turn me loose. I'll get it for ye quick as a flash. Oh, what will ye think of me?' she cried as she worked, taking down china, pouring milk into a jug, sugar-lumps into a bowl. 'Lazy in front of the fire, God bless us, instead of bein' about my work!'

'I'd think you were being wise for once, Fusty. You never rest. Don't I know that now.'

'Isn't it grand to see Miss Cecie out an' about?' Fusty said, scalding the teapot.

Fusty had been a mother to him when his own mother died. She more than anyone had brought him up, with his father, distraught with grief, not knowing what to do.

'It is that,' Harry answered her. 'There are roses in her cheeks this day. But the roses in yours would put the real ones to shame,' he added. He always flirted shamelessly with Fusty.

'Get on with you, Mr Harry,' she chortled now, pushing him away with a delighted face. 'Out with you now and I'll bring the tay out to you presently.'

'I wish you'd let me help you.'

'An' do me out of me job? Then where'd I be?'

He put up his hands in surrender. 'All right, Fusty,

246

I give up,' he said and retraced his steps to the rose garden.

He stopped just before he came into the arbour where the girls sat, partly to take a deep breath and partly to try to still the sudden thunderous beating of his heart.

Cecie was asleep. Her eyes were closed and her head rested on the cushion Sylvie had put behind her. Her pale face looked peaceful and calm as she lay there, her breathing shallow.

'She nodded off,' Sylvie whispered. 'She's been very excited. I think it's been a tiring day for her.'

'I didn't know she could go out at all,' Harry said, whispering too.

'Well, I asked if she could and Auntie Cora gave her permission. Cecie wanted it so much.'

'So it was your doing?'

Sylvie looked diffident. 'Well I suppose . . .' She shrugged.

It was such a kind, such a considerate thing to do, so generous that Harry felt himself almost suffocate with delight in her. He was staring intently at her and she blushed again. 'I feel as if I've known you all my life,' he said abruptly.

She looked at him, eyes startled, nodding. 'Yes,' she breathed. 'Yes. I know what you mean.'

'I knew, when I saw you, when I came upon you and Cecie, I knew something had happened. Something big . . . something stupendous.'

She shivered. 'Don't say anything. Don't say . . .' Tears sprang to her eyes. 'I'm afraid. It's all too much!'

'I know. But you must not be afraid, Sylvie. Ever again. I'll see you're never harmed. I'll protect you, I promise.'

He felt like a knight of old, chivalrous and gallant. He wanted to fight dragons for her, kill giants, joust with her scarf as his banner. Above all, protect her. She stirred the best in him and made him feel strong and wise.

She was looking at him, eyes swimming. 'But I'm not worth it,' she blurted out. He had to know. 'I'm such a failure,' she told him woefully, feeling she could tell him anything, her brave little mask crumbling.

'How can you *say* that?' he asked incredulously, stung to anger at her criticism of herself. No one should criticise her, not even herself. 'Never say that. Never.'

'No one ever wanted me before,' she confided, head drooping. He must know, he must understand before he committed himself.

'I was sent away by my mother,' she told him. There was no resentment in her voice, she was just stating facts. 'My father didn't want me either. The people who took me in, they – they didn't really care about me, they did it for the money. I don't honestly think I'm worth much, Harry, and you must think carefully before . . . before . . .' Her voice broke and he crossed to the stone bench where she sat and took her in his arms, gently as if she was a wounded bird. He stroked her hair, murmuring sweetly to her, 'Oh sweetheart, don't talk like that. My mother died when I was born and I've blamed myself ever since. It's not you. It's not me. It's life. And now I've found you I'll never let you go.' He smiled down at her, tilting her chin so that she could look into his eyes. 'Do you realise that all these years, all this time, there were the two of us, wandering about without direction, without mothers, lost in this big wide wonderful world, searching, searching, and now, at last, those two lost people have met and found what they were both looking for so desperately?'

'But so quickly? How can you be sure?'

'I don't know, my love. I simply am,' he told her, then asked, 'Are you?'

She nodded. 'When I saw you, when you appeared, just there, my breath left me and I thought I'd faint.'

'Well, I'm here now to look after you,' he said.

They talked like lovers the world over, as if they'd invented the age-old words. They sat together on the stone bench and Fusty brought the tea out and her tired old eyes rejoiced at what she saw. Cecie awakened and they drank as the light mellowed and the first star appeared over the sea. They fell silent then, and when dusk crept over the land Harry picked Cecie up and carried her inside, back to her room. Fusty came and helped Sylvie to undress her.

And that night Cecie slept peacefully without waking, a smile on her pale face.

Chapter Forty-nine

❦ ❧

Cora was functioning as if in a dream. She felt she'd lost the ability to feel. She moved through the days like an automaton. When she awakened and realised quite quickly that Roddy was not there beside her she felt no alarm or confusion. It had been bound to happen.

'He's with his tart,' she said to herself, then smiled at her reflection in the mirror as she applied a light dab of rouge, blending it into her flawless skin. 'I showed her!' she murmured, then quite calmly went down to breakfast.

The girls asked for their father. They too were surprised at this change of routine, but much more surprised by her reply. 'I think he's left me, dears,' she said calmly, ignoring their shock. They thought then that she was joking, but she shook her head. Oh no! She'd tell the truth and shame the devil. She was not going to protect her unfaithful husband. The children would find out what their father was *really* like. 'Dadda has another woman, a tart,' she told them in calm tones. 'A tart that he prefers to me. I'm afraid he's left me for her.' She buttered her toast and put some marmalade on the slice then ate it with relish.

Decla was crying. Her face was white with shock. Sylvie was trying awkwardly to comfort her and to efface herself as much as possible. Only Fidelma spoke.

'I don't believe it,' she said. 'What will people say? It's ridiculous, Mother. You've lost your reason. Dadda'd never look at another woman. You're the perfect wife.' Then she rose. 'I'm sending for Ossian or Monsignor Maguire. This nonsense will have to be nipped in the bud.'

For a moment Cora felt a suffocating fear but Decla cried, 'Don't you remember, they're in Rome.' Decla's tears were slow, her sobs harsh in her breast and her lips white with fear.

249

She kept pressing her hand over her mouth as if to trap the emotion inside her. 'Oh Mother, say it's not true.'

Fidelma sat down again, glaring at Cora. 'This is a mess, Mother, and I think you'd better sort it out *immediately*.' Her voice rose shrilly. 'I'm getting *married*, Christ's sake. Dadda is *Father-of-the-Bride*! And you say he's off with some fancy woman! In God's name who is she? Anyhow I don't believe it! I don't!'

'Rosie Daly! Her name is Rosie Daly. You've seen her at the theatre and parties and such and she's a vulgar, common woman. A tart!'

Sylvie was looking with horror at her aunt. She's enjoying this, she thought. Auntie Cora is lashing out right and left and she doesn't care who she's hurting.

She thought of the air-raids in London, of the families she had shared shelters with, and how she hated the arbitrary killing, how she resented bombs dropped on children, the innocent people who were not involved in the quarrel. Consideration of other people, of their right to be happy, was to Sylvie important.

At that moment Eamonn arrived. Unconscious of the others, or of the atmosphere in the room, he bounded in, hurried to the sideboard and busily helped himself to porridge which he brought to the table and began to scoff voraciously. No one spoke and Cora sat staring into space, sipping her tea.

Fidelma suddenly flounced out of the room without a word; Sylvie signalled Decla and the two excused themselves and went upstairs.

The atmosphere finally got to Eamonn. It penetrated his preoccupation with the hut and Shannon O'Brien and he turned to his mother questioningly. 'Mother, is everything okay?' he asked.

Cora looked at him and sighed. 'I'm afraid not, Eamonn,' she told him sadly. 'Your dadda's left me!'

'Oh, is that all?' Eamonn turned with relief back to his breakfast and tackled his porridge with the enthusiasm of the very hungry.

Sylvie and Decla went to Decla's attic-room where they mulled over developments.

'If only Ossian were here,' Decla wailed. She had sobbed

her heart out and was spent. Sylvie could see she was very shocked indeed and she shivered uncontrollably every now and then.

'I don't see what good he could do,' Sylvie said sensibly. 'Are you sure it's not a storm in a tea-cup?'

'How do you mean?'

'Well, does your mum go off the handle every so often? You know, create a fuss? Some people do. I stayed with a woman like that once. Her husband always said she was a real prima donna.'

Decla shook her head. 'No. Mother's always calm as calm. And if it's not true, where is Dadda? He's never in his life missed breakfast with us.'

Sylvie sighed. 'How can you find out the truth?'

Decla's face lit up. 'I know,' she said. 'I'll phone Shannon. His uncle, Mr O'Brien, is Dadda's best friend. He's bound to know.' She stood up. 'In fact,' she said, 'I'll go to the O'Brien house and talk to Mr O'Brien. Tell him what Mother said. Ask him what he knows and what I should do.' She looked at Sylvie. 'Will you come with me?' she asked.

'Only after I've seen Cecie and made plans for this afternoon,' Sylvie told her.

They went to Cecie's room but she slept on, like a baby. Sylvie scribbled a note saying she'd gone out with Decla and would be back in time to bring Cecie down to the rose garden in the afternoon. That was if she felt up to it. Then the two girls left the house to go and see Brendan O'Brien.

They walked into Dalkey, taking the back boreens, pulling at the cow-parsley and plucking the meadow-sweet, striding through the waist-high ferns.

Brendan O'Brien's house stood just outside Dalkey, back from the road, a gracious Georgian building like so many of the houses hereabouts. It was said that what Capri was to the Roman Emperors, so Dalkey had been to the British occupiers, and Brendan's house was a relic from that past.

Delores O'Brien sat in a rocking chair outside the front door, her hair in curlers, slippers on her feet and a cheerful smile on her face. She waved to the girls as they walked towards her, a little tired now after their long trek.

'Yer welcome, yer welcome to the O'Brien residence,' she called in her flat Dublin accent. 'C'mon, sit down'n have a cup o' tay. 'Tisn't often I get visitors. Now, who is it? Sure it's Decla Flood an' a pretty little stranger.'

'Yes, Mrs O'Brien, it's my cousin from London, Sylvie.'

'Oh, yiz are from London, are ye now! Oh, an' are ye the grand one, comin' from the capital of the world?'

Sylvie shook her head, a little taken aback. 'I'm sure I'm not grand, Mrs O'Brien,' she said.

'Well, it's nice te see ye. I don't get visitors much, shunned as I am by the snobs round here. Come'n rest awhile.'

The girls could see nowhere to sit but Mrs O'Brien's help, a slattern called Betsy, emerged through the front door carrying two wicker chairs and said in a voice like a foghorn, 'These do ye?' And with a toothless grin deposited one on each side of her mistress in the rocking chair. She looked at the two girls. 'Tay?' she asked. Her legs were bare and hairy and she smelled ripely. Sylvie and Decla stared at her in awed fascination, nodding their heads.

'Okey-dokey,' she said and returned indoors.

The girls sat and looked expectantly at Delores O'Brien, who stared back at them.

'Now what can I do for ye?' Mrs O'Brien asked eventually. 'For ye didn't walk this distance te bid me the time o' day.'

'Well, it's your husband we really want to see,' Decla said.

'Well, he's not here at the mo. He's in Dublin.' Delores' eyes narrowed shrewdly. 'But if it's about yer da now, there's not much I don't know. I may not get asked out an' about but not much happens I don't get wind of eventually, sometimes sooner than later. Me an' Betsy in there.'

Decla was looking at her fingers, which she was lacing and interlacing. 'Shannon there?' she asked, trying to sound casual, glancing into the house as if trying to decipher who was there.

Delores O'Brien shook her head. 'No he's not!' she said decisively. 'An' if I were you, girl, I'd stay away from the likes of him. He's a worthless corner-boy, a real gurrier, so he is, an' it's no use puttin' on that face for me. I'll speak my mind. I know what's been goin' on between ye two. But he's no good astore, no good for ye at all.' Her voice had softened. 'Yer a lovely wee girleen an' he's not worth a farthing.' She looked at both of them a moment, at Decla's mutinous face and Sylvie's sympathetic one. 'An' yer da is with Rosie Daly in Molesworth Street. I see no reason not tellin' the truth for ye'll find out sooner or later. They were here last night, my Brendan and yer da, both of them drunk as lords. Then yer da went in this morning an' Rosie Daly discharged herself from the Mater. Yer perfect mother, Decla, beat the be-Jasus outta her. An' they went back te her place, so they did, an' now the two of them are snug as pigs in a trough.'

'I think we better go, Mrs O'Brien.' Decla's voice was very tight. Sylvie could see she was reeling with the shock of plain speaking.

Delores O'Brien saw her droop alarmingly. 'Catch her, for Gawd's sake,' she cried and grabbed Decla's arm. 'Oh Jasus, I didn't mean to upset her, God forgive me!'

Sylvie caught the other arm.

Decla was swaying like a reed in the wind and the two of them pressed her into the wicker chair. Delores O'Brien pushed Decla's head between her knees. 'It's been too much for her, the poor wee lamb,' she said. 'Sylvie love, run in an' get Betsy to bring me the brandy and some water and rags. She needs a cloth wrung out with cold water on the back of her neck and a brandy inside her.'

Decla felt the world reel about her, lurch and slide away, then swim back like a surreal nightmare. She felt the shock of the icy-cold cloth on her neck and the fiery liquid run a scorching race down into her stomach. But it was the sharp, pungent smell of Betsy's body more than anything else that brought her round, gasping, and spluttering.

'It's not true,' she cried desperately, refusing to believe these awful lies Mrs O'Brien was telling them. 'My dadda never gets drunk. My mother wouldn't hurt a fly. Shannon is lovely, a real gentleman, and Dadda would never, *never* . . .'

'Feel like some tay?' Delores O'Brien asked, and presently they were sitting in the driveway sipping tea. Delores served it in an enamel teapot and it tasted strong and reviving. It was as if Delores O'Brien still lived in a crowded slum, Decla thought, and the things she had around from that slum, much more than anything Brendan had bought her, brought her comfort.

As if she read the girl's mind Delores O'Brien said, 'I'm uncomfortable here, in this place, an' it's no good tryin' to pretend otherwise. Janey Mac, I *did* try when me an' Brendan married. I tried at first. I went all la-di-da but I was as phony as powdered eggs an' they all sussed it. It didn't work an' I miss the old neighbourhood somethin' shockin'. Not a day goes past an' I don't wish I was back.'

She was reluctant to let the girls go before Brendan returned but Decla was suddenly galvanised and demanded Rosie Daly's number in Molesworth Street. Delores O'Brien gave it to her with a philosophical shrug. 'Sure yid find it in the telephone directory easy as easy if I didn't gev it you,' she said.

They left her there in the drive, Betsy pouring herself some thick black tay then sitting in the wicker chair vacated by Decla, joining her mistress in a cuppa.

'We'll get the tram to Dublin,' Decla said to Sylvie. 'Molesworth Street's on the way.'

'You sure about this?' Sylvie asked anxiously. The perfect family her mother had talked about was disintegrating in front of her by the minute.

Decla nodded, her forehead creased in a frown. 'Yes,' she told her cousin, 'I'm very sure. I won't have a moment's peace until I know the truth.'

Chapter Fifty

୨୭ ଓ୨

They stood at the stop waiting. 'What she mean about Shannon, Sylvie?' Decla asked.

Sylvie shrugged. 'I don't know,' she replied. 'I haven't a clue.'

'Well, I don't believe her, silly old bat,' Decla decided. 'It's all lies, lies, lies. Shannon's not a gurrier.'

'I don't know what that means,' Sylvie remarked.

'It means he's no good. Oh, it's the most muddled day of my life, Sylvie.' Decla's words caught in her throat and Sylvie took her hand and squeezed it. 'I'm so glad you're with me,' she whispered to her cousin.

Sylvie was thinking of Harry. She held him in her mind tenderly, keeping him there, a precious thing, a rare and magical being so extraordinary, so dear. You are my love, she whispered over and over to him in her thoughts, you are the dearest thing, the sweetest thing, my life.

She was not afraid. It was as if after all these years she had found a part of her that had always been missing. The important part of her. She knew she would not lose him. She was quite sure of that. Decla's confusion touched her and she wanted to help her cousin. Her love for Harry had made her unselfish, had brought out more strongly her desire to help. She felt full of love and wanted everyone to be as happy as she.

They took the tram to Molesworth Street. It was dark there. The sun had moved over the rooftops and left the street in shade. The tall houses glowered at them from either side.

They found the number, entered the hall, checked the names and pressed the bell to Rosie Daly's apartment.

Decla gripped Sylvie's hand. She was suddenly terrified. Suppose her dadda was there? But it was too late now to draw back.

Rosie opened the door a crack. 'Who is it?' she asked. There was a chain on the door.

'Decla Flood. And my cousin, Sylvie.'

'Oh no!' There was anguish in the voice behind the door. 'Leave me alone, can't you? Hasn't your mother done enough damage? Just go home and leave me be.'

'Let me in, please,' Decla cried. 'I don't mean to harm you, honestly. I just need to ask you and Dadda some questions.'

'No please, Decla honey, no! Just go away. Your dadda will explain it all to you soon. He's not here now. Don't you see, it's not my place to do so.'

'Please! You owe it to me.'

There was a pause, then the sound of the chain being unhooked.

'Oh all right.' The door opened and they saw Rosie Daly's back as she walked away from them. 'Close the door behind you please. Lock it. I'm very nervous these days.'

They did as she asked, then followed her into the living-room. She sat down heavily in an armchair. In the dim light from the window they could see the damage to her face, the bruising, now purple and greenish, liver-coloured where the stitches still were. She had not had her tooth replaced yet – the dentist who had seen her in the hospital had deemed it necessary to wait until the swelling had subsided and so there was a gap at the side of her mouth. Her nose looked awful and she had one arm in a sling.

'You know, these Jimmy Cagney movies are not very realistic,' she said conversationally. 'They never show the result of a beating in all the gory detail. It takes much longer to recover in real life.'

She looked at the two young girls, their faces creased with anxiety, and her expression softened. She beckoned with her good hand for them to sit. 'Oh come closer, do. I won't bite. I haven't got rabies.'

The girls sat side by side on the old sagging sofa. Decla looked around. It was a cluttered, untidy but very comfortable room. A room you could relax in.

'I'm not offering you refreshments, girls. You're too young for strong liquor at this time of day and I haven't the energy to make you tea or coffee. I've been in too much pain to get outta this chair and bestir myself. And I haven't a servant to do it for me.'

Decla blushed. 'I could do it,' she offered, but Rosie shook her head.

'No. If you can stand doing without I'd rather,' she told her.

'I want to know,' Decla began, 'I want to know, is it true?'

Rosie Daly fixed her with her good eye. 'What exactly?'

'You and Dadda.'

'You know it's true, Decla, otherwise you wouldn't be here.'

'I don't believe it.'

'Yes you do. You don't want to but you do.' Rosie sighed then winced. Her ribs still hurt her. 'Listen, Decla, when you're young you think your parents are quite perfect. It's normal to do so.'

'Mine are!' Decla protested, then added in a whisper, 'Were.'

'No,' Rosie contradicted her, 'they are human, like everyone else in this cock-eyed world. They were never superbeings like Mr Hitler was trying to breed. It's not possible. They are just people doing their best. Your father is a dear, sweet man and . . .' How to explain? Decla's eyes were hard and hostile, yet she seemed anxious to hear what Rosie had to say. She needed an explanation. 'I'm doing my best, Decla, and I don't know all the whys and wherefores. It seems to me that your mother was *too* perfect for your dadda. I'm not saying that's a bad thing. That's simply the way it is.' She winced again. Talking still hurt. 'Your dadda felt he needed to relax. Simply that. And rightly or wrongly he did not feel he could do that at home. So he came to me.'

Decla understood. She didn't want to but she did. She knew exactly what Rosie Daly was talking about and had often felt as Rosie said her father did. Aching for a place to just unwind. A place she could be untidy in, sprawl in. But she did not want to admit it. She felt it would be disloyal to her mother to do so.

Rosie's shrewd gaze saw the girl's dilemma. 'Don't take sides, Decla,' she advised. 'There is rarely one side all bad and one side all good. Very often both sides are right and wrong all mixed up. Try to coast a while.'

'What did . . .' Decla gulped. 'Did Mother really . . . Is it true? I mean, you . . .'

'I'm afraid so, Decla. She beat me up. I'd lie to you but you'd find out the truth eventually, and I think you know already. I'm sorry about it. It's a mess. But don't blame her either. I might have done the same thing in her shoes.'

'No you wouldn't.' Sylvie spoke for the first time, and she spoke decisively. 'No. You're too relaxed, too open. You wouldn't.'

Rosie Daly looked at her keenly. 'How would you know?' she asked.

'Well, keeping up a cheerful front,' Sylvie replied. 'I'm an expert. You have to bottle things up. Not let anyone see. And then you have to break sometime. Erupt. I know – I've had to do it all my life.' Sylvie giggled, then put her hand over her mouth. 'I don't mean erupt, I mean I've had to try *not* to. When I met Auntie Cora this time I could see she was a bit like me; all tensed, all tight and churning inside and outside calm as a pond on a summer day.' She shook her head. 'Oh, I'm not explaining it very well . . .'

'I think you're doing a fine job,' Rosie said.

'Well, it's like you hold on tight, tight, tight, pretending everything is perfect and it's not. It never is! Perfect, I mean. Life is constant turmoil. That's the way of it. So then, if you go on long enough like that you have to burst sometime. You just *have* to.'

'Unless you escape to someone you can be human with,' Rosie said softly. 'Unless you can run to someone who does not expect too much of you. Decla, I love your father and I would never do anything to hurt him. But I am the "other" woman and I quite understand it if you hate me. And I want you to know this. I did not want him to leave Rossbeg. I begged him to stay at home. But he refused.' She pushed herself out of the chair with her good hand. Her face showed the pain of effort. 'Now I'd like you to go. Think about it. Don't let emotion rule you. And remember, both your parents are good people. It's the situation that stinks.'

She shepherded them to the door. 'You seem a sensible girl,' she said to Sylvie. 'Talk it over with your cousin. It will pass, her anger. Her fear.' And they were suddenly outside the door again, in the entrance hall, and they could hear the clinking of the chain as Rosie bolted the door behind them.

Chapter Fifty-one

❧ ❧

Rome was very hot but Monsignor Maguire did not mind the heat. The flowers were in bloom and the sky was a delicate blue over the Eternal City, which looked elegant and grand. He loved this city, felt at home in the place, and welcomed the warm cloak of its ancient grandeur with delight.

However, most of his time was spent in the quiet corridors of the English College or the back rooms at the Vatican where the austere Pope held council, atrophied in piety, so totally out of touch with his flock that his pronouncements often appalled the College of Cardinals and forced them to reword his encyclicals. 'He lives in a different era,' Cardinal Montecelli remarked to his friend the Monsignor. The world is very small and very dear, His Holiness was fond of saying, and the Cardinals drew back their lips over their teeth and let out their collective breath in an exasperated hiss. The world may have been small and very dear to the pious pontiff living his remote life in prayer and fasting, but the more worldly clergy watched a world devouring itself, a world endeavouring to recover from an evil so dark that no one could have believed it possible. A world that had been devastated by a war to end all wars.

At this particular moment in time they watched General MacArthur blaze away in Korea, a round-the-clock bombing programme to demoralise the communists, and although that (they thought in private) was no bad thing – communism had to be rooted out – nevertheless the loss of human life was to be deplored, the destruction condemned. An atomic bomb had created devastation in Japan on a scale never before envisioned, and wherever one looked the communists flourished and the flame of Catholicism appeared to be flickering half-heartedly. People were less fervent, less accepting of the gospels, less accepting of the dictates of the Church. People were questioning the uncompromising attitude the Vatican took to such issues as birth control, divorce, the death penalty, homosexuality and other such burning topics, and those dissatisfied were drifting away. People were now far more questioning, far less gullible. The differences between Catholics and Protestants had become less clear, a little blurred, and that too was alarming. The Church was losing power and therefore money, and steps had to be taken to stop the drain, preserve the empire.

And now Ireland, Ireland the Island of Saints and Scholars, ardent seat of Catholicism, bastion of the faith beside renegade Britain, had been divided. Six counties in the North were under Protestant sway and the Catholics there were being persecuted for their faith, their allegiance to the recently freed Eire, and they had turned to Rome for help. What could be, should be done? No one knew, so Cardinal Montecelli had sent for his dear friend Roberto Maguire for enlightenment.

As luck would have it, Roberto, who was not due to take the group of young priests from Ireland, had been asked to do so when Father Martin was taken ill, which suited the Cardinal eminently and caused him to give thanks to what was obviously God's will in this matter.

The Cardinal was a handsome man with fine dark eyes and a deep voice. He had the olive skin of his race, smooth and soft, and his eyes would melt the soul of an angel. He sipped his fine wine and glanced at the Monsignor in the chair opposite him.

The room was high-ceilinged, shaded from the southern sun by closed shutters and heavy curtains. A chandelier dark with dust was its only source of light. An exquisite tapestry hung on one wall and there were bright discoloured patches on another where two Caravaggios had once hung.

'Mussolini "borrowed" them,' the Cardinal told Monsignor Maguire. 'We don't know where they got to yet. The Americans – or more likely the Russians – have them. But we'll get them back, you see if we don't. Plundering our treasures, outrageous!'

'I understand your—'

'Roberto, Roberto my friend, what can we do about this

business in Ireland? It is ridiculous! How can a small piece of a country opt out, heh? It makes no sense.'

'You should understand it, Eminence. Your own country was divided into small kingdoms, wasn't it? Not too long ago.'

'Ah, Garibaldi! Yes, and we fought all the time. Always attacking each other. The Milanese and the Venetians don't get on, neither do the Florentines and the Romans. Oh, why do people cling so fiercely to their place of birth? Eh? Why do we have to be so territorial? It has been the cause of so much violence.'

'And yet you, Eminence, are totally Roman. I would not wish to be in your presence if the place were insulted or reviled.'

'Nor would I, my dear friend, nor would I.' The Cardinal frowned. 'I wonder what it is that makes us like this? Is it our great desire for freedom? Or is it just ignorance?' He waved his hand as if to dismiss the argument, then leaned back in his winged chair. He smiled at the Monsignor. 'Well, Roberto?'

'Sean MacBride spoke about the problem the other day . . .'

'Who? Sean who?'

'Our Minister for External Affairs in Ireland. In the Free State.' Robert Maguire frowned in concentration. Politics was not his strong point. 'He seemed to believe the unification of the Republic of Ireland was only a matter of time.'

The prelate spread his hands. 'Then what's the problem?'

'I think he is unduly optimistic,' the Monsignor said, sipping his wine. 'It is, unfortunately, not as simple as that.'

'Explain, *per favore*.'

'MacBride said, "Even among our fiercest opponents there must be men of intelligence and objectivity who realise how untenable their case is!" It was a long speech, Eminence. He said that partitionists, by denying the right of the majority rule in the case of Ireland, were challenging the whole basis on which democracy rested.'

'He is right.'

The Monsignor leaned forward in his chair. 'He said that to propose a theory of local determination as against the accepted concept of national self-determination was

262

obviously an untenable position and would provide Russia with a good justification for setting up a communist state in any district of a country where there happened to be a local communist majority.'

The Cardinal pursed his full lips and shook his head. '*Jesu, Maria,* what a terrible thought!' He glanced again at his friend. 'But what is to be done?' he asked. 'Ireland is invaluable to us. It is important that she know she is protected by us here in the Holy City.'

Monsignor Maguire spread his hands in a gesture inherited from his mother. The Cardinal smiled. It amused him to see the two sides of the younger man's character battling for supremacy. He reckoned that in Italy the Latin side won hands down. Roberto became very much Roberto and less and less Maguire.

'I don't know, your Eminence. I really don't know. The Catholics in Northern Ireland lack power and position. They have been treated badly for many years now and they are . . .' He hesitated. 'Well . . .'

'*Mamma mia,* do not be afraid to say it; they are not too well able, either financially or intellectually, to put their case eloquently? Eh?'

'Precisely! We feel that will come better from Dublin.'

'But that, in itself, might cause problems. The Republic wants to get on with its affairs. The Archbishop of Dublin John Charles McQuaid tells me—'

Monsignor Maguire frowned. 'That man is so nearly Puritan as to be—'

'Well, well, let that be. We will not speak contentiously about our servants.'

The Monsignor sensed instantly that he'd overstepped the mark and he retreated hastily. Party political niceties had to be observed. Today's Archbishop might be – God forbid! – tomorrow's Pontiff.

'I think, your Eminence, that there is a small group in Dublin utterly opposed to partition and perhaps they could be made use of . . .'

'Be made use of, yes.' The Cardinal thought a while. 'Are they, er, violent? Or reasonable men?'

The Monsignor shrugged. 'Both kinds. There's the idealistic Irishman who talks endlessly and is certainly reasonable, though passionate. There is also the man of violence. The recent history of Ireland—'

'Oh no, dear Roberto, spare me that!' The Cardinal held up his hand in a gesture of denial. Then he continued, 'You have been most helpful, my friend.'

'I've told you nothing.'

'But you have! I have a clearer picture now. So! We will dine shortly.' He leaned forward in his chair. 'But tell me, Roberto, you! How are you? In yourself? You have a strained look. You are not the relaxed man I last saw here, how long ago was it?' He pursed his lips, pressed the tips of his fingers together and touched them to his lips. 'Eh?'

'How shrewd of your Eminence. Yes. If I'm honest I have to admit that I've been under considerable tension.'

'And what tension may that be? It is not like you to allow things to upset you.'

Robert Maguire told his friend of his predicament over delicious proscuitto and melon, a little pasta and an excellent escalope of veal with fresh fruit to follow.

Over the claret the Cardinal gave his friend the benefit of his advice. 'Keep away from that family, Roberto my friend. I know you are innocent of even the most minor offence, but mud sticks. It would be fatal for even a whisper of scandal to sully your name.'

'I've regretted my lack of vision in my dealings with the Floods,' the Monsignor told the Cardinal. 'Not that I could have guessed. But at the very least I should have sensed something – oh, I don't know, in her manner perhaps – but she never betrayed by the slightest . . .'

'I know, my friend, I know. You must not blame yourself. These things happen in the best of circles.'

'And I've regretted giving in to young Ossian Flood. It was stupid of me—'

'No, Jesuitical!'

'—but at the time I could not think what else to do.'

The Cardinal shook his head. 'No. I think, on the contrary, you did the right thing. It was extraordinarily clever of you.'

The Monsignor glanced at him, surprised. 'Really, your Eminence? I thought I'd acted in a cowardly fashion.' He was rinsing his fingers in the silver bowl provided and he looked enquiringly at the Cardinal. The bowl was half full of water and there were rose petals floating on the top. His fingers had been sticky from the apricots and white peaches they were eating.

The Cardinal was dissecting a ripe peach with the precision of a surgeon, nodding his head judiciously. 'Yes, wise. It prevented any precipitate action on the part of the young man. You certainly do not want him telling lies all over Dublin, and he sounds as if discretion is not his greatest attribute.'

'You may take my solemn, most sacred word for it, your Eminence, that there is absolutely no truth whatsoever in what he proposed to accuse me of.'

The Cardinal smiled. 'Of course, my dear fellow, I know that. Besides, if you were doing something of that sort, you are far too clever to let anyone find out. But as I have already said, mud sticks. You leave this young cleric to me. Bring him to me tomorrow. He is ambitious, you say?' The Monsignor nodded. 'Good. I'll let him know you were very frank with me and that I put no credence in his accusations. I'll give him to understand that if he plays those kinds of games he'll jeopardise any hope he has of advancement. I'll see to that personally. That should give him something to think about, no?' He glanced at his friend under his bushy brows and the Monsignor could not read the expression there. It was as enigmatic as the eyes in the portrait above the mantelpiece behind them.

'And, Roberto?'

'Yes, Eminence?'

'I think it is time we called you to Rome. I think you would adorn the Vatican and the Holy See would benefit from your presence.'

The Monsignor felt his heart beat warmly in joy beneath his jacket. He felt a surge of delight at the prospect so close to his heart. 'Thank you, your Eminence. I would like that very much indeed.'

The Cardinal stood. The meeting was over. He would work far into the night. '*Addio*, my friend,' he said, then as the Monsignor bent and kissed the prelate's ring he laid a hand on the Monsignor's head. '*Jesu Christo* be with you, dear boy.' And he turned and left the Monsignor alone in the ornate room. The Monsignor permitted himself a whoop of excitement at the prospect he had so long desired at last becoming a reality.

Chapter Fifty-two

෧෧ ஓෲ

Cardinal Montecelli sat next day in the same crimson winged chair he had the day before. Ireland was giving him a headache. He could think of absolutely nothing to do about the orange North and the Catholics there. If there was any way of avoiding the whole issue he would gladly have shrugged it away, but unfortunately this was not possible. Roberto had certainly helped him to understand the situation but he needed to take some positive action, set things in motion, however trivial that motion was. The powers that be had posed the question in the first place and they needed a report. They needed to be assured that action was being taken, that the matter was in capable hands, his hands, then they could all forget about it for a while, perhaps forever. Politics were notoriously fickle. Today's prime minister was tomorrow's outlaw and vice versa.

He would be uncomfortable getting into bed with the men of violence. The Vatican had been in enough trouble over the fascists (his mind slid away from that whole topic very quickly) so one had to be careful. On the other hand, if he could delegate responsibility to someone else, he could also apportion blame if power was misused. After all, he could not be held responsible in the event that another blundered.

There was a knock on the door, which he was expecting. He called, '*Avanti!*' and Father Sylvestre, his secretary, ushered a young man in. He had told Father Sylvestre to make the whole process as formal and intimidating as possible. Father Sylvestre, used to setting the scene for the Cardinal, understood perfectly.

Ossian Flood crossed the crimson carpet and the silken Oriental rugs that were older than the Vatican itself. It was a long walk and the previous day the Cardinal had met the Monsignor halfway. Now he did not stir and allowed the young man to march up to his chair across the vast expanse.

The Cardinal had to admire the young man's aplomb. He was certainly nervous, the Cardinal could see, but he held himself tall and obviously had his tension under control.

Watching him from under half-closed lids his Eminence saw he was a beautiful creature, but his eyes revealed his ambition, his cunning. This he had not yet learned to hide. His charm, the Cardinal decided, was, like all charm, superficial. Yes, the boy might be useful.

The Cardinal did not stand in greeting. He did not reveal his interest by the flicker of an eyelash.

Oh, he was so young, the Cardinal thought. How wonderful to be that young, that beautiful. Then he remembered that the young did not appreciate their youth. They were in such a hurry to mature. Greedy to 'get there', wherever 'there' was.

Ossian Flood stood before the older man and proffered his hand, but the Cardinal did not take it. Instead he held his hand out with his ring hanging heavily on his third finger, letting it droop over the arm of the chair so the boy had to kneel to kiss it. He then waved his visitor wordlessly to the chair opposite. Ossian, a little put out for he was used to his good looks and charm having an instant effect, turned and sat in the chair.

The Cardinal allowed him to sit there a while in silence. He could feel the young man's tension rise. Still, the Cardinal had to admit Ossian did a very good job of not showing it. The Cardinal continued to watch him covertly, then when he deemed it the right moment he announced, 'Well, young man. I have to tell you that I am not at all pleased with you.'

This took Ossian by surprise and he gasped aloud, but the Cardinal held up his hand. 'No, no. Hear me.' He settled back comfortably and scrutinised the boy closely. 'Yesterday,' he said, 'my dear friend, Monsignor Maguire sat in that very chair you are sitting in now.' He had to admire the young man. Except for a tightening of his jaw he gave no signs of alarm. He had been summoned here to these impressive apartments, he did not know why, into the august presence of His Eminence Cardinal Montecelli, he knew not what for, and was greeted with an unfriendly reception and an admonition, yet he was keeping his cool impressively.

'The Monsignor is a dear old friend of mine,' the Cardinal repeated. 'Perhaps you did not know that? The Monsignor has a lot of friends in high places.' He allowed that fact to sink in, then went on, 'He told me some things about you that alarmed me, I must say. He confided to me the terrible blackmail you subjected him to.' He turned the full force of his piercing eyes on Ossian and for the first time the boy showed discomposure and fear. The Cardinal's gaze had frightened more powerful and mature men and the import of his words astonished the young priest. He had certainly not expected the Monsignor to have discussed this sensitive subject with anyone as powerful as the Cardinal.

The trouble with youngsters like Ossian, the Cardinal reflected, watching the conflict in the boy's face, was that they were so inexperienced in sin and deception and they foolishly imagined that everyone would react and behave as they themselves would in the same situation. And because they themselves were guilty they could not foresee an innocent man's reaction. Could not imagine how he would behave. So Ossian Flood was nonplussed by the Monsignor's confiding to an old friend something that might damage him. Ossian himself, the Cardinal understood, would never trust anyone that far, even if he was innocent.

'He wanted to reassure himself that your vocation was, er, shall we say, sincere. In the light of the circumstances.' Then the Cardinal smiled. It was a shark-like smile and he had often used it to disconcert malcontents. The smile and the sudden piercing stare that followed would alarm a saint, and the young man before him was far from that. He showed distinct signs of disintegrating. He was swallowing hard and there was colour now in his pale cheeks, two bright hectic spots. But he remained silent and that showed courage and wisdom.

'You see, Father Flood, Monsignor Maguire has no secrets from me. He told me everything.' He glanced again at the young priest, who was biting the inside of his lip. 'He has been worried about your, well, let us call a spade a spade, your slander. And the fact that he was going to be accused of things he had never done if he refused to take you to Rome. Remember, Father Flood, I know Monsignor Maguire very well indeed and he is, pardon the expression, a genuinely holy man, something I doubt very much you'd understand.' He folded his hands and allowed his face to soften. 'Now, what's to be done about you, young man? That is the thing. Monsignor Maguire has nothing but good to say about you otherwise and he blames a lot of your reprehensible behaviour on the situation with your mother.' He saw Ossian's eyes widen. 'Oh yes, my son, when I say he told me everything that is exactly what I mean. Well, Monsignor Maguire has recommended leniency, though why he should is beyond me.' He was rewarded by a dawning of hope in the young priest's eyes. 'After all, up to now, according to the Monsignor your conduct has been impeccable.' He watched Ossian, trying to detect contrition, but all he could see was relief. He continued, 'So I have, on consideration, decided to give you the opportunity to undo your ill-advised actions.' He held up his hand again although this time Ossian Flood showed no inclination to speak. 'I was going to send you home in disgrace, but I have thought the better of it. Now, before you say anything, there are certain conditions. It is very foolish, young man, to flirt with the Devil. The Devil is at a disadvantage when up against the Holy Roman Catholic Church and we tend to beat him every time. You would do well to remember that. Whatever path you take is, in general, the one you will become unable to leave.' He looked at Ossian again. 'You must apologise to the Monsignor. Pray to God for the humility to make it a sincere repentance. You are, after all, Father, supposed to be a holy man too, never forget that. Using devious methods to get your own way will inevitably lead you into trouble, from which it is often impossible to extricate oneself. I do assure you of that. And,' he continued, 'and, I want you, when you return to Dublin, to do a little, er, shall we say, research for me.' He tapped the side of his nose with his finger. 'A secret between ourselves.'

He pondered a moment, gauging how much the young man should be told, and decided there was nothing to be lost by being frank. 'The Vatican is interested in trying to help the Catholic minority in Northern Ireland. So, fitting in with your duties, of course, I would be grateful if you would keep your eyes and ears open and let me know how feelings are running in Dublin vis-à-vis the Catholics in the North. See what you can find out. Let me know, discreetly of course. I trust your tact.'

Ossian had been too taken aback by the swift turn of events to say anything at all and now the Cardinal rose and Ossian, following his lead, stood too.

'You may write to me here. Send me a report.' He rang the small silver bell on the table beside his chair and Father Sylvestre instantly appeared. The Cardinal held out his hand, palm down once more and Ossian bowed and bent and kissed the ring. The Cardinal made the sign of the cross over the boy's head. '*In Nomine Patris, et Filii, et Spiritus Sancti. Amen.* Now go in peace, young man, and remember the apology. And my words.'

The Cardinal turned his back, saying, 'Father, show Father Flood out, if you please,' and, walking to the window, pulled open the slats of the shutters and looked out over the lush green of the Vatican gardens. He heard the door close behind Father Flood and he sighed in contentment. He could tell the college that the matter was in hand. He had a young Irish priest investigating. On the spot. Excellent. The ball was in Ossian's court. The boy was far too blinded by ambition to realise that success or failure would now be put down to him. The Cardinal was no longer responsible.

He saw the young man emerge from the building below him. He watched as Ossian lifted his face to the sun, blinking rapidly in the glare, then turned and walked purposefully away.

He sees himself the victor, the Cardinal ruminated ruefully. He is imagining himself Special Emissary to the Vatican, in charge of Irish Affairs, confidant of His Eminence Cardinal Montecelli. He has, in his own estimation, check-mated, trumped us all. I have a friend in high places, he is telling himself, and I work for him. I will go far. Mission accomplished. Journey to Rome a success.

The Cardinal shivered. There was evil in not being more severe with the boy, allowing him off the hook because he would be more useful working for the Cardinal in the knotty problem of the Irish situation.

The prelate shook his head. Ossian was disappearing in the crowd. Poor foolish boy, he did not realise that he was expendable.

It was when he rang the bell again to let Father Sylvestre know he was ready for his next appointment that he realised he had not heard the boy speak and he wondered how his voice sounded. Ah well, it was of no consequence. He did not think Rome would be bothered any more by the young priest's presence. Certainly the Cardinal had no intention of ever seeing Ossian Flood again.

Chapter Fifty-three

❧ ❧

Ossian left the offices on light feet. Nothing had worked out as he had planned but the end result was better than he had expected. The Cardinal had asked him to spy for Rome. That was what it amounted to. It was a triumph!

He had had some nasty moments in there, moments when his heart was in his throat and his stomach felt sick. The worst moments of his life. Worse even than when the Monsignor had told him he was not taking him to Rome.

Who would have thought that the Monsignor would tell the Cardinal everything? The Cardinal might not have believed that he was innocent. No smoke without fire. Ossian knew that *he* would never have risked it. But the Monsignor had told the Cardinal everything and had also recommended clemency. That seemed ridiculous to Ossian. Daft.

So Monsignor Maguire was not vindictive. Ossian would never have believed he could be so generous. *Nobody* was that generous. The older man's magnanimity astonished him. He would never have forgiven or forgotten if their situations had been reversed. Ossian decided that Robert Maguire was a fool and that he Ossian had benefited from that stupidity.

The next day he and the Monsignor left Rome for Dublin. They were on their way home. Ossian did not know why the Monsignor did not attempt conversation with him but instead of being embarrassed during the almost totally silent journey Ossian was glad he did not have to make conversation, did not have to step carefully through the minefield of subjects too dangerous to discuss. The problem with intrigue, Ossian decided, was that it curtailed spontaneity.

When they reached Collinstown they separated and Ossian, anxious to speak to his mother and sound her out about

273

the Monsignor, went directly to Rossbeg. Monsignor Maguire had been invited to spend a few days in the Archbishop's palace in Drumcondra to deliver his report from the Holy See. He was just as glad not to go home to the Abbey and instead stay a while with a dear old friend in the Archbishop's service. Being anywhere near Rossbeg at the moment was acutely distasteful to the priest, and as well as feeling a deep revulsion towards Ossian Flood and his mother he knew too that it would be tactless and could indeed be dangerous to remain in contact with that family. He knew that he needed to rid himself in prayer and meditation of any preoccupation with the Floods, as such thoughts often led to obsessive concentration on the very people one wanted to put out of one's mind. He did not want to invite Ossian and Cora to take up residence in his head, come between him and his breviary, hover over his thoughts and intrude in his sleep. He wanted them out of his brain.

He would, he knew, soon be leaving Ireland for Rome permanently and he was glad of this, not only because he could escape the Floods, but because his Italian blood called, had been calling for a long time now and this visit had whetted his appetite. He would take his mother with him. She ached for her home, the sun, the bright flowers, the Italian way of life. Although the Monsignor was quite content in Ireland the Italian part of him longed for the heat and the ancient beauty of Rome and his bright intelligence desired nothing more than an opportunity to work in the Vatican. There was corruption there as there always was near any seat of power and he longed to join the forces of good to battle with the evil, to take up the cudgels of right against the peddlers of greed, ambition and corruption.

He waved to Ossian and left him there to make his own way into Dublin as he hurried to the car waiting to take him to the Archbishop's palace. He had not told Ossian where he was headed and it amused him, in spite of himself, to see the young man stare with alarm at the large, luxurious limousine awaiting the Monsignor. He could almost hear the boy's consternation as the jumbled thoughts of the guilty clamoured in his brain. Would the Monsignor talk to others as well as the Cardinal? Would he be sent down in disgrace? Where was the Monsignor going? Had he, Ossian, done the wrong thing? Put his trust in the wrong person? It would always be like that for the boy and the Monsignor felt a pang of sorrow for him. Then he turned his face towards the verdant countryside and thought that he would miss this country too when he went to Italy. He reflected that the problem with parents of different nationalities was this divided loyalty. The feeling that when in Ireland he missed his Italian heritage and vice versa in Rome. But he'd spent a great many years here and he knew he could carry the beauty in his head and heart, and he knew too that he could visit. He smiled to himself and thought how lucky he was.

Ossian went home to Rossbeg, his mind full of questions about his mother. What exactly had happened between her and the Monsignor? He sensed that nothing physical had taken place; the Monsignor's behaviour was that of an innocent man and, reluctant as Ossian was to accept that fact, he grudgingly had to accept it as the truth. But he was curious to know what had passed between them, for of a surety *something* had.

And then, he decided, he'd be about the Church's business. He'd have to find out where the IRB meetings were held, what was happening on that front. He would send the Cardinal in Rome a report both comprehensive and detailed and the Cardinal would be astonished.

He got a bus to the Pillar. The Monsignor had had that huge car waiting for him at the airport and Ossian wondered why he had not been offered a lift. Surely it would have been polite? After all, he had apologised. It had been a mumbled apology on the plane, but he *had* apologised.

He boarded the Dalkey tram and went upstairs to the top deck. A couple of girls impressed by his good looks scanned him with flashing eyes across the aisle but, catching sight of his collar, dissolved into disappointed giggles.

He got out at Dalkey and walked to Rossbeg in the heat, carrying his bag and thinking longingly of tea and scones and Fusty's ginger cake.

Chapter Fifty-four

❧ ❧

Ossian found his mother in her room. Or rather the room she shared with Roddy. Or had, up to now.

She looked at her son with tragic eyes as he entered and without greeting him or asking him how his trip had been she told him in dramatic tones, 'He's left me!'

'Who, Mother?' Ossian was confused. He had arrived, worn out from the journey, looking for answers and tea and ginger cake, only to find Cora wild-eyed, talking nonsense.

'Dadda!' she said.

Ossian stared at her as if she'd taken leave of her senses, which was exactly the reaction she desired.

'Holy Mother of God! You're not serious, are you?'

'I'm perfectly serious, Ossian, and I want you to tell me what to do. You are the man of the house now.'

He could not believe his ears. 'Mother,' he said, 'let us talk this over calmly.'

'I'm perfectly calm, Ossian dear,' she replied. 'I just don't know exactly what to *do*! After all, I have no experience of this, none at all. This sort of thing doesn't happen to nice people.'

'You mean,' he said, struggling to make some kind of sense out of this latest bombshell, 'you mean to say *Dadda* has *left* you?'

She nodded, her eyes calm but tragic. 'That's what I'm trying to tell you, Ossian.'

'Because you had an affair with Monsignor Maguire?'

Perhaps the priest was guilty after all, and Ossian thought with admiration that perhaps the Monsignor was a bluffer of gigantic proportions. But his mother stared at him incredulously. 'An affair? With the Monsignor? Are you mad? *I've* never had an affair with anyone in my life! Are you insane, Ossian? How dare you speak to me like that. I'm your mother.'

Ossian was thrown. He felt like Alice in Wonderland when everything turned out wrong and the familiar became weird.

'Then why did Dadda leave? Tell me that.'

Cora rose and went to the window. She could see below her Cecie and cousin Sylvie sitting in her rose garden. Harry Devereau was chatting with them. He was, she reflected, probably making an attempt to see Fidelma and win her back. Cora was still bemused by her daughter's choice of fiancé.

Ossian was striding up and down behind her in the room, talking *at* her nineteen to the dozen, and she wondered what had gone wrong between Fidelma and Harry and why she hadn't asked her daughter about it. She had not been able to work up any curiosity about her children's affairs recently where once they had been her main concern. She filed a note in her head to rectify that as soon as possible. Cecie looked very tired, she saw, and decided that perhaps her daughter should spend tomorrow in her room resting. Too much too soon was not a good idea and she could go out the next day.

'Mother, I simply do not understand.' Ossian came and stood beside her at the window but he did not notice the little group below, so intent was he on what he was saying. Cora was suddenly and unexpectedly irritated with her eldest.

Monsignor Maguire, she reflected, would never lose his composure in the way Ossian was doing now. He was almost jumping up and down with impatience. Her son was a priest, after all, and should behave like one. The Monsignor *always* behaved like a priest.

She had censored their last meeting ruthlessly. It had been eradicated almost entirely, blotted out. It was the only way she could keep her sanity. In her mind nothing had happened. She'd said something inappropriate and he'd misunderstood. That was the whole of it. It was almost as if she'd been drunk then, suffering from delusions, and she'd explain it all to him sometime in the future, when she got around to it. He'd apologise and say he'd got the wrong idea, oh dear, how silly!

She had not, however, censored her meeting with Rosie

Daly, and every moment of that incident was clear in her mind. She felt detached from it though, as if she had a split personality. And she felt that terrified, guilty thrill that children get when they do something forbidden that they nevertheless enjoy.

'Rosie Daly,' she said now to stop Ossian babbling. 'He's left me for Rosie Daly.'

She did not know why she was so certain of this. Roddy had not been in communication with her since the incident. True, he had never before spent a night away from her, but one night and a day did not constitute *leaving* forever and he had not collected his clothes or told her what he was up to. But she knew. She knew Roddy. When he found out it was she who had, well, done that to Rosie Daly, and he would find out, fatalistically she knew that, he would never come home again. Never. Roddy would not be able to look her in the face. She knew that as certainly as she knew the sun would rise in the East and set in the West tomorrow.

'You are joking, Mother? You *must* be joking,' Ossian was spluttering. Oh, why couldn't he be calm, rational and sophisticated and not so emotional? Help her masterfully to sort this mess out? Instead he was letting her down, behaving like a child.

'I don't joke about things like this, Ossian,' she told him coldly. 'I thought you'd know that. I wish you'd stop behaving like a spoiled brat and give me some good advice.'

'Mother! You tell me Dadda is having an affair with Rosie Daly and expect me to stay calm? I'm not made of stone, Mother, not like you! You cannot *thrust* this piece of information on me and expect me to remain calm.'

'Oh look. Harry is kissing Sylvie! How odd! I thought he wanted to marry Fidelma. Oh well, now she's engaged to Lorcan I expect he's looking around for the nearest candidate. I know his father is very anxious to see him settled, and wouldn't that be perfect! He'd be in the family. I've always wanted a union between—'

'*Mother!*' Ossian shouted.

But Cora was not really listening. 'Go down, Ossian, and get Cecie up. The day is drawing out and I think she should come back up to her room.'

Ossian glanced down. Harry had his arm around Sylvie's

waist and he lifted a strand of hair tenderly from her face and pushed it back behind her ear. Then they both looked at Cecie and the three of them laughed. Harry bent down and lifted Cecie with care and began to walk towards the house, Sylvie following.

'They seem to be managing all right without me,' he said. He was not interested in Harry Devereau and Sylvie or, at the moment, Cecie.

'Mother, we'll call a family meeting,' he announced.

'Oh no, Ossian. I don't think that's necessary,' she protested. She did not want the incident with Rosie Daly to come out and it might if they all talked about it together.

'I insist, Mother. You asked me to help, well I'm helping. After dinner tonight we'll have a family gathering and talk this through,' he said decisively. 'You. Me. Fidelma and Decla. I think we ought to leave Cecie and Eamonn out of it. Oh, and Sylvie. It is, after all, none of her business.'

Cora opened her mouth to protest but he held up his hand. 'No, Mother. I won't listen to arguments. You owe it to us. This whole situation is grotesque and you and Father will have to be made to see reason.'

'But—'

'No buts, Mother. I won't hear another word now. We'll talk this thing through after dinner and that's an end to it.'

Chapter Fifty-five

❧ ❧

Ossian and Cora were not the only ones to witness the kiss in the garden. Fidelma, looking through the window on her way out, saw it too and froze in fury where she stood.

It was not a passionate kiss that Sylvie and Harry exchanged; not at all like the hot kisses Lorcan planted on her eager mouth, pushing his tongue between her teeth; French kissing, they called it and it was supposed to be a mortal sin. What angered her was the reverence inherent in Harry's attitude to her cousin. It was visible even at this distance, a gentle tenderness, as if he worshipped her. Fidelma watched, jealous and miserable, frustrated because she knew she could not *force* him, or anybody, to be like that with her. Tears sprang to her eyes and for a moment her guard dropped. 'Oh Harry! Harry!' she whispered, then drawing the back of her hand across her eyes she murmured, 'How *dare* he! It's not right! She's a scarecrow.' And she ran down the steps to where Lorcan was waiting, revving up the sports car's engine.

Harry was the first thing in her life that she'd wanted and could not have. She did not use logic, did not think it through, how'd she'd feel, really feel if she got him. She fed her resentment with irrational but to her conclusive reasons why Harry must not, as she put it, be allowed to make a fool of himself. Sylvie was not at all suitable for him. She would not fit in, would be an outsider, and eventually Harry, like Brendan O'Brien, would have to go places alone, leave her at home. Sylvie with her mended clothes, her lack of sophistication, would be a burden to poor Harry. She would not know how to run a house like Montpellier, wouldn't have a clue how to give dinner parties. Oh, she'd drag him down – if only he could see. Fidelma would have to *do* something to show

Sylvie that it was not at all the thing. She could not, just now, sitting beside Lorcan, the wind blowing her hair back, think of a way, but she would. She jolly well would. She'd bide her time and an opportunity would eventually present itself.

The lovers strolled together under the trees. They did not say much to each other; they did not need to. Their silence was full of thoughts communicated. They looked and their looks were eloquent and melting and said much more than mere words could. They were not excessively passionate; more romantic. Harry felt chivalrous and noble, and Sylvie was filled with the kind of trust and dependency she had ached for all her life but had been denied.

'Oh my love, my angel, my dearest one,' he whispered in her ear, the tendrils of her hair tickling his nose. She tucked her hand further into his, snuggled close to him. He had become, in so short a time, her world. She had unhesitatingly given him her heart, her hopes, and her dreams. Up to now life had held little promise. Moved from one place to the other, plucked from every environment she had stayed in, she knew at last she had come to rest.

Everything conspired to bless them. Cora, who would normally have been a serious stumbling block and would certainly have meddled, was otherwise occupied. Roddy, who would have been concerned, was not there. And Harry's father was only too happy his son was at last showing a decided interest in someone other than Fidelma Flood.

Chapter Fifty-six

❧ ❧

Dinner that night at Rossbeg was a sorry affair. At first the
girls were delighted to see their brother safely returned from
Rome and welcomed him enthusiastically.

'Oh Ossian, so soon!' Fidelma cried happily. 'We didn't
expect you back just yet.'

'What the devil do you mean, so soon?' Ossian to everyone's
surprise bit her head off. He smarted from the reminder that
of course he should have stayed in Rome longer and but for
the Monsignor he would have. The Monsignor and that
awkward business. 'I do as I'm *told*, Fidelma, you know that.
I'm a priest after all.'

Fidelma, taken aback, looked hurt and bewildered but
Ossian made no effort to smooth things over.

'What's the matter with you, Ossian?' Decla asked, astonishing her mother by adding, 'You really shouldn't speak to
Fidelma like that. It isn't fair.'

'I'll talk to her how I like,' Ossian further astonished them
all by snapping and Cora said, 'You sound like Eamonn,
Ossian, you really do. Please sit and try to control your
tongue.'

He was brusque and short-tempered through dinner,
which was a relatively silent meal. Cora could not help
thinking that all these years she had underestimated Roddy's
good-humoured influence on his family.

Surprised by Ossian's unusual crustiness, they drifted
into contemplation of their own concerns, hardly speaking at all.

It was not a comfortable silence. Sylvie felt it most. Always
sensitive to atmosphere, always fearful of other's moods,
for so often she had suffered if her guardians became
irritated, she sat self-effacing as usual, praying for the meal

to end. Fidelma was totally preoccupied with her forthcoming wedding and her thoughts were not joyful. She was agitated about what would happen if the Father-of-the-Bride was not available on the great day.

Decla was hashing and re-hashing the interview with Rosie Daly in her head. She felt torn and raw from the violence of the war within her. She liked and believed Rosie, knew deep down she was an honest person and she could see exactly why her father would need so soft, so relaxed and understanding a woman to escape the rigid discipline of his home-life. And yet, and yet she *hated* her with a fierce intensity, her whole being revolted against her father's disloyalty and carnality. Her idols had come crashing down at her feet. Cora and Roddy. Mother and Dadda, their images never to be mended.

Eamonn chewed and wondered how he could get Ossian alone and in a better mood. Ossian was *never* bad-tempered, yet tonight when Eamonn needed his big brother's advice Ossian, completely out of character, was being foul to everyone. Eamonn couldn't understand it. He wished grown-ups were more like the boys in school; like Martin Metcalf. You could *tell* with them. They said they were your friend; they'd be true to the death. Not blow hot and cold. Grown-ups had *moods*. They were, to say the least, inconsistent. All this rubbish about his dadda. He knew it was nonsense. Absolute twaddle. But his mother and sisters were turning it into World War Three.

His dadda, Eamonn knew, would never leave them. Not in a million years. His dadda would go away for a while, like he and Martin did, escape from it all, but he'd come back. Definitely.

His mother was *up there*. Like God, far away. Oh, she was present physically, but she was a deity above all else. He never *talked* to his mother, not really. She kissed him good morning and good night and talked *at* him. Gave him orders, instructions what to do and not to do. She was beautiful and good like the Saints. But Dadda was human. And it was Dadda he loved.

After dinner Ossian asked Sylvie rather abruptly to leave them. Decla protested, 'Oh, but her coffee . . .' but Ossian was firm. 'This is family business, Decla,' he told her, so obediently Sylvie hurried out and left them. Truth to tell, she was relieved. A family squabble or even a heated discussion filled her with fear and dread and she was only too happy to escape.

Fusty brought coffee into the drawing-room. She had been crying. Decla stared at her red eyes, a worried frown on her forehead. Fusty never cried.

Cora poured the coffee.

'Would you like a liqueur, Ossian? It's quite an Italian thing, is it not? To serve a liqueur after a dinner with the coffee?'

Ossian looked at his mother in disbelief. 'Are you quite mad, Mother?' he asked. 'Our whole world crumbling around us and all you can talk about is serving a liqueur!'

'Ossian, in polite society people do not shout,' Cora stated quietly.

'Dadda will be back all right,' Eamonn piped up. 'You don't have to worry . . .'

'Eamonn darling, of course Dadda will be back.' Cora held her son's hand and smiled down on him, then raised her eyes and glared at the assembly. 'Now you see what you've done!' she admonished. 'Up to bed with you, Eamonn. Off you go with Fusty. She'll help you.'

Eamonn in turn glared at his mother. 'I don't *need* Fusty to help me,' he protested. 'I was hoping that Ossian would . . .'

But his big brother was in no mood to pay attention to his requests. 'Get on with you, Eamonn. Off you go. Let the grown-ups talk.'

They'd squabble and bicker and solve nothing, Eamonn thought, and worried about who he could tell about Shannon O'Brien and his gun and his visits to the hut in the woods. He was not going to tell Ossian, that was for sure. He sighed and left the room.

'I preach about the sanctity of marriage all the time, Mother . . .' Ossian began as the door closed behind Eamonn.

'But you don't actually know anything about it, do you?' Decla asked reasonably. 'It's easy to lecture about stuff that you're not and never will be involved in.'

'I think you've all run insane.' Ossian looked around at them as if they were strangers.

Only Fidelma nodded, agreeing with him. 'Ossian's right, Mother. It can't go on. You and Dadda'll have to patch things up.'

Cora spread her hands, a helpless expression on her face. 'But, darlings, you don't seem to understand. It's Dadda who's left. I'm here! I told you. Dadda's having an affair with Rosie Daly and *he* has left *me*. What can I do about that?'

'Apologise to Rosie,' Decla said firmly and loudly. They all looked at her in amazement.

'*Apologise!* To Rosie Daly?' Ossian breathed, then let out a sibilant sigh of disbelief. 'Now I *know* you're nuts! Mother apologise to that whore? That adulteress? Good God, Decla, what are you dreaming of?'

'Only that I don't think you know the whole truth, Ossian, and I think you're being narrow-minded and sanctimonious and I hope I never have to go to you to confession. You can't see the wood for the trees.'

Fidelma looked from Decla to her mother and back again. 'What is she talking about, Ossian? Do you know something we don't? I don't understand any of this.'

'It's just that . . .' Decla was about to tell them of her visit to Rosie when she caught her mother's glance. There was such pleading there, such anguish, that Decla floundered. With her mother looking at her like that, eyes begging, all the words Decla ached to say, all the accusations, all the questions evaporated and she was struck dumb.

Ossian had seen the entreaty in his mother's eyes too, and he had seen Decla's response. He took over now, suddenly becoming calm and masterful. 'All right. That's enough waffle. We have to get our father home. That's the nub of the whole thing.'

Fidelma breathed, 'Oh yes. Please let's get Dadda back.'

'I'll deal with Dadda.' Ossian rose. 'I'll talk to him tomorrow, make him see reason.'

'Thank you, Ossian.' Cora sighed in relief. She had kept very quiet since her silent plea to Decla for she had realised with icy horror that Decla was going to blurt out what she had done to Rosie Daly. What would her children think of her then? It contradicted everything she had ever taught them, everything she stood for. Dignity. Control. And most of all, consideration and politeness.

But the crisis had been averted and for that Cora gave thanks, and, after all, in spite of his ill-humour Ossian was going to take charge. He would bring his father back. He had the Church behind him. Roddy would see reason.

After all, Ossian was a priest.

Chapter Fifty-seven

❧ ❧

Sylvie stood by the window of Cecie's room for a moment before she closed the shutters. It was a stilly night, moon-bathed and starry. The scents of the garden rose to her nostrils in a heavenly bouquet and she drank in the beauty all around her, resting for a little while in this peaceful moment. It was a habit she had acquired over the years: grasping the beauty of the here and now when available, for inevitably it would be snatched away from her. She had to rely on her store of memories for sustenance. This too might be snatched from her in spite of her prayers, for the family seemed headed for disaster, no matter how optimistically she tried to view the situation.

A black swan flew across the silver moon and Sylvie caught her breath at its grace.

Then she heard her name, like a whisper in the leaves, and leaning out she saw Harry Devereau below her, his face lit by the moonbeams and turned upward to her.

'Sylvie. Sylvie. It's me. Can you come down?'

She put her fingers to her lips and nodded. Glancing over her shoulder she saw that Cecie was asleep, mouth a little open, hands relaxed and curled on the counterpane, lashes motionless on her cheeks. Dr Sutton had pronounced his reluctant approval of the new treatment. 'Well, it's not harming her,' was his considered opinion. 'She's not had a relapse and the tuberculosis is not rampaging through the Flood household.'

Sylvie gently removed a pillow she had propped Cecie up with and let the girl's head drop smoothly back. She would sleep better that way. She closed the curtains and tiptoed out of the room, glancing back before she left to make sure every-thing was all right. Then she slipped silently downstairs.

She could hear them arguing in the drawing-room. Ossian's voice was loudest and most incisive.

Everyone talked about Ossian, Fidelma and Cora with awe and admiration, and Sylvie, though she did not dislike the two elder cousins and her aunt, found there was little to admire in them. She found in Decla and Cecie a generosity of spirit not visible in their exquisite mother, brother or sister, who seemed to Sylvie self-obsessed and selfish.

She hurried past the drawing-room and the angry voices emerging from behind the closed doors and let herself quietly out of the house.

Running across the lawn to Harry her heart thundered and a well of joy rose in her. Her vision was blurred and when she came to rest in his arms she was breathless.

'Oh, my darling,' he whispered, his lips in her hair. 'Oh my little dove.'

'Oh, I'm not! I'm not, Harry. I'm an ordinary person really, Harry. You'll be so disappointed in me. I know.'

'I've told you not to talk like that,' he admonished gently. 'Don't put yourself down. When you do that you put me down too.'

She pulled her head back, the better to see him. 'Oh no, Harry, I'd never do that.'

'Well you do. If you are terrible and I've chosen you,' he laughed, 'then it seems I have no taste.'

'Oh, that's not true! You have the best taste in the world!'

'Then? See? Oh, my dear one.' They laughed. 'See. My taste is impeccable.'

'You really love me, Harry?' she asked him, looking up at him. She had put on her smile, that smile that she'd been told was necessary if she wanted anyone to like her. 'Do it with a smile or you won't eat!' 'Smile, dear, or the lady won't want to have you to stay.' It was a heart-breaking and arid smile, a mechanical stretching of her mouth.

'You don't have to look like that for me,' Harry told her. 'It's the only thing I don't like you to do.'

Then he pressed his thumbs gently across her mouth, wiping the smile away. 'There's my lovely girl,' he said, kissing her nose. 'Now come with me. I've got someone I want you to meet.'

'Now?' she questioned anxiously, fearfully resisting him. If it was a test, she would fail, she knew she would. 'You want me to meet someone who has got to like me before you do?' she asked.

He stopped for a moment and looked at her very seriously. 'I *love* you,' he said simply. 'No matter what. I love you.' Then he pulled her along behind him. 'Come on, sweetheart, come with me.'

She was apprehensive in spite of his assurances. She was used to being rejected. Who was she to meet in this patched and mended dress, her hair untidy? She asked him again, calling to him anxiously, but Harry just ploughed on, his back to her, and wouldn't tell her. He drew her after him along the outskirts of the wood, then linked arms with her as they walked. Sylvie thought she caught a glimpse of Eamonn but Harry was drawing her on through the apple trees and gave her no time to check. Then, crossing a moonlit field, they wandered down a boreen bordered with waist-high purple fuchsia and up a wide driveway to the portals of a large and very imposing mansion.

'Oh Harry, where is this place?'

The mansion was grander than Rossbeg and when Harry told her it was his home she nearly fainted. She tried to stop, to run away from him and this new, and to her most unwelcome, piece of information, but he had a firm hold on her and steered her determinedly up the driveway and through the open front door. He guided her into a huge library off the hall, a dark but welcoming place, and, closing the door behind her, let her go at last.

She turned to run but a voice stopped her. A tall man with a kindly face, a face that showed great suffering, rose from behind his desk and with outstretched hands came to greet her. She could not resist the warmth of the smile in his eyes.

'My dear, oh my dear girl. Harry has told me all about you,' he said and embraced her. Then he held her shoulders and looked into her face. 'Ah yes, Harry,' he continued, 'you have good taste.'

Harry grinned and murmured to her, 'There, you see. I told you!'

'This one is wise and beautiful. Dear girl, you are welcome. Very welcome. Sit a moment with me, here beside the fire.'

Sylvie had fallen quite hopelessly for this charming old man. How could she not? Marcus Devereau had been charming people since he was four years old. His charm was based on a real liking of the human race and a compassion for its frailties. He understood people and he forgave them. In this moment he was doubly relieved. He was glad that his son had not brought Fidelma Flood with him for his blessing, and he was relieved that the girl his son was obviously in love with was, in his judgement, utterly delightful.

He had taken his shot of morphine before Harry had brought his girl to meet him so that he would not be grappling with the terrible pain of his body's decay.

'Harry, old fellow, I am thrilled with what I see,' he told his son, then looked at Sylvie. 'You are quite enchanting, my dear. What beautiful eyes you have. Pansies in the snow.' He coughed, then added, 'You must forgive an old man but I've been so afraid of what my son might bring home.' Sylvie opened her mouth to speak. 'No, don't say a word, my dear. Indulge me. He could have brought home Fidelma, your cousin, and that would have broken my heart, because Harry would have suffered and she would have eventually broken *his*.'

'But, Father, you know I wouldn't . . .'

'No I don't, my boy. How could I know that? Young people are so very unpredictable. You see, my dear, Fidelma used to be such a sweet child but they spoiled her. *We* spoiled her. Now you, my dear, bear a striking resemblance to my late wife, and as I look at you I realise that it is not in your looks but rather in your expression. The expression that reveals your soul. You have a compassionate spirit and I make you welcome in my home.'

'But sir, your son and I . . . we've only just met. We haven't planned . . .'

'Never fear, you'll be Mrs Devereau before the year is out. You see, Sylvie, a Devereau only falls in love once, and then for life. My father fell for his wife, a delightful Irishwoman named Maud, and he never looked at anyone else all his days. I fell for Harry's mother, and though she's been dead these twenty years, I've never wanted another woman. They've all seemed flavourless to me after her. Ah, your mother, Harry.'

'Oh Mr Devereau, I didn't mean to upset you.'

Sylvie, bemused by the speed of events, was still primarily concerned that Harry's father, who looked so frail and seemed so kind and welcoming, would not be upset.

'My dear,' the old man told her, 'there is only one thing that would upset me.'

'What's that?' she asked innocently.

'If you jilted my son. He'll never love another, you know.'

'Are you all right?' she asked.

He lifted eyes, clouded with pain, to hers. 'Yes, my dear. Now that I've seen you, I am. You'll be getting a good man in my son.' He glanced at Harry. 'If a little absent-minded sometimes. Make an old man happy.' He bit his lip. 'I'm rushing you, am I not?' he asked. 'Oh dear, oh dear. I've despaired of him, Sylvie. All the gorgeous girls of Wicklow and Dublin have been paraded before him and he has remained indifferent to them one and all. I was afraid he would never find the right one, until, one evening, he came back from Rossbeg and then I knew. It had happened.' He leaned forward and took her hand. 'All right, Sylvie. I'll try not to persuade you. All I can say is when you are making up your mind remember you'll be welcome here. Very, very welcome.' He let go of her hand and a spasm seemed to shake him. 'Get along with you now, the pair of you dear children. Go, go and let an old man rest.' His eyes were closed and an expression of acute pain crossed his face as they left the library.

'He insisted I bring you at once to meet him,' Harry told her in the hall. 'He sent me to Rossbeg to get you and bring you here. He's dying.'

He turned his face from her but Sylvie turned it back towards her and kissed him. 'My darling, I know. I could see that,' she said.

He put his arms around her, 'He doesn't think I know and he mustn't find out.'

She saw the sudden tears spring to his eyes and she whispered, 'Darling, my darling. It must be the worst thing in the world, to love someone like that and see them in pain.'

Harry did not say anything for a while, then he said, 'All he's waiting for is for me to marry. To have me settled. He was afraid I'd marry Fidelma Flood, but I told him, when I fall in love I'll know in an instant. Immediately. Then I'll marry. Only then. He was afraid he'd die before he saw it. When I saw you, in the rose garden with Cecie, I *knew*. At once I knew. I loved you instantly. There was no question in my mind, and, my darling, there never will be.'

He held her tenderly, kissing her hair, her cheeks, her lips. She returned his kisses fiercely, knowing she loved him passionately, knowing there would be no one else for her either but finding it hard to believe such happiness was hers. She who all her life had had to beg for the small portions of affection doled out to her was being offered a bountiful abundance of love and she could not quite credit it.

He paused, looking at her, scrutinising her face intently. 'Will you marry me, Sylvie? Be my wife?'

She returned his steady stare. 'Yes, my love. I will.'

They held on to each other, eyes squeezed shut, both of them pledging themselves silently to the other. They did not see the library door open and Marcus stepping into the hall. He too, when he saw them, murmured a blessing and sent up a prayer of gratitude.

Chapter Fifty-eight

≈ ∞

Eamonn saw Sylvie and Harry skirt the wood and go off towards Montpellier, but he was not interested in them, or where they went. He was on a quest. He wanted to find out, once and for all, what Shannon and the men in the hut were planning. It had to be criminal, else why the secrecy? People didn't meet at night in a garden hut to talk over wedding plans or a birthday party or Christmas. He had plumped for robbery. They were going to knock off Cleary's or Arnott's. Take all the jewellery out of Goldman's window in Grafton Street.

But what part was he to play? He was part of the plot whether they knew it or not. He could not make up his mind whether to join them and have an adventure and be rich for life or to tell the police and become a hero. On reflection he felt the latter to be the more profitable course. In all the movies he saw the robbers fell out among themselves and ended up either dead or in prison, the loot usually lost – scattered to the wind or back with its rightful owner. If that was going to happen he didn't want any part of it.

He didn't, however, think the police would believe his story – not what he had so far. He had wanted to ask Ossian about it, maybe have him come and see the men in their hut, but Ossian had been so totally unlike himself since his return from Rome that Eamonn decided to creep down to the hut alone and, if there was a meeting, listen, and if no one was there, have a little poke around.

He had discovered that the meetings were always on the nights that Shannon O'Brien dated Decla, so he figured that as he was not around tonight maybe the hut would be unoccupied.

The wood was very dark. Midsummer night had passed and

as the days shortened so the nights got darker. There were the usual rustlings and quiverings. An owl hooted and there was a badger snuffling around. The wood seemed full of ancient spells, the echoes of the Tuatha Dé Danann and Balor of the Evil Eye, of curses and old women's mutterings. 'Eye of newt, and toe of frog.' In his head he heard the cackling voices. 'Thrice the brinded cat hath mew'd. Thrice and once the hedge-pig whin'd.'

Witches had dwelt here in the past, Fusty had told him that. In the ancient times, long before Christianity, when heroes walked taller than the trees and great deeds of daring were done, witches and widow women had lived in the caves here, and some said the old oak in the middle of the wood was a witch metamorphosed into an ancient tree.

If Eamonn was scared by the wood in the mornings he was terrified by it at night. The darkness seemed impenetrable and he kept walking into trees, branches slapped his face and tore at his eyes, and he skidded all the time, missing his footing, falling. But he was determined and finally he saw the lights from the rear of the terrace of houses. He could even see the houses on the other side of the street, their front windows facing him, all lit up. It made him feel isolated and alone out there, like Jim Hawkins in *Treasure Island*. In one of the houses a man was undressing and in another a woman was closing the curtains against the night.

He was cold now and he hugged himself to get warm, slipping his hands against his upper arms.

In the houses that backed on to the wood lights shone everywhere. No one bothered to shut the night out at the rear and he could see wives cooking in tiny kitchens, husbands shaving, families around the table eating or talking or drinking tea. He wondered what it felt like to be them, to live in a dinky little house and have a teeny-weeny kitchen. He shivered more and more and was just going to move to the hut which, he saw, was in darkness when a hand fell heavily on his shoulder.

It terrified him. He wet his pants, something he'd never done in his life, and stood, too petrified to move or speak.

'Well, well, well, will ye lookit yerself! What's a little nipper like you doin' out in the night, in the dark?'

The hand turned him around and he found himself facing

the red-haired man from the hut. Eamonn stared at him, eyes wide as saucers, unable to utter a sound.

'Lost yer tongue?' The man sounded quite mild, not fierce as when he spoke to Shannon. Eamonn realised that the man was not at all suspicious of him.

'I'm lost, sir,' he said in a weak little voice that did not seem to belong to him at all.

'Oh now! An' where are you from?'

If the man found out he was someone who knew Shannon O'Brien Eamonn believed the fat would be in the fire good and proper. He was right to have predicted so swiftly the consequences of being honest and, thinking of the Devereaus and the old man who worked there, lied as blandly as he could. He hoped the man would put his nervousness down to his worry at being lost.

'I'm Declan Devanny's son from Montpellier,' he said.

'An' where's that exactly? I think I know where ye mean but . . .' The red-haired man looked at him anxiously. Eamonn could see he was concerned about him. He smelled stale and Eamonn coughed a little, his stomach rising in protest at the mixture of pints, cigarettes and bad teeth that came from the man as he leaned towards him.

'It's the other side of the wood,' Eamonn stammered, 'but I don't know which way to go. I lost my direction. I keep goin' round an' round, an' allus end up in the wrong place.'

He was quite proud of himself and his eloquence but decided not to embroider any more. He hoped he sounded reasonable, and apparently he did for the red-haired man said, 'If I take you to the other side of the wood, across there, will you be all right? I haven't time to take you all the way.'

Eamonn nodded emphatically.

'Then let's go,' the red-haired man said decisively.

He took Eamonn's hand. Eamonn wished he wouldn't but he felt to refuse would be rude. The man led him back through the trees. His large presence, noisy tread and rough pushing of the branches that barred the way quieted all forest life, banishing mystery and fear.

He made his way through without speaking and Eamonn hussied along beside him till they reached the other edge.

'Will this do?' the red-haired man asked. 'Can ye find

yer way from here?' Eamonn nodded. 'Okay then, off ye go.'

Eamonn shouted, 'Thank you, sir,' and ran full-tilt towards the Devereau place, only stopping when he crashed into Harry.

'Hey, little fella, where you harin' off to?'

Eamonn, weak with relief, cried, 'Home!'

'This isn't where you live, buster, or have you forgotten?'

'No, Harry. It's just . . . oh, I got lost in the woods' – he believed his own story now – 'and there was a man who showed me the way out but—'

'Hey, steady on. This doesn't ring true. *You* don't get lost hereabouts, now do you? That's not like you at all. Something fishy here.'

Eamonn liked Harry Devereau enormously. Next to his dadda and Ossian, Harry was his favourite. But he didn't want to tell him the secret yet. He wanted to think it through.

He knew he needed more information to convince Dadda, Ossian, or indeed Harry that his story had substance. Grown-ups never believed the young unless they had cast-iron proof. For some reason they were convinced that children spent their whole time lying, and in Eamonn's experience they had in general much more cause to believe a child's information than an adult's. Adults lied and exaggerated something shocking.

He looked up at Harry with an innocent expression on his face. 'I got in a muddle, okay? See, it's *very* late and I'm not supposed to be out. My mother would kill me if she found out.'

Harry grinned at him. 'Well, I won't say a word. Now I'll walk you home.' He smiled ruefully. 'Though I've just come from there.'

'Seeing Sylvie?' Eamonn thought he'd try to steer the conversation into safer channels.

Harry ruffled his hair and simply said, 'Come on, old fella, let's go. No, I won't take no for an answer. Soon as we reach Rossbeg you're on your own. Okay?'

'Okay.'

Harry laughed and strode out the way he'd just come. He

grinned at the boy and wondered if the small lad guessed how stupidly happy he was, figured he did not and surprised Eamonn by running down the road and vaulting over the three-barred gate into the fallow field yelling, 'Yahoo!', a huge smile on his face.

Chapter Fifty-nine

❧ ❧

Father Ossian Flood strode angrily down Grafton Street. People stood back to allow him to pass, admiring his tall energy, his amazing good looks. There was something about the impetus of his movement that made them retreat slightly from him, but if he'd said 'Follow me', quite a few of them would have. His arrogance prevented him from being able to divine their perception of him. If he had he might have put his energy to better use. If Ossian Flood had left his future in the hands of others he could hardly have failed to succeed. Left to himself he was bent on destruction.

He could not detach himself from events, could not see things with perspective or detachment. Monsignor Maguire had found this out and realised long before others would that Ossian Flood was not a leader. True, he looked the part. People on meeting him were bowled over and often invested in him a power and authority he did not possess, and he, in turn, overestimated his abilities.

He found the position he was in irksome. He did not doubt he could extricate himself, win his way back into Monsignor Maguire's good graces. It had dawned upon him a trifle belatedly that his situation was precarious to say the least. To be a confidant of Cardinal Montecelli was desirable, sure, but should things go wrong the Cardinal, who was after all the champion of Monsignor Maguire – he must not forget that – could, if he chose, wash his hands of the insignificant Father Flood, deny all knowledge of him. Dealing with the IRB was against the law in Ireland and they were a dangerous band of people to meddle with. After his first feelings of elation about his 'special mission' for the Cardinal, in the cold light of day he had awakened to the pitfalls of the venture and the harsh reality of a world where he could not go and ask the advice of his friend and mentor Monsignor Maguire. And a world without the Monsignor as a protector was a friendless world indeed.

So Ossian had come back to Ireland with an ambiguous and unwritten commission from a Cardinal in Rome, a father who was behaving like an idiot, breaking up the perfect family that Ossian had always felt strongly behind him, and an adored mother who seemed to have lost her senses and either had been in love with the Monsignor or still was. He could not make up his mind which it was and could get no sensible answers from her. Eventually it was his father that he decided to vent his pent-up anger upon.

He had not been able to locate Monsignor Maguire. The people at the Abbey said he was not there and they were not expecting him back in the near future. A Canon Dominguez visiting from Brazil had taken his place and if Ossian wanted advice or counsel the Brazilian father would be only too happy to oblige. Ossian slammed down the phone, his frustration getting the better of him.

Then at breakfast this morning Sylvie Flood, their mousy little cousin from London, announced in that soft apologetic way she had that she was going to marry Harry Devereau! The most eligible bachelor in Ireland – well, *one* of the most. Fidelma, though she claimed to be engaged to Lorcan Metcalf (not in the same league as Harry in Ossian's opinion), had taken the news very badly. Very badly indeed. Ossian turned into the Green, frowning. Fidelma's reaction was surprising in view of her own news. She had looked at Sylvie furiously. 'You sneak! You horrid little sneak!' she had hissed at her cousin, who looked pale enough to faint. 'You come here and you change everything!'

'But you're marrying Lorcan,' Sylvie had protested in that gentle voice of hers, stating only what everyone thought.

Fidelma had snarled, 'Lorcan! Lorcan! Much you know! Lorcan's just a . . . just a . . .' Then, catching sight of her mother's startled eyes and Decla's incredulous glance, she rose, threw down her napkin, knocked over her tea-cup and flounced from the room, leaving them all perplexed. Ossian had never before witnessed such a lack of restraint at the family breakfast before. On a Saturday too. Their relaxing together day. And his father not there. No wonder his mother was distraught. And Fidelma was behaving like a harridan, and who did that sly little intruder think she was, running off with the town's best catch? Ossian's fury had fuelled his journey and without noticing it he arrived at the house in Molesworth Street.

He found Rosie Daly's bell and rang it. His father opened the door. It was a father he did not recognise.

He wore a paisley silk dressing-gown, a garment Ossian knew his mother would have considered outré and tasteless. She would certainly have been appalled that he was still in it at eleven o'clock in the morning. Roddy's hair was tousled, something his son had never seen before, and he wore a relaxed grin on his face that Ossian, to his horror, wanted to slap off.

Roddy did not seem surprised to see Ossian outside the door. 'Come in, son, come in,' he invited. 'I guessed they'd send you eventually,' and he stood back to allow his son to pass him. Rosie Daly appeared, rising up from an armchair in what Ossian assumed was the living-room and to his horror he saw that she was *en déshabille*. She wore a pink satin dressing-gown that clung to her every curve and Ossian realised with distaste that she had nothing on underneath it. He moved gingerly past her, reluctantly breathing in the scent of her body mingled with the perfume she wore.

He looked around the living-room with distaste. Used only to Rossbeg and the austerity of the presbyteries and the seminary, he found Rosie Daly's living-room chaotic. How on earth could his father leave his mother, for this!

He sat on the only upright chair in the room. Dismayed, he saw his father take Rosie Daly's hand as they moved together and sat side by side on the sofa. It was so old and worn out that they sank down into it in a most undignified way, which would have been laughable if it had been anyone else. His father sat there, holding his floozie's hand, waiting for him to speak.

Ossian cleared his throat. He knew that whatever he said he'd sound pompous, and indeed he did.

'Well, Father,' – he could not call him Dadda, not under these circumstances – 'what on earth do you think you are up to? Don't you know what a terrible sin you are committing?'

Roddy laughed. Gently, kindly it was true, but he laughed when reminded of sin. He was, Ossian realised with a sinking heart, very far gone indeed. They had taught him that sin hardens one, that the repetition of an evil act, like murder or adultery, erodes conscience. He feared that this was the case with his father. Ossian could see now that his father was a lost soul. There was nothing to be gained by appealing to his morals.

'See, Father.' Rosie Daly spoke gently. She had the same kind of voice as Sylvie, Ossian realised. He did not want to listen to her but he had no choice short of leaving the room. 'Your father and I love each other. It is not a union sanctified by the Church, but Jesus always talked of love and he forgave, in his mercy, the adulteress, so we figure' – she glanced shyly at Roddy, her hazel eyes caressing him – 'we figure He'll forgive us for loving each other so much.'

'You are blaspheming, madam!' Ossian cut her short, his voice harsh. 'You speak against the clear directives of the Church.'

'The *Church*, Father, *not* Christ's teaching. And if you'll forgive me, the *Church* has made many a mistake. Think of Galileo. He was, I believe, under a death sentence by the Church for stating what we know today to be irrefutable fact – that the earth is round. Think of the Inquisition in Spain. The Church made a terrible mistake there, don't you think? And the Crusades? Hardly an untarnished record, I'd say.'

'I would be grateful if you would cease to talk about things you know nothing about,' Ossian said firmly. 'There were theological reasons . . .'

'Christ was not so hot on theology, dear Father, if my memory serves me right. In my humble opinion he came to challenge the dyed-in-the-wool adherence to the letter of the Bible and promote a more loving and human understanding. Love and compassion.'

Oh, she was far cleverer than she appeared, Ossian had to admit that. She'd put him firmly in the position of accuser by calling him his title. Father, not Ossian. As Father he could not play the pleading son and he'd been stupid to have taken a canonical stance. Pleading son would have been much more conducive to repentance for the sinner. And her knowledge of the Church was not shallow or ignorant as he had anticipated, and her arguments were well-thought out, if blasphemous.

'Excuse me, madam, but this is between me and my father,' Ossian rebuked her sternly.

'No, Ossian, it is not,' Roddy interrupted calmly. 'You are nearly twenty-two. At your age I was married and you were already born. This is between your mother and me—'

'And Eamonn. Do not forget Eamonn.'

He'd hit a vulnerable spot, he could tell. Rosie Daly's eyes widened and she looked at Roddy and his father's hand gripped hers harder. She did not wince but it must have hurt.

'Leave Eamonn to me,' Roddy said.

'Oh! And what? Are you going to explain to the boys in Clongoes that it is all right to commit adultery? Are you going to be there when Martin Metcalf teases him because his da's run off with a tart?' Roddy leapt to his feet but Ossian continued, 'For that's what they'll say, Father, you know they will.'

The anger went out of Roddy's stance. He could not argue that point. He knew the cruelty of children.

'Oh, if we lived in heathen England or America now it might be different. Divorce is not such a shocker there, the break-up of a family is not a public scandal. But it is here. It taints. How many families do you know where the father has left his home and his wife and gone to live with another woman? In this country? Eh?' Then, answering his own question, 'None!' he cried. 'Jack Doyle!' he continued contemptuously. 'Off with Movita! A film star. And look what the Dublin people did. Stoned the window of the hotel they were staying at. That's how they feel about adultery in this town.'

'Jealous, more like,' Roddy said. 'They were pissed off because he did what they wished they could.' Roddy shook his head for he knew the reason didn't matter to Ossian. It was the action that made the headlines. His son was right. Eamonn was in for a hard time.

'I'm going now, Father.' Ossian stood. He saw that Rosie Daly was looking at him with pity in her eyes. Why pity? he wondered. 'Just remember you've left Mother in a state of misery. Fidelma is equally upset. It should be the happiest time of her life, planning her wedding, but the father of the bride is not there to support and encourage her. All of society knows her father is with his floozie. Decla is broken-hearted and Cecie, who after all is just taking her first steps back into the bosom of her family, is asking for you.' She wasn't, but Roddy was not to know that. 'Where is Dadda, she asks, and who is to tell her the truth? Eh? And Eamonn, as I've said, is going to suffer horribly. Please, Father, come home. I urge you.' Ossian sighed. 'I leave it to you.'

Then he turned and looked at Rosie. 'And you. You seem intelligent.' It stuck in his throat, but he said it. 'Think about it, please. Set him free for his family's sake.'

And he left them there, satisfied with himself, satisfied that he'd done the Lord's work well.

When he'd gone Rosie smiled at Roddy, who said, 'He's a very good actor.'

And Rosie replied, 'He'll be a success, then, in the Church.'

Chapter Sixty

෴ ෴

'Hello, Shannon.'

'Hello, Decla.'

'You haven't called. I've been worried.'

She hadn't been able to think straight. She'd been demented, until this afternoon when the phone rang and Fusty said it was for her.

She couldn't wait to get to it in case he hung up. Although why he would do that she did not know. She was shocked by her anxiety. She was shocked by the fact that her father had left her mother and all she could think about was Shannon.

Why hadn't he phoned? How could he leave her like that, not knowing when he'd call again? Bathed in anxiety. She knew *she* couldn't leave him in suspense like that, but maybe girls were different to boys in that way. She tried to ask Fidelma but her sister told her to buzz off, not to bother her, she had more important things to do.

'No, I was busy,' Shannon told her now.

What sort of an answer was that?

'I missed you,' she said softly into the phone.

'Me too.'

That was better. The whole affair was not in the least like Fidelma's romances. No flowers. No passionate calls. No little notes saying 'I love you'. Decla sighed. It was hard going, like finding one's way through a minefield.

'When'll I see you?' Why did she have to ask?

'Tonight,' he suggested.

She'd have liked to ask him to dinner but with the family crisis at all systems go it did not seem appropriate. Suppose Fidelma sounded off, or Ossian lectured them all in one of his priestly tirades? Shannon might think them hateful and not up to standard. Though, Decla reasoned, that would be rather difficult, coming as he did from the chaotic O'Brien household. But he might reject her because her people were quarrelsome. Decla could not be sure and did not want to take the risk. She wanted everything to be perfect so that Shannon would go on loving her.

'At the lake,' she said.

'Yeah!'

'We can have a drink in the club.'

'Sure. And maybe go to a flick together after.'

'Oh, that'd be nice.'

See, she just had to be patient and he'd come up with suggestions. A movie would be grand. Sitting beside him in the dark, holding hands, kissing. Yes. It would all come out right in the end. It was hard, though. She couldn't help but be envious of Sylvie. She wasn't jealous exactly, but still it must be wonderful to be loved by Harry Devereau who hung around *all* the time and even asked you to meet his father.

She was not surprised, after she'd thought about it a bit, that Harry had fallen in love with Sylvie. They were both extraordinarily gentle and peaceable and she was so pretty. Not elegantly beautiful like Cora and Ossian and Fidelma, but pretty and fragile and sort of shining, glowing from within. She seemed so in need of protection too. Harry had always frowned at Fidelma's unkindnesses, her cruel little digs at other people's expense. It surprised Decla that her sister hadn't noticed that, but then Fidelma never noticed things about others unless it was to compare them unfavourably or to criticise.

Decla put on her new pale green voile dress. It had puff sleeves and a sash around her waist with tiny velvet daisies in a bunch at the bow. It was great being in the attic-room for Fidelma couldn't get at her there. Fidelma always said unkind things about Decla's appearance when she was all dressed up to go out. Her sister was worse than ever since her engagement, when you would have supposed she would be better. Decla imagined it was because Harry Devereau had proposed to Sylvie. Fidelma kept accusing Sylvie of chasing him, saying she'd trapped Harry into a proposal because she'd turned him down. Everyone knew that was nonsense. If he'd wanted to marry Fidelma nothing would have stopped Harry.

No one asked her where she was going. Fusty said there'd be enough salmon for eight and she'd serve it at the usual time and she could always use what was left over, if Decla didn't come home to eat, with salad tomorrow for lunch.

Harry called for Sylvie and Lorcan collected Fidelma. It depressed Decla that those sort of niceties never seemed to occur to Shannon.

At the curve of the drive a car was parked. She couldn't see who it was and she'd never seen the car before. As she approached, Anthony Linehan hoisted himself to sit on the back of the driving seat. The car was a red two-seater roadster, a snazzy sports MG.

'Hi, Decla. You seen this?' He indicated the car. His eyes were bright with excitement. 'I saw you comin', Dec,' he said, 'and I wanted you to see it. Dad gave her to me 'cause I got my college entrance. I go to UCD in September.' He looked with ardour at the car, and she smiled at them both.

'Isn't she gorgeous!' he exclaimed.

'Better than Marilyn Monroe?' Decla asked sarcastically.

He glanced at her, surprised. 'You sound like Fidelma, Dec. Don't. It's not nice.'

'I thought you *adored* her,' Decla said, making a face. 'I thought you were in love with my sister like all the other guys!'

Anthony shook his head. 'Whatever gave you that idea, Decla?' he asked. He sounded genuinely perplexed.

What did give me that idea? Decla wondered. She realised that Fidelma had. Fidelma often listed her admirers and Anthony Linehan came about fourth. Professor Linehan's son. But then, Decla reflected, Harry Devereau always topped the list. 'He'll marry me,' Fidelma used to boast, and he wasn't going to after all. So where did that leave all her sister's other boasts?

'You look very pretty, Decla,' Anthony was saying. 'Really pretty.'

She blushed. 'Thank you, Anthony.'

Why was she so shy so suddenly? She'd known Anthony Linehan all her life.

'You goin' somewhere special? Would you like a spin?'

'I'm meeting my boyfriend at the club.'

'Oh!' Anthony's face fell. He looked really disappointed.

'Who're you goin' with?' he asked.

'Shannon O'Brien,' she told him, enjoying the conversation. It was nice to know he thought her pretty. It was even nicer to know that he wanted to take her for a spin in his precious new car. It was delightful to drop into the conversation that she had a boyfriend. What power! No wonder Fidelma was spoiled. To know one could manipulate like this was a heady feeling indeed. But her triumph was shattered almost at once.

'That creep!' Anthony said in a disgusted tone of voice.

Decla was instantly on the defensive. 'What do you mean, creep? You wash out your mouth, Anthony Linehan. Shannon O'Brien and me are doin' a line and he's the nicest boy in the world, so he is.'

Anthony gave a great bellow – 'Ha!' – and started the ignition. 'Not for long!' he cried. 'You mark my words he's not a fixture here. He'll be gone one fine morning, you see if I'm not right.'

She was near to tears but he was not looking. He was fiddling with the dashboard of the car. 'You hop in, Dec, and I'll give you a lift anyway.'

'I'd rather die than get in your horrid old car. If you were the last man on earth, Anthony Linehan, I wouldn't take a lift from you.'

'Ha!' he exploded again, laughing. 'Your loss.' He reversed the car with much squealing of brakes and firm rotation of the wheel. 'And she's *not* horrid. She's beautiful,' he said, grinning at her. 'But not as beautiful as you look tonight, Decla Flood.' He laughed and screeched down the road with almost as much noise and fuss as Toad of Toad Hall.

Decla walked to the club. Very shortly she was furious with herself that she'd refused the lift. It might have been just the thing to spur Shannon on, her arriving in a red sports car with a handsome guy in tow. And it was a long, long walk to the club and her pale green suede shoes had cuban heels. She felt that she'd rather bitten off her nose to spite her face.

But what did he mean, Shannon was a creep? Why did everyone dislike Shannon? She felt deeply resentful of others' bad taste, as she saw it. Shannon was wonderful and she loved him. She just wished she knew what he *did*.

She wished too he'd not keep her waiting on tenter-hooks.

Still, tonight they'd meet at the black lake, have a drink in the club and go to the flicks. Magic!

It was nice though, what Anthony had said. Her cheeks got hot when she thought about it. He'd said she was pretty. Then he'd said she was prettier than his car – that was really something. She hoped Shannon would think so too.

She kicked a stone in front of her and gave a little skip. He'd wanted to give her a buzz in his new red roadster. That was really nice.

Come to think of it, he must have been on his way to Rossbeg to see her. Or maybe he was lying about Fidelma. But she didn't think so. He was an open type of guy and said what he meant and he'd said she was pretty. Wowee! That was terrific. He was a really nice boy, was Anthony Linehan. Really nice.

Then she reminded herself that she was going to meet Shannon O'Brien, her boyfriend, and she wondered why she suddenly felt flat. And then she berated herself for thinking that way. She loved Shannon. But she did wish he'd say complimentary stuff like that to her. She wished – oh, she wished . . . She stretched out her arms to the world, and the green diaphanous voile blew against her legs in the dusty boreen, and she sighed, yearning, to the countryside, to the milky blue sky, to the very air she breathed. Then she dropped her arms, wondered what she was doing, and resumed her walk.

Chapter Sixty-one

❧ ❧

Shannon was waiting for her at the lake. The trees blocked the light and a glowing red sunset cast a lurid shimmer on the water, making it look on fire.

'It's like a cauldron,' Decla said.

Shannon didn't seem interested. The black swan sat, utterly still on the red-gold burnished sheet, and stared at Decla.

'I walked,' Decla told him.

'Oh? Did you? It's not far really, is it?' Shannon said. He did not sound at all concerned. He stood awkwardly, back against a sycamore, staring into space.

'My father's left home,' she said. She didn't know why she told him. She hadn't meant to but it just came out. It was, after all, the event at the centre of her life just now and in the silence it was the first thing that sprang to her mind. If she'd wanted a reaction from him she certainly got one.

'What?' he cried as if stung. 'What?' he repeated, as if something earth-shattering had happened.

He turned to her and grabbed her by the arms, staring at her intently. 'Your da? Gone? Where?'

The trouble was, he didn't know who they were interested in. They'd bloody well kept him in the dark and they'd have to let him in on the secret soon. Would Roddy's absence make a difference? Shannon did not know how important that might be. 'Where?' he repeated.

'I don't know.' She didn't want to tell him about Rosie Daly. She felt that it somehow might reflect badly on herself. Shannon might think *her* a loose woman if he found out about Dadda and his fancy woman. She could not help the disloyal thought that entered her head, uninvited – that she would not have felt like this with Anthony. She would have confided in him without reservation, sure of a sympathetic ear. She banished the thought and cried,'You're hurting me, Shannon!'

His grip on her arms slackened. He had not realised how tightly he was holding her.

'You do know. Tell me,' he demanded, but in a gentler tone and with a gentler touch.

'He's gone to stay with Rosie Daly in Molesworth Street,' she said, shame-faced. 'Well, my brother, the priest is going to speak to him, get him to see reason, come home. My sister—'

'Listen, Decla, I gotta go. I gotta see someone.'

'But I just got here,' she protested.

'Well, I've got to split. Something's come up . . .'

'Nothing's come up!' she cried angrily. 'I've been here with you, how could it? Anyhow, you said we'd have a drink in the club and go to the movies.'

'Did I say that? Well, okay, but maybe, then, tomorrow.'

'No, Shannon, tonight. If you leave me now I'll never speak to you again. I mean it.'

What to do? How could he be sure that Roddy Flood's defection was not of paramount importance? How could he know whether his relationship with Decla was of more or less consequence? How in God's name could he know?

'Okay then, I'll tell you what,' he said desperately. 'We'll have the drink tomorrow and I'll definitely take you to the flicks. Promise. How's that?'

He had to get to Angus, let him know about Roddy Flood. He gave Decla a quick kiss and hurried away before she could do more than cry, 'But you said—' and he was gone.

She sat by the lake awhile, choking back tears that hurt her throat. Hunkering down beside the black water she stared at her reflection, not caring if her pretty dress got stained, trying hard to swallow, to gulp down the pain. Her face looked distorted in the sludgy depths, opaque and sinister, like the witch in Disney's *Snow White* when she started to change. Am I really so awful, he has to leave me as soon as he gets here? she asked herself. What did I say wrong? What did I do?

'You okay?' The voice startled her. Anthony Linehan.

She wanted to kill him. How dare he follow her! Maybe listen. Hear her boyfriend run away! Oh, shame!

She did not turn though, in case he saw the tears in her eyes.

He continued, his voice casual, 'I saw Shannon leave. I was up there in the bar. I guessed he was called away so I came to find you. This was the last place I looked.'

Whether he'd meant to or not he'd saved her face and she was grateful to him. She gulped and the tightness in her chest dissolved, the tears vanishing like dew on a sunny morning.

'It's spooky here, Dec. Let's go up to the clubhouse and I'll buy you a drink.'

She looked around at him. He was smiling at her, a soft look in his eyes. 'That is, if you can bear me for an hour or two?' His hand was stretched out to her, his eyes flirting with her, and his voice was soft and tender. She gave him her hand and he drew her to her feet. She hoped he wouldn't say anything more about Shannon and he didn't. He just stood holding her hand and looking at her in that affectionate way, then he gave a big grin and led her gently up to the clubhouse.

When they got there she excused herself. 'I'll order while you're in the little girls' room,' he said. 'What would you like?'

'Gin and It,' she told him. She felt very grown up saying it. Sophisticated. It was the first time a boy had bought her a drink. Shannon never had. Not a sophisticated one like gin and It.

She tidied herself up, surprised to see how brightly her eyes sparkled. Anthony Linehan was good-looking, a really nice fellow, and he seemed to like her. Life looked distinctly rosy, and she was not a wash-out after all.

Her face in the cracked mirror was very different from her reflection in the black lake. It was glowing and her eyes matched her dress, like large emeralds. Her hair seemed to have a life of its own and she marvelled that an invitation to have a drink could change a face so very much that the horrible Queen in *Snow White* suddenly looked like Scarlett O'Hara.

Chapter Sixty-two

❧ ❧

Eamonn knew Shannon had gone to the hut. He saw him hurry away from Decla and head across country towards the woods. He had been taken by Judge Metcalf to the club with Martin but had slouched away by himself when he saw Shannon arrive and then Decla.

He waited, though. He wanted to give Shannon a head start, time for him and the red-haired man to reach the hut before he followed them. He did not want a repetition of the other night. He was scared of being found again. This time he would not be so easily believed.

He was lucky his nocturnal outings had not been discovered by the family. Also that he'd been out with Martin, whose parents were not as strict as his own, and no one had imposed a curfew. He put this down to the fact that everyone at home seemed to be involved in some drama or other and they were all so tied up in their own troubles they had no time for him. Even his mother had forgotten to kiss him good night these evenings and he could hear her crying softly in her room when he passed it. And Fusty, who'd been a stern disciplinarian until a year ago, had with age become less vigilant and a little deaf.

Eamonn crept across in front of the clubhouse. They were all in the bar, carousing. The light glowed warmly in there, like pictures of Christmas, and Eamonn could see Decla in the centre of a group of fellas. She looked very pretty, her hair thick and shining, her eyes sparkling like the sea with the sun on it. She was surrounded by boys. Anthony Linehan seemed in charge, though, and had his arm over her shoulder in a very possessive way. Justin O'Brien was at her other side and quite a few others were trying to muscle in. Eamonn was glad for Decla. He knew Fidelma had up till now cornered all the boys in the neighbourhood. Her engagement to Lorcan seemed to have loosened her hold on the young available bucks and now they clustered around Decla.

He crept away from the window, being careful not to be seen. All it needed was for Martin's father or Mr O'Brien to spot him and he'd be a goner. He slid noiselessly into the bushes and down around the back of the clubhouse, and when he hit the road he began to run. This was the difficult bit. There was no shelter here between the clubhouse and the woods. He hugged the hedgerows until he reached the edge of the wood, whereupon he dived under the dark shelter of the trees.

As usual his flesh shrank in fear and his heart beat faster as he found himself shrouded in shadows, a blanket of stillness enveloping him, and all he could hear were the scuttlings and scurryings of the wood's inhabitants.

He hurried on, not worrying about noise tonight for he guessed that Shannon was long gone and the men were already in the hut. No one would be checking for followers.

Eamonn saw the light before he reached it. It shone like a beacon through the trees. Heart-in-mouth he crept around until he got under a window. He did not want to make the mistake of being seen through the glass again, albeit briefly, so he hid under the window opposite the one he'd peeked through before and found it blacked out. Then he remembered the flag that masked that window. So he went to the side of the hut and very, very cautiously pushed himself up on tiptoe.

He had a perfect side-on view. He could see Shannon, standing at ease now, in profile. Also in profile sat the big red-haired man and further away the little dapper fellow. And from here Eamonn could hear what they were saying. A corner of the glass was missing and the conversation filtered through, somewhat muffled, but clear enough to hear what they said.

'. . . It will be an easy job,' Angus was saying to Shannon. 'Just do it.'

'It's going to be very dangerous, sir,' Shannon said.

'He is to be killed. Understand? Or are you stupid?'

'I mean, it will be difficult to get away.' Shannon looked pinched and a little daunted.

313

'You do your job. If you have to suffer for Ireland, do you mind? Is that going to be a problem?' Angus's tone was sarcastic.

'Oh no, sir, but I may not be invited. On that day, to the event.'

'See that you are,' the dapper man said coldly.

'But the father—'

'It does not matter. The Taoiseach goes with a party. They'll all be there, in that party. We have all the information and our contact has seen the invitation list. Monsignor Maguire, the Floods, and you, Shannon, if you've played your cards right. We've been thorough. Very thorough indeed. Why do you think we chose the Floods? Eh?'

Eamonn's knees went wobbly and he sank into the under-growth at the mention of his family name. Then in case they'd heard he took to his heels and ran. This had something to do with his family. These meetings with Shannon and the red-haired man and the man like Dadda, it had something to do with *them*. The thought both terrified and confused him. He had been so certain that they were a bunch of crooks plotting a heist or a break-in that he'd never even considered an alternative, and what could they possibly want with his family? He was both baffled and scared.

He ran as fast as his legs would carry him, as if the Devil was behind him.

Who was this Tea ... thing person? It had a familiar ring to it, but he was not sure. What was this party they were all going to?

He fell, hitting his face on a stone. He touched it care-fully, looked at his hand as he stumbled along and found blood.

He could hear little panicky whining noises as he ran and realised that the sounds were whistling through his own nose as he crashed through the trees, careless now about discovery.

'Hey, hey, hey, buster, what's up? What's the rush? And what are you doing out at this time of night anyhow?'

He nearly died of fright at the sound. He started screaming and didn't stop until he felt strong arms about him and once more the reassuring hands of Harry Devereau holding on to him.

'Hey, little fella, what's up? Calm down. No one's going to hurt you.'

'I ... I ... they're planning, they'll ... they're going to murder us all, they ... they ...'

'Who, Eamonn? Who? Who is going to murder who?'

Harry was down now at his level, looking intently into his eyes.

'The big red man. Shannon O'Brien. In the hut.'

'What happened, Eamonn? Slowly now. Take it easy.'

'I followed him to the hut ...'

'Who?'

'Shannon O'Brien. I *said*.'

'All right. You followed Shannon. Then what? Where'd he go?'

'He went to the *hut*.' Eamonn shook his head, exasperated. 'The hut they use, behind the wood. Across from your house.' Why was everyone so stupid?

'The huts at the rear of Rothmere Terrace?'

'Yeah. I dunno! I s'pose.'

'Who are "they", Eamonn?'

'The big red man. A man like Dadda. And Shannon.'

'Show me.'

'No, no, no. They'll kill us. They'll kill us. Shannon has a gun. They told him to shoot.'

'Tell you what, Eamonn: you trust me, don't you? I'll let you ride on my shoulders and you show me the place. Just to be sure. It will be quite safe, old boy. I promise.'

Eamonn reluctantly allowed himself to be hoisted on to Harry's shoulders. His teeth were chattering and he wanted very badly to go home. The one place in the world he did not want to go was back into the wood or anywhere near that frightful hut.

Harry, however, marched right up near the Devereau mansion, doing a big detour around the wood. They were in full view now of anyone passing and Eamonn shivered in an agony of fear on his perch on Harry's shoulders, momentarily expecting the big red man or Shannon to leap out at them, twirling revolvers, killing them there on the Devereau lawns.

Montpellier seemed huge in the moonlight. There was no light in any of the windows except one on the ground

315

floor which spilled golden beams on to the gravel surround.

'It's my dad,' Harry told him. 'We'll go this way. Avoid the wood.'

Eamonn said nothing.

'My dad is old Eamonn. Nearing his end.' Harry's voice was very bleak. 'He's not sad to go. He misses my mother.'

Eamonn didn't care at that moment much about Mr Devereau. He did not realise Harry was talking for his sake, to distract him.

'I'm going to marry your cousin Sylvie. Did they tell you?' he asked Eamonn as he loped along. 'My father wants to see me settled, so all this' – he looked around at the huge house, the grounds – 'all this beauty will be well taken care of. Why he thinks I can't do it on my own is a mystery. But he's got it firmly into his head that without a wife who loves me and whom I love it will all go to rack and ruin.' Harry laughed. 'Parents get some funny ideas.'

Eamonn, who'd been trying his best not to listen, hadn't noticed that they'd reached Rothmere Terrace. Most of the backs of the little houses were lit up. Harry lifted him down from his shoulders. 'Let's cut along sideways from here,' he said softly, holding on to Eamonn's hand.

Eamonn held tightly, gripping Harry firmly. 'It's there . . . there,' he whispered excitedly.

But there was no light in the hut. Eamonn's heart sank. He pulled Harry up to the broken window he'd looked through but there was nothing there. No one sat inside any more; there were no chairs to sit on and the table, Eamonn could see, was folded up and laid on its side in a corner. There was no flag and the place looked deserted.

'Well, buster, I reckon we're out of luck. Must've missed them.'

'But they *were* here, you believe me?' Eamonn cried anxiously.

'Sure. If you say so, Eamonn. 'Course I believe you.'

But Eamonn couldn't be sure if Harry really meant what he said.

He carried Eamonn back to Rossbeg on his shoulders. All the doors were locked and Eamonn began, at last, to cry – from strain and excitement and shock and fear and, lastly, apprehension. Fusty would kill him. His mother would be cold and angry and his father when he came home would stop his pocket money and he was saving for new skates.

'I tell you what,' Harry whispered, 'I'll wake Sylvie. She'll let you in. No sweat.' He didn't add, and she'll know what to do with you – a little boy stressed out, overtired and upset.

Eamonn looked at him with relief.

'Which is her room?' Harry asked.

'That one,' Eamonn pointed, his face streaked with tears but his voice eager. He needed desperately at this moment a woman's soft comforting arms, a consoling breast and words of reassurance. 'But be careful not to get that one,' Eamonn whispered as Harry raised a handful of gravel to throw. 'The one beside it is Fidelma's an' she'd make a storm, raise the roof so she would an' you get *her*!' His little tear-stained, scratched and bloody face creased in a grin and Harry wanted to hug him. He decided however that this was not the right time for such a gesture. Eamonn might feel himself regulated back to the nursery and that would not do at all, so Harry contented himself with a wink and, as accurately as he could, aimed the shower of gravel at Sylvie's window. In moments it shot up and Sylvie's face appeared. She took in the anxious face of her lover and the small bedraggled figure of her little cousin. She put her finger to her lips and her face vanished.

Very shortly she appeared at the side of the house, an old flannel dressing-gown wrapped around her. She beckoned them inside into the kitchen.

She bathed Eamonn's face, hugged him and made much of him just as he had craved. However, he pretended he didn't care but she held him to her just the same, understanding that he needed to be tamed into accepting such a demonstration of affection.

She made him cocoa, fed him biscuits and put iodine on his cuts.

He told his story once more: about Shannon and the big red man and the dapper one and the gun. He repeated the talk of the Floods and the 'party', but they didn't ask him any questions. Both their faces wore worried concerned expressions but there was no understanding of what had happened. They thought he was imagining things.

317

Harry carried him up to bed and Sylvie tucked him in, kissed him and said Gentle Jesus with him, and quite suddenly he drifted off into sleep.

He dreamed of Shannon and his gun and the big red man and Harry, in full armour, riding Salty, Vinny's pony, into the wood, hacking back the branches and charging to his rescue.

Chapter Sixty-three

❦ ❧

'Well? What do you think?'

They sat across from each other, Harry in Fusty's rocking chair, Sylvie on Mary Mac's stool. They whispered though no one could possibly have heard – the kitchen was cut off from the rest of the house, and the only room connected to it was the dining-room, where there would not of course, be anyone at this time of night.

Sylvie frowned. 'He's so sure. It's bizarre, but he's so certain.'

'And he hasn't changed his story. Not one iota,' Harry said. 'But it's nuts! There was nothing there. Nothing at all. It looked disused. A dusty old garden shed, empty and deserted. And Eamonn jabbering about a big red man and Shannon and guns.'

'All the same, Eamonn is not stupid,' said Sylvie. 'He's realistic in his own way.'

'But he loves to scare himself. And he's had all the upset with his father leaving. Who knows how it might affect him?'

Sylvie shook her head. She looked so lovely, delicate as a snowdrop, he thought and smiled at her with tenderness and love. 'I trust him though,' she said softly. 'Evidence or no.'

'You would!' he said. He stood and drew her up into his arms. 'I love you so much, sweet girl.' He smiled at her. 'You melt everything in me.' He held her close, so close. 'I want you, dearest, want you so badly, want you now.'

'Then you can have me now,' she said simply, looking up at him, her dark velvet eyes wide with passion.

He groaned. 'Don't, beloved, don't tempt me. I'd never take advantage of you, never.'

'Why does it matter? Don't you understand you would not

319

be taking advantage of me? I would be giving freely. And,' she smiled, 'you heard your father; we'll be married before the end of the year.'

'And if I get you pregnant? What then? If I had an accident and died and you were left . . .'

'Hush. Don't!' She put her finger to his lips. 'Your father would look after me. You know he would. He'd be delighted and he'd make himself live until I was looked after and the baby born; you know that to be true.'

He knew, and he could feel his blood rising, his body hardening, desperate to cleave to hers, desperate to make them one.

She did not want to part her body from his but she also did not want him to make love to her here, in the kitchen. She drew him after her into the hall, putting her finger to her lips, up the stairs and to her room.

'Fidelma!' he mouthed to her but she shook her head and put her lips close to his ear. 'Separated by the bathroom,' she whispered. 'We'll be quiet.'

The room was full of moonlight and he untied her old flannel dressing-gown and lifted her nightdress over her head and she stood naked, like a nymph, before him.

She crossed her arms over her breasts and stood before him, her desire for his approval obvious in her eyes. He gently drew her arms away and looked at her. 'Oh my darling, how beautiful you are,' he whispered over and over as he kissed her.

They were young, their passion for each other acute, their blood hot. Their love-making was amateur and fumbling but fierce and urgent. He entered her standing, pressing her softly rounded buttocks to him and she, winding her legs around his waist, gave herself up utterly to his ardent thrusting.

His eyes were open looking at her, kissing her mouth, and when he came into her she could feel it deep in her and a flood of ecstasy shook her from top to toe. They fell on to the carpet and his seed entered her womb, just as he knew it would, and Marcus Devereau's dearest wish was granted.

Chapter Sixty-four

༄ ༄

Cora lay in bed fingering her rosary. She felt the misery of anti-climax gnaw at her as she lay rigidly on her side of the bed, not, for some reason, being able to relax and spread herself into Roddy's half even though he was not there.

The days had passed and Roddy had not returned and life had altered considerably. No more social round, no gay whirl. She did not go to the club any more. She *could* have braved the crowd – there was nothing and no one to stop her – but she just could not bring herself to face possible humiliation. She did not feel she could swan in without Roddy. She would not have an escort. Everyone had an escort. A lone woman without her man was an untenable position for Cora Flood, she, the matriarch of the perfect family. Oh, she'd often gone to the club without her husband, but that was different. They were a couple then and people knew that. They'd known there'd been a good reason for Roddy's absence. Now everyone would know he wasn't there because he was dallying with Rosie Daly.

And who'd pay the bills? She'd never paid a bill in her life. Who'd organise things for her, enable her to be the perfect wife?

She didn't go to the theatre, the dances they'd been invited to, the picnics they'd agreed to attend, the summer fête, the garden party at the French Consulate, all for the same reason.

She'd bought herself a New Look outfit by Dior to swank in at the Phoenix Park races in the Taoiseach's party next Saturday, but now she'd not be able to wear it. She would not be able to attend without Roddy. It was a great honour to be asked by Ireland's leader, a great man to be included in their group, but he would not want any breath of scandal to sully

321

his good name, in case it sullied his party, for people might think he condoned that sort of behaviour in holy Catholic Ireland, and that would never do. She felt she could not bear the humiliation of being eased quietly away from this, the most important group, and that was what would most probably happen if she braved the storm and simply went.

She had so looked forward to it. Making an entrance in her Dior, surrounded by her beautiful family, her hand on her husband's arm. But now that delight would be denied her. Oh, it was too bad.

Life had become very boring. Fidelma whined. Ossian ranted, and Decla looked at her with reproachful eyes, reminding her of events she would rather forget.

And she had no one to advise her. Her thoughts still shied away from the memory of Monsignor Maguire. She had acquired the habit of shutting them down whenever he came into her mind and quickly saying the Our Father.

Naturally she had no one to replace him. She could not bring herself to look for someone else – who would she ask? Where would she go? The whole country, it seemed, knew of her shame, knew of Roddy's infidelity.

At first the drama of it had excited her, but now the loss of her status as the perfect wife was dawning on her in its full horror. People liked Roddy and there were a lot who'd take his side against her, never mind the facts of the case. The Old Boy's Club, for a start. And there were many who were jealous of her and would not be able to conceal their delight at her downfall.

And where was she in all the mess? Abandoned! Alone and house-bound and insecure. It would make a saint cross.

Suddenly she sat up, alert. There was someone outside on the landing and then a knock on her door.

'Mother. Mother.' Fidelma's voice. She got up and put on her satin *robe de chambre.* What on earth could be the matter now? She opened the door and Fidelma stood there, her finger to her lips. She was pointing at Decla's room.

'What . . . ?' Cora began, but Fidelma whispered, 'Hush!' then, 'There. Listen,' and she led her mother close to the door.

Cora listened outside the door, then froze in horror. She heard them, those sounds that made her feel sick, animal sounds, sounds she'd asked Roddy so often to control, sounds that made her blush and her skin hot. Sounds that revolted her. Dirty! Dirty! Disgusting.

She stood, frozen for a moment, immobilised by her revulsion, looking in horror at Fidelma, thinking, Decla, how could you! Then she reminded herself that it must be the appalling Shannon O'Brien seducing her daughter under her parents' roof. She flung the door open and burst into the room full of righteous fury.

'Decla!' she cried. But it was Sylvie and Harry Devereau! The honourable and upright Harry Devereau and that ingratiating little chit Sylvie.

She had forgotten all about her daughter's change of room and the visitor. There they lay, *on the floor*, naked, legs all twined like those lascivious statues in Rome. She could never understand why the Pope allowed them!

At first she felt only relief. Decla was intact and tucked away in bed in the attic-room. Then anger flooded her, pent-up rage spewed forth from her lips as if an abscess had burst.

'You filthy little whore, cover yourself instantly! You underhanded scum, Harry Devereau, what would your father say? You foul disgusting pair, get out of my house now. Depraved, you are. Disgusting! Disgusting! Dirty!'

She was screaming, her face contorted, shaking as if she had the ague.

Harry rose. He pulled on his trousers slowly, not hurrying, staring at her all the time with pity in his eyes. Where had she seen that look before?

He handed the flannel dressing-gown to Sylvie who, with dignity, put it on in silence. Then Harry took her hand and led her from the room.

Cora wondered where they'd go to in the middle of the night, then realised she didn't care. She'd be glad to be rid of them. They had despoiled the sanctity of her home and she never wanted to see either of them again.

She left the room, slamming the door behind her. Fidelma was nowhere to be seen. She must have returned to her own room, Cora supposed. Cora decided she'd have Fusty give Decla's room a good clear-out next morning, scrub and clean it again, get rid of anything that wasn't Decla's. Then the household could revert to the way it was before. Before . . .

Except for Roddy. How could she sort that out? How could she return their lives to their normal serene pattern and not have Roddy *in situ*? She didn't know and she was too tired to tackle it now.

As she looked down the landing she realised that a tousled Eamonn, eyes wild and scared, was standing, one foot on top of the other, in the doorway of his bedroom.

'Go back to bed, sweetheart,' she said.

'Mamma . . . I want . . . I want to tell you . . .'

'Not now, sweetheart. Go back to bed.'

'But Mamma . . . it's important.'

'I said not now, Eamonn. Are you deaf? Now go to bed.'

'Sorry, Mother.'

'There's a good boy. Good night.'

'Good night, Mamma.'

Chapter Sixty-five

❧ ❧

Harry brought her to his bed in Montpellier. He took off the old flannel dressing-gown for a second time that night and tucked her in. The bed smelled of him and she smiled up at him tremulously from between the sheets.

'Don't worry, my beloved,' he told her. They had not spoken since they left Rossbeg. Harry was too angry to trust himself to say anything.

'I'm not,' she told him tranquilly.

'It will be all right, dearest,' he said.

'I know,' she replied.

'You do trust me, don't you.' It was a statement more than a question.

'You know I do, Harry. With all my heart.'

He left her there, the counterpane just under her chin, her wide-eyed gaze trusting him, making him feel heroic.

His father was still up, dozing in the library. He sat before a huge log fire, for even in this weather the cold bit his bones and aggravated his pain. He glanced up as his son entered and listened intently to his confession.

'. . . And then Mrs Flood burst into the room. She screamed at us to get out. She never wanted to see us again. And she was yelling something about us being dirty and disgusting. So I brought Sylvie with me here.'

Marcus chortled. He chuckled and giggled and laughed. It was a long time since his son had seen him so overcome with mirth.

'That must have shaken her.' Marcus wiped his eyes. 'What a prude dear Cora Flood is,' he said. 'I'll bet she's frigid.' He looked up at his son from beneath bushy eyebrows. 'Marry the girl, now!' he instructed. Then he added, 'Be wonderful if Sylvie was pregnant. Just great. We Devereaus do that. Your mother . . .' He stopped, then his chin sank on his breast. 'A lot of the time, boy, I forget she's not here,' he said softly.

After a moment when both of them were silent he looked at Harry and said, 'Keep her here in Montpellier. But not in the same bed as you, son. I don't want talk. Let us do all things properly.'

'Okay.' The idea appealed to Harry's chivalrous nature.

'You sleep in one of the guest rooms, Harry. It will only be for a short time. Tomorrow I'll send for Father Bannister.'

'How soon can we marry?' Harry asked.

'Three weeks. Well, two and a few days. Three weekends. The banns must be read. And she must send to London for her baptism and birth certificates. Let's hope the records are intact and haven't been destroyed by one of Mr Hitler's doodlebugs.'

'She's got them with her. She said the people who fostered her always had to have them so she got in the habit of carrying them around with her.'

'Well, good, good, couldn't be better.' Marcus glanced at his son. 'Let's show em, eh?' he said. 'Let's have a lovely weddin' day here in Montpellier. Get married in the chapel here. Have a grand breakfast. Invite everyone.'

'The Floods?'

'Of course the Floods, Harry. A social gathering would not be the same without the Floods.' He grinned to himself. 'It will be a right royal battle!'

'What, Father?'

'Cora Flood's battle with herself. To go to a big social gathering in Montpellier, or refuse on the grounds of a moral issue. I wonder how long the struggle will last?' He sighed and laid his head on the back of the chair and closed his eyes.

'Will you be able to . . . I mean, Father, are you . . . ?'

'I'll bear up, boy, you see if I don't. It's my dearest wish come true. Love is written all over your face. I know the signs. And all I want is for you to be as happy as I was with your mother.' He waved his hand. 'Now go to bed,' he said wearily. 'But not with Sylvie! I want to be able to look Cora Flood straight in the eyes.' He glanced up at Harry. 'For she'll come, depend on it. Her love of social

326

position will win out every time over her moral code. Bet upon it.'

'She'll probably want to organise it,' Harry said, laughing.

'You could be right, son, and that may be a very fine idea. Well, I want to be able to tell her – truthfully mind – "Not in my house, they didn't".'

Harry bent and kissed his father's head. 'I'll not let you down,' he assured the old man. 'You can count on me, Father.'

The following day Cecie was distraught when she discovered Sylvie's absence. 'I want to go to Montpellier,' she told Cora when it was discovered where Sylvie was. In a telephone call Marcus Devereau informed Cora that the marriage banns of her niece and his son would be announced in the parish church as from Sunday. Cora received the news in silence. 'Now don't give me any hassle, Cora,' Marcus instructed her firmly. 'I know what happened must have horrified you. And my God, Cora, seeing two young people engaged in sex must have shocked the pants off you.' Cora snorted. How coarse the man was. But he *was* a French aristocrat and therefore not to be alienated and, as a bright idea struck her, she thought that this might be the answer to all her problems. 'Let bygones be bygones, woman, and join me in wishing them well,' Marcus finished.

'If you'll let me be hostess, Marcus,' Cora replied quickly, 'then I'll gladly drop the whole . . . thing.' It was an opportunity not to be missed. Even without Roddy, as 'Mother-of-the-Bride' she'd be in a position of unassailable rectitude. She would be socially prominent and backed by an impeccable position with an impeccable family. No one could cut her. It was a perfect opportunity to get back into the social whirl again. 'After all, she is my niece, Marcus,' she said.

The days passed and still Roddy did not return. Ossian was livid. Eamonn did not come across Harry or Sylvie, who were not to be found around Rossbeg these days. He tried very hard to speak to his mother and Ossian but to no avail. He lurked around the hut on one or two nights but it was always deserted.

Decla was seeing a lot of Shannon. When he phoned her the day after his desertion and asked her out she told him she'd think about it and put the phone down. He began to haunt Rossbeg after that, bringing her flowers, taking her to the movies and for coffees. He would never be gallant, make pretty speeches, nor did she expect him suddenly to become eloquent, but it flattered her to think she'd changed him. Made him think. And it was hard to get away from him. He kept angling to join their party at the big Phoenix Park race meeting. He seemed very anxious to do that and she kept him on tenter-hooks.

Anthony Linehan was around a lot too. As the long summer days shortened and the twilight came earlier, a group was often to be seen on the periphery of the apple orchard at dusk, Decla on the swing, and, as awkward as two men could be with each other, Shannon on one side of her and Anthony on the other. Decla was enjoying herself and the situation thoroughly.

Of the Flood family she was the only one who was. Cora, though flattered and mollified by Marcus Devereau allowing her to organise the wedding up at Montpellier, nevertheless was still very put out about her husband's defection. She was also cross that the wedding she was arranging with such indecent haste was not Fidelma's.

'Nothing happened in *my* house, Cora,' Marcus said when she went to see him about the forthcoming nuptials. He gave her a piercing look. 'And I'm sure nothing happened in *yours*. You have always been above reproach.'

What could she say to that? She had no choice but to bow gracefully and accept that her eldest daughter was lumbered with Mister Second-best and that her mousy niece from London had run off (well, had been asked to leave, by herself, in a rage) with Harry Devereau, the pick of the bunch. That her youngest son was fast becoming a juvenile delinquent, that Ossian was useless in a crisis and that Cecie had had a relapse. It was not at all a happy picture.

Fidelma was constantly in an ill-humour and Lorcan had begun to wear the anxious, hang-dog expression that Roddy used to have before he met Rosie Daly. Ossian complained and hectored them all about rebuilding the family but had no practical suggestions as to how exactly he envisioned that. He went down to the Pro Cathedral for Benediction one day and in the middle of the *Salve Regina* spotted the Monsignor with the Archbishop and Cardinal Gregorivich, the exiled Polish prelate recently released from a communist prison and over on a visit. Ossian tried to catch the Monsignor's attention – he would have liked to meet the Pole and perhaps be photographed outside the cathedral with him and the Monsignor, see himself on the inside page of the *Irish Times* or *Independent* – but the Monsignor bowed briefly to him and neither smiled at him nor greeted him. He might have been someone the Monsignor had just met and would never lay eyes on again, the most casual of acquaintances.

Ossian had tried, since he returned, to gather some information on the banned organisation the IRB but to date had had no success. He had begun to realise that if he had taken one step forward by becoming Cardinal Montecelli's detective in Ireland, he had concurrently taken two back by alienating Monsignor Maguire. The Monsignor was the catalyst, the link between the powerful prelate and Ireland. He would, in the long run, have been much more useful to Ossian than the Cardinal, an Italian living far away in Rome. Monsignor Maguire was here, at the heart of things, and Ossian was realist enough to be aware that though the Monsignor wished him no ill, he would nevertheless stall any advancement up the ladder that Ossian might be proposed for. He could hear the Monsignor in his deep calm voice confiding that the young priest needed to learn patience, humility and obedience before he was rewarded with a role more important than that of substitute priest. Ossian chafed ill-humouredly in the trap he'd set for himself, and so preoccupied was he in trying to work out plans of campaign to escape from that trap, plans to rebuild a friendship badly damaged and at the same time find out enough about the IRB to fill a report for the Cardinal that he totally missed his little brother's need to talk to him.

Eamonn despaired of grown-ups. He had made strenuous efforts to pass on the information he'd received but no one would listen and Sylvie and Harry were up at Montpellier and unavailable. So he gave up.

And in the meantime Cecie lay upstairs and listened to the rumblings of discontent within Rossbeg and turned her face helplessly to the wall. The fragile foundation her happiness had been built on had crumbled and left her much worse off than before.

It was terrible now that she'd had a taste of freedom and friendship. She felt let down and betrayed. No one told her that Cora had banished Sylvie and in her isolation and ignorance she thought Sylvie had forgotten about her.

'She's gone to Montpellier to live with Harry,' Eamonn told her.

'I don't believe you!' Cecie cried and Eamonn bit his lip. Grown people never believed him and he decided they were dim.

They were talking through the door again. Everything had reverted to the way it was before Sylvie came to Rossbeg. Except for Fusty, but then Fusty's behaviour never really changed.

'Well, it's true. You'll find out soon enough.'

'But why, Eamonn?'

''Cause they're in love. And Mother is going to do the wedding up there in Montpellier and it will be very grand.'

'Why didn't she say goodbye to me?' Cecie asked.

'Dunno. Girls get soppy when they're in love. Maybe she didn't have time. Maybe she forgot.' Eamonn couldn't think why she didn't say goodbye. His mind was on other things. 'Cecie, can I tell you something?' he whispered.

'Oh, don't bother me now, Eamonn. I just can't understand Sylvie. How could she be so unkind? How?'

Eamonn went down the corridor to his room, sighing. Would no one ever pay him any attention?

Chapter Sixty-six

Rosie curled herself around her lover and breathed in the masculine smell of him. Doting on him as she did she was well aware of his unhappiness and it pained her that she was the cause of it.

Roddy was simply not cut out for scandal and intrigue. He could not live peacefully with what he thought of as dishonourable behaviour. Deserting his wife and children was not something a decent man did. It was not how things should be.

He was also not cut out for living in a small apartment in crowded conditions, feminine accoutrements everywhere. All his life he'd had space and the luxuries money could buy. Little by little and very reluctantly, these were the conclusions Rosie came to.

It would be so easy for her to blind herself to these truths, so easy just to pretend these trifling objections didn't exist and that everything was just fine and dandy with her and Roddy living in Molesworth Street. But Rosie Daly was too honest and loving a person to take advantage like that. She could see Roddy's painful efforts to fit in and adapt to life with her in a four-roomed flat. He tried so hard and she felt such sympathy for him, her heart aching to ease his bewilderment. Roddy had never taken into account the little essential practicalities that make life bearable and that up to now he had taken for granted.

She could also sense his loneliness away from his family. Roddy was a family man and without his family around him he felt incomplete. She knew that he had not anticipated these feelings and was angry with himself for having them. He worried about them, about Ossian and Fidelma, about Decla and Eamonn, and most of all about Cecie. Rosie loved him too much to inflict that kind of lonely separation on him.

There had been hate mail and nasty phone calls at the apartment in Molesworth Street though he and she were not exactly Jack the Ripper or Lizzie Borden to warrant such vicious backlash, but Rosie knew that if they went on living there the situation would worsen. Sick people would get all worked up and take out old hatreds and resentments on her. She was the scarlet woman. She shouldered the real anger for, after all, Roddy was a man.

Rosie was aware that Roddy depended heavily on the goodwill of people. He was a gregarious chap and he felt very distressed when people made their feelings of distaste obvious. Here he was in the centre of a scandal, everyone in the circles he had moved in talking about him, criticising him, and the poor bewildered man, between the Devil and the deep blue sea, did not know which way to turn.

In Rosie's arms he was sublimely happy. In her arms he could do anything, conquer unpopularity, brave society, forget the storm raging outside, but he could not be in her arms twenty-four hours a day.

She too was finding his constant presence a bit difficult. She wanted to keep the little secrets of her boudoir to herself. She did not want to reveal to her lover the pain and the powder, the mechanics of her allure, but in the small apartment it was impossible to hide them. She liked to be made-up prettily, dressed especially for him when he arrived so that she could set the scene for sexual excitement but that was impossible under the circumstances.

'My love,' she shook him awake one morning, 'my precious heart of my heart, I think you should go home.'

It hurt her to say it. The pain stabbed at her heart and she blurted it out before she lost her courage.

He leapt up, incredulous, gazing at her with consternation in his eyes.

'Don't look like that,' she begged. 'I'm not throwing you out of my life, my darling. I'm just asking you to put things back the way they were. It will please your family.'

'And you? How will you feel?' he asked her. He was like a little boy being sent out to play alone in the cold. His confusion made her smile and she hugged him close to her

332

'I never want you to be away from me, my dearest one,' she said, 'and I won't let you go if you think for one moment that I do.' She kissed his cheek and laid her hand on his heart. 'But think about it, my love. You're unhappy . . .'

'Oh Rosie, I'm not. I've never been happier . . .'

'No, Roddy, listen. You've been happy, I know. You've been at rest in my arms, in my home, but you've been . . . uncomfortable. You've missed your family very much. Too much. The family to you is vital. Now admit it.'

'Of course I've missed them. Any man would. But I wouldn't swap them for you any day.'

'I'm not talking about swap. You don't have to swap. It isn't a choice. Why, dearest, all I'm suggesting is that you go back to the way we were. You in Rossbeg with wife and family, preserving the status quo, and me, a couple of nights, stay over, during the week. Those would be your terms. Put it to her. Say, I'll be here in Rossbeg, master of the house, but I'll spend a few nights from home each week. Then we can all be comfortable again.'

'She'll never agree,' he said. 'She'll not have me back if I still see you.'

Rosie smiled. 'Oh yes, I think she will. People say she's not been anywhere since you left. Cora is social. She'll be very anxious to have you home, believe me. As long as you don't ram me down her throat . . . understand?'

Roddy nodded. It was what he wanted more than anything and he knew she was suggesting it because she loved him. But it seemed to him that she was getting a very bad bargain.

'What about you, my sweet?' he asked her and she read his thought. 'You've got no husband, no protector, no position. I don't think that's fair.'

'I would never get you for a husband anyway, Roddy. I don't think you realise that. We could never remarry in Ireland, and, God help us, you'd come to hate me if we became exiles. You're not the sort of man who could just nip off to England or some outlandish place on the Continent and have to live there, away from all we know. No,' she sighed, 'I wouldn't want that either. I love this town. I love the Green. I love the Shelbourne, the Country Shop, Davy Byrne's and the Bailey. I'd be lost without Switzers, Brown Thomas, Mitchells and Fullers.' She glanced at him. 'So would you, Roddy, so would you. So that's out. And I want you happy with me able to giggle, able to have a laugh together and sod 'em. He saw her eyes twinkling and he kissed the little scar lef by Cora's attack.

'I love you so much, my darling one,' he said softly, hi heart in his eyes. 'Oh, how I love you.'

She smiled at him and her heart sank. Against all reason she had wanted him to stay with her, tell her he couldn't live apart from her, make her run off with him. If only I had the courage to make him stay and damn the consequences, i only I was ruthless enough not to care about his well-being she thought. She had the power over him at this moment, and she might never have it again. All she lacked was courage, and in its place had an overwhelming unselfishness, a love that put his welfare first.

And Roddy did not suggest that they run away. He did no suggest that, nor contradict her rationale.

She realised with a heavy heart that she'd persuaded him to return to Rossbeg. She'd won and she wished she hadn't 'C'mere,' she said and wrapped her arms around him. There were tears in her eyes as she kissed him, feeling him grow hard for her.

'Oh, how'll I manage without your lovely body beside me all the time,' he cried, his voice thick with desire. 'What'll I do on the long weekends without you at Rossbeg, alone and aching for you?'

And she knew he'd already decided that he'd come to her Tues, Wed and Thurs. 'Long weekends' meant he'd be home Friday to Monday inclusive. The plan had clicked into place in his brain and was more or less arranged, and she had had little to do with the arranging. She gave a sad sigh. 'You'll manage, my darling,' she said, wondering why her heart fell like a stone. After all, it had been her idea. It would never have entered his head if she had not suggested it. She loved him, though. Oh, how she loved this man. She kissed him tenderly, then gave herself over to the passion of the moment.

Chapter Sixty-seven

✑ ✎

Roddy's reappearance in Rossbeg was never talked about, never debated. He had disappeared, then appeared again without explanation and that was that. He came to breakfast, chauffeured up the drive in Charlie's Ford. He came to the table; groomed, Brylcreemed, shaved, immaculately dressed, sat down, shook out his napkin and said, 'Good morning everyone!'

Cora, smooth as silk, said, 'Good morning, dear. The *Irish Times* is beside your plate.'

Fidelma opened her mouth to speak but her mother kicked her hard and sharp under the table. Fidelma's eyes flew open and she gasped and looked in astonishment at her mother, then closed her mouth with a snap and remained silent.

Eamonn said not a word but looked at his father with such gratitude that Roddy felt tears prick the back of his eyelids. Fusty's hand shook as she poured the coffee into his cup but she too said nothing, and Decla smiled at him ecstatically.

Ossian was not there and Roddy was relieved. The last thing he wanted was a lecture from his eldest.

Breakfast progressed smoothly, as if he'd never been away, and afterwards Roddy followed Cora up to the bedroom. Cora's beautiful face was serene as the black lake and underneath the façade just as turbulent. But Roddy had everything under control.

He closed the door behind him. 'Cora,' he began, and she cried, 'How *could* you?' All set to play a big scene. He held up his hand. 'I have no intention, Cora, of discussing this *at all.* I'm prepared to come home, but not to this room. I'll move into Decla's room for the moment. Sylvie has gone to Montpellier, I believe. I think that arrangement would suit us both much better. I'll build a small bedroom and dressing-room off my study downstairs.'

'But, Roddy—'

He ignored her interruption and continued firmly, 'I'll be here, if it is agreeable to you, every weekend. From Friday to Monday. I intend to spend Tuesday, Wednesday and Thursday away from home on business.'

Cora knew precisely what he meant by that. She compressed her lips, understanding the ultimatum. Roddy would be with Rosie Daly mid-week, but he'd save her face and continue here if she said nothing, did nothing to cause trouble. If she rocked the boat the deal would be off and he'd leave. She had no illusions that he would not keep his word. She had no choice. If she wanted to lead her old social life again she had to give in to his wishes.

Either way she was the loser. But at least this way she would be able to keep up appearances, she could hold her head up in society, she could go to her parties, her balls, to the club. She could flaunt her Dior.

She nodded wordlessly. She knew defeat when it stared her in the eye and she knew how to compromise. That made her the perfect wife, after all.

'All right, Roddy,' she said, tight-lipped.

'Good. Then, my dear, I take it it's on for the races tomorrow?'

She brightened up. 'Yes,' she replied.

'And the family?'

'I'll put it to them at supper. I expect Fidelma will bring Lorcan. I'm not sure about Ossian, but Decla will probably be with that ghastly Shannon. I really must talk to you about them, Roddy.' How easily she fell back into the habit of marital conversation.

'Well, we'll check this evening, dear,' he said. 'Now I'll go to my study and sort out the bills. They must have piled up.'

'Oh do, dear.' Cora sounded very relieved. He was back in the role of protector.

'See you at dinner then.' And he was gone.

Cora sat at her dressing-table, staring at her face in the mirror. She felt old. I'll never be young again, she thought, and gave an angry snort. Was this what it was all about?

She thought briefly of the Monsignor, his austere and handsome face, the sprinkle of grey in his hair, the gentle curve of his mouth, the lips that looked so tender, and she banged her fist on the dressing-table, savagely cutting off her thoughts. She winced as the salt tears stung her eyes, but banged her fist again, over and over, whispering, 'Damn, damn, damn.'

Where had they all gone? The hopes and dreams of youth? The certainty that one day, somehow, the rainbow would illuminate *her* sky, *her* world would become Technicolor instead of sepia?

She had compromised and by doing so had forfeited freedom. She was no longer her own mistress, could no longer be proud and independent.

She was not sure why this was, she only knew it was so and she was filled with a great sense of loss and failure. 'If only I had the courage,' she whispered, unconscious that she was echoing her arch rival. 'If only.' But like Rosie she knew she had not. She would compromise, and compromise until her freedom had been whittled away. After all, was not that what made her the perfect wife?

Chapter Sixty-eight

❧ ❧

Everyone was there. The sound of the military band playing 'Stars and Stripes Forever', and 'Over There' greeted them as they arrived at Phoenix Park. The visiting band of the United States Air Force were giving a concert in the presence of Sean T. O'Kelly, the President of Ireland, and his wife, that evening and had graciously accepted an invitation to play for the Taoiseach, Mr Costello, at the Phoenix Park races that afternoon. The music was stirring, it made the feet feel light and the heart lift in excitement and pleasure.

It was a fashionable crowd. Women wore hats, mostly wide-brimmed and gorgeously decorated with flowers that put the real ones in the gardens to shame. Men wore top hats and grey trousers and waistcoats with their black cut-away coats. Buttonholes proliferated. The women's dresses were like bouquets of multi-coloured blossoms, bright wide skirts over petticoats. Slyne's of Grafton Street had been bought out quite literally during the previous week. With their new frocks the woman wore white gloves and carried envelope handbags under their arms. It was difficult managing a glass of champagne, a race-card and pencil, and a cigarette all at the same time, but they managed.

The Floods made their entrance just before the Taoiseach's party arrived. It was a spectacular one and caused a flurry of intense interest. Roddy was back with Cora! Cora had won the battle. Smiles of satisfaction wreathed the faces of the fashionable crowd. Anything that threatened the sanctity of marriage was not to be condoned. It was very good to see the Floods on each other's arms, virtue triumphant, morality the winner.

Cora looked, all agreed, unbelievably beautiful in her model Dior gown, white silk with huge black dots. She wore it with a breath-taking, wide-brimmed black straw hat decorated with a circle of white cabbage-roses around the crown. She waved at some, stopped to greet others on what was almost a royal progress to the enclosure. No one could detect triumph in her eyes and they reiterated their affirmations about her virtue.

Roddy looked his usual benign self and the gossips paused, wondering if perhaps their information had been a tad incorrect. They speculated if perhaps someone had been, as Brendan O'Brien delicately put it, 'taking the piss'. Protecting his friend he had steadfastly refused to indulge in speculation about the Floods and what exactly was happening at Rossbeg. He had scoffed at the experts who insisted Roddy Flood had left Cora for good, left the perfect wife. He had said it was all nonsense, even though Roddy was seen abroad with the glamorous widow Rosie Daly. His expression now irritated quite a few people, but they could not doubt the evidence of their own eyes. There was Cora, making her way to the Taoiseach's box, looking ravishing, leaning on her husband's arm, her devoted family in attendance.

Ossian had heard the Monsignor would be in the Taoiseach's party so he was there in his best black suit, his white reversed collar causing a stir of regret in many a female heart, a tribute for all to see to a devoted Catholic mother's training. Fidelma, breath-taking in lilac voile and a hat with a huge floppy brim was accompanied by her fiancé Lorcan Metcalf. She wore an enormous diamond ring on the third finger of her left hand which she flashed around quite a lot, having taken off her cotton glove.

Decla had chosen Anthony Linehan as her escort, much to her parents' delight. She was wearing a shade of moss-green that matched her eyes and she made heads turn as she moved confidently through the crowd, and people muttered about how beautiful she was. 'Oho! Decla'll outdo Fidelma by the looks of things,' they whispered. 'Fidelma'll need to watch out.'

Eamonn, very smart in his miniature morning outfit, seemed anxious and a bit on edge, which everyone thought cute. 'The little man wants to be a credit to his big brother,' Brendan O'Brien remarked, much to Eamonn's disgust. That was *not* what was bothering him at all.

Brendan O'Brien was not a guest of the Taoiseach, but Roddy, not unmindful of his support in his time of trouble, made a date to have a jar with him after the third race.

'Black Bohal is going to win in the first,' Brendan told Roddy.

'Yeah! Listen, Brendan, I better go. Cora is waiting.' He gave Brendan a pregnant look.

'All they'll serve will be cat's pee,' Brendan informed him, referring to the champagne, which in his opinion was not a man's drink. 'So I'll order us a stiff Paddy, okay?' Roddy nodded. As the Flood party moved on Brendan caught Decla's arm. 'I thought you were going with Shannon?' he asked gently, so that Anthony would not hear. Decla shook her head. 'No. No, I told him last night that Anthony was taking me.' Her face, he noticed, was radiant, eyes glittering with excitement, and he, like everyone else, thought what a beauty she was. 'That's funny,' he said to her. 'He told me he was taking you.'

'Wishful thinking,' she retorted, smiling. 'No, Mr O'Brien, Shannon was very casual with me. He sometimes didn't turn up for a date at all.' She shrugged. 'He lost out!' And with a little wave to Brendan she turned back to Anthony.

They made their way to the centre of the stand where, under an awning, a box had been decorated for the Taoiseach and his party. The Devereaus had already arrived and were sipping champagne. Marcus, who was full of drugs, looked skeletal and gaunt, pale as a ghost, but nevertheless appeared in fine good humour. He kissed Cora's hand and there was an ironic gleam in his eye as he caught hers. He procured a glass of champagne for her. 'It's a long time, Cora, since I've been so excited,' he told her. 'These two young people have given me a new lease of life.'

He turned to Harry and Sylvie, his face shining with affection. Cora couldn't help thinking that they were indeed a sweet pair. Harry, looking like an advertisement for health and happiness, was bending down, talking to his bride-to-be in a confidential way and she, fragile as a flower, was gazing at him adoringly. She laughed at what he said and he kissed her cheek. His whole attitude towards her was protective and caring. They reminded Cora of the illustrations in Victorian books of poetry. Young Lochinvar and his bride from Netherby Hall. They made her feel very sad and she did not know why.

'Well, Cora, brings back memories of youth and passion, does it not?' Marcus remarked, glancing at the young pair, then back at her with an evil grin. She surprised him by looking at him directly, eyes starred by tears, and saying softly, 'It must be nice to feel like that. I expect I missed it.'

He pressed her hand, instantly sympathetic, and replied, 'Maybe you are lucky, Cora. I didn't and it's hellishly painful.'

Cora greeted Harry and Sylvie graciously, as if nothing had happened, and the conversation became general. It helped that Roddy knew nothing of the episode in Decla's bedroom and he jovially congratulated his niece and Harry and said he believed his wife was arranging the festivities.

'Cora tells me you are staying with Harry at Montpellier,' he said innocently to Sylvie.

'They're under my protection, Roddy,' Marcus said.

'I didn't mean anything, Marcus,' Roddy protested, looking around, suddenly sensing something. 'Am I missing something here?' he hazarded.

'No. No. And I know you didn't mean anything,' Marcus said smoothly. 'Now let me fill up your glasses.' Then, looking up, 'Ah! Here are the big guns arriving.'

The Earl of Longford, a gargantuan man, theatrical producer for the Dublin Gate Theatre, and his playwright wife, a frail bird-like little woman, were slowly processing from the paddock where the horses were parading. Lord Killanin, a rotund and benevolent charmer, and his elegant wife were with them, as was Monsignor Maguire. Ossian moved determinedly forward.

If there was any awkwardness in the little group with the arrival of the Monsignor it was not visible to anyone watching. Cora's face was impassive and she acknowledged the Monsignor's arrival with grace and gentle condescension, and he too bowed over her hand but forbore to kiss it. Roddy embraced him enthusiastically. The two men clasped hands and slapped shoulders in delighted greeting. Then the Monsignor shook hands with the girls and, turning, inclined his head to Ossian.

'Father Flood,' he said briefly, then went across to Lord

Longford and engaged him in lively conversation about the latest production in the Gate.

There was a fanfare, trumpets tooted and drums rolled. A storm of applause broke out spontaneously as the Taoiseach's party arrived. It was still a new enough fact, Ireland having its own leader and government, not to have lost its magic. Ireland no longer ruled by Westminster.

Roddy remarked to Marcus Devereau, 'Indeed, it's a great and glorious thing, to govern ourselves at last.'

Marcus nodded in agreement.

'Aye, but we don't!' a voice proclaimed in Roddy's ear and he turned to see Shannon O'Brien beside him.

'What are you doing here?' Roddy asked.

'Is he with you, sir?' a Garda asked. 'He came in the gate an' I follied him here. He gev no ticket. He keeps sayin' he's with ye.'

'I came to be with Decla,' Shannon said. 'She's doin' a line with me.' He sounded distraught and not at all romantic. But the National Anthem was playing and all conversation stopped.

As it ended the hubbub broke out and excitement rose as the horses came on to the race course. Roddy, anxious to watch the first race, cried – more to remove the problem and allow him to concentrate – 'Yes, yes, yes. He's with us.' And he put his binoculars to his eyes as the horses, restive at the starting gate, pinned back their ears to hear the starting shot.

Decla had seen Shannon. She glared at him. 'What are you doing here?' she hissed. 'I told you you couldn't come. You look ridiculous.'

Shannon was wearing his thick tweed jacket which looked very out of place in the fashionable group and on such a hot day. Only Eamonn knew there was a gun underneath it.

The starter's gun went off and Eamonn jumped and let out a little yelp. Harry looked at him, frowning. 'He really has the most vivid imagination,' he told Sylvie.

The Taoiseach was following the race and like most of the party had his binoculars glued to his face. Eamonn had run to his father's side and was pulling at his coat. 'What is it, son?' Roddy asked. Eamonn mouthed something at him, shouting, but Roddy couldn't hear. The crowd was

roaring, so Roddy bent to try to hear what his son was
telling.

'Dadda . . . Dadda . . .'

'What is it, son? What's the matter?' Roddy was concerned
for Eamonn had begun to whimper.

'Dadda . . . the gun. He's got a gun!'

''Course he has, silly boy. It's to start the horses.'

'No, Dadda, no.'

Roddy was irritated. He wanted to test the going, watch
the race, but his son was pointing. Reluctantly Roddy's
eyes flickered to where his son indicated and he too saw
the gun.

Shannon O'Brien was producing it from beneath his
jacket. Decla, who was just behind him, screamed but the
sound was lost in the din as the horses thundered past and
Shannon raised the gun and aimed it at the Taoiseach's
head.

What happened next was so muddled that there were many
differing versions afterwards and indeed some swore nothing
at all had happened and that Marcus Devereau had died of
his cancer quite naturally. If you could call cancer natural.

Marcus, standing between the Taoiseach and Shannon,
heard Decla scream. He was the only one who did, except
for Anthony Linehan who was beside her. Roddy, utterly
horrified, had thoughts only for his son and dived to cover
Eamonn's body with his own, and Anthony darted forward
to grab Shannon. But Shannon fired the gun, just as a roar
went up from the crowd and Black Bohal romped home
first, and Marcus Devereau deliberately stepped in front of
the Taoiseach and stopped the bullet with his body.

Chapter Sixty-nine

సి ఐ

The whole affair was hushed up. It would have bee
politically awkward when some of the facts were sorted an
the truth of the matter emerged. It would be very awkwar
indeed for the Government to publicise the evidence tha
the IRB had tried to assassinate the Taoiseach, one o
their own.

Marcus had whispered to Harry in his last moments, 'Don
let this stop you, lad, right?'

'Right, Father.'

'And, Harry. I'm glad to be joining your mother at last. S
don't weep for me.'

'You are very brave, Father,' Harry said.

'Not bravery, boy. Reflex.' And he passed away peacefull

They took him out discreetly, the back way. The St John
Ambulancemen were not used to victims of violence. All the
were ever expected to deal with were casualties of the heat o
the crowds and the odd punter the worse for booze. Howeve
they rose to the occasion manfully and drove Marcus's bod
to the Mater Hospital and in a ward not far from wher
Rosie Daly had recovered from the wounds Cora Floo
had inflicted, Marcus Devereau was pronounced dead fro
a bullet wound to the chest. And, it was added, he was riddle
with cancer.

Then someone spoke to someone and Harry was called i
in confidence and the death certificate read: *Cause of Deatι
Incurable Cancer*. The words 'bullet wound' fell off the pag
and eventually disappeared.

Anthony did not manage to hold on to Shannon unt
the Gardi arrived. He gave him a darned good trouncin;
all agreed afterwards, disarmed him, bloodied his nose, bι
before he could deliver the coup de gráce Shannon ha

344

wriggled desperately away from him, slid under the flap at the far side of the tent, and run for his life into the Park.

Decla had turned to Anthony, enthralled by his bravery, and kissed him ardently on the lips.

Roddy had turned his attention to Eamonn. What the boy told them, and later two men from the Security Forces, appalled his mother and father. It appeared that, during their troubled time, their small son had been cavorting across the countryside spying on a banned and dangerous group of fanatics. The eyes of the Security men met over his head in shocked recognition as he told them of the big red-haired man and the small dapper one. Oh yes, little Eamonn, hiding outside the tennis club, on tiptoe outside the hut behind Rothmere Terrace, left his parents speechless with horror. Cora groped for her husband's hand and he took hers and pressed it between his own. They silently vowed to give their boy the attention he deserved and indeed was entitled to.

'I *tried* to tell you, Mother. And Ossian. And you, Dadda, weren't here. I tried to tell you but you wouldn't listen,' he cried pathetically and Roddy and Cora felt shamed.

'It won't happen again, dearest,' Cora promised.

'You were a very brave boy, Eamonn,' Roddy said. 'But if *ever* anything like this happens again you've *got* to tell us.'

'I tried,' Eamonn insisted and decided that grown-ups were, as he had always thought, dim.

Chapter Seventy

⊷ ⊷

Even a perfect family is entitled to a blip or two. The Floods were very soon put back on their pedestal.

'Did you *see* Cora Flood's outfit at the races? She only looked divine! And Roddy all over her! Who said they were splitting up? Nonsense! They're quite perfect. The perfect couple.'

'And the family. Decla has turned into a stunner. Going out with the Linehan boy. Oh, that'll be a grand match, no mistake.'

'And isn't Cora the pious one? That son of hers makes a lovely priest. A gorgeous priest. And Fidelma is engaged to Lorcan Metcalf. Yes, one of *the* Metcalfs. God bless us, aren't they the perfect family altogether.'

But Fidelma didn't marry Lorcan Metcalf, one of *the* Metcalfs. He cried off at the last moment, jilting her the very morning of the wedding when the presents had been acknowledged, the bride was at the church and the wedding feast all set. He ran away.

His father was apologetic, then he too took off for the Listowel races and left the Floods to cope. Like Miss Havisham, Fidelma sat in her room in her wedding finery and stared at the clock in fury.

The biggest problem for Fidelma was to save face. Cora instantly hustled her off to the Abbey. As it happened, Monsignor Maguire was there, packing, and he proved a great help.

Cora had arrived with a bedraggled red-eyed Fidelma who was so full of self-pity the Monsignor wanted to slap her. She was hustled off in the care of Sister Agnes, the same Sister Agnes who nursed Cecie, and Cora, reverting to her role of penitent to the Monsignor's Father Confessor and forgetting

346

all about the contretemps on her last visit, asked his advice in a distraught fashion.

'Leave her awhile,' he advised. 'Let her lick her wounds. There has been a terrible blow to the pride and as I've often said, Cora, it's one of the hardest things to swallow, being made to look a fool.'

'Yes. Yes. I'll leave her here. Will she be all right?'

'The Sisters will find occupation for her that will help her take her mind off things,' the Monsignor said placatingly. He had always had the power to reassure her. 'I'll have a word with the Reverend Mother.'

'Thank you, Monsignor.'

For a moment she nearly asked his forgiveness for her 'lunatic behaviour' as she put it to herself but something in his severe face forbade such an unburdening. She understood, if imperfectly, that there were certain amends one could not make.

'Are you all right otherwise, Cora?' he asked. His tone was concerned but formal. It rejected intimacy.

She nodded. 'Yes,' she told him. 'Only Fidelma's wedding . . .'

He bent his head in affirmation. 'I know. I know,' he murmured and rose. 'Leave Fidelma to Sister Agnes for the time being.' He guided her to the door without touching her.

'It's goodbye then, Cora, I'm afraid,' he told her. 'I'm going to Rome. I've been honoured with a very attractive post within the Vatican, so I'll take my mother there with me.'

'Will you go soon?' Her voice was light, airy almost, but within her something died. Like the last of a dream slipping away. For a moment, one brief moment, she had thought maybe, just maybe, they could renew their old routine, the Friday visits, the calm theological conversations so intellectually satisfying, obtain his advice and guidance, but his words dashed that hope.

'Immediately,' he replied. 'My mother can't wait.'

Suddenly, briefly, she hated that Italian woman he so obviously loved – his mother. She who had given him that beautiful Italian face. Then she shrugged the thought off as unworthy. 'I hope you'll be very happy there,' she said.

He looked at her quizzically. 'Happiness is not something I search for, Cora. I've discovered it is a by-product of generosity of spirit. It is that I seek. I see it a lot in the

347

faces here of the sisters who give so much and ask so little. I have not reached their simplicity, their humility, yet, and therefore I do not look for the happiness they have without even knowing they have it.'

To his surprise she nodded. 'Yes,' she said sadly. 'I think you don't know you've been happy until you've lost it.'

'How wise of you, Cora,' he said and opened the door. 'Goodbye, my dear lady. I wish you well.'

'And I you.'

'Keep me in your prayers,' he asked her, turning. His noble profile was to her, the wing of his thick black hair, the gentle curve of his lips and his long olive fingers curled over the edge of the door. What had it all been about? She could not imagine. Her feeling now was one of loss and a great yearning for something undiscovered, she could not think what. She was aware that out there, out in the realms of danger, places she had not dared travel for fear of the loss of that perfect image, there lay the answer. 'The children of light are wiser in their generation than . . .' – what? Was exploring a good thing? Did understanding of not only the realm of love and perfection but also of the abysses of darkness and sin lead to serenity? She did not know, but was uncomfortably aware that it was too late for her. She looked at the Monsignor. He had taken her so close, so very close. 'Goodbye, Monsignor Maguire,' she said, and left him standing there.

It was the last time she ever saw him.

Chapter Seventy-one

❧ ❧

Fidelma never left the Abbey. After a long illness she announced that she was taking the veil. The illness, it appeared, was the breaking down of a stubborn will and an iron determination to do and get and have all the wrong things.

The Reverend Mother told Cora that she believed Fidelma had a real vocation.

Cora was summoned for an interview which took place in the library where she had spent such pleasant hours with the Monsignor. In her innocence it had never occurred to her that anyone else used this peaceful place and she had thought of it as his sole territory. But the little Sister Benedict said, 'Come in, come in, Mrs Flood. She's in the library, I think. She always sees people there.'

The Reverend Mother was a large woman with an untidy body under her robes. Her face was moon-like but her eyes were shrewd and intelligent.

'You must not run away with the idea, Mrs Flood, that we encourage girls to become postulants,' she told Cora. 'Far from it. Any encouraging is done when they are at school. Then they are told to look deep in their hearts to see if God has called them to this special service. Now it won't surprise you to learn that most romantic young girls, immediately after this lesson, decide they want to become nuns. Quite inappropriately, I'm afraid. It's a combination of fear of the adult world and fear of their budding sensuality.'

Cora winced. Things had certainly changed from her day, when such a word would never have been used.

'So we weed them out ruthlessly,' the Reverend Mother continued. 'A convent is not a place to take refuge *from* life, Mrs Flood. Quite the contrary.' She stared at Cora.

'But in Fidelma's case I sense strongly that she actually h[as] a vocation.' She shook her head, her homely countenan[ce] expressing gentle surprise, her fine uncompromising ga[ze] fixed on Cora. Cora did not think she dared contradict th[e] Head. Not that she wanted to. 'Fidelma ran away from a[n] awkward situation to us, that is certainly true, but with us sh[e] discovered her true self. Within these walls she has found [a] deep spirituality. I have advised her not to rush. Take h[er] time. I have counselled her to realise that she would, wit[h] her beauty, have no problem finding a husband, and I fe[el] absolutely certain that what happened to her before will n[ot] happen again. But she has persuaded me that she was [as] reluctant to marry Mr Metcalf as he was to marry her.'

'Then why did she become engaged to him?' Cora aske[d] puzzled.

'Apparently a young man from a house near yours turne[d] her down. She proposed and he rejected.'

'Harry Devereau,' Cora breathed.

'Yes. That's the one. She asked him, told him, accordin[g] to her, to marry her and he said no.'

'That was my fault,' Cora said, 'I urged her to—'

'That is not important, Mrs Flood.' The Reverend Moth[er] shook her head. 'It was a process leading her to us. O[ut] of the humiliation of rejection, as she saw it, she accepte[d] poor Mr Metcalf's offer of marriage and became more an[d] more miserable. She says that if he had not backed out sh[e] would have married him out of spite and been desperate[ly] unhappy. It took her time here, within these walls, to reac[h] the conclusion, on mature reflection, that she did not wa[nt] to marry at all. And for a girl like Fidelma, who has bee[n] brought up to believe marriage is the only worthwhile goa[l] that is really quite something.'

Cora found her daughter strangely remote. She had [to] agree, though, that she seemed absolutely certain abo[ut] her vocation and appeared to have no doubts that sh[e] was doing the right thing. There was a new sweetne[ss] about Fidelma, as if for the first time in her life sh[e] felt relaxed and at ease. She seemed happy too, thoug[h] Cora thought she was drifting away from her mother an[d] try as she might she could not catch hold of her an[y] more. It was as if her spirit had escaped somewhere els[e] somewhere unreachable, and Cora had perforce to leave her there.

Eventually Fidelma took the veil and she became Sister Cecelia. Her brother Father Ossian Flood officiated at the concelebration ceremony and once more people murmured what a wonderful mother Cora Flood was, how sainted she must be with her son a priest and now her daughter a nun.

Chapter Seventy-two

❧ ❧

Ossian Flood was eaten up with frustration. The magnificent future he envisaged for himself seemed each day further and further away. He wrote the letter to Rome, to Cardinal Montecelli, explaining the actual circumstances of the shooting with himself as a slightly more important protagonist than he had actually been. It did not dawn on the priest that Monsignor Maguire might also be in communication with the Cardinal. He was proud of the research he did about the IRB, proud of his efforts, which he felt were worthy of praise. The fact that the report was far from dispassionate did not strike him as inappropriate, nor the fact that his extreme right-wing slant somewhat detracted from the impartiality necessary for a really scholarly account.

He waited for a reply. And waited. But he heard nothing. There was no answer from the Vatican, not even an acknowledgement. He wrote again and this time got a brief note signed not by the Cardinal but by his secretary Father Sylvestre, stating only that his communication had been received and its contents noted. And after that, nothing.

So his big dream dwindled, and as his acceptance of life on its own mundane terms eluded him, so did peace of mind.

He was not even given a parish of his own in Ireland, but seemed doomed to wander the face of the country, spending time in tiny hamlets and villages in the role of relief priest. Whenever a priest got ill Father Flood was dispatched to fill in until the sick padre recovered. He was a substitute and he resented such a position.

Full of anger and frustration he began to imbibe the communion wine. A sip or two relaxed him. Goddammit, he needed it. Was anyone in the world more put-upon than he? Had anyone in this world with his talents and good looks drawn such unlucky cards? Anyone bandied about like chaff on the wind would do the same. After all, Christ turned the water into wine. Life was not fair. There was a conspiracy against him started by Monsignor Maguire, and when Ossian had had half a bottle, then a full bottle, and lately a full litre, he'd tell all who would listen the tale of his suffering at the hands of this treacherous but important cleric in Rome.

'He was jealous of me. He knew. He knew about me, my potential. But he was jealous and he squashed it. He tried to seduce my mother,' he'd tell his audience, winking one eye, 'and when I found out he blackened my name to his most important friends in Rome and to the Archbishop in Dublin. And look at me now.' Spreading his hands out in a gesture of helplessness. As those he confided these slanders to were for the most part fellow imbibers or unambitious holy men in the service of God, the first would not remember the next morning and the second were not disposed to give his stories credence or his self-pity much sympathy. They'd take the wine from their relief priest and write asking the authorities not to send them Father Flood again. They would prefer to be short-handed than have his angry presence in their midst.

Eventually he was posted to a Dublin slum, an appallingly dirty and poverty-ridden place where he could drink himself into oblivion for all anyone cared. Everyone else there did, so why not their priest?

If at the Profession of his sister he stumbled over the prayers and up the altar steps, sure wasn't he overcome with emotion? And wouldn't anyone, with their sister looking like a saint from heaven, right off the wall of an Italian church, be moved to a religious ecstasy and find it difficult to rise to their feet without help? So when Father Flood put his head in his hands and seemed to drift off into another world and Father Doherty had to take over the ceremony, they all said it was piety and Father Flood had been overcome with spiritual rapture. It was only the very cynical who whispered that the good Father Flood was dead drunk.

Chapter Seventy-three

❦ ❦

Sylvie married Harry and she produced a male heir for Montpellier within a few days of the requisite nine months.

Marcus they had buried in the family vault with all the early de Vereaus. Harry missed him dreadfully, but he remembered his father's instructions to wed soon, so early one Saturday when most of Dalkey still slept he and Sylvie had gone to the little local church and got married in a simple, quiet ceremony. Father Bannister officiated and the young couple went on honeymoon to Paris.

They were sublimely happy. It irritated Cora to watch their simple joy in each other. Others who were jealous tried to puncture their adoration of each other but none succeeded. Before they left Dalkey Sylvie went to Rossbeg to see Cecie.

Cecie lay once more in darkness, imprisoned in her room. Dr Sutton had decided that her relapse had come from being allowed out of it in the first place. When Cecie explained that she could not fight the disease without her friend Sylvie, Dr Sutton, who had been, truth to tell, a little jealous of Sylvie Flood, tut-tutted and said nonsense.

Sylvie explained what had happened, how Cora had found them together in Decla's bedroom, and drew a giggle from her cousin. She told Cecie that when she and Harry returned from Paris they wanted her to come and live with them in Montpellier.

And so she did. She never recovered completely. She was never strong, but she helped Sylvie with the running of the huge house, with her children, for a girl followed quickly on a boy and another boy followed the girl in that very happy household.

But no one ever called the Devereau family perfect.

Chapter Seventy-four

❧ ❧

Decla married Anthony Linehan. Anthony graduated in law. He was extremely ambitious and applied to do postgraduate work at Harvard Law School in Boston. He excelled himself there and he and Decla set up house in that city and Anthony was invited to join the prestigious firm of Hermann, Ossito and James. Anthony soon became a partner and moved easily into Boston society with his beautiful wife on his arm, and when Decla heard of Anthony's little peccadilloes she took a leaf from her mother's book and settled for an armed truce. So one could say Decla was as happy as she allowed herself to be.

Eamonn grew up to be a detective in the Garda. He always claimed it was his experience with the IRB that inspired him, that those nights outside the Nissen hut at the back of Rothmere Terrace had perfectly prepared him for his work. He married a charming young lady but never had any children.

Shannon searched for Angus O'Laughlin, striding up and down the mean little streets in an agony of apprehension. He asked but no one knew where the red-haired man had run to ground. But Shannon, half-crazed with fear, the Security forces on his tail, at last found his employer.

He was hiding out with the Doyles and when Shannon demanded to speak with him he stood in their doorway, face taut with rage, lips narrow in hatred and contempt. 'Piss off, ye little shite,' he hissed at Shannon, standing out on the pavement, shivering in the darkness. 'Piss off an' don't bother me ever again.'

'But, sir . . .'

'Yer a total failure! You're useless, Shannon O'Brien. A disgrace to Ireland, so ye are. A blot on the face of nationalism.

Yiv made us the laughing stock of the organisation, so ye hav
brought shame on me. Get outta Ireland. Get back to where
came from. We don't want your sort with us. Yer a disgrac

Shannon reeled away from the house. He rambled abo
the city, a fugitive, penniless and friendless. He had nev
before in his life felt so isolated and bereft. To be cast out
the Brotherhood, told to disappear, rejected and unwant
by the only people he really cared about was more than
could bear.

He thought wistfully about Decla. Not that he felt in a
way drawn to her. There was no capacity for love in hi
but he contemplated, as he pushed his way down the stre
of Dublin and Dalkey, the apparent closeness and lovi
kindness of her family. The welcoming atmosphere th
created, the politeness of their acceptance and the relax
warmth that embraced all who spent time with them. It w
a gift they bestowed and one he could not accept.

His ramblings led him finally to the black lake. Sick a
hungry, tired and hopeless, he halted at the brink, th
stretched his arms out to the velvet sky in a gesture
bewilderment.

Then he threw himself in. The water closed instantly ov
him, sucking him down into its mysterious black depths wi
a gulp like a sink emptying.

No one looked for him. No one cared. No one knew
his dark and watery grave. He disappeared as requested
the organisation, by Angus O'Laughlin, a last order implici
obeyed.

In the end Cora and Roddy were left alone in Rossbe
They lived a pleasant, civilised existence and Roddy did n
weep too much when Rosie Daly up and married a retir
English colonel whom she met at a party in Dublin and wh
had a great sense of humour. He made her double up, sh
told Roddy.

Eight years had passed since Cora had attacked her an
Rosie, as she phrased it herself, was not getting any younge
'It's my last chance, Roddy,' she said, 'to be a married wom:
and hold my head up. You can't count poor Peadar. He w
a wash-out and I was ashamed of him.'

'Like you're ashamed of me?'

'Ah no, Roddy darlin', don't say that. No, but Rodd

'm tired of being pointed at, being called Roddy Flood's loozie.'

Their love-making had become chore-like since the upheaval', as Roddy called it. 'The joy has disappeared,' Rosie said. 'We just go through the motions, Roddy. I think t's time we let each other go.'

He had to agree and didn't begrudge her a new start in ife as the Colonel's lady. But he watched her go wistfully, as one watching the last of one's youth disappear.

Rosie and her new husband went to the Cotswolds and pought a picturesque little pub on a riverside, far enough off the motorway for peace, near enough for customers to easily find their way there. She proved to be a wonderful andlady and he a most jovial landlord. They soon had a levoted following and a crowded house every evening and Rosie began to let rooms for a night or two. This likewise was a great success. She bloomed and blossomed like a glorious ndian summer. She had a new freedom and a happiness she had never dared to hope for. Sometimes when she put on her make-up she'd touch the small scar over her right eyebrow and smile a little sadly for love gone. Then she'd hear her Benjy singing in the shower and she'd grin with relief and know that everything was as it should be. She might not now have passion but she had tenderness and great fun. What more could any woman want?

They still talked about the Floods in Dublin, Wicklow and Dalkey. What a perfect family they were, what beauty and good fortune, an example to everyone.

In their old age Roddy and Cora often smiled at each other and reassured each other that their lives had indeed been wonderful.

'Never a bad day,' Cora would say complacently. And Roddy would nod emphatically.

'It's been perfect,' he'd say. 'Perfect.'

And she'd echo, 'Perfect!'

FOUL APPETITE

*A compelling story of hope,
despair − and the power of love . . .*

Dublin, 1950s. For the wealthy Masters family, a time
of Country Club suppers, tennis parties and tea on
the lawn. Also a time of celebration: Felicity, the older
daughter, has just become engaged to Derry Devlin,
friend of the family and a very suitable match, while
Meriel, her younger sister, has started dating properly
with her friend Bobby Mitchell.

As the talk turns to receptions and bridesmaids' dresses,
the Masterses remain happily unaware that in another
part of Dublin, Lonny Clebber, an undertaker's
assistant, has just walked out of court a free man, with
only a suspended sentence for a brutal rape.

Now he is on the hunt for his next victim. And only
Detective Inspector O'Malley, who made the arrest,
knows how to curb his foul appetite . . .

The Lovely American
'Read the book. You won't be able to put it down'
Lancashire Evening Telegraph

The Palucci Vendetta
'Gripping stuff' − *Women's Realm*

Other best selling Warner titles available by mail:

☐	The Palucci Vendetta	Genevieve Lyons	£4.99
☐	Summer in Dranmore	Genevieve Lyons	£4.99
☐	Demara's Dream	Genevieve Lyons	£5.99
☐	Foul Appetite	Genevieve Lyons	£5.99
☐	The Lovely American	Genevieve Lyons	£5.99

The prices shown above are correct at time of going to press, however the publishers reserve the right to increase prices on covers from those previously advertised, without further notice.

W
WARNER BOOKS

WARNER BOOKS
Cash Sales Department, P.O. Box 11, Falmouth, Cornwall, TR10 9EN
Tel: +44 (0) 1326 372400, Fax: +44 (0) 1326 374888
Email: books@barni.avel.co.uk

POST AND PACKING
Payments can be made as follows: cheque, postal order (payable to Warner Books) or by credit cards. Do not send cash or currency.

All U.K Orders	**FREE OF CHARGE**	Please note: Our Mail order service
E.E.C. & Overseas	20% of order value	is international and we can supply to
		any address throughout the world.

Name (Block Letters) _____

Address _____

_____

Post/zip code: _____

☐ Please keep me in touch with future Warner publications
☐ I enclose my remittance £ _____
☐ I wish to pay by Visa/Access/Mastercard/Eurocard

Card Expiry Date

☐☐☐☐☐☐☐☐☐☐☐☐☐☐☐☐☐☐   _____